[See p. 146

DENISON HIMSELF, VERY EXCITED, JUMPED OUT AND DASHED INTO
THE LABORATORY

THE CRAIG KENNEDY SERIES

THE
WAR TERROR

BY
ARTHUR B. REEVE

FRONTISPIECE BY
WILL FOSTER

HARPER & BROTHERS·PUBLISHERS
NEW YORK AND LONDON

CONTENTS

CHAPTER   PAGE

Introduction   vii

I. The War Terror   1

II. The Electro-magnetic Gun   .   .   .   11

III. The Murder Syndicate   22

IV. The Air Pirate   35

V. The Ultra-violet Ray   45

VI. The Triple Mirror   55

VII. The Wireless Wiretappers   .   .   .   66

VIII. The Houseboat Mystery   .   .   .   75

IX. The Radio Detective   85

X. The Curio Shop   96

XI. The "Pillar of Death"   107

XII. The Arrow Poison   118

XIII. The Radium Robber   129

XIV. The Spinthariscope   139

XV. The Asphyxiating Safe   .   .   .   149

XVI. The Dead Line   161

XVII. The Paste Replica   172

XVIII. The Burglar's Microphone   .   .   .   184

XIX. The Germ Letter   195

XX. The Artificial Kidney   205

XXI. The Poison Bracelet   216

XXII. The Devil Worshipers   227

CONTENTS

CHAPTER		PAGE
XXIII.	The Psychic Curse	235
XXIV.	The Serpent's Tooth	245
XXV.	The "Happy Dust"	254
XXVI.	The Binet Test	263
XXVII.	The Lie Detector	273
XXVIII.	The Family Skeleton	281
XXIX.	The Lead Poisoner	291
XXX.	The Electrolytic Murder	303
XXXI.	The Eugenic Bride	314
XXXII.	The Germ Plasm	324
XXXIII.	The Sex Control	334
XXXIV.	The Billionaire Baby	346
XXXV.	The Psychanalysis	355
XXXVI.	The Ends of Justice	368

INTRODUCTION

As I look back now on the sensational events of the past months since the great European War began, it seems to me as if there had never been a period in Craig Kennedy's life more replete with thrilling adventures than this.

In fact, scarcely had one mysterious event been straightened out from the tangled skein, when another, even more baffling, crowded on its very heels.

As was to have been expected with us in America, not all of these remarkable experiences grew either directly or indirectly out of the war, but there were several that did, and they proved to be only the beginning of a succession of events which kept me busy chronicling for the *Star* the exploits of my capable and versatile friend.

Altogether, this period of the war was, I am sure, quite the most exciting of the many series of episodes through which Craig has been called upon to go. Yet he seemed to meet each situation as it arose with a fresh mind, which was amazing even to me who have known him so long and so intimately.

As was naturally to be supposed, also, at such a time, it was not long before Craig found himself entangled in the marvelous spy system of the warring European nations. These systems revealed their devious and dark ways, ramifying as they did tentacle-like even across the ocean in their efforts to gain their ends in neutral America. Not only so, but, as I shall some day endeavor to show later, when the ban of silence imposed by neutrality is raised after the war, many of the horrors of the war were brought home intimately to us.

I have, after mature consideration, decided that even at present nothing but good can come from the publication at least of some part of the strange series of adventures through which Kennedy and I have just gone, especially those which might, if we had not succeeded, have caused most important changes in current history. As for the other adventures, no question can be raised about the propriety of their publication.

At any rate, it came about that early in August, when the war cloud was just beginning to loom blackest, Kennedy was unexpectedly called into one of the strangest, most dangerous situations in which his peculiar and perilous profession had ever involved him.

THE WAR TERROR

CHAPTER I

THE WAR TERROR

"I MUST see Professor Kennedy—where is he?—
I must see him, for God's sake!"

I was almost carried off my feet by the inrush
of a wild-eyed girl, seemingly half crazed with excitement, as she cried out Craig's name.

Startled by my own involuntary exclamation of
surprise which followed the vision that shot past
me as I opened our door in response to a sudden,
sharp series of pushes at the buzzer, Kennedy
bounded swiftly toward me, and the girl almost flung
herself upon him.

"Why, Miss—er—Miss—my dear young lady—
what's the matter?" he stammered, catching her by
the arm gently.

As Kennedy forced our strange visitor into a
chair, I observed that she was all a-tremble. Her
teeth fairly chattered. Alternately her nervous,
peaceless hands clutched at an imaginary something
in the air, as if for support, then, finding none, she
would let her wrists fall supine, while she gazed
about with quivering lips and wild, restless eyes.
Plainly, there was something she feared. She was
almost over the verge of hysteria.

She was a striking girl, of medium height and

I

slender form, but it was her face that fascinated me, with its delicately molded features, intense unfathomable eyes of dark brown, and lips that showed her idealistic, high-strung temperament.

"Please," he soothed, "get yourself together, please—try! What is the matter?"

She looked about, as if she feared that the very walls had eyes and ears. Yet there seemed to be something bursting from her lips that she could not restrain.

"My life," she cried wildly, "my life is at stake. Oh—help me, help me! Unless I commit a murder to-night, I shall be killed myself!"

The words sounded so doubly strange from a girl of her evident refinement that I watched her narrowly, not sure yet but that we had a plain case of insanity to deal with.

"A murder?" repeated Kennedy incredulously. *"You* commit a murder?"

Her eyes rested on him, as if fascinated, but she did not flinch as she replied desperately, "Yes— Baron Kreiger—you know, the German diplomat and financier, who is in America raising money and arousing sympathy with his country."

"Baron Kreiger!" exclaimed Kennedy in surprise, looking at her more keenly.

We had not met the Baron, but we had heard much about him, young, handsome, of an old family, trusted already in spite of his youth by many of the more advanced of old world financial and political leaders, one who had made a most favorable impression on democratic America at a time when such impressions were valuable.

Glancing from one of us to the other, she seemed suddenly, with a great effort, to recollect herself, for she reached into her chatelaine and pulled out a card from a case.

It read simply, "Miss Paula Lowe."

"Yes," she replied, more calmly now to Kennedy's repetition of the Baron's name, "you see, I belong to a secret group." She appeared to hesitate, then suddenly added, "I am an anarchist."

She watched the effect of her confession and, finding the look on Kennedy's face encouraging rather than shocked, went on breathlessly: "We are fighting war with war—this iron-bound organization of men and women. We have pledged ourselves to exterminate all kings, emperors and rulers, ministers of war, generals—but first of all the financiers who lend money that makes war possible."

She paused, her eyes gleaming momentarily with something like the militant enthusiasm that must have enlisted her in the paradoxical war against war.

"We are at least going to make another war impossible!" she exclaimed, for the moment evidently forgetting herself.

"And your plan?" prompted Kennedy, in the most matter-of-fact manner, as though he were discussing an ordinary campaign for social betterment. "How were you to—reach the Baron?"

"We had a drawing," she answered with amazing calmness, as if the mere telling relieved her pent-up feelings. "Another woman and I were chosen. We knew the Baron's weakness for a pretty face. We planned to become acquainted with him—lure him on."

Her voice trailed off, as if, the first burst of confidence over, she felt something that would lock her secret tighter in her breast.

A moment later she resumed, now talking rapidly,

disconnectedly, giving Kennedy no chance to interrupt or guide the conversation.

"You don't know, Professor Kennedy," she began again, "but there are similar groups to ours in European countries and the plan is to strike terror and consternation everywhere in the world at once. Why, at our headquarters there have been drawn up plans and agreements with other groups and there are set down the time, place, and manner of all the—the removals."

Momentarily she seemed to be carried away by something like the fanaticism of the fervor which had at first captured her, even still held her as she recited her incredible story.

"Oh, can't you understand?" she went on, as if to justify herself. "The increase in armies, the frightful implements of slaughter, the total failure of the peace propaganda—they have all defied civilization!

"And then, too, the old, red-blooded emotions of battle have all been eliminated by the mechanical conditions of modern warfare in which men and women are just so many units, automata. Don't you see? To fight war with its own weapons—that has become the only last resort."

Her eager, flushed face betrayed the enthusiasm which had once carried her into the "Group," as she called it. I wondered what had brought her now to us.

"We are no longer making war against man," she cried. "We are making war against picric acid and electric wires!"

I confess that I could not help thinking that there was no doubt that to a certain type of mind the reasoning might appeal most strongly.

"And you would do it in war time, too?" asked Kennedy quickly.

She was ready with an answer. "King George of Greece was killed at the head of his troops. Remember Nazim Pasha, too. Such people are easily reached in time of peace and in time of war, also, by sympathizers on their own side. That's it, you see—we have followers of all nationalities."

She stopped, her burst of enthusiasm spent. A moment later she leaned forward, her clean-cut profile showing her more earnest than before. "But, oh, Professor Kennedy," she added, "it is working itself out to be more terrible than war itself!"

"Have any of the plans been carried out yet?" asked Craig, I thought a little superciliously, for there had certainly been no such wholesale assassination yet as she had hinted at.

She seemed to catch her breath. "Yes," she murmured, then checked herself as if in fear of saying too much. "That is, I—I think so."

I wondered if she were concealing something, perhaps had already had a hand in some such enterprise and it had frightened her.

Kennedy leaned forward, observing the girl's discomfiture. "Miss Lowe," he said, catching her eye and holding it almost hypnotically, "why have you come to see me?"

The question, pointblank, seemed to startle her. Evidently she had thought to tell only as little as necessary, and in her own way. She gave a little nervous laugh, as if to pass it off. But Kennedy's eyes conquered.

"Oh, can't you understand yet?" she exclaimed, rising passionately and throwing out her arms in appeal. "I was carried away with my hatred of war. I hate it yet. But now——the sudden realization of what this compact all means has——well, caused something in me to——to snap. I don't care what oath I have taken. Oh, Professor Kennedy, you——you must save him!"

I looked up at her quickly. What did she mean? At first she had come to be saved herself. "You must save him!" she implored.

Our door buzzer sounded.

She gazed about with a hunted look, as if she felt that some one had even now pursued her and found out.

"What shall I do?" she whispered. "Where shall I go?"

"Quick——in here. No one will know," urged Kennedy, opening the door to his room. He paused for an instant, hurriedly. "Tell me——have you and this other woman met the Baron yet? How far has it gone?"

The look she gave him was peculiar. I could not fathom what was going on in her mind. But there was no hesitation about her answer. "Yes," she replied, "I——we have met him. He is to come back to New York from Washington to-day——this afternoon——to arrange a private loan of five million dollars with some bankers secretly. We were to see him to-night——a quiet dinner, after an automobile ride up the Hudson——"

"Both of you?" interrupted Craig.

"Yes——that——that other woman and myself," she repeated, with a peculiar catch in her voice. "To-night was the time fixed in the drawing for the——"

The word stuck in her throat. Kennedy understood. "Yes, yes," he encouraged, "but who is the other woman?"

Before she could reply, the buzzer had sounded again and she had retreated from the door. Quickly Kennedy closed it and opened the outside door.

It was our old friend Burke of the Secret Service.

Without a word of greeting, a hasty glance seemed to assure him that Kennedy and I were alone. He closed the door himself, and, instead of sitting down, came close to Craig.

"Kennedy," he blurted out in a tone of suppressed excitement, "can I trust you to keep a big secret?"

Craig looked at him reproachfully, but said nothing.

"I beg your pardon—a thousand times," hastened Burke. "I was so excited, I wasn't thinking——"

"Once is enough, Burke," laughed Kennedy, his good nature restored at Burke's crestfallen appearance.

"Well, you see," went on the Secret Service man, "this thing is so very important that—well, I forgot."

He sat down and hitched his chair close to us, as he went on in a lowered, almost awestruck tone.

"Kennedy," he whispered, "I'm on the trail, I think, of something growing out of these terrible conditions in Europe that will tax the best in the Secret Service. Think of it, man. There's an organization, right here in this city, a sort of assassin's club, as it were, aimed at all the powerful men the world over. Why, the most refined and intellectual reformers have joined with the most red-handed anarchists and——"

"Sh! not so loud," cautioned Craig. "I think I have one of them in the next room. Have they done anything yet to the Baron?"

It was Burke's turn now to look from one to the other of us in unfeigned surprise that we should already know something of his secret.

"The Baron?" he repeated, lowering his voice. "What Baron?"

It was evident that Burke knew nothing, at least of this new plot which Miss Lowe had indicated. Kennedy beckoned him over to the window furthest from the door to his own room.

"What have you discovered?" he asked, forestalling Burke in the questioning. "What has happened?"

"You haven't heard, then?" replied Burke.

Kennedy nodded negatively.

"Fortescue, the American inventor of fortescite, the new explosive, died very strangely this morning."

"Yes," encouraged Kennedy, as Burke came to a full stop to observe the effect of the information.

"Most incomprehensible, too," he pursued. "No cause, apparently. But it might have been overlooked, perhaps, except for one thing. It wasn't known generally, but Fortescue had just perfected a successful electro-magnetic gun — powderless, smokeless, flashless, noiseless and of tremendous power. To-morrow he was to have signed the contract to sell it to England. This morning he is found dead and the final plans of the gun are gone!"

Kennedy and Burke were standing mutely looking at each other.

"Who is in the next room?" whispered Burke hoarsely, recollecting Kennedy's caution of silence.

Kennedy did not reply immediately. He was evidently much excited by Burke's news of the wonderful electro-magnetic gun.

"Burke," he exclaimed suddenly, "let's join forces.

I think we are both on the trail of a world-wide conspiracy—a sort of murder syndicate to wipe out war!"

Burke's only reply was a low whistle that involuntarily escaped him as he reached over and grasped Craig's hand, which to him represented the sealing of the compact.

As for me, I could not restrain a mental shudder at the power that their first murder had evidently placed in the hands of the anarchists, if they indeed had the electro-magnetic gun which inventors had been seeking for generations. What might they not do with it—perhaps even use it themselves and turn the latest invention against society itself!

Hastily Craig gave a whispered account of our strange visit from Miss Lowe, while Burke listened, open-mouthed.

He had scarcely finished when he reached for the telephone and asked for long distance.

"Is this the German embassy in Washington?" asked Craig a few moments later when he got his number. "This is Craig Kennedy, in New York. The United States Secret Service will vouch for me —mention to them Mr. Burke of their New York office who is here with me now. I understand that Baron Kreiger is leaving for New York to meet some bankers this afternoon. He must not do so. He is in the gravest danger if he—What? He left last night at midnight and is already here?"

Kennedy turned to us blankly.

The door to his room opened suddenly.

There stood Miss Lowe, gazing wild-eyed at us. Evidently her supernervous condition had heightened the keenness of her senses. She had heard what we were saying. I tried to read her face. It

2

was not fear that I saw there.   It was rage; it was jealousy.

"The traitress—it is Marie!" she shrieked.

For a moment, obtusely, I did not understand.

"She has made a secret appointment with him," she cried.

At last I saw the truth.   Paula Lowe had fallen in love with the man she had sworn to kill!

CHAPTER II

THE ELECTRO-MAGNETIC GUN

"What shall we do?" demanded Burke, instantly taking in the dangerous situation that the Baron's sudden change of plans had opened up.

"Call O'Connor," I suggested, thinking of the police bureau of missing persons, and reaching for the telephone.

"No, no!" almost shouted Craig, seizing my arm. "The police will inevitably spoil it all. No, we must play a lone hand in this if we are to work it out. How was Fortescue discovered, Burke?"

"Sitting in a chair in his laboratory. He must have been there all night. There wasn't a mark on him, not a sign of violence, yet his face was terribly drawn as though he were gasping for breath or his heart had suddenly failed him. So far, I believe, the coroner has no clue and isn't advertising the case."

"Take me there, then," decided Craig quickly. "Walter, I must trust Miss Lowe to you on the journey. We must all go. That must be our starting point, if we are to run this thing down."

I caught his significant look to me and interpreted it to mean that he wanted me to watch Miss Lowe especially. I gathered that taking her was in the nature of a third degree and as a result he expected

to derive some information from her. Her face
was pale and drawn as we four piled into a taxicab for a quick run downtown to the laboratory of
Fortescue from which Burke had come directly to
us with his story.

"What do you know of these anarchists?" asked
Kennedy of Burke as we sped along. "Why do you
suspect them?"

It was evident that he was discussing the case so
that Paula could overhear, for a purpose.

"Why, we received a tip from abroad—I won't
say where," replied Burke guardedly, taking his cue.
"They call themselves the 'Group,' I believe, which
is a common enough term among anarchists. It
seems they are composed of terrorists of all nations."

"The leader?" inquired Kennedy, leading him on.

"There is one, I believe, a little florid, stout German. I think he is a paranoiac who believes there
has fallen on himself a divine mission to end all
warfare. Quite likely he is one of those who have
fled to America to avoid military service. Perhaps,
why certainly, you must know him—Annenberg, an
instructor in economics now at the University?"

Craig nodded and raised his eyebrows in mild surprise. We had indeed heard of Annenberg and
some of his radical theories which had sometimes
quite alarmed the conservative faculty. I felt that
this was getting pretty close home to us now.

"How about Mrs. Annenberg?" Craig asked, recalling the clever young wife of the middle-aged professor.

At the mere mention of the name, I felt a sort of
start in Miss Lowe, who was seated next to me in
the taxicab. She had quickly recovered herself, but

not before I saw that Kennedy's plan of breaking down the last barrier of her reserve was working.

"She is one of them, too," Burke nodded. "I have had my men out shadowing them and their friends. They tell me that the Annenbergs hold salons—I suppose you would call them that—attended by numbers of men and women of high social and intellectual position who dabble in radicalism and all sorts of things."

"Who are the other leaders?" asked Craig. "Have you any idea?"

"Some idea," returned Burke. "There seems to be a Frenchman, a tall, wiry man of forty-five or fifty with a black mustache which once had a military twist. There are a couple of Englishmen. Then there are five or six Americans who seem to be active. One, I believe, is a young woman."

Kennedy checked him with a covert glance, but did not betray by a movement of a muscle to Miss Lowe that either Burke or himself suspected her of being the young woman in question.

"There are three Russians," continued Burke, "all of whom have escaped from Siberia. Then there is at least one Austrian, a Spaniard from the Ferrer school, and Tomasso and Enrico, two Italians, rather heavily built, swarthy, bearded. They look the part. Of course there are others. But these in the main, I think, compose what might be called 'the inner circle' of the 'Group.'"

It was indeed an alarming, terrifying revelation, as we began to realize that Miss Lowe had undoubtedly been telling the truth. Not alone was there this American group, evidently, but all over Europe the lines of the conspiracy had apparently spread. It was not a casual gathering of ordinary malcontents.

It went deeper than that. It included many who in their disgust at war secretly were not unwilling to wink at violence to end the curse. I could not but reflect on the dangerous ground on which most of them were treading, shaking the basis of all civilization in order to cut out one modern excrescence.

The big fact to us, just at present, was that this group had made America its headquarters, that plans had been studiously matured and even reduced to writing, if Paula were to be believed. Everything had been carefully staged for a great simultaneous blow or series of blows that would rouse the whole world.

As I watched I could not escape observing that Miss Lowe followed Burke furtively now, as though he had some uncanny power.

Fortescue's laboratory was in an old building on a side street several blocks from the main thoroughfares of Manhattan. He had evidently chosen it, partly because of its very inaccessibility in order to secure the quiet necessary for his work.

"If he had any visitors last night," commented Kennedy when our cab at last pulled up before the place, "they might have come and gone unnoticed."

We entered. Nothing had been disturbed in the laboratory by the coroner and Kennedy was able to gain a complete idea of the case rapidly, almost as well as if we had been called in immediately.

Fortescue's body, it seemed, had been discovered sprawled out in a big armchair, as Burke had said, by one of his assistants only a few hours before when he had come to the laboratory in the morning to open it. Evidently he had been there undisturbed all night, keeping a gruesome vigil over his looted treasure house.

As we gleaned the meager facts, it became more evident that whoever had perpetrated the crime must have had the diabolical cunning to do it in some ordinary way that aroused no suspicion on the part of the victim, for there was no sign of any violence anywhere.

As we entered the laboratory, I noted an involuntary shudder on the part of Paula Lowe, but, as far as I knew, it was no more than might have been felt by anyone under the circumstances.

Fortescue's body had been removed from the chair in which it had been found and lay on a couch at the other end of the room, covered merely by a sheet. Otherwise, everything, even the armchair, was undisturbed.

Kennedy pulled back a corner of the sheet, disclosing the face, contorted and of a peculiar, purplish hue from the congested blood vessels. He bent over and I did so, too. There was an unmistakable odor of tobacco on him. A moment Kennedy studied the face before us, then slowly replaced the sheet.

Miss Lowe had paused just inside the door and seemed resolutely bound not to look at anything. Kennedy meanwhile had begun a most minute search of the table and floor of the laboratory near the spot where the armchair had been sitting.

In my effort to glean what I could from her actions and expressions I did not notice that Craig had dropped to his knees and was peering into the shadow under the laboratory table. When at last he rose and straightened himself up, however, I saw that he was holding in the palm of his hand a half-smoked, gold-tipped cigarette, which had evidently fallen on the floor beneath the table where it had burned itself out, leaving a blackened mark on the wood.

An instant afterward he picked out from the pile of articles found in Fortescue's pockets and lying on another table a silver cigarette case. He snapped it open. Fortescue's cigarettes, of which there were perhaps a half dozen in the case, were cork-tipped.

Some one had evidently visited the inventor the night before, had apparently offered him a cigarette, for there were any number of the cork-tipped stubs lying about. Who was it? I caught Paula looking with fascinated gaze at the gold-tipped stub, as Kennedy carefully folded it up in a piece of paper and deposited it in his pocket. Did she know something about the case, I wondered?

Without a word, Kennedy seemed to take in the scant furniture of the laboratory at a glance and a quick step or two brought him before a steel filing cabinet. One drawer, which had not been closed as tightly as the rest, projected a bit. On its face was a little typewritten card bearing the inscription: "E-M GUN."

He pulled the drawer open and glanced over the data in it.

"Just what is an electro-magnetic gun?" I asked, interpreting the initials on the drawer.

"Well," he explained as he turned over the notes and sketches, "the primary principle involved in the construction of such a gun consists in impelling the projectile by the magnetic action of a solenoid, the sectional coils or helices of which are supplied with current through devices actuated by the projectile itself. In other words, the sections of helices of the solenoid produce an accelerated motion of the projectile by acting successively on it, after a principle involved in the construction of electro-magnetic rock drills and dispatch tubes.

"All projectiles used in this gun of Fortescue's evidently must have magnetic properties and projectiles of iron or containing large portions of iron are necessary. You see, many coils are wound around the barrel of the gun. As the projectile starts it does so under the attraction of those coils ahead which the current makes temporary magnets. It automatically cuts off the current from those coils that it passes, allowing those further on only to attract it, and preventing those behind from pulling it back."

He paused to study the scraps of plans. "Fortescue had evidently also worked out a way of changing the poles of the coils as the projectile passed, causing them then to repel the projectile, which must have added to its velocity. He seems to have overcome the practical difficulty that in order to obtain service velocities with service projectiles an enormous number of windings and a tremendously long barrel are necessary as well as an abnormally heavy current beyond the safe carrying capacity of the solenoid which would raise the temperature to a point that would destroy the coils."

He continued turning over the prints and notes in the drawer. When he finished, he looked up at us with an expression that indicated that he had merely satisfied himself of something he had already suspected.

"You were right, Burke," he said. "The final plans are gone."

Burke, who, in the meantime, had been telephoning about the city in a vain effort to locate Baron Kreiger, both at such banking offices in Wall Street

as he might be likely to visit and at some of the hotels most frequented by foreigners, merely nodded.
He was evidently at a loss completely how to proceed.

In fact, there seemed to be innumerable problems—to warn Baron Kreiger, to get the list of the
assassinations, to guard Miss Lowe against falling
into the hands of her anarchist friends again, to find
the murderer of Fortescue, to prevent the use of the
electro-magnetic gun, and, if possible, to seize the
anarchists before they had a chance to carry further
their plans.

"There is nothing more that we can do here," remarked Craig briskly, betraying no sign of hesitation. "I think the best thing we can do is to go
to my own laboratory. There at least there is something I must investigate sooner or later."

No one offering either a suggestion or an objection, we four again entered our cab. It was quite
noticeable now that the visit had shaken Paula
Lowe, but Kennedy still studiously refrained from
questioning her, trusting that what she had seen and
heard, especially Burke's report as to Baron Kreiger,
would have its effect.

Like everyone visiting Craig's laboratory for the
first time, Miss Lowe seemed to feel the spell of the
innumerable strange and uncanny instruments which
he had gathered about him in his scientific warfare
against crime. I could see that she was becoming
more and more nervous, perhaps fearing even that
in some incomprehensible way he might read her
own thoughts. Yet one thing I did not detect. She
showed no disposition to turn back on the course on
which she had entered by coming to us in the first
place.

Kennedy was quickly and deftly testing the stub of the little thin, gold-tipped cigarette.

"Excessive smoking," he remarked casually, "causes neuroses of the heart and tobacco has a specific affinity for the coronary arteries as well as a tremendous effect on the vagus nerve. But I don't think this was any ordinary smoke."

He had finished his tests and a quiet smile of satisfaction flitted momentarily over his face. We had been watching him anxiously, wondering what he had found.

As he looked up he remarked to us, with his eyes fixed on Miss Lowe, "That was a ladies' cigarette. Did you notice the size? There has been a woman in this case—presumably."

The girl, suddenly transformed by the rapid-fire succession of discoveries, stood before us like a specter.

"The 'Group,' as anarchists call it," pursued Craig, "is the loosest sort of organization conceivable, I believe, with no set membership, no officers, no laws—just a place of meeting with no fixity, where the comrades get together. Could you get us into the inner circle, Miss Lowe?"

Her only answer was a little suppressed scream. Kennedy had asked the question merely for its effect, for it was only too evident that there was no time, even if she could have managed it, for us to play the "stool pigeon."

Kennedy, who had been clearing up the materials he had used in the analysis of the cigarette, wheeled about suddenly. "Where is the headquarters of the inner circle?" he shot out.

Miss Lowe hesitated. That had evidently been one of the things she had determined not to divulge.

"Tell me," insisted Kennedy. "You must!"

If it had been Burke's bulldozing she would never have yielded. But as she looked into Kennedy's eyes she read there that he had long since fathomed the secret of her wildly beating heart, that if she would accomplish the purpose of saving the Baron she must stop at nothing.

"At—Maplehurst," she answered in a low tone, dropping her eyes from his penetrating gaze, "Professor Annenberg's home—out on Long Island."

"We must act swiftly if we are to succeed," considered Kennedy, his tone betraying rather sympathy with than triumph over the wretched girl who had at last cast everything in the balance to outweigh the terrible situation into which she had been drawn. "To send Miss Lowe for that fatal list of assassinations is to send her either back into the power of this murderous group and let them know that she has told us, or perhaps to involve her again in the completion of their plans."

She sank back into a chair in complete nervous and physical collapse, covering her face with her hands at the realization that in her new-found passion to save the Baron she had bared her sensitive soul for the dissection of three men whom she had never seen before.

"We must have that list," pursued Kennedy decisively. "We must visit Annenberg's headquarters."

"And I?" she asked, trembling now with genuine fear at the thought that he might ask her to accompany us as he had on our visit to Fortescue's laboratory that morning.

"Miss Lowe," said Kennedy, bending over her, "you have gone too far now ever to turn back. You are not equal to the trip. Would you like to remain here? No one will suspect. Here at least you will be safe until we return."

Her answer was a mute expression of thanks and confidence.

CHAPTER III

THE MURDER SYNDICATE

QUICKLY now Craig completed his arrangements for the visit to the headquarters of the real anarchist leader. Burke telephoned for a high-powered car, while Miss Lowe told frankly of the habits of Annenberg and the chances of finding his place unguarded, which were good in the daytime. Kennedy's only equipment for the excursion consisted in a small package which he took from a cabinet at the end of the room, and, with a parting reassurance to Paula Lowe, we were soon speeding over the bridge to the borough across the river.

We realized that it might prove a desperate undertaking, but the crisis was such that it called for any risk.

Our quest took us to a rather dilapidated old house on the outskirts of the little Long Island town. The house stood alone, not far from the tracks of a trolley that ran at infrequent intervals. Even a hasty reconnoitering showed that to stop our motor at even a reasonable distance from it was in itself to arouse suspicion.

Although the house seemed deserted, Craig took no chances, but directed the car to turn at the next crossroad and then run back along a road back of and parallel to that on which Annenberg's was situated. It was perhaps a quarter of a mile away,

across an open field, that we stopped and ran the
car up along the side of the road in some bushes.
Annenberg's was plainly visible and it was not at all
likely that anyone there would suspect trouble from
that quarter.

A hasty conference with Burke followed, in which
Kennedy unwrapped his small package, leaving part
of its contents with him, and adding careful instructions.

Then Kennedy and I retraced our steps down the
road, across by the crossroad, and at last back to
the mysterious house.

To all appearance there had been no need of such
excessive caution. Not a sound or motion greeted
us as we entered the gate and made our way around
to the rear of the house. The very isolation of the
house was now our protection, for we had no in-
quisitive neighbors to watch us for the instant when
Kennedy, with the dexterity of a yeggman, inserted
his knife between the sashes of the kitchen window
and turned the catch which admitted us.

We made our way on cautious tiptoe through a
dining room to a living room, and, finding nothing,
proceeded upstairs. There was not a soul, apparently, in the house, nor in fact anything to indicate that it was different from most small suburban
homes, until at last we mounted to the attic.

It was finished off in one large room across the
back of the house and two in front. As we opened
the door to the larger room, we could only gaze
about in surprise. This was the rendezvous, the
arsenal, literary, explosive and toxicological of the
"Group." Ranged on a table were all the materials
for bomb-making, while in a cabinet I fancied there
were poisons enough to decimate a city.

On the walls were pictures, mostly newspaper prints, of the assassins of McKinley, of King Humbert, of the King of Greece, of King Carlos and others, interspersed with portraits of anarchist and anti-militarist leaders of all lands.

Kennedy sniffed. Over all I, too, could catch the faint odor of stale tobacco. No time was to be lost, however, and while Craig set to work rapidly going through the contents of a desk in the corner, I glanced over the contents of a drawer of a heavy mission table.

"Here's some of Annenberg's literature," I remarked, coming across a small pile of manuscript, entitled "The Human Slaughter House."

"Read it," panted Kennedy, seeing that I had about completed my part of the job. "It may give a clue."

Hastily I scanned the mad, frantic indictment of war, while Craig continued in his search:

"I see wild beasts all around me, distorted unnaturally, in a life and death struggle, with bloodshot eyes, with foaming, gnashing mouths. They attack and kill one another and try to mangle each other. I leap to my feet. I race out into the night and tread on quaking flesh, step on hard heads, and stumble over weapons and helmets. Something is clutching at my feet like hands, so that I race away like a hunted deer with the hounds at his heels—and ever over more bodies—breathless . . . out of one field into another. Horror is crooning over my head. Horror is crooning beneath my feet. And nothing but dying, mangled flesh!

"Of a sudden I see nothing but blood before me. The heavens have opened and the red blood pours in through the windows. Blood wells up on an altar.

The walls run blood from the ceiling to the floor and . . . a giant of blood stands before me. His beard and his hair drip blood. He seats himself on the altar and laughs from thick lips. The black executioner raises his sword and whirls it above my head. Another moment and my head will roll down on the floor. Another moment and the red jet will spurt from my neck.

"Murderers! Murderers! None other than murderers!"

I paused in the reading. "There's nothing here," I remarked, glancing over the curious document for a clue, but finding none.

"Well," remarked Craig contemplatively, "one can at least easily understand how sensitive and imaginative people who have fallen under the influence of one who writes in that way can feel justified in killing those responsible for bringing such horrors on the human race. Hello—what's this?"

He had discovered a false back of one of the drawers in the desk and had jimmied it open. On the top of innumerable papers lay a large linen envelope. On its face it bore in typewriting, just like the card on the drawer at Fortescue's, "E-M GUN."

"It is the original envelope that contained the final plans of the electro-magnetic gun," he explained, opening it.

The envelope was empty. We looked at each other a moment in silence. What had been done with the plans?

Suddenly a bell rang, startling me beyond measure. It was, however, only the telephone, of which an extension reached up into the attic-arsenal. Some one, who did not know that we were there, was evidently calling up.

2

Kennedy quickly unhooked the receiver with a hasty motion to me to be silent.

"Hello," I heard him answer. "Yes, this is it."

He had disguised his voice. I waited anxiously and watched his face to gather what response he received.

"The deuce!" he exclaimed, with his hand over the transmitter so that his voice would not be heard at the other end of the line.

"What's the matter?" I asked eagerly.

"It was Mrs. Annenberg—I am sure. But she was too keen for me. She caught on. There must be some password or form of expression that they use, which we don't know, for she hung up the receiver almost as soon as she heard me."

Kennedy waited a minute or so. Then he whistled into the transmitter. It was done apparently to see whether there was anyone listening. But there was no answer.

"Operator, operator!" he called insistently, moving the hook up and down. "Yes, operator. Can you tell me what number that was which just called?"

He waited impatiently.

"Bleecker—7180," he repeated after the girl. "Thank you. Information, please."

Again we waited, as Craig tried to trace the call up.

"What is the street address of Bleecker, 7180?" he asked. "Five hundred and one East Fifth—a tenement. Thank you."

"A tenement?" I repeated blankly.

"Yes," he cried, now for the first time excited. "Don't you begin to see the scheme? I'll wager that Baron Kreiger has been lured to New York to purchase the electro-magnetic gun which they have stolen from Fortescue and the British. That is the bait that is held out to him by the woman. Call up Miss Lowe at the laboratory and see if she knows the place."

I gave central the number, while he fell to at the little secret drawer of the desk again. The grinding of the wheels of a passing trolley interfered somewhat with giving the number and I had to wait a moment.

"Ah—Walter—here's the list!" almost shouted Kennedy, as he broke open a black-japanned dispatch box in the desk.

I bent over it, as far as the slack of the telephone wire of the receiver at my ear would permit. Annenberg had worked with amazing care and neatness on the list, even going so far as to draw at the top, in black, a death's head. The rest of it was elaborately prepared in flaming red ink.

Craig gasped to observe the list of world-famous men marked for destruction in London, Paris, Berlin, Rome, Vienna, St. Petersburg, and even in New York and Washington.

"What is the date set?" I asked, still with my ear glued to the receiver.

"To-night and to-morrow," he replied, stuffing the fateful sheet into his pocket.

Rummaging about in the drawer of the table, I had come to a package of gold-tipped cigarettes which had interested me and I had left them out. Kennedy was now looking at them curiously.

"What is to be the method, do you suppose?" I asked.

"By a poison that is among the most powerful, approaching even cyanogen," he replied confidently, tapping the cigarettes. "Do you smell the odor in this room? What is it like?"

"Stale tobacco," I replied.

"Exactly—nicotine. Two or three drops on the mouth-end of a cigar or cigarette. The intended victim thinks it is only natural. But it is the purest form of the deadly alkaloid—fatal in a few minutes, too."

He examined the thin little cigarettes more carefully. "Nicotine," he went on, "was about the first alkaloid that was recovered from the body by chemical analysis in a homicide case. That is the penetrating, persistent odor you smelled at Fortescue's and also here. It's a very good poison—if you are not particular about being discovered. A pound of ordinary smoking tobacco contains from a half to an ounce of it. It is almost entirely consumed by combustion; otherwise a pipeful would be fatal. Of course they may have thought that investigators would believe that their victims were inveterate smokers. But even the worst tobacco fiend wouldn't show traces of the weed to such an extent."

Miss Lowe answered at last and Kennedy took the telephone.

"What is at five hundred and one East Fifth?" he asked.

"A headquarters of the Group in the city," she answered. "Why?"

"Well, I believe that the plans of that gun are there and that the Baron——"

"You damned spies!" came a voice from behind us.

Kennedy dropped the receiver, turning quickly, his automatic gleaming in his hand.

There was just a glimpse of a man with glitter-
ing bright blue eyes that had an almost fiendish, bale-
ful glare.   An instant later the door which had so
unexpectedly opened banged shut, we heard a key
turn in the lock—and the man dropped to the floor
before even Kennedy's automatic could test its ability to penetrate wood on a chance at hitting something the other side of it.

We were prisoners!

My mind worked automatically.   At this very
moment, perhaps, Baron Kreiger might be nego-
tiating for the electro-magnetic gun.   We had found
out where he was, in all probability, but we were
powerless to help him.   I thought of Miss Lowe,
and picked up the receiver which Kennedy had
dropped.

She did not answer.   The wire had been cut.   We
were isolated!

Kennedy had jumped to the window.   I followed
to restrain him, fearing that he had some mad
scheme for climbing out.   Instead, quickly he placed
a peculiar arrangement, from the little package he
had brought, holding it to his eye as if sighting it,
his right hand grasping a handle as one holds a
stereoscope.   A moment later, as I examined it more
closely, I saw that instead of looking at anything he
had before him a small parabolic mirror turned
away from him.

His finger pressed alternately on a button on the
handle and I could see that there flashed in the little
mirror a minute incandescent lamp which seemed to
have a special filament arrangement.

The glaring sun was streaming in at the window
and I wondered what could possibly be accom-

plished by the little light in competition with the sun itself.

"Signaling by electric light in the daytime may sound to you ridiculous," explained Craig, still industriously flashing the light, "but this arrangement with Professor Donath's signal mirror makes it possible, all right.

"I hadn't expected this, but I thought I might want to communicate with Burke quickly. You see, I sight the lamp and then press the button which causes the light in the mirror to flash. It seems a paradox that a light like this can be seen from a distance of even five miles and yet be invisible to one for whom it was not intended, but it is so. I use the ordinary Morse code—two seconds for a dot, six for a dash with a four-second interval."

"What message did you send?" I asked.

"I told him that Baron Kreiger was at five hundred and one East Fifth, probably; to get the secret service office in New York by wire and have them raid the place, then to come and rescue us. That was Annenberg. He must have come up by that trolley we heard passing just before."

The minutes seemed ages as we waited for Burke to start the machinery of the raid and then come for us.

"No—you can't have a cigarette—and if I had a pair of bracelets with me, I'd search you myself," we heard a welcome voice growl outside the door a few minutes later. "Look in that other pocket, Tom."

The lock grated back and there stood Burke holding in a grip of steel the undersized Annenberg, while the chauffeur who had driven our car swung open the door.

"I'd have been up sooner," apologized Burke, giving the anarchist an extra twist just to let him know that he was at last in the hands of the law, "only I figured that this fellow couldn't have got far away in this God-forsaken Ducktown and I might as well pick him up while I had a chance. That's a great little instrument of yours, Kennedy. I got you, fine."

Annenberg, seeing we were now four to one, concluded that discretion was the better part of valor and ceased to struggle, though now and then I could see he glanced at Kennedy out of the corner of his eye. To every question he maintained a stolid silence.

A few minutes later, with the arch anarchist safely pinioned between us, we were speeding back toward New York, laying plans for Burke to dispatch warnings abroad to those whose names appeared on the fatal list, and at the same time to round up as many of the conspirators as possible in America.

As for Kennedy, his main interest now lay in Baron Kreiger and Paula. While she had been driven frantic by the outcome of the terrible pact into which she had been drawn, some one, undoubtedly, had been trying to sell Baron Kreiger the gun that had been stolen from the American inventor. Once they had his money and he had received the plans of the gun, a fatal cigarette would be smoked. Could we prevent it?

On we tore back to the city, across the bridge and down through the canyons of East Side streets.

At last we pulled up before the tenement at five hundred and one. As we did so, one of Burke's men jumped out of the doorway.

"Are we in time?" shouted Burke.

"It's an awful mix-up," returned the man. "I can't make anything out of it, so I ordered 'em all held here till you came."

We pushed past without a word of criticism of his wonderful acumen.

On the top floor we came upon a young man, bending over the form of a girl who had fainted. On the floor of the middle of the room was a mass of charred papers which had evidently burned a hole in the carpet before they had been stamped out. Near by was an unlighted cigarette, crushed flat on the floor.

"How is she?" asked Kennedy anxiously of the young man, as he dropped down on the other side of the girl.

It was Paula. She had fainted, but was just now coming out of the borderland of unconsciousness.

"Was I in time? Had he smoked it?" she moaned weakly, as there swam before her eyes, evidently, a hazy vision of our faces.

Kennedy turned to the young man.

"Baron Kreiger, I presume?" he inquired.

The young man nodded.

"Burke of the Secret Service," introduced Craig, indicating our friend. "My name is Kennedy. Tell what happened."

"I had just concluded a transaction," returned Kreiger in good but carefully guarded English. "Suddenly the door burst open. She seized these papers and dashed a cigarette out of my hands. The next instant she had touched a match to them and had fallen in a faint almost in the blaze. Strangest experience I ever had in my life. Then all these other fellows came bursting in—said they were Secret Service men, too."

Kennedy had no time to reply, for a cry from Annenberg directed our attention to the next room where on a couch lay a figure all huddled up.

As we looked we saw it was a woman, her head sweating profusely, and her hands cold and clammy. There was a strange twitching of the muscles of the face, the pupils of her eyes were widely dilated, her pulse weak and irregular. Evidently her circulation had failed so that it responded only feebly to stimulants, for her respiration was slow and labored, with loud inspiratory gasps.

Annenberg had burst with superhuman strength from Burke's grasp and was kneeling by the side of his wife's deathbed.

"It—was all Paula's fault——" gasped the woman. "I—knew I had better—carry it through —like the Fortescue visit—alone."

I felt a sense of reassurance at the words. At least my suspicions had been unfounded. Paula was innocent of the murder of Fortescue.

"Severe, acute nicotine poisoning," remarked Kennedy, as he rejoined us a moment later. "There is nothing we can do—now."

Paula moved at the words, as though they had awakened a new energy in her. With a supreme effort she raised herself.

"Then I—I failed?" she cried, catching sight of Kennedy.

"No, Miss Lowe," he answered gently. "You won. The plans of the terrible gun are destroyed. The Baron is safe. Mrs. Annenberg has herself smoked one of the fatal cigarettes intended for him."

Kreiger looked at us, uncomprehending. Kennedy picked up the crushed, unlighted cigarette and laid it in the palm of his hand beside another, half smoked, which he had found beside Mrs. Annen-berg.

"They are deadly," he said simply to Kreiger. "A few drops of pure nicotine hidden by that pretty gilt tip would have accomplished all that the bitterest anarchist could desire."

All at once Kreiger seemed to realize what he had escaped so narrowly. He turned toward Paula. The revulsion of her feelings at seeing him safe was too much for her shattered nerves.

With a faint little cry, she tottered.

Before any of us could reach her, he had caught her in his arms and imprinted a warm kiss on the insensible lips.

"Some water—quick!" he cried, still holding her close.

CHAPTER IV

THE AIR PIRATE

ROUNDING up the "Group" took several days, and it proved to be a great story for the *Star*. I was pretty fagged when it was all over, but there was a great deal of satisfaction in knowing that we had frustrated one of the most daring anarchist plots of recent years.

"Can you arrange to spend the week-end with me at Stuyvesant Verplanck's at Bluffwood?" asked Kennedy over the telephone, the afternoon that I had completed my work on the newspaper of undoing what Annenberg and the rest had attempted.

"How long since society took you up?" I asked airily, adding, "Is it a large house party you are getting up?"

"You have heard of the so-called 'phantom bandit' of Bluffwood, haven't you?" he returned rather brusquely, as though there was no time now for bantering.

I confess that in the excitement of the anarchists I had forgotten it, but now I recalled that for several days I had been reading little paragraphs about robberies on the big estates on the Long Island shore of the Sound. One of the local correspondents had called the robber a "phantom bandit," but I had thought it nothing more than an attempt to make good copy out of a rather ordinary occurrence.

"Well," he hurried on, "that's the reason why I have been 'taken up by society,' as you so elegantly phrase it. From the secret hiding-places of the boudoirs and safes of fashionable women at Bluff-wood, thousands of dollars' worth of jewels and other trinkets have mysteriously vanished. Of course you'll come along. Why, it will be just the story to tone up that alleged page of society news you hand out in the Sunday *Star*. There—we're quits now. Seriously, though, Walter, it really seems to be a very baffling case, or rather series of cases. The whole colony out there is terrorized. They don't know who the robber is, or how he operates, or who will be the next victim, but his skill and success seem almost uncanny. Mr. Ver-planck has put one of his cars at my disposal and I'm up here at the laboratory gathering some ap-paratus that may be useful. I'll pick you up any-where between this and the Bridge—how about Co-lumbus Circle in half an hour?"

"Good," I agreed, deciding quickly from his tone and manner of assurance that it would be a case I could not afford to miss.

The Stuyvesant Verplancks, I knew, were among the leaders of the rather recherché society at Bluff-wood, and the pace at which Bluffwood moved and had its being was such as to guarantee a good story in one way or another.

"Why," remarked Kennedy, as we sped out over the picturesque roads of the north shore of Long Island, "this fellow, or fellows, seems to have taken the measure of all the wealthy members of the ex-clusive organizations out there—the Westport Yacht Club, the Bluffwood Country Club, the North Shore Hunt, and all of them. It's a positive scandal, the

ease with which he seems to come and go without
detection, striking now here, now there, often at
places that it seems physically impossible to get at,
and yet always with the same diabolical skill and
success. One night he will take some baubles worth
thousands, the next pass them by for something apparently of no value at all, a piece of bric-à-brac, a
bundle of letters, anything."

"Seems purposeless, insane, doesn't it?" I put in.

"Not when he always takes something—often
more valuable than money," returned Craig.

He leaned back in the car and surveyed the
glimpses of bay and countryside as we were whisked
by the breaks in the trees.

"Walter," he remarked meditatively, "have you
ever considered the possibilities of blackmail if the
right sort of evidence were obtained under this new
'white-slavery act'? Scandals that some of the fast
set may be inclined to wink at, that at worst used
to end in Reno, become felonies with federal prison
sentences looming up in the background. Think
it over."

Stuyvesant Verplanck had telephoned rather hurriedly to Craig earlier in the day, retaining his services, but telling only in the briefest way of the extent of the depredations, and hinting that more than
jewelry might be at stake.

It was a pleasant ride, but we finished it in silence. Verplanck was, as I recalled, a large master-
ful man, one of those who demanded and liked large
things—such as the estate of several hundred acres
which we at last entered.

It was on a neck of land with the restless waters
of the Sound on one side and the calmer waters of
the bay on the other. Westport Bay lay in a beau-

tifully wooded, hilly country, and the house itself
was on an elevation, with a huge sweep of terraced
lawn before it down to the water's edge. All around,
for miles, were other large estates, a veritable colony of wealth.

As we pulled up under the broad stone porte-
cochère, Verplanck, who had been expecting us, led
the way into his library, a great room, literally
crowded with curios and objects of art which he had
collected on his travels. It was a superb mental
workshop, overlooking the bay, with a stretch of
several miles of sheltered water.

"You will recall," began Verplanck, wasting no
time over preliminaries, but plunging directly into
the subject, "that the prominent robberies of late
have been at seacoast resorts, especially on the
shores of Long Island Sound, within, say, a hundred
miles of New York. There has been a great deal of
talk about dark and muffled automobiles that have
conveyed mysterious parties swiftly and silently
across country.

"My theory," he went on self-assertively, "is that
the attack has been made always along water routes.
Under shadow of darkness, it is easy to slip into one
of the sheltered coves or miniature fiords with which
the north coast of the Island abounds, land a cut-
throat crew primed with exact information of the
treasure on some of these estates. Once the booty
is secured, the criminal could put out again into the
Sound without leaving a clue."

He seemed to be considering his theory. "Perhaps the robberies last summer at Narragansett,
Newport, and a dozen other New England places
were perpetrated by the same cracksman. I believe," he concluded, lowering his voice, "that there

plies to-day on the wide waters of the Sound a slim, swift motor boat which wears the air of a pleasure craft, yet is as black a pirate as ever flew the Jolly Roger. She may at this moment be anchored off some exclusive yacht club, flying the respectable burgee of the club—who knows?"

He paused as if his deductions settled the case so far. He would have resumed in the same vein, if the door had not opened. A lady in a cobwebby gown entered the room. She was of middle age, but had retained her youth with a skill that her sisters of less leisure always envy. Evidently she had not expected to find anyone, yet nothing seemed to disconcert her.

"Mrs. Verplanck," her husband introduced, "Professor Kennedy and his associate, Mr. Jameson—those detectives we have heard about. We were discussing the robberies."

"Oh, yes," she said, smiling, "my husband has been thinking of forming himself into a vigilance committee. The local authorities are all at sea."

I thought there was a trace of something veiled in the remark and fancied, not only then but later, that there was an air of constraint between the couple.

"You have not been robbed yourself?" queried Craig tentatively.

"Indeed we have," exclaimed Verplanck quickly. "The other night I was awakened by the noise of some one down here in this very library. I fired a shot, wild, and shouted, but before I could get down here the intruder had fled through a window, and half rolling down the terraces. Mrs. Verplanck was awakened by the rumpus and both of us heard a peculiar whirring noise."

"Like an automobile muffled down," she put in.

"No," he asserted vigorously, "more like a powerful motor boat, one with the exhaust under water."

"Well," she shrugged, "at any rate, we saw no one."

"Did the intruder get anything?"

"That's the lucky part. He had just opened this safe apparently and begun to ransack it. This is my private safe. Mrs. Verplanck has another built into her own room upstairs where she keeps her jewels."

"It is not a very modern safe, is it?" ventured Kennedy. "The fellow ripped off the outer casing with what they call a 'can-opener.'"

"No. I keep it against fire rather than burglars. But he overlooked a box of valuable heirlooms, some silver with the Verplanck arms. I think I must have scared him off just in time. He seized a package in the safe, but it was only some business correspondence. I don't relish having lost it, particularly. It related to a gentlemen's agreement a number of us had in the recent cotton corner. I suppose the Government would like to have it. But—here's the point. If it is so easy to get in and get away, no one in Bluffwood is safe."

"Why, he robbed the Montgomery Carter place the other night," remarked Mrs. Verplanck, "and almost got a lot of old Mrs. Carter's jewels as well as stuff belonging to her son, Montgomery, Junior. That was the first robbery. Mr. Carter, that is Junior—Monty, everyone calls him—and his chauffeur almost captured the fellow, but he managed to escape in the woods."

"In the woods?" repeated Craig.

Mrs. Verplanck nodded. "But they saved the loot he was about to take."

"Oh, no one is safe any more," reiterated Verplanck. "Carter seems to be the only one who has had a real chance at him, and he was able to get away neatly."

"But he's not the only one who got off without a loss," she put in significantly. "The last visit——" Then she paused.

"Where was the last attempt?" asked Kennedy.

"At the house of Mrs. Hollingsworth—around the point on this side of the bay. You can't see it from here."

"I'd like to go there," remarked Kennedy.

"Very well. Car or boat?"

"Boat, I think."

"Suppose we go in my little runabout, the *Streamline II?* She's as fast as any ordinary automobile."

"Very good. Then we can get an idea of the harbor."

"I'll telephone first that we are coming," said Verplanck.

"I think I'll go, too," considered Mrs. Verplanck, ringing for a heavy wrap.

"Just as you please," said Verplanck.

The *Streamline* was a three-stepped boat which Verplanck had built for racing, a beautiful craft, managed much like a racing automobile. As she started from the dock, the purring drone of her eight cylinders sent her feathering over the waves like a skipping stone. She sank back into the water, her bow leaping upward, a cloud of spray in her wake, like a waterspout.

Mrs. Hollingsworth was a wealthy divorcée, living rather quietly with her two children, of whom the courts had awarded her the care. She was a striking woman, one of those for whom the new

4

styles of dress seem especially to have been designed. I gathered, however, that she was not on
very good terms with the little Westport clique in
which the Verplancks moved, or at least not with
Mrs. Verplanck. The two women seemed to regard
each other rather coldly, I thought, although Mr.
Verplanck, man-like, seemed to scorn any distinc-
tions and was more than cordial. I wondered why
Mrs. Verplanck had come.

The Hollingsworth house was a beautiful little
place down the bay from the Yacht Club, but not
as far as Verplanck's, or the Carter estate, which
was opposite.

"Yes," replied Mrs. Hollingsworth when the reason for our visit had been explained, "the attempt
was a failure. I happened to be awake, rather late,
or perhaps you would call it early. I thought I
heard a noise as if some one was trying to break
into the drawing-room through the window. I
switched on all the lights. I have them arranged so
for just that purpose of scaring off intruders. Then,
as I looked out of my window on the second floor, I
fancied I could see a dark figure slink into the
shadow of the shubbery at the side of the house.
Then there was a whirr. It might have been an
automobile, although it sounded differently from
that—more like a motor boat. At any rate, there
was no trace of a car that we could discover in the
morning. The road had been oiled, too, and a car
would have left marks. And yet some one was here.
There were marks on the drawing-room window just
where I heard the sounds."

Who could it be? I asked myself as we left. I
knew that the great army of chauffeurs was infested
with thieves, thugs and gunmen. Then, too, there

were maids, always useful as scouts for these corsairs who prey on the rich.   Yet so adroitly had everything been done in these cases that not a clue seemed to have been left behind by which to trace the thief.

We returned to Verplanck's in the *Streamline* in record time, dined, and then found McNeill, a local detective, waiting to add his quota of information. McNeill was of the square-toed, double-chinned, bull-necked variety, just the man to take along if there was any fighting.   He had, however, very little to add to the solution of the mystery, apparently believing in the chauffeur-and-maid theory.

It was too late to do anything more that night, and we sat on the Verplanck porch, overlooking the beautiful harbor.   It was a black, inky night, with no moon, one of those nights when the myriad lights on the boats were mere points in the darkness.   As we looked out over the water, considering the case which as yet we had hardly started on, Kennedy seemed engrossed in the study in black.

"I thought I saw a moving light for an instant across the bay, above the boats, and as though it were in the darkness of the hills on the other side. Is there a road over there, above the Carter house?" he asked suddenly.

"There is a road part of the way on the crest of the hill," replied Mrs. Verplanck.   "You can see a car on it, now and then, through the trees, like a moving light."

"Over there, I mean," reiterated Kennedy, indicating the light as it flashed now faintly, then disappeared, to reappear further along, like a gigantic firefly in the night.

"N-no," said Verplanck.   "I don't think the road

runs down as far as that. It is further up the bay."

"What is it then?" asked Kennedy, half to him-self. "It seems to be traveling rapidly. Now it must be about opposite the Carter house. There—it has gone."

We continued to watch for several minutes, but it did not reappear. Could it have been a light on the mast of a boat moving rapidly up the bay and perhaps nearer to us than we suspected? Nothing further happened, however, and we retired early, expecting to start with fresh minds on the case in the morning. Several watchmen whom Verplanck employed both on the shore and along the drive-ways were left guarding every possible entrance to the estate.

Yet the next morning as we met in the cheery east breakfast room, Verplanck's gardener came in, hat in hand, with much suppressed excitement.

In his hand he held an orange which he had found in the shrubbery underneath the windows of the house. In it was stuck a long nail and to the nail was fastened a tag.

Kennedy read it quickly.

"If this had been a bomb, you and your detectives would never have known what struck you.
                                        "AQUAERO."

CHAPTER V

THE ULTRA-VIOLET RAY

"GOOD Gad, man!" exclaimed Verplanck, who had read it over Craig's shoulder. "What do you make of *that?*"

Kennedy merely shook his head. Mrs. Verplanck was the calmest of all.

"The light," I cried. "You remember the light? Could it have been a signal to some one on this side of the bay, a signal light in the woods?"

"Possibly," commented Kennedy absently, adding, "Robbery with this fellow seems to be an art as carefully strategized as a promoter's plan or a merchant's trade campaign. I think I'll run over this morning and see if there is any trace of anything on the Carter estate."

Just then the telephone rang insistently. It was McNeill, much excited, though he had not heard of the orange incident. Verplanck answered the call.

"Have you heard the news?" asked McNeill. "They report this morning that that fellow must have turned up last night at Belle Aire."

"Belle Aire? Why, man, that's fifty miles away and on the other side of the island. He was here last night," and Verplanck related briefly the find of the morning. "No boat could get around the

45

island in that time and as for a car—those roads
are almost impossible at night."

"Can't help it," returned McNeill doggedly.
"The Halstead estate out at Belle Aire was robbed
last night. It's spooky all right."

"Tell McNeill I want to see him—will meet him
in the village directly," cut in Craig before Verplanck had finished.

We bolted a hasty breakfast and in one of Verplanck's cars hurried to meet McNeill.

"What do you intend doing?" he asked helplessly, as Kennedy finished his recital of the queer
doings of the night before.

"I'm going out now to look around the Carter
place. Can you come along?"

"Surely," agreed McNeill, climbing into the car.
"You know him?"

"No."

"Then I'll introduce you. Queer chap, Carter.
He's a lawyer, although I don't think he has much
practice, except managing his mother's estate."

McNeill settled back in the luxurious car with
an exclamation of satisfaction.

"What do you think of Verplanck?" he asked.

"He seems to me to be a very public-spirited
man," answered Kennedy discreetly.

That, however, was not what McNeill meant and
he ignored it. And so for the next ten minutes we
were entertained with a little retail scandal of Westport and Bluffwood, including a tale that seemed to
have gained currency that Verplanck and Mrs. Hollingsworth were too friendly to please Mrs. Verplanck. I set the whole thing down to the hostility
and jealousy of the towns people who misinterpret
everything possible in the smart set, although I could

not help recalling how quickly she had spoken when we had visited the Hollingsworth house in the *Streamline* the day before.

Montgomery Carter happened to be at home and, at least openly, interposed no objection to our going about the grounds.

"You see," explained Kennedy, watching the effect of his words as if to note whether Carter himself had noticed anything unusual the night before, "we saw a light moving over here last night. To tell the truth, I half expected you would have a story to add to ours, of a second visit."

Carter smiled. "No objection at all. I'm simply nonplussed at the nerve of this fellow, coming back again. I guess you've heard what a narrow squeak he had with me. You're welcome to go anywhere, just so long as you don't disturb my study down there in the boathouse. I use that because it overlooks the bay—just the place to study over knotty legal problems."

Back of, or in front of the Carter house, according as you fancied it faced the bay or not, was the boathouse, built by Carter's father, who had been a great yachtsman in his day and commodore of the club. His son had not gone in much for water sports and had converted the corner underneath a sort of observation tower into a sort of country law office.

"There has always seemed to me to be something strange about that boathouse since the old man died," remarked McNeill in a half whisper as we left Carter. "He always keeps it locked and never lets anyone go in there, although they say he has it fitted beautifully with hundreds of volumes of law books, too."

Kennedy had been climbing the hill back of the house and now paused to look about. Below was the Carter garage.

"By the way," exclaimed McNeill, as if he had at last hit on a great discovery, "Carter has a new chauffeur, a fellow named Wickham. I just saw him driving down to the village. He's a chap that it might pay us to watch—a newcomer, smart as a steel trap, they say, but not much of a talker."

"Suppose you take that job—watch him," encouraged Kennedy. "We can't know too much about strangers here, McNeill."

"That's right," agreed the detective. "I'll follow him back to the village and get a line on him."

"Don't be easily discouraged," added Kennedy, as McNeill started down the hill to the garage. "If he is a fox he'll try to throw you off the trail. Hang on."

"What was that for?" I asked as the detective disappeared. "Did you want to get rid of him?"

"Partly," replied Craig, descending slowly, after a long survey of the surrounding country.

We had reached the garage, deserted now except for our own car.

"I'd like to investigate that tower," remarked Kennedy with a keen look at me, "if it could be done without seeming to violate Mr. Carter's hospitality."

"Well," I observed, my eye catching a ladder beside the garage, "there's a ladder. We can do no more than try."

He walked over to the automobile, took a little package out, slipped it into his pocket, and a few minutes later we had set the ladder up against the side of the boathouse farthest away from the house.

It was the work of only a moment for Kennedy to scale it and prowl across the roof to the tower, while I stood guard at the foot.

"No one has been up there recently," he panted breathlessly as he rejoined me.   "There isn't a sign."

We took the ladder quietly back to the garage, then Kennedy led the way down the shore to a sort of little summerhouse cut off from the boathouse and garage by the trees, though over the top of a hedge one could still see the boathouse tower.

We sat down, and Craig filled his lungs with the good salt air, sweeping his eye about the blue and green panorama as though this were a holiday and not a mystery case.

"Walter," he said at length, "I wish you'd take the car and go around to Verplanck's.   I don't think you can see the tower through the trees, but I should like to be sure."

I found that it could not be seen, though I tried all over the place and got myself disliked by the gardener and suspected by a watchman with a dog.

It could not have been from the tower of the boathouse that we had seen the light, and I hurried back to Craig to tell him so.   But when I returned, I found that he was impatiently pacing the little rustic summerhouse, no longer interested in what he had sent me to find out.

"What has happened?" I asked eagerly.

"Just come out here and I'll show you something," he replied, leaving the summerhouse and approaching the boathouse from the other side of the hedge, on the beach, so that the house itself cut us off from observation from Carter's.

"I fixed a lens on the top of that tower when I

was up there," he explained, pointing up at it. "It must be about fifty feet high. From there, you see, it throws a reflection down to this mirror. I did it because through a skylight in the tower I could read whatever was written by anyone sitting at Carter's desk in the corner under it."

"Read?" I repeated, mystified.

"Yes, by invisible light," he continued. "This invisible light business, you know, is pretty well understood by this time. I was only repeating what was suggested once by Professor Wood of Johns Hopkins. Practically all sources of light, you understand, give out more or less ultraviolet light, which plays no part in vision whatever. The human eye is sensitive to but few of the light rays that reach it, and if our eyes were constituted just the least bit differently we should have an entirely different set of images.

"But by the use of various devices we can, as it were, translate these ultraviolet rays into terms of what the human eye can see. In order to do it, all the visible light rays which show us the thing as we see it—the tree green, the sky blue—must be cut off. So in taking an ultraviolet photograph a screen must be used which will be opaque to these visible rays and yet will let the ultraviolet rays through to form the image. That gave Professor Wood a lot of trouble. Glass won't do, for glass cuts off the ultraviolet rays entirely. Quartz is a very good medium, but it does not cut off all the visible light. In fact there is only one thing that will do the work, and that is metallic silver."

I could not fathom what he was driving at, but the fascination of Kennedy himself was quite sufficient.

"Silver," he went on, "is all right if the objects can be illuminated by an electric spark or some other source rich in the rays. But it isn't entirely satisfactory when sunlight is concerned, for various reasons that I need not bore you with. Professor Wood has worked out a process of depositing nickel on glass. That's it up there," he concluded, wheeling a lower reflector about until it caught the image of the afternoon sun thrown from the lens on the top of the tower.

"You see," he resumed, "that upper lens is concave so that it enlarges tremendously. I can do some wonderful tricks with that."

I had been lighting a cigarette and held a box of safety wind matches in my hand.

"Give me that matchbox," he asked.

He placed it at the foot of the tower. Then he went off, I should say, without exaggeration, a hundred feet.

The lettering on the matchbox could be seen in the silvered mirror, enlarged to such a point that the letters were plainly visible!

"Think of the possibilities in that," he added excitedly. "I saw them at once. You can read what some one is writing at a desk a hundred, perhaps two hundred feet away."

"Yes," I cried, more interested in the practical aspects of it than in the mechanics and optics. "What have you found?"

"Some one came into the boathouse while you were away," he said. "He had a note. It read, 'Those new detectives are watching everything. We must have the evidence. You must get those letters to-night, without fail.' "

"Letters—evidence," I repeated. "Who wrote it? Who received it?"

"I couldn't see over the hedge who had entered the boathouse, and by the time I got around here he was gone."

"Was it Wickham—or intended for Wickham?" I asked.

Kennedy shrugged his shoulders.

"We'll gain nothing by staying here," he said. "There is just one possibility in the case, and I can guard against that only by returning to Verplanck's and getting some of that stuff I brought up here with me. Let us go."

Late in the afternoon though it was, after our return, Kennedy insisted on hurrying from Verplanck's to the Yacht Club up the bay. It was a large building, extending out into the water on made land, from which ran a long, substantial dock. He had stopped long enough only to ask Verplanck to lend him the services of his best mechanician, a Frenchman named Armand.

On the end of the yacht club dock Kennedy and Armand set up a large affair which looked like a mortar. I watched curiously, dividing my attention between them and the splendid view of the harbor which the end of the dock commanded on all sides.

"What is this?" I asked finally. "Fireworks?"

"A rocket mortar of light weight," explained Kennedy, then dropped into French as he explained to Armand the manipulation of the thing.

There was a searchlight near by on the dock.

"You can use that?" queried Kennedy.

"Oh, yes. Mr. Verplanck, he is vice-commodore

of the club. Oh, yes, I can use that. **Why, Monsieur?**"

Kennedy had uncovered a round brass case. It did not seem to amount to much, as compared to some of the complicated apparatus he had used. In it was a four-sided prism of glass—I should have said, cut off the corner of a huge glass cube.

He handed it to us.

"Look in it," he said.

It certainly was about the most curious piece of crystal gazing I had ever done. Turn the thing any way I pleased and I could see my face in it, just as in an ordinary mirror.

"What do you call it?" Armand asked, much interested.

"A triple mirror," replied Kennedy, and again, half in English and half in French, neither of which I could follow, he explained the use of the mirror to the mechanician.

We were returning up the dock, leaving Armand with instructions to be at the club at dusk, when we met McNeill, tired and disgusted.

"What luck?" asked Kennedy.

"Nothing," he returned. "I had a 'short' shadow and a 'long' shadow at Wickham's heels all day. You know what I mean. Instead of one man, two— the second sleuthing in the other's tracks. If he escaped Number One, Number Two would take it up, and I was ready to move up into Number Two's place. They kept him in sight about all the time. Not a fact. But then, of course, we don't know what he was doing before we took up tailing him. Say," he added, "I have just got word from an agency with which I correspond in New York that it is reported that a yeggman named 'Australia

Mac,' a very daring and clever chap, has been at-
tempting to dispose of some of the goods which we
know have been stolen through one of the worst
'fences' in New York."

"Is that all?" asked Craig, with the mention of
Australia Mac showing the first real interest yet in
anything that McNeill had done since we met him
the night before.

"All so far. I wired for more details immediately."

"Do you know anything about this Australia
Mac?"

"Not much. No one does. He's a new man, it
seems, to the police here."

"Be here at eight o'clock, McNeill," said Craig,
as we left the club for Verplanck's. "If you can
find out more about this yeggman, so much the better."

"Have you made any progress?" asked Verplanck
as we entered the estate a few minutes later.

"Yes," returned Craig, telling only enough to
whet his interest. "There's a clue, as I half expected, from New York, too. But we are so far
away that we'll have to stick to my original plan.
You can trust Armand?"

"Absolutely."

"Then we shall transfer our activity to the Yacht
Club to-night," was all that Kennedy vouchsafed.

CHAPTER VI

IT was the regular Saturday night dance at the club, a brilliant spectacle, faces that radiated pleasure, gowns that for startling combinations of color would have shamed a Futurist, music that set the feet tapping irresistibly—a scene which I shall pass over because it really has no part in the story.

The fascination of the ballroom was utterly lost on Craig. "Think of all the houses only half guarded about here to-night," he mused, as we joined Armand and McNeill on the end of the dock. I could not help noting that that was the only idea which the gay, variegated, sparkling tango throng conveyed to him.

In front of the club was strung out a long line of cars, and at the dock several speed boats of national and international reputation, among them the famous *Streamline II*, at our instant beck and call. In it Craig had already placed some rather bulky pieces of apparatus, as well as a brass case containing a second triple mirror like that which he had left with Armand.

With McNeill, I walked back along the pier, leaving Kennedy with Armand, until we came to the wide porch, where we joined the wallflowers and the rocking-chair fleet. Mrs. Verplanck, I observed, was

55

a beautiful dancer. I picked her out in the throng immediately, dancing with Carter.

McNeill tugged at my sleeve. Without a word I saw what he meant me to see. Verplanck and Mrs. Hollingsworth were dancing together. Just then, across the porch I caught sight of Kennedy at one of the wide windows. He was trying to attract Verplanck's attention, and as he did so I worked my way through the throng of chatting couples leaving the floor until I reached him. Verplanck, oblivious, finished the dance; then, seeming to recollect that he had something to attend to, caught sight of us, and ran off during the intermission from the gay crowd to which he resigned Mrs. Hollingsworth.

"What is it?" he asked.

"There's that light down the bay," whispered Kennedy.

Instantly Verplanck forgot about the dance.

"Where?" he asked.

"In the same place."

I had not noticed, but Mrs. Verplanck, woman-like, had been able to watch several things at once. She had seen us and had joined us.

"Would you like to run down there in the *Streamline?*" he asked. "It will only take a few minutes."

"Very much."

"What is it—that light again?" she asked, as she joined us in walking down the dock.

"Yes," answered her husband, pausing to look for a moment at the stuff Kennedy had left with Armand. Mrs. Verplanck leaned over the *Streamline,* turned as she saw me, and said: "I wish I could go with you. But evening dress is not the thing for a shivery night in a speed boat. I think I know as

much about it as Mr. Verplanck. Are you going to
leave Armand?"

"Yes," replied Kennedy, taking his place beside
Verplanck, who was seated at the steering wheel.
"Walter and McNeill, if you two will sit back there,
we're ready. All right."

Armand had cast us off and Mrs. Verplanck
waved from the end of the float as the *Streamline*
quickly shot out into the night, a buzzing, throbbing
shape of mahogany and brass, with her exhausts
sticking out like funnels and booming like a pipe
organ. It took her only seconds to eat into the
miles.

"A little more to port," said Kennedy, as Verplanck swung her around.

Just then the steady droning of the engine seemed
a bit less rhythmical. Verplanck throttled her
down, but it had no effect. He shut her off. Something was wrong. As he crawled out into the space
forward of us where the engine was, it seemed as
if the *Streamline* had broken down suddenly and
completely.

Here we were floundering around in the middle of
the bay.

"Chuck-chuck-chuck," came in quick staccato out
of the night. It was Montgomery Carter, alone, on
his way across the bay from the club, in his own
boat.

"Hello—Carter," called Verplanck.

"Hello, Verplanck. What's the matter?"

"Don't know. Engine trouble of some kind. Can
you give us a line?"

"I've got to go down to the house," he said,
ranging up near us. "Then I can take you back.
Perhaps I'd better get you out of the way of any

5

other boats first. You don't mind going over and then back?"

Verplanck looked at Craig. "On the contrary," muttered Craig, as he made fast the welcome line.

The Carter dock was some three miles from the club on the other side of the bay. As we came up to it, Carter shut off his engine, bent over it a moment, made fast, and left us with a hurried, "Wait here."

Suddenly, overhead, we heard a peculiar whirring noise that seemed to vibrate through the air. Something huge, black, monster-like, slid down a board runway into the water, traveled a few feet, in white suds and spray, rose in the darkness—and was gone!

As the thing disappeared, I thought I could hear a mocking laugh flung back at us.

"What is it?" I asked, straining my eyes at what had seemed for an instant like a great flying fish with finny tail and huge fins at the sides and above.

"'Aquaero,'" quoted Kennedy quickly. "Don't you understand—a hydroaeroplane—a flying boat. There are hundreds of privately owned flying boats now wherever there is navigable water. That was the secret of Carter's boathouse, of the light we saw in the air."

"But this Aquaero—who is he?" persisted McNeill. "Carter—Wickham—Australia Mac?"

We looked at each other blankly. No one said a word. We were captured, just as effectively as if we were ironed in a dungeon. There were the black water, the distant lights, which at any other time I should have said would have been beautiful.

Kennedy had sprung into Carter's boat.

"The deuce," he exclaimed. "He's put her out
ɛf business."

Verplanck, chagrined, had been going over his
own engine feverishly. "Do you see that?" he
asked suddenly, holding up in the light of a lantern
a little nut which he had picked out of the complicated machinery. "It never belonged to this engine.
Some one placed it there, knowing it would work its
way into a vital part with the vibration."

Who was the person, the only one who could have
done it? The answer was on my lips, but I repressed it. Mrs. Verplanck herselt had been bending over the engine when last I saw her. All at
once it flashed over me that she knew more about
the phantom bandit than she had admitted. Yet
what possible object could she have had in putting
the *Streamline* out of commission?

My mind was working rapidly, piecing together
the fragmentary facts. The remark of Kennedy,
long before, instantly assumed new significance.
What were the possibilities of blackmail in the right
sort of evidence? The yeggman had been after
what was more valuable than jewels—letters!
Whose? Suddenly I saw the situation. Carter had
not been robbed at all. He was in league with the
robber. That much was a blind to divert suspicion.
He was a lawyer—some one's lawyer. I recalled the
message about letters and evidence, and as I did so
there came to mind a picture of Carter and the
woman he had been dancing with. In return for
his inside information about the jewels of the
wealthy homes of Bluffwood, the yeggman was to
get something of interest and importance to his
client.

The situation called for instant action. Yet what

could we do, marooned on the other side of the bay?

From the Club dock a long finger of light swept out into the night, plainly enough near the dock, but diffused and disclosing nothing in the distance. Armand had trained it down the bay in the direction we had taken, but by the time the beam reached us it was so weak that it was lost.

Craig had leaped up on the Carter dock and was capping and uncapping with the brass cover the package which contained the triple mirror.

Still in the distance I could see the wide path of light, aimed toward us, but of no avail.

"What are you doing?" I asked.

"Using the triple mirror to signal to Armand. It is something better than wireless. Wireless requires heavy and complicated apparatus. This is portable, heatless, almost weightless, a source of light depending for its power on another source of light at a great distance."

I wondered how Armand could ever detect its feeble ray.

"Even in the case of a rolling ship," Kennedy continued, alternately covering and uncovering the mirror, "the beam of light which this mirror reflects always goes back, unerring, to its source. It would do so from an aeroplane, so high in the air that it could not be located. The returning beam is invisible to anyone not immediately in the path of the ray, and the ray always goes to the observer. It is simply a matter of pure mathematics practically applied. The angle of incidence equals the angle of reflection. There is not a variation of a foot in two miles."

"What message are you sending him?" asked Verplanck.

"To tell Mrs. Hollingsworth to hurry home immediately," Kennedy replied, still flashing the letters according to his code.

"Mrs. Hollingsworth?" repeated Verplanck, looking up.

"Yes. This hydroaeroplane yeggman is after something besides jewels to-night. Were those letters that were stolen from you the only ones you had in the safe?"

Verplanck looked up quickly. "Yes, yes. Of course."

"You had none from a woman——"

"No," he almost shouted. Of a sudden it seemed to dawn on him what Kennedy was driving at—the robbery of his own house with no loss except of a packet of letters on business, followed by the attempt on Mrs. Hollingsworth. "Do you think I'd keep dynamite, even in the safe?"

To hide his confusion he had turned and was bending again over the engine.

"How is it?" asked Kennedy, his signaling over.

"Able to run on four cylinders and one propeller," replied Verplanck.

"Then let's try her. Watch the engine. I'll take the wheel."

Limping along, the engine skipping and missing, the once peerless *Streamline* started back across the bay. Instead of heading toward the club, Kennedy pointed her bow somewhere between that and Verplanck's.

"I wish Armand would get busy," he remarked, after glancing now and then in the direction of the club. "What can be the matter?"

"What do you mean?" I asked.

There came the boom as if of a gun far away in the direction in which he was looking, then another.

"Oh, there it is. Good fellow. I suppose he had to deliver my message to Mrs. Hollingsworth himself first."

From every quarter showed huge balls of fire, rising from the sea, as it were, with a brilliantly luminous flame.

"What is it?" I asked, somewhat startled.

"A German invention for use at night against torpedo and aeroplane attacks. From that mortar Armand has shot half a dozen bombs of phosphide of calcium which are hurled far into the darkness. They are so constructed that they float after a short plunge and are ignited on contact by the action of the salt water itself."

It was a beautiful pyrotechnic display, lighting up the shore and hills of the bay as if by an unearthly flare.

"There's that thing now!" exclaimed Kennedy.

In the glow we could see a peculiar, birdlike figure flying through the air over toward the Hollingsworth house. It was the hydroaeroplane.

Out from the little stretch of lawn under the accentuated shadow of the trees, she streaked into the air, swaying from side to side as the pilot operated the stabilizers on the ends of the planes to counteract the puffs of wind off the land.

How could she ever be stopped?

The *Streamline,* halting and limping, though she was, had almost crossed the bay before the light bombs had been fired by Armand. Every moment brought the flying boat nearer.

She swerved. Evidently the pilot had seen us at

last and realized who we were. I was so engrossed watching the thing that I had not noticed that Kennedy had given the wheel to Verplanck and was standing in the bow, endeavoring to sight what looked like a huge gun.

In rapid succession half a dozen shots rang out. I fancied I could almost hear the ripping and tearing of the tough rubber-coated silken wings of the hydroaeroplane as the wind widened the perforation the gun had made.

She had not been flying high, but now she swooped down almost like a gull, seeking to rest on the water. We were headed toward her now, and as the flying boat sank I saw one of the passengers rise in his seat, swing his arm, and far out something splashed in the bay.

On the water, with wings helpless, the flying boat was no match for the *Streamline* now. She struck at an acute angle, rebounded in the air for a moment, and with a hiss skittered along over the waves, planing with the help of her exhaust under the step of the boat.

There she was, a hull, narrow, scow-bowed, like a hydroplane, with a long pointed stern and a cockpit for two men, near the bow. There were two wide, winglike planes, on a light latticework of wood covered with silk, trussed and wired like a kite frame, the upper plane about five feet above the lower, which was level with the boat deck. We could see the eight-cylindered engine which drove a two-bladed wooden propeller, and over the stern were the air rudder and the horizontal planes. There she was, the hobbled steed now of the phantom bandit who had accomplished the seemingly impossible.

In spite of everything, however, the flying boat reached the shore a trifle ahead of us. As she did so both figures in her jumped, and one disappeared quickly up the bank, leaving the other alone.

"Verplanck, McNeill—get him," cried Kennedy, as our own boat grated on the beach. "Come, Walter, we'll take the other one."

The man had seen that there was no safety in flight. Down the shore he stood, without a hat, his hair blown pompadour by the wind.

As we approached Carter turned superciliously, unbuttoning his bulky khaki life preserver jacket.

"Well?" he asked coolly.

Not for a moment did Kennedy allow the assumed coolness to take him back, knowing that Carter's delay did not cover the retreat of the other man.

"So," Craig exclaimed, "you are the—the air pirate?"

Carter disdained to reply.

"It was you who suggested the millionaire households, full of jewels, silver and gold, only half guarded; you, who knew the habits of the people; you, who traded that information in return for another piece of thievery by your partner, Australia Mac—Wickham he called himself here in Bluffwood. It was you——"

A car drove up hastily, and I noted that we were still on the Hollingsworth estate. Mrs. Hollingsworth had seen us and had driven over toward us.

"Montgomery!" she cried, startled.

"Yes," said Kennedy quickly, "air pirate and lawyer for Mrs. Verplanck in the suit which she contemplated bringing——"

Mrs. Hollingsworth grew pale under the ghastly, flickering light from the bay.

"Oh!" she cried, realizing at what Kennedy hinted, "the letters!"

"At the bottom of the harbor, now," said Kennedy. "Mr. Verplanck tells me he has destroyed his. The past is blotted out as far as that is concerned. The future is—for you three to determine. For the present I've caught a yeggman and a blackmailer."

CHAPTER VII

THE WIRELESS WIRETAPPERS

KENNEDY did not wait at Bluffwood longer than was necessary. It was easy enough now to silence Montgomery Carter, and the reconciliation of the Verplancks was assured. In the *Star* I made the case appear at the time to involve merely the capture of Australia Mac.

When I dropped into the office the next day as usual, I found that I had another assignment that would take me out on Long Island. The story looked promising and I was rather pleased to get it.

"Bound for Seaville, I'll wager," sounded a familiar voice in my ear, as I hurried up to the train entrance at the Long Island corner of the Pennsylvania Station.

I turned quickly, to find Kennedy just behind me, breathless and perspiring.

"Er—yes," I stammered in surprise at seeing him so unexpectedly, "but where did you come from? How did you know?"

"Let me introduce Mr. Jack Waldon," he went on, as we edged our way toward the gate, "the brother of Mrs. Tracy Edwards, who disappeared so strangely from the houseboat *Lucie* last night at Seaville. That is the case you're going to write up, isn't it?"

It was then for the first time that I noticed

the excited young man beside Kennedy was really his companion.

I shook hands with Waldon, who gave me a grip that was both a greeting and an added impulse in our general direction through the wicket.

"Might have known the *Star* would assign you to this Edwards case," panted Kennedy, mopping his forehead, for the heat in the terminal was oppressive and the crowd, though not large, was closely packed. "Mr. Jameson is my right-hand man," he explained to Waldon, taking us each by the arm and urging us forward. "Waldon was afraid we might miss the train or I should have tried to get you, Walter, at the office."

It was all done so suddenly that they quite took away what remaining breath I had, as we settled ourselves to swelter in the smoker instead of in the concourse. I did not even protest at the matter-of-fact assurance with which Craig assumed that his deduction as to my destination was correct.

Waldon, a handsome young fellow in a flannel suit and yachting cap somewhat the worse for his evidently perturbed state of mind, seemed to eye me for the moment doubtfully, in spite of Kennedy's cordial greeting.

"I've had all the first editions of the evening papers," I hinted as we sped through the tunnel, "but the stories seemed to be quite the same—pretty meager in details."

"Yes," returned Waldon with a glance at Kennedy, "I tried to keep as much out of the papers as I could just now for Lucie's sake."

"You needn't fear Jameson," remarked Kennedy. He fumbled in his pocket, then paused a moment and shot a glance of inquiry at Waldon, who nodded a mute acquiescence to him.

"There seem to have been a number of very peculiar disappearances lately," resumed Kennedy, "but this case of Mrs. Edwards is by far the most extraordinary. Of course the *Star* hasn't had that— yet," he concluded, handing me a sheet of notepaper.

"Mr. Waldon didn't give it out, hoping to avoid scandal."

I took the paper and read eagerly, in a woman's hand:

"MY DEAR MISS FOX: I have been down here at Seaville on our houseboat, the *Lucie,* for several days for a purpose which now is accomplished.

"Already I had my suspicions of you, from a source which I need not name. Therefore, when the *Kronprinz* got into wireless communication with the station at Seaville I determined through our own wireless on the *Lucie* to overhear whether there would be any exchange of messages between my husband and yourself.

"I was able to overhear the whole thing and I want you to know that your secret is no longer a secret from me, and that I have already told Mr. Edwards that I know it. You ruin his life by your intimacy which you seem to want to keep up, although you know you have no right to do it, but you shall not ruin mine.

"I am thoroughly disillusioned now. I have not decided on what steps to take, but——"

Only a casual glance was necessary to show me that the writing seemed to grow more and more weak as it progressed, and the note stopped abruptly, as if the writer had been suddenly interrupted or some new idea had occurred to her.

Hastily I tried to figure it out. Lucie Waldon, as everybody knew, was a famous beauty, a marvel of charm and daintiness, slender, with big, soulful, wistful eyes. Her marriage to Tracy Edwards, the wealthy plunger and stockbroker, had been a great social event the year before, and it was reputed at the time that Edwards had showered her with jewels and dresses to the wonder and talk even of society.

As for Valerie Fox, I knew she had won quick recognition and even fame as a dancer in New York during the previous winter, and I recalled reading three or four days before that she had just returned on the *Kronprinz* from a trip abroad.

"I don't suppose you have had time to see Miss Fox," I remarked. "Where is she?"

"At Beach Park now, I think," replied Waldon, " a resort a few miles nearer the city on the south shore, where there is a large colony of actors."

I handed back the letter to Kennedy.

"What do you make of it?" he asked, as he folded it up and put it back into his pocket.

"I hardly know what to say," I replied. "Of course there have been rumors, I believe, that all was not exactly like a honeymoon still with the Tracy Edwardses."

"Yes," returned Waldon slowly, "I know myself that there has been some trouble, but nothing definite until I found this letter last night in my sister's room. She never said anything about it either to mother or myself. They haven't been much together during the summer, and last night when she disappeared Tracy was in the city. But I hadn't thought much about it before, for, of course, you know he has large financial interests that make him keep in pretty close touch with New York and this summer hasn't been a particularly good one on the stock exchange."

"And," I put in, "a plunger doesn't always make the best of husbands. Perhaps there is temperament to be reckoned with here."

"There seem to be a good many things to be reckoned with," Craig considered. "For example, here's a houseboat, the *Lucie,* a palatial affair, cruising about aimlessly, with a beautiful woman on it. She gives a little party, in the absence of her husband, to her brother, his fiancée and her mother, who visit her from his yacht, the *Nautilus.* They break up, those living on the *Lucie* going to their rooms and the rest back to the yacht, which is anchored out further in the deeper water of the bay.

"Some time in the middle of the night her maid, Juanita, finds that she is not in her room. Her brother is summoned back from his yacht and finds that she has left this pathetic, unfinished letter. But otherwise there is no trace of her. Her husband is notified and hurries out there, but he can find no clue. Meanwhile, Mr. Waldon, in despair, hurries down to the city to engage me quietly."

"You remember I told you," suggested Waldon, "that my sister hadn't been feeling well for several days. In fact it seemed that the sea air wasn't doing her much good, and some one last night suggested that she try the mountains."

"Had there been anything that would foreshadow the—er—disappearance?" asked Kennedy.

"Only as I say, that for two or three days she seemed to be listless, to be sinking by slow and easy stages into a sort of vacant, moody state of ill health."

"She had a doctor, I suppose?" I asked.

"Yes, Dr. Jermyn, Tracy's own personal physician came down from the city several days ago."

"What did he say?"

"He simply said that it was congestion of the
lungs. As far as he could see there was no apparent
cause for it. I don't think he was very enthusiastic
about the mountain air idea. The fact is he was
like a good many doctors under the circumstances,
noncommittal—wanted her under observation, and
all that sort of thing."

"What's your opinion?" I pressed Craig. "Do
you think she has run away?"

"Naturally, I'd rather not attempt to say yet,"
Craig replied cautiously. "But there are several
possibilities. Yes, she might have left the houseboat in some other boat, of course. Then there is
the possibility of accident. It was a hot night. She
might have been leaning from the window and have
lost her balance. I have even thought of drugs, that
she might have taken something in her despondency
and have fallen overboard while under the influence
of it. Then, of course, there are the two deductions
that everyone has made already—either suicide or
murder."

Waldon had evidently been turning something
over in his mind.

"There was a wireless outfit aboard the houseboat," he ventured at length.

"What of that?" I asked, wondering why he was
changing the subject so abruptly.

"Why, only this," he replied. "I have been reading about wireless a good deal lately, and if the
theories of some scientists are correct, the wireless
age is not without its dangers as well as its wonders. I recall reading not long ago of a German

professor who says there is no essential difference between wireless waves and the X-rays, and we know the terrible physical effects of X-rays. I believe he estimated that only one three hundred millionth part of the electrical energy generated by sending a message from one station to another near by is actually used up in transmitting the message. The rest is dispersed in the atmosphere. There must be a good deal of such stray electrical energy about Seaville. Isn't it possible that it might hit some one somewhere who was susceptible?"

Kennedy said nothing. Waldon's was at least a novel idea, whether it was plausible or not. The only way to test it out, as far as I could determine, was to see whether it fitted with the facts after a careful investigation of the case itself.

It was still early in the day and the trains were not as crowded as they would be later. Consequently our journey was comfortable enough and we found ourselves at last at the little vine-covered station at Seaville.

One could almost feel that the gay summer colony was in a state of subdued excitement. As we left the quaint station and walked down the main street to the town wharf where we expected some one would be waiting for us, it seemed as if the mysterious disappearance of the beautiful Mrs. Edwards had put a damper on the life of the place. In the hotels there were knots of people evidently discussing the affair, for as we passed we could tell by their faces that they recognized us. One or two bowed and would have joined us, if Waldon had given any encouragement. But he did not stop, and we kept on down the street quickly.

I myself began to feel the spell of mystery about

the case as I had not felt it among the distractions of the city. Perhaps I imagined it, but there even seemed to be something strange about the houseboat which we could descry at anchor far down the bay as we approached the wharf.

We were met, as Waldon had arranged, by a high-powered runabout, the tender to his own yacht, a slim little craft of mahogany and brass, driven like an automobile, and capable of perhaps twenty-five or thirty miles an hour. We jumped in and were soon skimming over the waters of the bay like a skipping stone.

It was evident that Waldon was much relieved at having been able to bring assistance, in which he had as much confidence as he reposed in Kennedy. At any rate it was something to be nearing the scene of action again.

The *Lucie* was perhaps seventy feet long and a most attractive craft, with a hull yachty in appearance and of a type which could safely make long runs along the coast, a stanch, seaworthy boat, of course without the speed of the regularly designed yacht, but more than making up in comfort for those on board what was lost in that way. Waldon pointed out with obvious pride his own trim yacht swinging gracefully at anchor a half mile or so away.

As we approached the houseboat I looked her over carefully. One of the first things I noticed was that there rose from the roof the primitive inverted V aërial of a wireless telegraph. I thought immediately of the unfinished letter and its contents, and shaded my eyes as I took a good look at the powerful transatlantic station on the spit of sand perhaps three or four miles distant, with its tall steel masts.

6

of the latest inverted L type and the cluster of little houses below, in which the operators and the plant were.

Waldon noticed what I was looking at, and remarked, "It's a wonderful station—and well worth a visit, if you have the time—one of the most powerful on the coast, I understand."

"How did the *Lucie* come to be equipped with wireless?" asked Craig quickly. "It's a little unusual for a private boat."

"Mr. Edwards had it done when she was built," explained Waldon. "His idea was to use it to keep in touch with the stock market on trips."

"And it has proved effective?" asked Craig.

"Oh, yes—that is, it was all right last winter when he went on a short cruise down in Florida. This summer he hasn't been on the boat long enough to use it much."

"Who operates it?"

"He used to hire a licensed operator, although I believe the engineer, Pedersen, understands the thing pretty well and could use it if necessary."

"Do you think it was Pedersen who used it for Mrs. Edwards?" asked Kennedy.

"I really don't know," confessed Waldon. "Pedersen denies absolutely that he has touched the thing for weeks. I want you to quiz him. I wasn't able to get him to admit a thing."

CHAPTER VIII

WE had by this time swung around to the side of the houseboat. I realized as we mounted the ladder that the marine gasoline engine had materially changed the old-time houseboat from a mere scow or barge with a low flat house on it, moored in a bay or river, and only with difficulty and expense towed from one place to another. Now the houseboat was really a fair-sized yacht.

The *Lucie* was built high in order to give plenty of accommodation for the living quarters. The staterooms, dining rooms and saloon were really rooms, with seven or eight feet of head room, and furnished just as one would find in a tasteful and expensive house.

Down in the hull, of course, was the gasoline motor which drove the propeller, so that when the owner wanted a change of scene all that was necessary was to get up anchor, start the motor and navigate the yacht-houseboat to some other harbor.

Edwards himself met us on the deck. He was a tall man, with a red face, a man of action, of outdoor life, apparently a hard worker and a hard player. It was quite evident that he had been waiting for the return of Waldon anxiously.

"You find us considerably upset, Professor Kennedy," he greeted Craig, as his brother-in-law introduced us.

Edwards turned and led the way toward the saloon. As he entered and bade us be seated in the costly cushioned wicker chairs I noticed how sumptuously it was furnished, and particularly its mechanical piano, its phonograph and the splendid hardwood floor which seemed to invite one to dance in the cool breeze that floated across from one set of open windows to the other. And yet in spite of everything, there was that indefinable air of something lacking, as in a house from which the woman is gone.

"You were not here last night, I understand," remarked Kennedy, taking in the room at a glance.

"Unfortunately, no," replied Edwards. "Business has kept me with my nose pretty close to the grindstone this summer. Waldon called me up in the middle of the night, however, and I started down in my car, which enabled me to get here before the first train. I haven't been able to do a thing since I got here except just wait—wait—wait. I confess that I don't know what else to do. Waldon seemed to think we ought to have some one down here— and I guess he was right. Anyhow, I'm glad to see you."

I watched Edwards keenly. For the first time I realized that I had neglected to ask Waldon whether he had seen the unfinished letter. The question was unnecessary. It was evident that he had not.

"Let me see, Waldon, if I've got this thing straight," Edwards went on, pacing restlessly up and down the saloon. "Correct me if I haven't. Last night, as I understand it, there was a sort of little family party here, you and Miss Verrall and

your mother from the *Nautilus,* and Mrs. Edwards
and Dr. Jermyn."

"Yes," replied Waldon with, I thought, a touch
of defiance at the words "family party." He paused
as if he would have added that the *Nautilus* would
have been more congenial, anyhow, then added, "We
danced a little bit, all except Lucie. She said she
wasn't feeling any too well."

Edwards had paused by the door. "If you'll excuse me a minute," he said, "I'll call Jermyn and
Mrs. Edwards' maid, Juanita. You ought to go
over the whole thing immediately, Professor Kennedy."

"Why didn't you say anything about the letter to
him?" asked Kennedy under his breath.

"What was the use?" returned Waldon. "I didn't
know how he'd take it. Besides, I wanted your advice on the whole thing. Do you want to show it
to him?"

"Perhaps it's just as well," ruminated Kennedy.
"It may be possible to clear the thing up without
involving anybody's name. At any rate, some one
is coming down the passage this way."

Edwards entered with Dr. Jermyn, a clean-shaven
man, youthful in appearance, yet approaching middle age. I had heard of him before. He had
studied several years abroad and had gained considerable reputation since his return to America.

Dr. Jermyn shook hands with us cordially enough,
made some passing comment on the tragedy, and
stood evidently waiting for us to disclose our hands.

"You have been Mrs. Edwards' physician for
some time, I believe?" queried Kennedy, fencing for
an opening.

"Only since her marriage," replied the doctor briefly.

"She hadn't been feeling well for several days, had she?" ventured Kennedy again.

"No," replied Dr. Jermyn quickly. "I doubt whether I can add much to what you already know. I suppose Mr. Waldon has told you about her illness. The fact is, I suppose her maid Juanita will be able to tell you really more than I can."

I could not help feeling that Dr. Jermyn showed a great deal of reluctance in talking.

"You have been with her several days, though, haven't you?"

"Four days, I think. She was complaining of feeling nervous and telegraphed me to come down here. I came prepared to stay over night, but Mr. Edwards happened to run down that day, too, and he asked me if I wouldn't remain longer. My practice in the summer is such that I can easily leave it with my assistant in the city, so I agreed. Really, that is about all I can say. I don't know yet what was the matter with Mrs. Edwards, aside from the nervousness which seemed to be of some time standing."

He stood facing us, thoughtfully stroking his chin, as a very pretty and petite maid nervously entered and stood facing us in the doorway.

"Come in, Juanita," encouraged Edwards. "I want you to tell these gentlemen just what you told me about discovering that Madame had gone—and anything else that you may recall now."

"It was Juanita who discovered that Madame was gone, you know," put in Waldon.

"How did you discover it?" prompted Craig.

"It was very hot," replied the maid, "and often

on hot nights I would come in and fan Madame since she was so wakeful. Last night I went to the door and knocked. There was no reply. I called to her, 'Madame, madame.' Still there was no answer. The worst I supposed was that she had fainted. I continued to call."

"The door was locked?" inquired Kennedy.

"Yes, sir. My call aroused the others on the boat. Dr. Jermyn came and he broke open the door with his shoulder. But the room was empty. Madame was gone."

"How about the windows?" asked Kennedy.

"Open. They were always open these nights. Sometimes Madame would sit by the window when there was not much breeze."

"I should like to see the room," remarked Craig, with an inquiring glance at Edwards.

"Certainly," he answered, leading the way down a corridor.

Mrs. Edwards' room was on the starboard side, with wide windows instead of portholes. It was furnished magnificently and there was little about it that suggested the nautical, except the view from the window.

"The bed had not been slept in," Edwards remarked as we looked about curiously.

Kennedy walked over quickly to the wide series of windows before which was a leather-cushioned window seat almost level with the window, several feet above the level of the water. It was by this window, evidently, that Juanita meant that Mrs. Edwards often sat. It was a delightful position, but I could readily see that it would be comparatively easy for anyone accidentally or purposely to fall.

"I think myself," Waldon remarked to Kennedy,

"that it must have been from the open window that she made her way to the outside. It seems that all agree that the door was locked, while the window was wide open."

"There had been no sound—no cry to alarm you?" shot out Kennedy suddenly to Juanita.

"No, sir, nothing. I could not sleep myself, and I thought of Madame."

"You heard nothing?" he asked of Dr. Jermyn.

"Nothing until I heard the maid call," he replied briefly.

Mentally I ran over again Kennedy's first list of possibilities—taken off by another boat, accident, drugs, suicide, murder.

Was there, I asked myself, sufficient reason for suicide? The letter seemed to me to show too proud a spirit for that. In fact the last sentence seemed to show that she was contemplating the surest method of revenge, rather than surrender. As for accident, why should a person fall overboard from a large houseboat into a perfectly calm harbor? Then, too, there had been no outcry. Somehow, I could not seem to fit any of the theories in with the facts. Evidently it was like many another case, one in which we, as yet, had insufficient data for a conclusion.

Suddenly I recalled the theory that Waldon himself had advanced regarding the wireless, either from the boat itself or from the wireless station. For the moment, at least, it seemed plausible that she might have been seated at the window, that she might have been affected by escaped wireless, or by electrolysis. I knew that some physicians had described a disease which they attributed to wireless, a sort of anemia with a marked diminution in the

number of red corpuscles in the blood, due partly
to the overetherization of the air by reason of the
alternating currents used to generate the waves.

"I should like now to inspect the little wireless
plant you have here on the *Lucie*," remarked
Kennedy. "I noticed the mast as we were approaching a few minutes ago."

I had turned at the sound of his voice in time to
catch Edwards and Dr. Jermyn eyeing each other
furtively. Did they know about the letter, after all,
I wondered? Was each in doubt about just how
much the other knew?

There was no time to pursue these speculations.
"Certainly," agreed Mr. Edwards promptly, leading
the way.

Kennedy seemed keenly interested in inspecting
the little wireless plant, which was of a curious type
and not exactly like any that I had seen before.

"Wireless apparatus," he remarked, as he looked
it over, "is divided into three parts, the source of
power whether battery or dynamo, the making and
sending of wireless waves, including the key, spark,
condenser and tuning coil, and the receiving apparatus, head telephones, antennæ, ground and detector."

Pedersen, the engineer, came in while we were
looking the plant over, but seemed uncommunicative
to all Kennedy's efforts to engage him in conversation.

"I see," remarked Kennedy, "that it is a very
compact system with facilities for a quick change
from one wave length to another."

"Yes," grunted Pedersen, as averse to talking,
evidently, as others on the *Lucie*.

"Spark gap, quenched type," I heard Kennedy
mutter almost to himself, with a view to showing

Pedersen that he knew something about it. "Break system relay—operator can overhear any interference while transmitting—transformation by a single throw of a six-point switch which tunes the oscillating and open circuits to resonance. Very clever—very efficient. By the way, Pedersen, are you the only person aboard who can operate this?"

"How should I know?" he answered almost surlily.

"You ought to know, if anybody," answered Kennedy unruffled. "I know that it has been operated within the past few days."

Pedersen shrugged his shoulders. "You might ask the others aboard," was all he said. "Mr. Edwards pays me to operate it only for himself, when he has no other operator."

Kennedy did not pursue the subject, evidently from fear of saying too much just at present.

"I wonder if there is anyone else who could have operated it," said Waldon, as we mounted again to the deck.

"I don't know," replied Kennedy, pausing on the way up. "You haven't a wireless on the *Nautilus,* have you?"

Waldon shook his head. "Never had any particular use for it myself," he answered.

"You say that Miss Verrall and her mother have gone back to the city?" pursued Kennedy, taking care that as before the others were out of earshot.

"Yes."

"I'd like to stay with you to-night, then," decided Kennedy. "Might we go over with you now? There doesn't seem to be anything more I can do here, unless we get some news about Mrs. Edwards."

Waldon seemed only too glad to agree, and no one on the *Lucie* insisted on our staying.

We arrived at the *Nautilus* a few minutes later, and while we were lunching Kennedy dispatched the tender to the Marconi station with a note.

It was early in the afternoon when the tender returned with several packages and coils of wire. Kennedy immediately set to work on the *Nautilus* stretching out some of the wire.

"What is it you are planning?" asked Waldon, to whom every action of Kennedy seemed to be a mystery of the highest interest.

"Improvising my own wireless," he replied, not averse to talking to the young man to whom he seemed to have taken a fancy. "For short distances, you know, it isn't necessary to construct an aerial pole or even to use outside wires to receive messages. All that is needed is to use just a few wires stretched inside a room. The rest is just the apparatus."

I was quite as much interested as Waldon. "In wireless," he went on, "the signals are not sent in one direction, but in all, so that a person within range of the ethereal disturbance can get them if only he has the necessary receiving apparatus. This apparatus need not be so elaborate and expensive as used to be thought needful if a sensitive detector is employed, and I have sent over to the station for a new piece of apparatus which I knew they had in almost any Marconi station. Why, I've got wireless signals using only twelve feet of number eighteen copper wire stretched across a room and grounded with a water pipe. You might even use a wire mattress on an iron bedstead."

"Can't they find out by—er, interference?" I
asked, repeating the term I had so often heard.

Kennedy laughed. "No, not for radio apparatus
which merely receives radiograms and is not
equipped for sending. I am setting up only one side
of a wireless outfit here. All I want to do is to hear
what is being said. I don't care about saying anything."

He unwrapped another package which had been
loaned to him by the radio station and we watched
him curiously as he tested it and set it up. Some
parts of it I recognized such as the very sensitive
microphone, and another part I could have sworn
was a phonograph cylinder, though Craig was so
busy testing his apparatus that now we could not
ask questions.

It was late in the afternoon when he finished, and
we had just time to run up to the dock at Seaville
and stop off at the *Lucie* to see if anything had happened in the intervening hours before dinner. There
was nothing, except that I found time to file a message to the *Star* and meet several fellow newspaper
men who had been sent down by other papers on
the chance of picking up a good story.

We had the *Nautilus* to ourselves, and as she was
a very comfortable little craft, we really had a very
congenial time, a plunge over her side, a good dinner, and then a long talk out on deck under the
stars, in which we went over every phase of the
case. As we discussed it, Waldon followed keenly,
and it was quite evident from his remarks that he
had come to the conclusion that Dr. Jermyn at least
knew more than he had told about the case.

Still, the day wore away with no solution yet of
the mystery.

CHAPTER IX

THE RADIO DETECTIVE

It was early the following morning when a launch drew up beside the *Nautilus*. In it were Edwards and Dr. Jermyn, wildly excited.

"What's the matter?" called out Waldon.

"They—they have found the body," Edwards blurted out.

Waldon paled and clutched the rail. He had thought the world of his sister, and not until the last moment had he given up hope that perhaps she might be found to have disappeared in some other way than had become increasingly evident.

"Where?" cried Kennedy. "Who?"

"Over on Ten Mile Beach," answered Edwards. "Some fishermen who had been out on a cruise and hadn't heard the story. They took the body to town, and there it was recognized. They sent word out to us immediately."

Waldon had already spun the engine of his tender, which was about the fastest thing afloat about Seaville, had taken Edwards over, and we were off in a cloud of spray, the nose of the boat many inches above the surface of the water.

In the little undertaking establishment at Seaville lay the body of the beautiful young matron about whom so much anxiety had been felt. I could not help thinking what an end was this for the incom-

85

parable beauty. At the very height of her brief career the poor little woman's life had been suddenly snuffed out. But by what? The body had been found, but the mystery had been far from solved.

As Kennedy bent over the body, I heard him murmur to himself, "She had everything—everything except happiness."

"Was it drowning that caused her death?" asked Kennedy of the local doctor, who also happened to be coroner and had already arrived on the scene.

The doctor shook his head. "I don't know," he said doubtfully. "There was congestion of the lungs—but I—I can't say but what she might have been dead before she fell or was thrown into the water."

Dr. Jermyn stood on one side, now and then putting in a word, but for the most part silent unless spoken to. Kennedy, however, was making a most minute examination.

As he turned the beautiful head, almost reverently, he saw something that evidently attracted his attention. I was standing next to him and, between us, I think we cut off the view of the others. There on the back of the neck, carefully, had been smeared something transparent, almost skin-like, which had easily escaped the attention of the rest.

Kennedy tried to pick it off, but only succeeded in pulling off a very minute piece to which the flesh seemed to adhere.

"That's queer," he whispered to me. "Water, naturally, has no effect on it, else it would have been washed off long before. Walter," he added, "just slip across the street quietly to the drug store and get me a piece of gauze soaked with acetone."

As quickly and unostentatiously as I could I did so and handed him the wet cloth, contriving at the same time to add Waldon to our barrier, for I could see that Kennedy was anxious to be observed as little as possible.

"What is it?" I whispered, as he rubbed the transparent skin-like stuff off, and dropped the gauze into his pocket.

"A sort of skin varnish," he remarked under his breath, "waterproof and so adhesive that it resists pulling off even with a knife without taking the cuticle with it."

Beneath, as the skin varnish slowly dissolved under his gentle rubbing, he had disclosed several very small reddish spots, like little cuts that had been made by means of a very sharp instrument. As he did so, he gave them a hasty glance, turned the now stony beautiful head straight again, stood up, and resumed his talk with the coroner, who was evidently getting more and more bewildered by the case.

Edwards, who had completed the arrangements with the undertaker for the care of the body as soon as the coroner released it, seemed completely unnerved.

"Jermyn," he said to the doctor, as he turned away and hid his eyes, "I can't stand this. The undertaker wants some stuff from the—er—boat," his voice broke over the name which had been hers. "Will you get it for me? I'm going up to a hotel here, and I'll wait for you there. But I can't go out to the boat—yet."

"I think Mr. Waldon will be glad to take you out in his tender," suggested Kennedy. "Besides, I feel that I'd like a little fresh air as a bracer, too, after such a shock."

"What were those little cuts?" I asked as Waldon and Dr. Jermyn preceded us through the crowd outside to the pier.

"Some one," he answered in a low tone, "has severed the pneumogastric nerves."

"The pneumogastric nerves?" I repeated.

"Yes, the vagus or wandering nerve, the so-called tenth cranial nerve. Unlike the other cranial nerves, which are concerned with the special senses or distributed to the skin and muscles of the head and neck, the vagus, as its name implies, strays downward into the chest and abdomen supplying branches to the throat, lungs, heart and stomach and forms an important connecting link between the brain and the sympathetic nervous system."

We had reached the pier, and a nod from Kennedy discouraged further conversation on the subject.

A few minutes later we had reached the *Lucie* and gone up over her side. Kennedy waited until Jermyn had disappeared into the room of Mrs. Edwards to get what the undertaker had desired. A moment and he had passed quietly into Dr. Jermyn's own room, followed by me. Several quick glances about told him what not to waste time over, and at last his eye fell on a little portable case of medicines and surgical instruments. He opened it quickly and took out a bottle of golden yellow liquid.

Kennedy smelled it, then quickly painted some on the back of his hand. It dried quickly, like an artificial skin. He had found a bottle of skin varnish in Dr. Jermyn's own medicine chest!

We hurried back to the deck, and a few minutes later the doctor appeared with a large package.

"Did you ever hear of coating the skin by a substance which is impervious to water, smooth and elastic?" asked Kennedy quietly as Waldon's tender sped along back to Seaville.

"Why—er, yes," he said frankly, raising his eyes and looking at Craig in surprise. "There have been a dozen or more such substances. The best is one which I use, made of pyroxylin, the soluble cotton of commerce, dissolved in amyl acetate and acetone with some other substances that make it perfectly sterile. Why do you ask?"

"Because some one has used a little bit of it to cover a few slight cuts on the back of the neck of Mrs. Edwards."

"Indeed?" he said simply, in a tone of mild surprise.

"Yes," pursued Kennedy. "They seem to me to be subcutaneous incisions of the neck with a very fine scalpel dividing the two great pneumogastric nerves. Of course you know what that would mean —the victim would pass away naturally by slow and easy stages in three or four days, and all that would appear might be congestion of the lungs. They are delicate little punctures and elusive nerves to locate, but after all it might be done as painlessly, as simply and as safely as a barber might remove some dead hairs. A country coroner might easily pass over such evidence at an autopsy—especially if it was concealed by skin varnish."

I was surprised at the frankness with which Kennedy spoke, but absolutely amazed at the coolness of Jermyn. At first he said absolutely nothing. He seemed to be as set in his reticence as he had been when we first met.

I watched him narrowly. Waldon, who was driving the boat, had not heard what was said, but

7

I had, and I could not conceive how anyone could take it so calmly.

Finally Jermyn turned to Kennedy and looked him squarely in the eye. "Kennedy," he said slowly, "this is extraordinary—most extraordinary," then, pausing, added, "if true."

"There can be no doubt of the truth," replied Kennedy, eyeing Dr. Jermyn just as squarely.

"What do you propose to do about it?" asked the doctor.

"Investigate," replied Kennedy simply. "While Waldon takes these things up to the undertaker's, we may as well wait here in the boat. I want him to stop on the way back for Mr. Edwards. Then we shall go out to the *Lucie*. He must go, whether he likes it or not."

It was indeed a most peculiar situation as Kennedy and I sat in the tender with Dr. Jermyn waiting for Waldon to return with Edwards. Not a word was spoken.

The tenseness of the situation was not relieved by the return of Waldon with Edwards. Waldon seemed to realize without knowing just what it was, that something was about to happen. He drove his boat back to the *Lucie* again in record time. This was Kennedy's turn to be reticent. Whatever it was he was revolving in his mind, he answered in scarcely more than monosyllables whatever questions were put to him.

"You are not coming aboard?" inquired Edwards in surprise as he and Jermyn mounted the steps of the houseboat ladder, and Kennedy remained seated in the tender.

"Not yet," replied Craig coolly.

"But I thought you had something to show me. Waldon told me you had."

"I think I shall have in a short time," returned Kennedy. "We shall be back immediately. I'm just going to ask Waldon to run over to the *Nautilus* for a few minutes. We'll tow back your launch, too, in case you need it."

Waldon had cast off obediently.

"There's one thing sure," I remarked. "Jermyn can't get away from the *Lucie* until we return—unless he swims."

Kennedy did not seem to pay much attention to the remark, for his only reply was: "I'm taking a chance by this maneuvering, but I think it will work out that I am correct. By the way, Waldon, you needn't put on so much speed. I'm in no great hurry to get back. Half an hour will be time enough."

"Jermyn? What did you mean by Jermyn?" asked Waldon, as we climbed to the deck of the *Nautilus*.

He had evidently learned, as I had, that it was little use to try to quiz Kennedy until he was ready to be questioned and had decided to try it on me.

I had nothing to conceal and I told him quite fully all that I knew. Actually, I believe if Jermyn had been there, it would have taken both Kennedy and myself to prevent violence. As it was I had a veritable madman to deal with while Kennedy gathered up leisurely the wireless outfit he had installed on the deck of Waldon's yacht. It was only by telling him that I would certainly demand that Kennedy leave him behind if he did not control his feelings that I could calm him before Craig had finished his work on the yacht.

Waldon relieved himself by driving the tender

back at top speed to the *Lucie,* and now it seemed that Kennedy had no objection to traveling as fast as the many-cylindered engine was capable of going.

As we entered the saloon of the houseboat, I kept close watch over Waldon.

Kennedy began by slipping a record on the phonograph in the corner of the saloon, then facing us and addressing Edwards particularly.

"You may be interested to know, Mr. Edwards," he said, "that your wireless outfit here has been put to a use for which you never intended it."

No one said anything, but I am sure that some one in the room then for the first time began to suspect what was coming.

"As you know, by the use of an aerial pole, messages may be easily received from any number of stations," continued Craig. "Laws, rules and regulations may be adopted to shut out interlopers and plug busybody ears, but the greater part of whatever is transmitted by the Hertzian waves can be snatched down by other wireless apparatus.

"Down below, in that little room of yours," went on Craig, "might sit an operator with his ear-phone clamped to his head, drinking in the news conveyed surely and swiftly to him through the wireless signals—plucking from the sky secrets of finance and," he added, leaning forward, "love."

In his usual dramatic manner Kennedy had swung his little audience completely with him.

"In other words," he resumed, "it might be used for eavesdropping by a wireless wiretapper. Now," he concluded, "I thought that if there was any radio detective work being done, I might as well do some, too."

He toyed for a moment with the phonograph record. "I have used," he explained, "Marconi's radiotelephone, because in connection with his receivers Marconi uses phonographic recorders and on them has captured wireless telegraph signals over hundreds of miles.

"He has found that it is possible to receive wireless signals, although ordinary records are not loud enough, by using a small microphone on the repeating diaphragm and connected with a loud-speaking telephone. The chief difficulty was to get a microphone that would carry a sufficient current without burning up. There were other difficulties, but they have been surmounted and now wireless telegraph messages may be automatically recorded and made audible."

Kennedy started the phonograph, running it along, stopping it, taking up the record at a new point.

"Listen," he exclaimed at length, "there's something interesting, the WXY call—Seaville station—from some one on the *Lucie* only a few minutes ago, sending a message to be relayed by Seaville to the station at Beach Park. It seems impossible, but buzzing and ticking forth is this message from some one off this very houseboat. It reads: "Miss Valerie Fox, Beach Park. I am suspected of the murder of Mrs. Edwards. I appeal to you to help me. You must allow me to tell the truth about the messages I intercepted for Mrs. Edwards which passed between yourself on the ocean and Mr. Edwards in New York via Seaville. You rejected me and would not let me save you. Now you must save me."

Kennedy paused, then added, "The message is signed by Dr. Jermyn!"

At once I saw it all. Jermyn had been the unsuccessful suitor for Miss Fox's affections. But before I could piece out the rest of the tragic story, Kennedy had started the phonograph record at an earlier point which he had skipped for the present.

"Here's another record—a brief one—also to Valerie Fox from the houseboat: 'Refuse all interviews. Deny everything. Will see you as soon as present excitement dies down.'"

Before Kennedy could finish, Waldon had leaped forward, unable longer to control his feelings. If Kennedy had not seized his arm, I verily believe he would have cast Dr. Jermyn into the bay into which his sister had fallen two nights before in her terribly weakened condition.

"Waldon," cried Kennedy, "for God's sake, man —wait! Don't you understand? The second message is signed Tracy Edwards."

It came as quite as much a shock of surprise to me as to Waldon.

"Don't you understand?" he repeated. "Your sister first learned from Dr. Jermyn what was going on. She moved the *Lucie* down here near Seaville in order to be near the wireless station when the ship bearing her rival, Valerie Fox, got in touch with land. With the help of Dr. Jermyn she intercepted the wireless messages from the *Kronprinz* to the shore—between her husband and Valerie Fox."

Kennedy was hurrying on now to his irresistible conclusion. "She found that he was infatuated with the famous stage beauty, that he was planning to marry another, her rival. She accused him of it, threatened to defeat his plans. He knew she knew his unfaithfulness. Instead of being your sister's murderer, Dr. Jermyn was helping her get the evidence that would save both her and perhaps win Miss Fox back to himself."

Kennedy had turned sharply on Edwards.

"But," he added, with a glance that crushed any lingering hope that the truth had been concealed, "the same night that Dr. Jermyn arrived here, you visited your wife. As she slept you severed the nerves that meant life or death to her. Then you covered the cuts with the preparation which you knew Dr. Jermyn used. You asked him to stay, while you went away, thinking that when death came you would have a perfect alibi—perhaps a scape-goat. Edwards, the radio detective convicts you!"

CHAPTER X

THE CURIO SHOP

EDWARDS crumpled up as Kennedy and I faced him. There was no escape. In fact our greatest difficulty was to protect him from Waldon.

Kennedy's work in the case was over when we had got Edwards ashore and in the hands of the authorities. But mine had just begun and it was late when I got my story on the wire for the *Star*.

I felt pretty tired and determined to make up for it by sleeping the next day. It was no use, however.

"Why, what's the matter, Mrs. Northrop?" I heard Kennedy ask as he opened our door the next morning, just as I had finished dressing.

He had admitted a young woman, who greeted us with nervous, wide-staring eyes.

"It's—it's about Archer," she cried, sinking into the nearest chair and staring from one to the other of us.

She was the wife of Professor Archer Northrop, director of the archeological department at the university. Both Craig and I had known her ever since her marriage to Northrop, for she was one of the most attractive ladies in the younger set of the faculty, to which Craig naturally belonged. Archer had been of the class below us in the university. We

96

had hazed him, and out of the mild hazing there had, strangely enough, grown a strong friendship.

I recollected quickly that Northrop, according to last reports, had been down in the south of Mexico on an archeological expedition. But before I could frame, even in my mind, the natural question in a form that would not alarm his wife further, Kennedy had it on his lips.

"No bad news from Mitla, I hope?" he asked gently, recalling one of the main working stations chosen by the expedition and the reported unsettled condition of the country about it. She looked up quickly.

"Didn't you know—he—came back from Vera Cruz yesterday?" she asked slowly, then added, speaking in a broken tone, "and—he seems—suddenly—to have disappeared. Oh, such a terrible night of worry! No word—and I called up the museum, but Doctor Bernardo, the curator, had gone, and no one answered. And this morning—I couldn't stand it any longer—so I came to you."

"You have no idea, I suppose, of anything that was weighing on his mind?" suggested Kennedy.

"No," she answered promptly.

In default of any further information, Kennedy did not pursue this line of questioning. I could not determine from his face or manner whether he thought the matter might involve another than Mrs. Northrop, or, perhaps, something connected with the unsettled condition of the country from which her husband had just arrived.

"Have you any of the letters that Archer wrote home?" asked Craig, at length.

"Yes," she replied eagerly, taking a little packet

from her handbag. "I thought you might ask that. I brought them."

"You are an ideal client," commented Craig encouragingly, taking the letters. "Now, Mrs. Northrop, be brave. Trust me to run this thing down, and if you hear anything let me know immediately."

She left us a moment later, visibly relieved.

Scarcely had she gone when Craig, stuffing the letters into his pocket unread, seized his hat, and a moment later was striding along toward the museum with his habitual rapid, abstracted step which told me that he sensed a mystery.

In the museum we met Doctor Bernardo, a man slightly older than Northrop, with whom he had been very intimate. He had just arrived and was already deeply immersed in the study of some new and beautiful colored plates from the National Museum of Mexico City.

"Do you remember seeing Northrop here yesterday afternoon?" greeted Craig, without explaining what had happened.

"Yes," he answered promptly. "I was here with him until very late. At least, he was in his own room, working hard, when I left."

"Did you see him go?"

"Why—er—no," replied Bernardo, as if that were a new idea. "I left him here—at least, I didn't see him go out."

Kennedy tried the door of Northrop's room, which was at the far end, in a corner, and communicated with the hall only through the main floor of the museum. It was locked. A pass-key from the janitor quickly opened it.

Such a sight as greeted us, I shall never forget.

There, in his big desk-chair, sat Northrop, absolutely rigid, the most horribly contorted look on his features that I have ever seen—half of pain, half of fear, as if of something nameless.

Kennedy bent over. His hands were cold. Northrop had been dead at least twelve hours, perhaps longer. All night the deserted museum had guarded its terrible secret.

As Craig peered into his face, he saw, in the fleshy part of the neck, just below the left ear, a round red mark, with just a drop or two of now black coagulated blood in the center. All around we could see a vast amount of miscellaneous stuff, partly unpacked, partly just opened, and waiting to be taken out of the wrappings by the now motionless hands.

"I suppose you are more or less familiar with what Northrop brought back?" asked Kennedy of Bernardo, running his eye over the material in the room.

"Yes, reasonably," answered Bernardo. "Before the cases arrived from the wharf, he told me in detail what he had managed to bring up with him."

"I wish, then, that you would look it over and see if there is anything missing," requested Craig, already himself busy in going over the room for other evidence.

Doctor Bernardo hastily began taking a mental inventory of the stuff. While they worked, I tried vainly to frame some theory which would explain the startling facts we had so suddenly discovered.

Mitla, I knew, was south of the city of Oaxaca, and there, in its ruined palaces, was the crowning achievement of the old Zapotec kings. No ruins in

America were more elaborately ornamented or richer in lore for the archeologist.

Northrop had brought up porphyry blocks with quaint grecques and much hieroglyphic painting. Already unpacked were half a dozen copper axes, some of the first of that particular style that had ever been brought to the United States. Besides the sculptured stones and the mosaics were jugs, cups, vases, little gods, sacrificial stones—enough, almost, to equip a new alcove in the museum.

Before Northrop was an idol, a hideous thing on which frogs and snakes squatted and coiled. It was a fitting piece to accompany the gruesome occupant of the little room in his long, last vigil. In fact, it almost sent a shudder over me, and if I had been inclined to the superstitious, I should certainly have concluded that this was retribution for having disturbed the *lares* and *penates* of a dead race.

Doctor Bernardo was going over the material a second time. By the look on his face, even I could guess that something was missing.

"What is it?" asked Craig, following the curator closely.

"Why," he answered slowly, "there was an inscription—we were looking at it earlier in the day —on a small block of porphyry. I don't see it."

He paused and went back to his search before we could ask him further what he thought the inscription was about.

I thought nothing myself at the time of his reticence, for Kennedy had gone over to a window back of Northrop and to the left. It was fully twenty feet from the downward slope of the campus there, and, as he craned his neck out, he noted that the copper leader of the rain pipe ran past it a few feet away.

I, too, looked out. A thick group of trees hid the window from the avenue beyond the campus wall, and below us, at a corner of the building, was a clump of rhododendrons. As Craig bent over the sill, he whipped out a pocket lens.

A moment later he silently handed the glass to me. As nearly as I could make out, there were five marks on the dust of the sill.

"Finger-prints!" I exclaimed. "Some one has been clinging to the edge of the ledge."

"In that case," Craig observed quietly, "there would have been only four prints."

I looked again, puzzled. The prints were flat and well separated.

"No," he added, "not finger-prints—toe-prints."

"Toe-prints?" I echoed.

Before he could reply, Craig had dashed out of the room, around, and under the window. There, he was carefully going over the soft earth around the bushes below.

"What are you looking for?" I asked, joining him.

"Some one—perhaps two—has been here," he remarked, almost under his breath. "One, at least, has removed his shoes. See those shoe-prints up to this point? The print of a boot-heel in soft earth shows the position and contour of every nail head. Bertillon has made a collection of such nails, certain types, sizes, and shapes used in certain boots, showing often what country the shoes came from. Even the number and pattern are significant. Some factories use a fixed number of nails and arrange them in a particular manner. I have made my own col-

lection of such prints in this country. These were
American shoes. Perhaps the clue will not lead us
anywhere, though, for I doubt whether it was an
American foot."

Kennedy continued to study the marks.

"He removed his shoes—either to help in climbing or to prevent noise—ah—here's the foot!
Strange—see how small it is—and broad, how pre-
hensile the toes—almost like fingers. Surely that
foot could never have been encased in American
shoes all its life. I shall make plaster casts of these,
to preserve later."

He was still scouting about on hands and knees
in the dampness of the rhododendrons. Suddenly
he reached his long arm in among the shrubs and
picked up a little reed stick. On the end of it was
a small cylinder of buff brown.

He looked at it curiously, dug his nail into the soft
mass, then rubbed his nail over the tip of his tongue
gingerly.

With a wry face, as if the taste were extremely
acrid, he moistened his handkerchief and wiped off
his tongue vigorously.

"Even that minute particle that was on my nail
makes my tongue tingle and feel numb," he remarked, still rubbing. "Let us go back again. I
want to see Bernardo."

"Had he any visitors during the day?" queried
Kennedy, as he reëntered the ghastly little room,
while the curator stood outside, completely unnerved
by the tragedy which had been so close to him without his apparently knowing it. Kennedy was squeez-
ing out from the little wound on Northrop's neck
a few drops of liquid on a sterilized piece of glass.

"No; no one," Bernardo answered, after a moment.

"Did you see anyone in the museum who looked suspicious?" asked Kennedy, watching Bernardo's face keenly.

"No," he hesitated. "There were several people wandering about among the exhibits, of course. One, I recall, late in the afternoon, was a little dark-skinned woman, rather good-looking."

"A Mexican?"

"Yes, I should say so. Not of Spanish descent, though. She was rather of the Indian type. She seemed to be much interested in the various exhibits, asked me several questions, very intelligently, too. Really, I thought she was trying to—er—flirt with me."

He shot a glance at Craig, half of confession, half of embarrassment.

"And—oh, yes—there was another—a man, a little man, as I recall, with shaggy hair. He looked like a Russian to me. I remember, because he came to the door, peered around hastily, and went away. I thought he might have got into the wrong part of the building and went to direct him right—but before I could get out into the hall, he was gone. I remember, too, that, as I turned, the woman had followed me and soon was asking other questions—which, I will admit—I was glad to answer."

"Was Northrop in his room while these people were here?"

"Yes; he had locked the door so that none of the students or visitors could disturb him."

"Evidently the woman was diverting your attention while the man entered Northrop's room by the window," ruminated Craig, as we stood for a moment in the outside doorway.

He had already telephoned to our old friend Doctor Leslie, the coroner, to take charge of the case, and now was ready to leave. The news had spread, and the janitor of the building was waiting to lock the campus door to keep back the crowd of students and others.

Our next duty was the painful one of breaking the news to Mrs. Northrop. I shall pass it over. Perhaps no one could have done it more gently than Kennedy. She did not cry. She was simply dazed. Fortunately her mother was with her, had been, in fact, ever since Northrop had gone on the expedition.

"Why should anyone want to steal tablets of old Mixtec inscriptions?" I asked thoughtfully, as we walked sadly over the campus in the direction of the chemistry building. "Have they a sufficient value, even on appreciative Fifth Avenue, to warrant murder?"

"Well," he remarked, "it does seem incomprehensible. Yet people do just such things. The psychologists tell us that there is a veritable mania for possessing such curios. However, it is possible that there may be some deeper significance in this case," he added, his face puckered in thought.

Who was the mysterious Mexican woman, who the shaggy Russian? I asked myself. Clearly, at least, if she existed at all, she was one of the millions not of Spanish but of Indian descent in the country south of us. As I reasoned it out, it seemed to me as if she must have been an accomplice. She could not have got into Northrop's room either before or after Doctor Bernardo left. Then, too, the

toe- and shoe-prints were not hers.   But, I figured,
she certainly had a part in the plot.

While I was engaged in the vain effort to un-
ravel the tragic affair by pure reason, Kennedy was
at work with practical science.

He began by examining the little dark cylinder on
the end of the reed.   On a piece of the stuff, broken
off, he poured a dark liquid from a brown-glass
bottle.   Then he placed it under a microscope.

"Microscopically," he said slowly, "it consists almost wholly of minute, clear granules which give a
blue reaction with iodine.   They are starch.   Mixed
with them are some larger starch granules, a few
plant cells, fibrous matter, and other foreign particles.   And then, there is the substance that gives
that acrid, numbing taste."   He appeared to be
vacantly studying the floor.

"What do you think it is?" I asked, unable to
restrain myself.

"Aconite," he answered slowly, "of which the active principle is the deadly poisonous alkaloid,
aconitin."

He walked over and pulled down a well-thumbed
standard work on toxicology, turned the pages, then
began to read aloud:

Pure aconitin is probably the most actively poisonous substance with which we are acquainted and, if
administered hypodermically, the alkaloid is even
more powerfully poisonous than when taken by the
mouth.

As in the case of most of the poisonous alkaloids,
aconitin does not produce any decidedly characteristic post-mortem appearances.   There is no way to
distinguish it from other alkaloids, in fact, no re-

8

liable chemical test. The physiological effects before death are all that can be relied on.

Owing to its exceeding toxic nature, the smallness of the dose required to produce death, and the lack of tests for recognition, aconitin possesses rather more interest in legal medicine than most other poisons.

It is one of the few substances which, in the present state of toxicology, might be criminally administered and leave no positive evidence of the crime. If a small but fatal dose of the poison were to be given, especially if it were administered hypodermically, the chances of its detection in the body after death would be practically none.

CHAPTER XI

THE "PILLAR OF DEATH"

I was looking at him fixedly as the diabolical nature of what must have happened sank into my mind. Here was a poison that defied detection. I could see by the look on Craig's face that that problem, alone, was enough to absorb his attention. He seemed fully to realize that we had to deal with a criminal so clever that he might never be brought to justice.

An idea flashed over me.

"How about the letters?" I suggested.

"Good, Walter!" he exclaimed.

He untied the package which Mrs. Northrop had given him and glanced quickly over one after another of the letters.

"Ah!" he exclaimed, fairly devouring one dated at Mitla. "Listen—it tells about Northrop's work and goes on:

" 'I have been much interested in a cavern, or *subterraneo*, here, in the shape of a cross, each arm of which extends for some twelve feet underground. In the center it is guarded by a block of stone popularly called "the Pillar of Death." There is a superstition that whoever embraces it will die before the sun goes down.

" 'From the *subterraneo* is said to lead a long, underground passage across the court to another sub-

107

terranean chamber which is full of Mixtec treasure. Treasure hunters have dug all around it, and it is said that two old Indians, only, know of the immense amount of buried gold and silver, but that they will not reveal it.' "

I started up. Here was the missing link which I had been waiting for.

"There, at least, is the motive," I blurted out. "That is why Bernardo was so reticent. Northrop, in his innocence of heart, had showed him that inscription."

Kennedy said nothing as he finally tied up the little packet of letters and locked it in his safe. He was not given to hasty generalizations; neither was he one who clung doggedly to a preconceived theory.

It was still early in the afternoon. Craig and I decided to drop into the museum again in order to see Doctor Bernardo. He was not there, and we sat down to wait.

Just then the letter box in the door clicked. It was the postman on his rounds. Kennedy walked over and picked up the letter.

The postmark bore the words, "Mexico City," and a date somewhat later than that on which Northrop had left Vera Cruz. In the lower corner, underscored, were the words, "Personal—Urgent."

"I'd like to know what is in that," remarked Craig, turning it over and over.

He appeared to be considering something, for he rose suddenly and shoved the letter into his pocket.

I followed, and a few moments later, across the campus in his laboratory, he was working quickly over an X-ray apparatus. He had placed the letter in it.

"These are what are known as 'low' tubes," he explained. "They give out 'soft rays.'" He continued to work for a few moments, then handed me the letter.

"Now, Walter," he said, "if you will just hurry back to the museum and replace that letter, I think I will have something that will astonish you—though whether it will have any bearing on the case, remains to be seen."

"What is it?" I asked, a few minutes later, when I had rejoined him, after returning the letter. He was poring intently over what looked like a negative.

"The possibility of reading the contents of documents inclosed in a sealed envelope," he replied, still studying the shadowgraph closely, "has already been established by the well-known English scientist, Doctor Hall Edwards. He has been experimenting with the method of using X-rays recently discovered by a German scientist, by which radiographs of very thin substances, such as a sheet of paper, a leaf, an insect's body, may be obtained. These thin substances through which the rays used formerly to pass without leaving an impression, can now be radiographed."

I looked carefully as he traced out something on the negative. On it was easily possible, following his guidance, to read the words inscribed on the sheet of paper inside. So admirably defined were all the details that even the gum on the envelope and the edges of the sheet of paper inside the envelope could be distinguished.

"Any letter written with ink having a mineral basis can be radiographed," added Craig. "Even when the sheet is folded in the usual way, it is possible by taking a radiograph stereoscopically, to distinguish the writing, every detail standing out in relief. Besides, it can be greatly magnified, which aids in deciphering it if it is indistinct or jumbled up. Some of it looks like mirror writing. Ah," he added, "here's something interesting!"

Together we managed to trace out the contents of several paragraphs, of which the significant parts were as follows:

I am expecting that my friend Señora Herreria will be in New York by the time you receive this, and should she call on you, I know you will accord her every courtesy. She has been in Mexico City for a few days, having just returned from Mitla, where she met Professor Northrop. It is rumored that Professor Northrop has succeeded in smuggling out of the country a very important stone bearing an inscription which, I understand, is of more than ordinary interest. I do not know anything definite about it, as Señora Herreria is very reticent on the matter, but depend on you to find out if possible and let me know of it.

According to the rumors and the statements of the *señora,* it seems that Northrop has taken an unfair advantage of the situation down in Oaxaca, and I suppose she and others who know about the inscription feel that it is really the possession of the government.

You will find that the *señora* is an accomplished antiquarian and scholar. Like many others down here just now, she has a high regard for the Japanese. As you know, there exists a natural sympathy between some Mexicans and Japanese, owing to what is believed to be a common origin of the two races.

In spite of the assertions of many to the contrary,

there is little doubt left in the minds of students that the Indian races which have peopled Mexico were of Mongolian stock.   Many words in some dialects are easily understood by Chinese immigrants.   A secretary of the Japanese legation here was able recently to decipher old Mixtec inscriptions found in the ruins of Mitla.

Señora Herreria has been much interested in establishing the relationship and, I understand, is acquainted with a Japanese curio dealer in New York who recently visited Mexico for the same purpose. I believe that she wishes to collaborate with him on a monograph on the subject, which is expected to have a powerful effect on the public opinion both here and at Tokyo.

In regard to the inscription which Northrop has taken with him, I rely on you to keep me informed. There seems to be a great deal of mystery connected with it, and I am simply hazarding a guess as to its nature.   If it should prove to be something which might interest either the Japanese or ourselves, you can see how important it may be, especially in view of the forthcoming mission of General Francisco to Tokyo.

Very sincerely yours,
DR. EMILIO SANCHEZ, Director.

"Bernardo is a Mexican," I exclaimed, as Kennedy finished reading, "and there can be no doubt that the woman he mentioned was this Señora Herreria."

Kennedy said nothing, but seemed to be weighing the various paragraphs in the letter.

"Still," I observed, "so far, the only one against whom we have any direct suspicion in the case is the shaggy Russian, whoever he is."

"A man whom Bernardo says looked like a Russian," corrected Craig.

He was pacing the laboratory restlessly.

"This is becoming quite an international affair," he remarked finally, pausing before me, his hat on. "Would you like to relax your mind by a little excursion among the curio shops of the city? I know something about Japanese curios—more, perhaps, than I do of Mexican. It may amuse us, even if it doesn't help in solving the mystery. Meanwhile, I shall make arrangements for shadowing Bernardo. I want to know just how he acts after he reads that letter."

He paused long enough to telephone his instructions to an uptown detective agency which could be depended on for such mere routine work, then joined me with the significant remark: "Blood is thicker than water, anyhow, Walter. Still, even if the Mexicans are influenced by sentiment, I hardly think that would account for the interest of our friends from across the water in the matter."

I do not know how many of the large and small curio shops of the city we visited that afternoon. At another time, I should have enjoyed the visits immensely, for anyone seeking articles of beauty will find the antique shops of Fifth and Fourth Avenues and the side streets well worth visiting.

We came, at length, to one, a small, quaint, dusty rookery, down in a basement, entered almost directly from the street. It bore over the door a little gilt sign which read simply, "Sato's."

As we entered, I could not help being impressed by the wealth of articles in beautiful cloisonné enamel, in mother-of-pearl, lacquer, and champlevé. There were beautiful little koros, or incense burners, vases, and teapots. There were enamels incrusted, translucent, and painted, works of the famous Namikawa, of Kyoto, and Namikawa, of Tokyo. Satsuma vases, splendid and rare examples of the potter's art, crowded gorgeously embroidered screens depicting all sorts of brilliant scenes, among others the sacred Fujiyama rising in the stately distance. Sato himself greeted us with a ready smile and bow.

"I am just looking for a few things to add to my den," explained Kennedy, adding, "nothing in particular, but merely whatever happens to strike my fancy."

"Surely, then, you have come to the right shop," greeted Sato. "If there is anything that interests you, I shall be glad to show it."

"Thank you," replied Craig. "Don't let me trouble you with your other customers. I will call on you if I see anything."

For several minutes, Craig and I busied ourselves looking about, and we did not have to feign interest, either.

"Often things are not as represented," he whispered to me, after a while, "but a connoiseur can tell spurious goods. These are the real thing, mostly."

"Not one in fifty can tell the difference," put in the voice of Sato, at his elbow.

"Well, you see I happen to know," Craig replied, not the least disconcerted. "You can't always be too sure."

A laugh and a shrug was Sato's answer. "It's well all are not so keen," he said, with a frank acknowledgment that he was not above sharp practices.

I glanced now and then at the expressionless face

of the curio dealer. Was it merely the natural blankness of his countenance that impressed me, or was there, in fact, something deep and dark hidden in it, something of "East is East and West is West" which I did not and could not understand? Craig was admiring the bronzes. He had paused before one, a square metal fire-screen of odd design, with the title on a card, "Japan Gazing at the World."

It represented Japan as an eagle, with beak and talons of burnished gold, resting on a rocky island about which great waves dashed. The bird had an air of dignity and conscious pride in its strength, as it looked out at the world, a globe revolving in space.

"Do you suppose there is anything significant in that?" I asked, pointing to the continent of North America, also in gold and prominently in view.

"Ah, honorable sir," answered Sato, before Kennedy could reply, "the artist intended by that to indicate Japan's friendliness for America and America's greatness."

He was inscrutable. It seemed as if he were watching our every move, and yet it was done with a polite cordiality that could not give offense.

Behind some bronzes of the Japanese Hercules destroying the demons and other mythical heroes was a large alcove, or *tokonoma,* decorated with peacock, stork, and crane panels. Carvings and lacquer added to the beauty of it. A miniature chrysanthemum garden heightened the illusion. Carved *hinoki* wood framed the panels, and the roof was supported by columns in the old Japanese style, the whole being a compromise between the very simple and quiet and the polychromatic. The dark woods, the lanterns, the floor tiles of dark red, and the

cushions of rich gold and yellow were most allur-
ing. It had the genuine fascination of the Orient.

"Will the gentlemen drink a little *sake?*" Sato
asked politely.

Craig thanked him and said that we would.

"Otaka!" Sato called.

A peculiar, almost white-skinned attendant answered, and a moment later produced four cups and
poured out the rice brandy, taking his own quietly,
apart from us. I watched him drink, curiously. He
took the cup; then, with a long piece of carved wood,
he dipped into the *sake,* shaking a few drops on the
floor to the four quarters. Finally, with a deft
sweep, he lifted his heavy mustache with the piece
of wood and drank off the draft almost without taking breath.

He was a peculiar man of middle height, with a
shock of dark, tough, woolly hair, well formed and
not bad-looking, with a robust general physique, as
if his ancestors had been meat eaters. His forehead was narrow and sloped backward; the cheek-
bones were prominent; nose hooked, broad and wide,
with strong nostrils; mouth large, with thick lips,
and not very prominent chin. His eyes were perhaps the most noticeable feature. They were dark
gray, almost like those of a European.

As Otaka withdrew with the empty cups, we rose
to continue our inspection of the wonders of the
shop. There were ivories of all descriptions. Here
was a two-handled sword, with a very large ivory
handle, a weirdly carved scabbard, and wonderful
steel blade. By the expression of Craig's face, Sato
knew that he had made a sale.

Craig had been rummaging among some warlike
instruments which Sato, with the instincts of a true

salesman, was now displaying, and had picked up
a bow. It was short, very strong, and made of pine
wood. He held it horizontally and twanged the
string. I looked up in time to catch a pleased expression on the face of Otaka.

"Most people would have held·it the other way,"
commented Sato.

Craig said nothing, but was examining an arrow,
almost twenty inches long and thick, made of cane,
with a point of metal very sharp but badly fastened.
He fingered the deep blood groove in the scooplike
head of the arrow and looked at it carefully.

"I'll take that," he said, "only I wish it were one
with the regular reddish-brown lump in it."

"Oh, but, honorable sir," apologized Sato, "the
Japanese law prohibits that, now. There are few
of those, and they are very valuable."

"I suppose so," agreed Craig. "This will do,
though. You have a wonderful shop here, Sato.
Some time, when I feel richer, I mean to come in
again. No, thank you, you need not send them; I'll
carry them."

We bowed ourselves out, promising to come again
when Sato received a new consignment from the
Orient which he was expecting.

"That other Jap is a peculiar fellow," I observed,
as we walked along uptown again.

"He isn't a Jap," remarked Craig. "He is an
Ainu, one of the aborigines who have been driven
northward into the island of Yezo."

"An Ainu?" I repeated.

"Yes. Generally thought, now, to be a white
race and nearer of kin to Europeans than Asiatics.
The Japanese have pushed them northward and are
now trying to civilize them. They are a dirty, hairy

race, but when they are brought under civilizing influences they adapt themselves to their environment and make very good servants.   Still, they are on about the lowest scale of humanity."

"I thought Otaka was very mild," I commented.

"They are a most inoffensive and peaceable people usually," he answered, "good-natured and amenable to authority.   But they become dangerous when driven to despair by cruel treatment.   The Japanese government is very considerate of them—but not all Japanese are."

CHAPTER XII

THE ARROW POISON

FAR into the night Craig was engaged in some very delicate and minute microscopic work in the laboratory.

We were about to leave when there was a gentle tap on the door. Kennedy opened it and admitted a young man, the operative of the detective agency who had been shadowing Bernardo. His report was very brief, but, to me at least, significant. Bernardo, on his return to the museum, had evidently read the letter, which had agitated him very much, for a few moments later he hurriedly left and went downtown to the Prince Henry Hotel. The operative had casually edged up to the desk and overheard whom he asked for. It was Señora Herreria. Once again, later in the evening, he had asked for her, but she was still out.

It was quite early the next morning, when Kennedy had resumed his careful microscopic work, that the telephone bell rang, and he answered it mechanically. But a moment later a look of intense surprise crossed his face.

"It was from Doctor Leslie," he announced, hanging up the receiver quickly. "He has a most peculiar case which he wants me to see—a woman."

Kennedy called a cab, and, at a furious pace, we dashed across the city and down to the Metropolitan

Hospital, where Doctor Leslie was waiting. He met us eagerly and conducted us to a little room where, lying motionless on a bed, was a woman.

She was a striking-looking woman, dark of hair and skin, and in life she must have been sensuously attractive. But now her face was drawn and contorted—with the same ghastly look that had been on the face of Northrop.

"She died in a cab," explained Doctor Leslie, "before they could get her to the hospital. At first they suspected the cab driver. But he seems to have proved his innocence. He picked her up last night on Fifth Avenue, reeling—thought she was intoxicated. And, in fact, he seems to have been right. Our tests have shown a great deal of alcohol present, but nothing like enough to have had such a serious effect."

"She told nothing of herself?" asked Kennedy.

"No; she was pretty far gone when the cabby answered her signal. All he could get out of her was a word that sounded like 'Curio-curio.' He says she seemed to complain of something about her mouth and head. Her face was drawn and shrunken; her hands were cold and clammy, and then convulsions came on. He called an ambulance, but she was past saving when it arrived. The numbness seemed to have extended over all her body; swallowing was impossible; there was entire loss of her voice as well as sight, and death took place by syncope."

"Have you any clue to the cause of her death?" asked Craig.

"Well, it might have been some trouble with her heart, I suppose," remarked Doctor Leslie tentatively.

"Oh, she looks strong that way. No, hardly anything organic."

"Well, then I thought she looked like a Mexican," went on Doctor Leslie. "It might be some new tropical disease. I confess I don't know. The fact is," he added, lowering his voice, "I had my own theory about it until a few moments ago. That was why I called you."

"What do you mean?" asked Craig, evidently bent on testing his own theory by the other's ignorance.

Doctor Leslie made no answer immediately, but raised the sheet which covered her body and disclosed, in the fleshy part of the upper arm, a curious little red swollen mark with a couple of drops of darkened blood.

"I thought at first," he added, "that we had at last a genuine 'poisoned needle' case. You see, that looked like it. But I have made all the tests for curare and strychnin without results."

At the mere suggestion, a procession of hypodermic-needle and white-slavery stories flashed before me.

"But," objected Kennedy, "clearly this was not a case of kidnaping. It is a case of murder. Have you tested for the ordinary poisons?"

Doctor Leslie shook his head. "There was no poison," he said, "absolutely none that any of our tests could discover."

Kennedy bent over and squeezed out a few drops of liquid from the wound on a microscope slide, and covered them.

"You have not identified her yet," he added, looking up. "I think you will find, Leslie, that there is a Señora Herreria registered at the Prince Henry who is missing, and that this woman will agree with the description of her. Anyhow, I wish you would look it up and let me know."

Half an hour later, Kennedy was preparing to continue his studies with the microscope when Doctor Bernardo entered. He seemed most solicitous to know what progress was being made on the case, and, although Kennedy did not tell much, still he did not discourage conversation on the subject.

When we came in the night before, Craig had unwrapped and tossed down the Japanese sword and the Ainu bow and arrow on a table, and it was not long before they attracted Bernardo's attention.

"I see you are a collector yourself," he ventured, picking them up.

"Yes," answered Craig, offhand; "I picked them up yesterday at Sato's. You know the place?"

"Oh, yes, I know Sato," answered the curator, seemingly without the slightest hesitation. "He has been in Mexico—is quite a student."

"And the other man, Otaka?"

"Other man—Otaka? You mean his wife?"

I saw Kennedy check a motion of surprise and came to the rescue with the natural question: "His wife—with a beard and mustache?"

It was Bernardo's turn to be surprised. He looked at me a moment, then saw that I meant it, and suddenly his face lighted up.

"Oh," he exclaimed, "that must have been on account of the immigration laws or something of the sort. Otaka is his wife. The Ainus are much sought after by the Japanese as wives. The women, you know, have a custom of tattooing mustaches on themselves. It is hideous, but they think it is beautiful."

9

"I know," I pursued, watching Kennedy's interest in our conversation, "but this was not tattooed."

"Well, then, it must have been false," insisted Bernardo.

The curator chatted a few moments, during which I expected Kennedy to lead the conversation around to Señora Herreria. But he did not, evidently fearing to show his hand.

"What did you make of it?" I asked, when he had gone. "Is he trying to hide something?"

"I think he has simplified the case," remarked Craig, leaning back, his hands behind his head, gazing up at the ceiling. "Hello, here's Leslie! What did you find, Doctor?" The coroner had entered with a look of awe on his face, as if Kennedy had directed him by some sort of necromancy.

"It was Señora Herreria!" he exclaimed. "She has been missing from the hotel ever since late yesterday afternoon. What do you think of it?"

"I think," replied Kennedy, speaking slowly and deliberately, "that it is very much like the Northrop case. You haven't taken that up yet?"

"Only superficially. What do you make of it?" asked the coroner.

"I had an idea that it might be aconitin poisoning," he said.

Leslie glanced at him keenly for a moment. "Then you'll never prove anything in the laboratory," he said.

"There are more ways of catching a criminal, Leslie," put in Craig, "than are set down in the medico-legal text-books. I shall depend on you and Jameson to gather together a rather cosmopolitan crowd here to-night."

He said it with a quiet confidence which I could

not gainsay, although I did not understand. However, mostly with the official aid of Doctor Leslie, I followed out his instructions, and it was indeed a strange party that assembled that night. There were Doctor Bernardo; Sato, the curio dealer; Otaka, the Ainu, and ourselves. Mrs. Northrop, of course, could not come.

"Mexico," began Craig, after he had said a few words explaining why he had brought us together, "is full of historical treasure. To all intents and purposes, the government says, 'Come and dig.' But when there are finds, then the government swoops down on them for its own national museum. The finder scarcely gets a chance to export them. However, now seemed to be the time to Professor Northrop to smuggle his finds out of the country.

"But evidently it could not be done without exciting all kinds of rumors and suspicions. Stories seem to have spread far and fast about what he had discovered. He realized the unsettled condition of the country—perhaps wanted to confirm his reading of a certain inscription by consultation with one scholar whom he thought he could trust. At any rate, he came home."

Kennedy paused, making use of the silence for emphasis. "You have all read of the wealth that Cortez found in Mexico. Where are the gold and silver of the *conquistadores?* Gone to the melting pot, centuries ago. But is there none left? The Indians believe so. There are persons who would stop at nothing—even at murder of American professors, murder of their own comrades, to get at the secret."

He laid his hand almost lovingly on his power-

ful little microscope as he resumed on another line
of evidence.

"And while we are on the subject of murders,
two very similar deaths have occurred," he went on.
"It is of no use to try to gloss them over. Frankly,
I suspected that they might have been caused by
aconite poisoning. But, in the case of such poisoning, not only is the lethal dose very small but our
chemical methods of detection are *nil*. The dose of
the active principle, aconitin nitrate, is about one
six-hundredth of a grain. There are no color tests,
no reactions, as in the case of the other organic
poisons."

I wondered what he was driving at. Was there,
indeed, no test? Had the murderer used the safest
of poisons—one that left no clue? I looked covertly
at Sato's face. It was impassive. Doctor Bernardo was visibly uneasy as Kennedy proceeded.
Cool enough up to the time of the mention of the
treasure, I fancied, now, that he was growing more
and more nervous.

Craig laid down on the table the reed stick with
the little darkened cylinder on the end.

"That," he said, "is a little article which I picked
up beneath Northrop's window yesterday. It is a
piece of *anno-noki*, or *bushi*." I fancied I saw just
a glint of satisfaction in Otaka's eyes.

"Like many barbarians," continued Craig, "the
Ainus from time immemorial have prepared virulent
poisons with which they charged their weapons of
the chase and warfare. The formulas for the
preparations, as in the case of other arrow poisons
of other tribes, are known only to certain members,
and the secret is passed down from generation to
generation as an heirloom, as it were. But in this

case it is no longer a secret. It has now been proved that the active principle of this poison is aconite."

"If that is the case," broke in Doctor Leslie, "it is hopeless to connect anyone directly in that way with these murders. There is no test for aconitin."

I thought Sato's face was more composed and impassive than ever. Doctor Bernardo, however, was plainly excited.

"What—no test—*none?*" asked Kennedy, leaning forward eagerly. Then, as if he could restrain the answer to his own question no longer, he shot out: "How about the new starch test just discovered by Professor Reichert, of the University of Pennsylvania? Doubtless you never dreamed that starch may be a means of detecting the nature of a poison in obscure cases in criminology, especially in cases where the quantity of poison necessary to cause death is so minute that no trace of it can be found in the blood.

"The starch method is a new and extremely inviting subject to me. The peculiarities of the starch of any plant are quite as distinctive of the plant as are those of the hemoglobin crystals in the blood of an animal. I have analyzed the evidence of my microscope in this case thoroughly. When the arrow poison is introduced subcutaneously—say, by a person shooting a poisoned dart, which he afterward removes in order to destroy the evidence—the lethal constituents are rapidly absorbed.

"But the starch remains in the wound. It can be recovered and studied microscopically and can be definitely recognized. Doctor Reichert has published a study of twelve hundred such starches from all sorts of plants. In this case, it not only proves to be aconitin but the starch granules themselves can be recognized. They came from this piece of arrow poison."

Every eye was fixed on him now.

"Besides," he rapped out, "in the soft soil beneath the window of Profesor Northrop's room, I found footprints. I have only to compare the impressions I took there and those of the people in this room, to prove that, while the real murderer stood guard below the window, he sent some one more nimble up the rain pipe to shoot the poisoned dart at Professor Northrop, and, later, to let down a rope by which he, the instigator, could gain the room, remove the dart, and obtain the key to the treasure he sought."

Kennedy was looking straight at Professor Bernardo.

"A friend of mine in Mexico has written me about an inscription," he burst out. "I received the letter only to-day. As nearly as I can gather, there was an impression that some of Northrop's stuff would be valuable in proving the alleged kinship between Mexico and Japan, perhaps to arouse hatred of the United States."

"Yes—that is all very well," insisted Kennedy. "But how about the treasure?"

"Treasure?" repeated Bernardo, looking from one of us to another.

"Yes," pursued Craig relentlessly, "the treasure. You are an expert in reading the hieroglyphics. By your own statement, you and Northrop had been going over the stuff he had sent up. You know it."

Bernardo gave a quick glance from Kennedy to me. Evidently he saw that the secret was out.

"Yes," he said huskily, in a low tone, "Northrop and I were to follow the directions after we had plotted them out and were to share it together on the next expedition, which I could direct as a Mexican without so much suspicion. I should still have shared it with his widow if this unfortunate affair had not exposed the secret."

Bernardo had risen earnestly.

"Kennedy," he cried, "before God, if you will get back that stone and keep the secret from going further than this room, I will prove what I have said by dividing the Mixtec treasure with Mrs. Northrop and making her one of the richest widows in the country!"

"That is what I wanted to be sure of," nodded Craig. "Bernardo, Señora Herreria, of whom your friend wrote to you from Mexico, has been murdered in the same way that Professor Northrop was. Otaka was sent by her husband to murder Northrop, in order that they might obtain the so-called 'Pillar of Death' and the key to the treasure. Then, when the *señora* was no doubt under the influence of *sake* in the pretty little Oriental bower at the curio shop, a quick jab, and Otaka had removed one who shared the secret with them."

He had turned and faced the pair.

"Sato," he added, "you played on the patriotism of the *señora* until you wormed from her the treasure secret. Evidently rumors of it had spread from Mexican Indians to Japanese visitors. And then, Otaka, all jealousy over one whom she, no doubt, justly considered a rival, completed your work by sending her forth to die, unknown, on the street. Walter, ring up First Deputy O'Connor. The stone is hidden somewhere in the curio shop. We can find it without Sato's help. The quicker such a criminal is lodged safely in jail, the better for humanity.''

Sato was on his feet, advancing cautiously toward Craig. I knew the dangers, now, of *anno-noki*, as well as the wonders of *jujutsu*, and, with a leap, I bounded past Bernardo and between Sato and Kennedy.

How it happened, I don't know, but, an instant later, I was sprawling.

Before I could recover myself, before even Craig had a chance to pull the hair-trigger of his automatic, Sato had seized the Ainu arrow poison from the table, had bitten the little cylinder in half, and had crammed the other half into the mouth of Otaka.

CHAPTER XIII

THE RADIUM ROBBER

KENNEDY simply reached for the telephone and called an ambulance. But it was purely perfunctory. Dr. Leslie himself was the only official who could handle Sato's case now.

We had planned a little vacation for ourselves, but the planning came to naught. The next night we spent on a sleeper. That in itself is work to me.

It all came about through a hurried message from Murray Denison, president of the Federal Radium Corporation. Nothing would do but that he should take both Kennedy and myself with him post-haste to Pittsburgh at the first news of what had immediately been called "the great radium robbery."

Of course the newspapers were full of it. The very novelty of an ultra-modern cracksman going off with something worth upward of a couple of hundred thousand dollars—and all contained in a few platinum tubes which could be tucked away in a vest pocket—had something about it powerfully appealing to the imagination.

"Most ingenious, but, you see, the trouble with that safe is that it was built to keep radium *in*—not cracksmen *out*," remarked Kennedy, when Denison had rushed us from the train to take a look at the little safe in the works of the Corporation.

129

"Breaking into such a safe as this," added Kennedy, after a cursory examination, "is simple enough, after all."

It was, however, a remarkably ingenious contrivance, about three feet in height and of a weight of perhaps a ton and a half, and all to house something weighing only a few grains.

"But," Denison hastened to explain, "we had to protect the radium not only against burglars, but, so to speak, against itself. Radium emanations pass through steel and experiments have shown that the best metal to contain them is lead. So, the difficulty was solved by making a steel outer case enclosing an inside leaden shell three inches thick."

Kennedy had been toying thoughtfully with the door.

"Then the door, too, had to be contrived so as to prevent any escape of the emanations through joints. It is lathe turned and circular, a 'dead fit.' By means of a special contrivance any slight looseness caused by wear and tear of closing can be adjusted. And another feature. That is the appliance for preventing the loss of emanation when the door is opened. Two valves have been inserted into the door and before it is opened tubes with mercury are passed through which collect and store the emanation."

"All very nice for the radium," remarked Craig cheerfully. "But the fellow had only to use an electric drill and the gram or more of radium was his."

"I know that—now," ruefully persisted Denison. "But the safe was designed for us specially. The fellow got into it and got away, as far as I can see, without leaving a clue."

"Except one, of course," interrupted Kennedy quickly.

Denison looked at him a moment keenly, then nodded and said, "Yes—you are right. You mean one which he must bear on himself?"

"Exactly. You can't carry a gram or more of radium bromide long with impunity. The man to look for is one who in a few days will have somewhere on his body a radium burn which will take months to heal. The very thing he stole is a veritable Frankenstein's monster bent on the destruction of the thief himself!"

Kennedy had meanwhile picked up one of the Corporation's circulars lying on a desk. He ran his eye down the list of names.

"So, Hartley Haughton, the broker, is one of your stockholders," mused Kennedy.

"Not only one but *the* one," replied Denison with obvious pride.

Haughton was a young man who had come recently into his fortune, and, while no one believed it to be large, he had cut quite a figure in Wall Street.

"You know, I suppose," added Denison, "that he is engaged to Felicie Woods, the daughter of Mrs. Courtney Woods?"

Kennedy did not, but said nothing.

"A most delightful little girl," continued Denison thoughtfully. "I have known Mrs. Woods for some time. She wanted to invest, but I told her frankly that this is, after all, a speculation. We may not be able to swing so big a proposition, but, if not, no one can say we have taken a dollar of money from widows and orphans."

"I should like to see the works," nodded Kennedy approvingly.

"By all means."

The plant was a row of long low buildings of brick on the outskirts of the city, once devoted to the making of vanadium steel. The ore, as Denison explained, was brought to Pittsburgh because he had found here already a factory which could readily be turned into a plant for the extraction of radium. Huge baths and vats and crucibles for the various acids and alkalis and other processes used in treating the ore stood at various points.

"This must be like extracting gold from sea water," remarked Kennedy jocosely, impressed by the size of the plant as compared to the product.

"Except that after we get through we have something infinitely more precious than gold," replied Denison, "something which warrants the trouble and outlay. Yes, the fact is that the percentage of radium in all such ores is even less than of gold in sea water."

"Everything seems to be most carefully guarded," remarked Kennedy as we concluded our tour of the well-appointed works.

He had gone over everything in silence, and now at last we had returned to the safe.

"Yes," he repeated slowly, as if confirming his original impression, "such an amount of radium as was stolen wouldn't occasion immediate discomfort to the thief, I suppose, but later no infernal machine could be more dangerous to him."

I pictured to myself the series of fearful works of mischief and terror that might follow, a curse on the thief worse than that of the weirdest curses of the Orient, the danger to the innocent, and the fact that in the hands of a criminal it was an instrument for committing crimes that might defy detection.

"There is nothing more to do here now," he concluded. "I can see nothing for the present except to go back to New York. The telltale burn may not be the only clue, but if the thief is going to profit by his spoils we shall hear about it best in New York or by cable from London, Paris, or some other European city."

Our hurried departure from New York had not given us a chance to visit the offices of the Radium Corporation for the distribution of the salts themselves. They were in a little old office building on William Street, near the drug district and yet scarcely a moment's walk from the financial district.

"Our head bookkeeper, Miss Wallace, is ill," remarked Denison when we arrived at the office, "but if there is anything I can do to help you, I shall be glad to do it. We depend on Miss Wallace a great deal. Haughton says she is the brains of the office."

Kennedy looked about the well-appointed suite curiously.

"Is this another of those radium safes?" he asked, approaching one similar in appearance to that which had been broken open already.

"Yes, only a little larger."

"How much is in it?"

"Most of our supply. I should say about two and a half grams. Miss Wallace has the record."

"It is of the same construction, I presume," pursued Kennedy. "I wonder whether the lead lining fits closely to the steel?"

"I think not," considered Denison. "As I remember there was a sort of insulating air cushion or something of the sort."

Denison was quite eager to show us about. In fact ever since he had hustled us out to view the scene of the robbery, his high nervous tension had given us scarcely a moment's rest. For hours he had talked radium, until I felt that he, like his metal, must have an inexhaustible emanation of words. He was one of those nervous, active little men, a born salesman, whether of ribbons or radium.

"We have just gone into furnishing radium water," he went on, bustling about and patting a little glass tank.

I looked closely and could see that the water glowed in the dark with a peculiar phosphorescence.

"The apparatus for the treatment," he continued, "consists of two glass and porcelain receptacles. Inside the larger receptacle is placed the smaller, which contains a tiny quantity of radium. Into the larger receptacle is poured about a gallon of filtered water. The emanation from that little speck of radium is powerful enough to penetrate its porcelain holder and charge the water with its curative properties. From a tap at the bottom of the tank the patient draws the number of glasses of water a day prescribed. For such purposes the emanation within a day or two of being collected is as good as radium itself. Why, this water is five thousand times as radioactive as the most radioactive natural spring water."

"You must have control of a comparatively large amount of the metal," suggested Kennedy.

"We are, I believe, the largest holders of radium in the world," he answered. "I have estimated that all told there are not much more than ten grams, of which Madame Curie has perhaps three, while Sir Ernest Cassel of London is the holder of perhaps as much. We have nearly four grams, leaving about six or seven for the rest of the world."

Kennedy nodded and continued to look about.

"The Radium Corporation," went on Denison, "has several large deposits of radioactive ore in Utah in what is known as the Poor Little Rich Valley, a valley so named because from being about the barrenest and most unproductive mineral or agricultural hole in the hills, the sudden discovery of the radioactive deposits has made it almost priceless."

He had entered a private office and was looking over some mail that had been left on his desk during his absence.

"Look at this," he called, picking up a clipping from a newspaper which had been laid there for his attention. "You see, we have them aroused."

We read the clipping together hastily:

PLAN TO CORNER WORLD'S RADIUM

LONDON.—Plans are being matured to form a large corporation for the monopoly of the existing and future supply of radium throughout the world. The company is to be called Universal Radium, Limited, and the capital of ten million dollars will be offered for public subscription at par simultaneously in London, Paris and New York.

The company's business will be to acquire mines and deposits of radioactive substances as well as the control of patents and processes connected with the production of radium. The outspoken purpose of the new company is to obtain a world-wide monopoly and maintain the price.

"Ah—a competitor," commented Kennedy, handing back the clipping.

"Yes. You know radium salts used always to come from Europe. Now we are getting ready to do some exporting ourselves. Say," he added excitedly, "there's an idea, possibly, in that."

"How?" queried Craig.

"Why, since we should be the principal competitors to the foreign mines, couldn't this robbery have been due to the machinations of these schemers? To my mind, the United States, because of its supply of radium-bearing ores, will have to be reckoned with first in cornering the market. This is the point, Kennedy. Would those people who seem to be trying to extend their new company all over the world stop at anything in order to cripple us at the start?"

How much longer Denison would have rattled on in his effort to explain the robbery, I do not know. The telephone rang and a reporter from the *Record*, who had just read my own story in the *Star*, asked for an interview. I knew that it would be only a question of minutes now before the other men were wearing a path out on the stairs, and we managed to get away before the onrush began.

"Walter," said Kennedy, as soon as we had reached the street. "I want to get in touch with Halsey Haughton. How can it be done?"

I could think of nothing better at that moment than to inquire at the *Star's* Wall Street office, which happened to be around the corner. I knew the men down there intimately, and a few minutes later we were whisked up in the elevator to the office.

They were as glad to see me as I was to see them, for the story of the robbery had interested the financial district perhaps more than any other.

"Where can I find Halsey Haughton at this hour?" I asked.

"Say," exclaimed one of the men, "what's the matter? There have been all kinds of rumors in

the Street about him to-day.   Did you know he was
ill?"

"No," I answered.   "Where is he?"

"Out at the home of his fiancée, who is the daughter of Mrs. Courtney Woods, at Glenclair."

"What's the matter?" I persisted.

"That's just it.   No one seems to know.   They
say—well—they say he has a cancer."

Halsey Haughton suffering from cancer?   It was
such an uncommon thing to hear of a young man that
I looked up quickly in surprise.   Then all at once it
flashed over me that Denison and Kennedy had discussed the matter of burns from the stolen radium.
Might not this be, instead of cancer, a radium
burn?

Kennedy, who had been standing a little apart
from me while I was talking with the boys, signaled
to me with a quick glance not to say too much, and
a few minutes later we were on the street again.

I knew without being told that he was bound by
the next train to the pretty little New Jersey suburb
of Glenclair.

It was late when we arrived, yet Kennedy had
no hesitation in calling at the quaint home of Mrs.
Courtney Woods on Woodridge Avenue.

Mrs. Woods, a well-set-up woman of middle age,
who had retained her youth and good looks in a remarkable manner, met us in the foyer.   Briefly,
Kennedy explained that we had just come in from
Pittsburgh with Mr. Denison and that it was very
important that we should see Haughton at once.

We had hardly told her the object of our visit
when a young woman of perhaps twenty-two or
three, a very pretty girl, with all the good looks of
her mother and a freshness which only youth can

10

possess, tiptoed quietly downstairs. Her face told plainly that she was deeply worried over the illness of her fiancé.

"Who is it, mother?" she whispered from the turn in the stairs. "Some gentlemen from the company? Hartley's door was open when the bell rang, and he thought he heard something said about the Pittsburgh affair."

Though she had whispered, it had not been for the purpose of concealing anything from us, but rather that the keen ears of her patient might not catch the words. She cast an inquiring glance at us.

"Yes," responded Kennedy in answer to her look, modulating his tone. "We have just left Mr. Denison at the office. Might we see Mr. Haughton for a moment? I am sure that nothing we can say or do will be as bad for him as our going away, now that he knows that we are here."

The two women appeared to consult for a moment.

"Felicie," called a rather nervous voice from the second floor, "is it some one from the company?"

"Just a moment, Hartley," she answered, then, lower to her mother, added, "I don't think it can do any harm, do you, mother?"

"You remember the doctor's orders, my dear."

Again the voice called her.

"Hang the doctor's orders," the girl exclaimed, with an air of almost masculinity. "It can't be half so bad as to have him worry. Will you promise not to stay long? We expect Dr. Bryant in a few moments, anyway."

CHAPTER XIV

THE SPINTHARISCOPE

WE followed her upstairs and into Haughton's room, where he was lying in bed, propped up by pillows. Haughton certainly was ill. There was no mistake about that. He was a tall, gaunt man with an air about him that showed that he found illness very irksome. Around his neck was a bandage, and some adhesive tape at the back showed that a plaster of some sort had been placed there.

As we entered his eyes traveled restlessly from the face of the girl to our own in an inquiring manner. He stretched out a nervous hand to us, while Kennedy in a few short sentences explained how we had become associated with the case and what we had seen already.

"And there is not a clue?" he repeated as Craig finished.

"Nothing tangible yet," reiterated Kennedy. "I suppose you have heard of this rumor from London of a trust that is going into the radium field internationally?"

"Yes," he answered, "that is the thing you read to me in the morning papers, you remember, Felicie. Denison and I have heard such rumors before. If it is a fight, then we shall give them a fight. They can't hold us up, if Denison is right in thinking that they are at the bottom of this—this robbery."

"Then you think he may be right?" shot out Kennedy quickly.

Haughton glanced nervously from Kennedy to me.

"Really," he answered, "you see how impossible it is for me to have an opinion? You and Denison have been over the ground. You know much more about it than I do. I am afraid I shall have to defer to you."

Again we heard the bell downstairs, and a moment later a cheery voice, as Mrs. Woods met some one down in the foyer, asked, "How is the patient to-night?"

We could not catch the reply.

"Dr. Bryant, my physician," put in Haughton. "Don't go. I will assume the responsibility for your being here. Hello, Doctor. Why, I'm much the same to-night, thank you. At least no worse since I took your advice and went to bed."

Dr. Bryant was a bluff, hearty man, with the personal magnetism which goes with the making of a successful physician. He had mounted the stairs quietly but rapidly, evidently prepared to see us.

"Would you mind waiting in this little dressing room?" asked the doctor, motioning to another, smaller room adjoining.

He had taken from his pocket a little instrument with a dial face like a watch, which he attached to Haughton's wrist.

"A pocket instrument to measure blood pressure," whispered Craig, as we entered the little room.

While the others were gathered about Haughton, we stood in the next room, out of earshot. Kennedy had leaned his elbow on a chiffonier. As he looked about the little room, more from force of

habit than because he thought he might discover
anything, Kennedy's eye rested on a glass tray on
the top in which lay some pins, a collar button or
two, which Haughton had apparently just taken off,
and several other little unimportant articles.

Kennedy bent over to look at the glass tray more
closely, a puzzled look crossed his face, and with a
glance at the other room he gathered up the tray
and its contents.

"Keep up a good courage," said Dr. Bryant.
"You'll come out all right, Haughton."   Then as
he left the bedroom he added to us, "Gentlemen, I
hope you will pardon me, but if you could postpone
the remainder of your visit until a later day, I am
sure you will find it more satisfactory."

There was an air of finality about the doctor,
though nothing unpleasant in it.   We followed him
down the stairs, and as we did so, Felicie, who had
been waiting in a reception room, appeared before
the portieres, her earnest eyes fixed on his kindly
face.

"Dr. Bryant," she appealed, "is he—is he, really
—so badly?"

The Doctor, who had apparently known her all
her life, reached down and took one of her hands,
patting it with his own in a fatherly way.   "Don't
worry, little girl," he encouraged.   "We are going
to come out all right—all right."

She turned from him to us and, with a bright
forced smile which showed the stuff she was made
of, bade us good night.

Outside, the Doctor, apparently regretting that he
had virtually forced us out, paused before his car.
"Are you going down toward the station? Yes?

I am going that far. I should be glad to drive you there."

Kennedy climbed into the front seat, leaving me in the rear where the wind wafted me their brief conversation as we sped down Woodbridge Avenue.

"What seems to be the trouble?" asked Craig.

"Very high blood pressure, for one thing," replied the Doctor frankly.

"For which the latest thing is the radium water cure, I suppose?" ventured Kennedy.

"Well, radioactive water is one cure for hardening of the arteries. But I didn't say he had hardening of the arteries. Still, he is taking the water, with good results. You are from the company?"

Kennedy nodded.

"It was the radium water that first interested him in it. Why, we found a pressure of 230 pounds, which is frightful, and we have brought it down to 150, not far from normal."

"Still that could have nothing to do with the sore on his neck," hazarded Kennedy.

The Doctor looked at him quickly, then ahead at the path of light which his motor shed on the road.

He said nothing, but I fancied that even he felt there was something strange in his silence over the new complication. He did not give Kennedy a chance to ask whether there were any other such sores.

"At any rate," he said, as he throttled down his engine with a flourish before the pretty little Glenclair station, "that girl needn't worry."

There was evidently no use in trying to extract anything further from him. He had said all that medical ethics or detective skill could get from him.

We thanked him and turned to the ticket window to see how long we should have to wait.

"Either that doctor doesn't know what he is talking about or he is concealing something," remarked Craig, as we paced up and down the platform. "I am inclined to read the enigma in the latter way."

Nothing more passed between us during the journey back, and we hurried directly to the laboratory, late as it was. Kennedy had evidently been revolving something over and over in his mind, for the moment he had switched on the light, he unlocked one of his air- and dust-proof cabinets and took from it an instrument which he placed on a table before him.

It was a peculiar-looking instrument, like a round glass electric battery with a cylinder atop, smaller and sticking up like a safety valve. On that were an arm, a dial, and a lens fixed in such a way as to read the dial. I could not see what else the rather complicated little apparatus consisted of, but inside, when Kennedy brought near it the pole of a static electric machine two delicate thin leaves of gold seemed to fly wide apart when it was charged.

Kennedy had brought the glass tray near the thing. Instantly the leaves collapsed and he made a reading through the lens.

"What is it?" I asked.

"A radioscope," he replied, still observing the scale. "Really a very sensitive gold leaf electroscope, devised by one of the students of Madame Curie. This method of detection is far more sensitive even than the spectroscope."

"What does it mean when the leaves collapse?" I asked.

"Radium has been near that tray," he answered.

"It is radioactive. I suspected it first when I saw that violet color. That is what radium does to that kind of glass. You see, if radium exists in a gram of inactive matter only to the extent of one in ten-thousand million parts its presence can be readily detected by this radioscope, and everything that has been rendered radioactive is the same. Ordinarily the air between the gold leaves is insulating. Bringing something radioactive near them renders the air a good conductor and the leaves fall under the radiation."

"Wonderful!" I exclaimed, marveling at the delicacy of it.

"Take radium water," he went on, "sufficiently impregnated with radium emanations to be luminous in the dark, like that water of Denison's. It would do the same. In fact all mineral waters and the so-called curative muds like fango are slightly radioactive. There seems to be a little radium everywhere on earth that experiments have been made, even in the interiors of buildings. It is ubiquitous. We are surrounded and permeated by radiations— that soil out there on the campus, the air of this room, all. But," he added contemplatively, "there is something different about that tray. A lot of radium has been near that, and recently."

"How about that bandage about Haughton's neck?" I asked suddenly. "Do you think radium could have had anything to do with that?"

"Well, as to burns, there is no particular immediate effect usually, and sometimes even up to two weeks or more, unless the exposure has been long and to a considerable quantity. Of course radium keeps itself three or four degrees warmer than other things about it constantly. But that isn't what does the harm. It is continually emitting little corpuscles, which I'll explain some other time, traveling all the way from twenty to one hundred and thirty thousand miles a second, and these corpuscles blister and corrode the flesh like quick-moving missiles bombarding it. The gravity of such lesions increases with the purity of the radium. For instance I have known an exposure of half an hour to a comparatively small quantity through a tube, a box and the clothes to produce a blister fifteen days later. Curie said he wouldn't trust himself in a room with a kilogram of it. It would destroy his eyesight, burn off his skin and kill him eventually. Why, even after a slight exposure your clothes are radioactive—the electroscope will show that."

He was still fumbling with the glass plate and the various articles on it.

"There's something very peculiar about all this," he muttered, almost to himself.

Tired by the quick succession of events of the past two days, I left Kennedy still experimenting in his laboratory and retired, still wondering when the real clue was to develop. Who could it have been who bore the tell-tale burn? Was the mark hidden by the bandage about Haughton's neck the brand of the stolen tubes? Or were there other marks on his body which we could not see?

No answer came to me, and I fell asleep and woke up without a radiation of light on the subject. Kennedy spent the greater part of the day still at work at his laboratory, performing some very delicate experiments. Finding nothing to do there, I went down to the *Star* office and spent my time reading the reports that came in from the small army of reporters who had been assigned to run down clues in

the case which was the sensation of the moment. I
have always felt my own lips sealed in such cases,
until the time came that the story was complete and
Kennedy released me from any further need of silence. The weird and impossible stories which came
in not only to the *Star* but to the other papers surely
did make passable copy in this instance, but with my
knowledge of the case I could see that not one of
them brought us a step nearer the truth.

One thing which uniformly puzzled the newspapers was the illness of Haughton and his enforced
idleness at a time which was of so much importance
to the company which he had promoted and indeed
very largely financed. Then, of course, there was
the romantic side of his engagement to Felicie
Woods.

Just what connection Felicie Woods had with the
radium robbery if any, I was myself unable quite to
fathom. Still, that made no difference to the papers.
She was pretty and therefore they published her picture, three columns deep, with Haughton and Denison, who were intimately concerned with the real
loss in little ovals perhaps an inch across and two
inches in the opposite dimension.

The late afternoon news editions had gone to
press, and I had given up in despair, determined to
go up to the laboratory and sit around idly watching
Kennedy with his mystifying experiments, in prefer-
ence to waiting for him to summon me.

I had scarcely arrived and settled myself to an
impatient watch, when an automobile drove up furiously, and Denison himself, very excited, jumped out
and dashed into the laboratory.

"What's the matter?" asked Kennedy, looking
up from a test tube which he had been examining,

with an air for all the world expressive of "Why so hot, little man?"

"I've had a threat," ejaculated Denison.

He laid on one of the laboratory tables a letter, without heading and without signature, written in a disguised hand, with an evident attempt to simulate the cramped script of a foreign penmanship.

"I know who did the Pittsburgh job. The same party is out to ruin Federal Radium. Remember Pittsburgh and be prepared!

"A Stockholder."

"Well?" demanded Kennedy, looking up.

"That can have only one meaning," asserted Denison.

"What is that?" inquired Kennedy coolly, as if to confirm his own interpretation.

"Why, another robbery—here in New York, of course."

"But who would do it?" I asked.

"Who?" repeated Denison. "Some one representing that European combine, of course. That is only part of the Trust method—ruin of competitors whom they cannot absorb."

"Then you have refused to go into the combine? You know who is backing it?"

"No—no," admitted Denison reluctantly. "We have only signified our intent to go it alone, as often as anyone either with or without authority has offered to buy us out. No, I do not even know who the people are. They never act in the open. The only hints I have ever received were through perfectly reputable brokers acting for others."

"Does Haughton know of this note?" asked Kennedy.

"Yes. As soon as I received it, I called him up."

"What did he say?"

"He said to disregard it. But—you know what condition he is in. I don't know what to do, whether to surround the office by a squad of detectives or remove the radium to a regular safety deposit vault, even at the loss of the emanation. Haughton has left it to me."

Suddenly the thought flashed across my mind that perhaps Haughton could act in this uninterested fashion because he had no fear of ruin either way. Might he not be playing a game with the combination in which he had protected himself so that he would win, no matter what happened?

"What shall I do?" asked Denison. "It is getting late."

"Neither," decided Kennedy.

Denison shook his head. "No," he said, "I shall have some one watch there, anyhow."

CHAPTER XV

THE ASPHYXIATING SAFE

DENISON had scarcely gone to arrange for some one to watch the office that night, when Kennedy, having gathered up his radioscope and packed into a parcel a few other things from various cabinets, announced: "Walter, I must see that Miss Wallace, right away. Denison has already given me her address. Call a cab while I finish clearing up here. I don't like the looks of this thing, even if Haughton does neglect it."

We found Miss Wallace at a modest boarding-house in an old but still respectable part of the city. She was a very pretty girl, of the slender type, rather a business woman than one given much to amusement. She had been ill and was still ill. That was evident from the solicitous way in which the motherly landlady scrutinized two strange callers.

Kennedy presented a card from Denison, and she came down to the parlor to see us.

"Miss Wallace," began Kennedy, "I know it is almost cruel to trouble you when you are not feeling like office work, but since the robbery of the safe at Pittsburgh, there have been threats of a robbery of the New York office."

She started involuntarily, and it was evident, I thought, that she was in a very highstrung state.

149

"Oh," she cried, "why, the loss means ruin to Mr. Denison!"

There were genuine tears in her eyes as she said it.

"I thought you would be willing to aid us," pursued Kennedy sympathetically. "Now, for one thing, I want to be perfectly sure just how much radium the Corporation owns, or rather owned before the first robbery."

"The books will show it," she said simply.

"They will?" commented Kennedy. "Then if you will explain to me briefly just the system you used in keeping account of it, perhaps I need not trouble you any more."

"I'll go down there with you," she answered bravely. "I'm better to-day, anyhow, I think."

She had risen, but it was evident that she was not as strong as she wanted us to think.

"The least I can do is to make it as easy as possible by going in a car," remarked Kennedy, following her into the hall where there was a telephone.

The hallway was perfectly dark, yet as she preceded us I could see that the diamond pin which held her collar in the back sparkled as if a lighted candle had been brought near it. I had noticed in the parlor that she wore a handsome tortoiseshell comb set with what I thought were other brilliants, but when I looked I saw now that there was not the same sparkle to the comb which held her dark hair in a soft mass. I noticed these little things at the time, not because I thought they had any importance, but merely by chance, wondering at the sparkle of the one diamond which had caught my eye.

"What do you make of her?" I asked as Kennedy finished telephoning.

"A very charming and capable girl," he answered noncommittally.

"Did you notice how that diamond in her neck sparkled?" I asked quickly.

He nodded. Evidently it had attracted his attention, too.

"What makes it?" I pursued.

"Well, you know radium rays will make a diamond fluoresce in the dark."

"Yes," I objected, "but how about those in the comb?"

"Paste, probably," he answered tersely, as we heard her foot on the landing. "The rays won't affect paste."

It was indeed a shame to take advantage of Miss Wallace's loyalty to Denison, but she was so game about it that I knew only the utmost necessity on Kennedy's part would have prompted him to do it. She had a key to the office so that it was not necessary to wait for Denison, if indeed we could have found him.

Together she and Kennedy went over the records. It seemed that there were in the safe twenty-five platinum tubes of one hundred milligrams each, and that there had been twelve of the same amount at Pittsburgh. Little as it seemed in weight it represented a fabulous fortune.

"You have not the combination?" inquired Kennedy.

"No. Only Mr. Denison has that. What are you going to do to protect the safe to-night?" she asked.

"Nothing especially," evaded Kennedy.

"Nothing?" she repeated in amazement.

"I have another plan," he said, watching her intently. "Miss Wallace, it was too much to ask you to come down here. You are ill."

She was indeed quite pale, as if the excitement had been an overexertion.

"No, indeed," she persisted. Then, feeling her own weakness, she moved toward the door of Denison's office where there was a leather couch. "Let me rest here a moment. I do feel queer. I——"

She would have fallen if he had not sprung forward and caught her as she sank to the floor, overcome by the exertion.

Together we carried her in to the couch, and as we did so the comb from her hair clattered to the floor.

Craig threw open the window, and bathed her face with water until there was a faint flutter of the eyelids.

"Walter," he said, as she began to revive, "I leave her to you. Keep her quiet for a few moments. She has unintentionally given me just the opportunity I want."

While she was yet hovering between consciousness and unconsciousness on the couch, he had unwrapped the package which he had brought with him. For a moment he held the comb which she had dropped near the radioscope. With a low exclamation of surprise he shoved it into his pocket.

Then from the package he drew a heavy piece of apparatus which looked as if it might be the motor part of an electric fan, only in place of the fan he fitted a long, slim, vicious-looking steel bit. A flexible wire attached the thing to the electric light circuit and I knew that it was an electric drill. With

his coat off he tugged at the little radium safe until
he had moved it out, then dropped on his knees behind it and switched the current on in the electric
drill.

It was a tedious process to drill through the steel
of the outer casing of the safe and it was getting
late. I shut the door to the office so that Miss Wallace could not see.

At last by the cessation of the low hum of the
boring, I knew that he had struck the inner lead lining. Quietly I opened the door and stepped out.
He was injecting something from an hermetically
sealed lead tube into the opening he had made and
allowing it to run between the two linings of lead
and steel. Then using the tube itself he sealed the
opening he had made and dabbed a little black over
it.

Quickly he shoved the safe back, then around it
concealed several small coils with wires also concealed and leading out through a window to a court.

"We'll catch the fellow this time," he remarked
as he worked. "If you ever have any idea, Walter,
of going into the burglary business, it would be well
to ascertain if the safes have any of these little
selenium cells as suggested by my friend, Mr. Ham-
mer, the inventor. For by them an alarm can be
given miles away the moment an intruder's bull's-
eye falls on a hidden cell sensitive to light."

While I was delegated to take Miss Wallace
home, Kennedy made arrangements with a small
shopkeeper on the ground floor of a building that
backed up on the court for the use of his back room
that night, and had already set up a bell actuated
by a system of relays which the weak current from
the selenium cells could operate.

It was not until nearly midnight that he was ready to leave the laboratory again, where he had been busily engaged in studying the tortoiseshell comb which Miss Wallace in her weakness had forgotten.

The little shopkeeper let us in sleepily and Kennedy deposited a large round package on a chair in the back of the shop, as well as a long piece of rubber tubing. Nothing had happened so far.

As we waited the shopkeeper, now wide awake and not at all unconvinced that we were bent on some criminal operation, hung around. Kennedy did not seem to care. He drew from his pocket a little shiny brass instrument in a lead case, which looked like an abbreviated microscope.

"Look through it," he said, handing it to me.

I looked and could see thousands of minute sparks.

"What is it?" I asked.

"A spinthariscope. In that it is possible to watch the bombardment of the countless little corpuscles thrown off by radium, as they strike on the zinc blende crystal which forms the base. When radium was originally discovered, the interest was merely in its curious properties, its power to emit invisible rays which penetrated solid substances and rendered things fluorescent, of expending energy without apparent loss.

"Then came the discovery," he went on, "of its curative powers. But the first results were not convincing. Still, now that we know the reasons why radium may be dangerous and how to protect ourselves against them we know we possess one of the most wonderful of curative agencies."

I was thinking rather of the dangers than of the

beneficence of radium just now, but Kennedy continued.

"It has cured many malignant growths that seemed hopeless, brought back destroyed cells, exercised good effects in diseases of the liver and intestines and even the baffling diseases of the arteries. The reason why harm, at first, as well as good came, is now understood. Radium emits, as I told you before, three kinds of rays, the alpha, beta, and gamma rays, each with different properties. The emanation is another matter. It does not concern us in this case, as you will see."

Fascinated as I was by the mystery of the case, I began to see that he was gradually arriving at an explanation which had baffled everyone else.

"Now, the alpha rays are the shortest," he launched forth, "in length let us say one inch. They exert a very destructive effect on healthy tissue. That is the cause of injury. They are stopped by glass, aluminum and other metals, and are really particles charged with positive electricity. The beta rays come next, say, about an inch and a half. They stimulate cell growth. Therefore they are dangerous in cancer, though good in other ways. They can be stopped by lead, and are really particles charged with negative electricity. The gamma rays are the longest, perhaps three inches long, and it is these rays which effect cures, for they check the abnormal and stimulate the normal cells. They penetrate lead. Lead seems to filter them out from the other rays. And at three inches the other rays don't reach, anyhow. The gamma rays are not charged with electricity at all, apparently."

He had brought a little magnet near the spinthariscope. I looked into it.

"A magnet," he explained, "shows the difference between the alpha, beta, and gamma rays. You see those weak and wobbly rays that seem to fall to one side? Those are the alpha rays. They have a strong action, though, on tissues and cells. Those falling in the other direction are the beta rays. The gamma rays seem to flow straight."

"Then it is the alpha rays with which we are concerned mostly now?" I queried, looking up.

"Exactly. That is why, when radium is unprotected or insufficiently protected and comes too near, it is destructive of healthy cells, produces burns, sores, which are most difficult to heal. It is with the explanation of such sores that we must deal."

It was growing late. We had waited patiently now for some time. Kennedy had evidently reserved this explanation, knowing we should have to wait. Still nothing happened.

Added to the mystery of the violet-colored glass plate was now that of the luminescent diamond. I was about to ask Kennedy point-blank what he thought of them, when suddenly the little bell before us began to buzz feebly under the influence of a current.

I gave a start. The faithful little selenium cell burglar alarm had done the trick. I knew that selenium was a good conductor of electricity in the light, poor in the dark. Some one had, therefore, flashed a light on one of the cells in the Corporation office. It was the moment for which Kennedy had prepared.

Seizing the round package and the tubing, he dashed out on the street and around the corner. He tried the door opening into the Radium Corporation hallway. It was closed, but unlocked. As it yielded and we stumbled in, up the old worn wooden stairs of the building, I knew that there must be some one there.

A terrific, penetrating, almost stunning odor seemed to permeate the air even in the hall.

Kennedy paused at the door of the office, tried it, found it unlocked, but did not open it.

"That smell is ethyldichloracetate," he explained. "That was what I injected into the air cushion of that safe between the two linings. I suppose my man here used an electric drill. He might have used thermit or an oxyacetylene blowpipe for all I would care. These fumes would discourage a cracksman from 'soup'—to nuts," he laughed, thoroughly pleased at the protection modern science had enabled him to devise.

As we stood an instant by the door, I realized what had happened. We had captured our man. He was asphyxiated!

Yet how were we to get to him? Would Craig leave him in there, perhaps to die? To go in ourselves meant to share his fate, whatever might be the effect of the drug.

Kennedy had torn the wrapping off the package. From it he drew a huge globe with bulging windows of glass in the front and several curious arrangements on it at other points. To it he fitted the rubber tubing and a little pump. Then he placed the globe over his head, like a diver's helmet, and fastened some air-tight rubber arrangement about his neck and shoulders.

"Pump, Walter!" he shouted. "This is an oxygen helmet such as is used in entering mines filled with deadly gases."

Without another word he was gone into the black-

ness of the noxious stifle which filled the Radium
Corporation office since the cracksman had struck
the unexpected pocket of rapidly evaporating stuff.

I pumped furiously.

Inside I could hear him blundering around. What
was he doing?

He was coming back slowly. Was he, too, overcome?

As he emerged into the darkness of the hallway
where I myself was almost sickened, I saw that he
was dragging with him a limp form.

A rush of outside air from the street door seemed
to clear things a little. Kennedy tore off the oxygen
helmet and dropped down on his knees beside the
figure, working its arms in the most approved manner of resuscitation.

"I think we can do it without calling on the pul-
motor," he panted. "Walter, the fumes have cleared
away enough now in the outside office. Open a window—and keep that street door open, too."

I did so, found the switch and turned on the
lights.

It was Denison himself!

For many minutes Kennedy worked over him. I
bent down, loosened his collar and shirt, and looked
eagerly at his chest for the tell-tale marks of the
radium which I felt sure must be there. There was
not even a discoloration.

Not a word was said, as Kennedy brought the
stupefied little man around.

Denison, pale, shaken, was leaning back now in
a big office chair, gasping and holding his head.

Kennedy, before him, reached down into his
pocket and handed him the spinthariscope.

"You see that?" he demanded.

Denison looked through the eyepiece.

"Wh—where did you get so much of it?" he asked, a queer look on his face.

"I got that bit of radium from the base of the collar button of Hartley Haughton," replied Kennedy quietly, "a collar button which some one intimate with him had substituted for his own, bringing that deadly radium with only the minutest protection of a thin strip of metal close to the back of his neck, near the spinal cord and the medulla oblongata which controls blood pressure. That collar button was worse than the poisoned rings of the Borgias. And there is more radium in the pretty gift of a tortoiseshell comb with its paste diamonds which Miss Wallace wore in her hair. Only a fraction of an inch, not enough to cut off the deadly alpha rays, protected the wearers of those articles."

He paused a moment, while surging through my mind came one after another the explanations of the hitherto inexplicable. Denison seemed almost to cringe in the chair, weak already from the fumes.

"Besides," went on Kennedy remorselessly, "when I went in there to drag you out, I saw the safe open. I looked. There was nothing in those pretty platinum tubes, as I suspected. European trust—bah! All the cheap devices of a faker with a confederate in London to send a cablegram—and another in New York to send a threatening letter."

Kennedy extended an accusing forefinger at the man cowering before him.

"This is nothing but a get-rich-quick scheme, Denison. There never was a milligram of radium in the Poor Little Rich Valley, not a milligram here in all the carefully kept reports of Miss Wallace— except what was bought outside by the Corporation with the money it collected from its dupes. Haughton has been fleeced. Miss Wallace, blinded by her loyalty to you—you will always find such a faithful girl in such schemes as yours—has been fooled.

"And how did you repay it? What was cleverer, you said to yourself, than to seem to be robbed of what you never had, to blame it on a bitter rival who never existed? Then to make assurance doubly sure, you planned to disable, perhaps get rid of the come-on whom you had trimmed, and the faithful girl whose eyes you had blinded to your gigantic swindle.

"Denison," concluded Kennedy, as the man drew back, his very face convicting him, "Denison, you are the radium robber—robber in another sense!"

CHAPTER XVI

THE DEAD LINE

MAIDEN LANE, no less than Wall Street, was deeply interested in the radium case. In fact, it seemed that one case in this section of the city led to another.

Naturally, the *Star* and the other papers made much of the capture of Denison. Still, I was not prepared for the host of Maiden Lane cases that followed. Many of them were essentially trivial. But one proved to be of extreme importance.

"Professor Kennedy, I have just heard of your radium case, and I—I feel that I can—trust you."

There was a note of appeal in the hesitating voice of the tall, heavily veiled woman whose card had been sent up to us with a nervous "Urgent" written across its face.

It was very early in the morning, but our visitor was evidently completely unnerved by some news which she had just received and which had sent her posting to see Craig.

Kennedy met her gaze directly with a look that arrested her involuntary effort to avoid it again. She must have read in his eyes more than in his words that she might trust him.

"I—I have a confession to make," she faltered.

"Please sit down, Mrs. Moulton," he said simply.

"It is my business to receive confidences—and to keep them."

She sank into, rather than sat down in, the deep leather rocker beside his desk, and now for the first time raised her veil.

Antoinette Moulton was indeed stunning, an exquisite creature with a wonderful charm of slender youth, brightness of eye and brunette radiance.

I knew that she had been on the musical comedy stage and had had a rapid rise to a star part before her marriage to Lynn Moulton, the wealthy lawyer, almost twice her age. I knew also that she had given up the stage, apparently without a regret. Yet there was something strange about the air of secrecy of her visit. Was there a hint in it of a disagreement between the Moultons, I wondered, as I waited while Kennedy reassured her.

Her distress was so unconcealed that Craig, for the moment, laid aside his ordinary inquisitorial manner. "Tell me just as much or just as little as you choose, Mrs. Moulton," he added tactfully. "I will do my best."

A look almost of gratitude crossed her face.

"When we were married," she began again, "my husband gave me a beautiful diamond necklace. Oh, it must have been worth a hundred thousand dollars easily. It was splendid. Everyone has heard of it. You know, Lynn—er—Mr. Moulton, has always been an enthusiastic collector of jewels."

She paused again and Kennedy nodded reassuringly. I knew the thought in his mind. Moulton had collected one gem that was incomparable with all the hundred thousand dollar necklaces in existence.

"Several months ago," she went on rapidly, still

avoiding his eyes and forcing the words from her reluctant lips, "I—oh, I needed money—terribly."

She had risen and faced him, pressing her daintily gloved hands together in a little tremble of emotion which was none the less genuine because she had studied the art of emotion.

"I took the necklace to a jeweler, Herman Schloss, of Maiden Lane, a man with whom my husband had often had dealings and whom I thought I could trust. Under a promise of secrecy he loaned me fifty thousand dollars on it and had an exact replica in paste made by one of his best workmen. This morning, just now, Mr. Schloss telephoned me that his safe had been robbed last night. My necklace is gone!"

She threw out her hands in a wildly appealing gesture.

"And if Lynn finds that the necklace in our wall safe is of paste—as he will find, for he is an expert in diamonds—oh—what shall I do? Can't you—can't you find my necklace?"

Kennedy was following her now eagerly. "You were blackmailed out of the money?" he queried casually, masking his question.

There was a sudden, impulsive drooping of her mouth, an evasion and keen wariness in her eyes. "I can't see that that has anything to do with the robbery," she answered in a low voice.

"I beg your pardon," corrected Kennedy quickly. "Perhaps not. I'm sorry. Force of habit, I suppose. You don't know anything more about the robbery?"

"N—no, only that it seems impossible that it could have happened in a place that has the wonderful burglar alarm protection that Mr. Schloss described to me."

"You know him pretty well?"

"Only through this transaction," she replied hastily. "I wish to heaven I had never heard of him."

The telephone rang insistently.

"Mrs. Moulton," said Kennedy, as he returned the receiver to the hook, "it may interest you to know that the burglar alarm company has just called me up about the same case. If I had need of an added incentive, which I hope you will believe I have not, that might furnish it. I will do my best," he repeated.

"Thank you—a thousand times," she cried fervently, and, had I been Craig, I think I should have needed no more thanks than the look she gave him as he accompanied her to the door of our apartment.

It was still early and the eager crowds were pushing their way to business through the narrow network of downtown streets as Kennedy and I entered a large office on lower Broadway in the heart of the jewelry trade and financial district.

"One of the most amazing robberies that has ever been attempted has been reported to us this morning," announced James McLear, manager of the Hale Electric Protection, adding with a look half of anxiety, half of skepticism, "that is, if it is true."

McLear was a stocky man, of powerful build and voice and a general appearance of having been once well connected with the city detective force before an attractive offer had taken him into this position of great responsibility.

"Herman Schloss, one of the best known of Maiden Lane jewelers," he continued, "has been robbed of goods worth two or three hundred thousand dollars—and in spite of every modern protection. So that you will get it clearly, let me show you what we do here."

He ushered us into a large room, on the walls of which were hundreds of little indicators. From the front they looked like rows of little square compartments, tier on tier, about the size of ordinary post-office boxes. Closer examination showed that each was equipped with a delicate needle arranged to oscillate backward and forward upon the very minutest interference with the electric current. Under the boxes, each of which bore a number, was a series of drops and buzzers numbered to correspond with the boxes.

"In nearly every office in Maiden Lane where gems and valuable jewelry are stored," explained McLear, "this electrical system of ours is installed. When the safes are closed at night and the doors swung together, a current of electricity is constantly shooting around the safes, conducted by cleverly concealed wires. These wires are picked up by a cable system which finds its way to this central office. Once here, the wires are safeguarded in such manner that foreign currents from other wires or from lightning cannot disturb the system."

We looked with intense interest at this huge electrical pulse that felt every change over so vast and rich an area.

"Passing a big dividing board," he went on, "they are distributed and connected each in its place to the delicate tangent galvanometers and sensitive indicators you see in this room. These instantly announce the most minute change in the working of the current, and each office has a distinct separate metallic circuit. Why, even a hole as small as a lead pencil in anything protected would sound the alarm here."

Kennedy nodded appreciatively.

"You see," continued McLear, glad to be able to talk to one who followed him so closely, "it is another evidence of science finding for us greater security in the use of a tiny electric wire than in massive walls of steel and intricate lock devices. But here is a case in which, it seems, every known protection has failed. We can't afford to pass that by. If we have fallen down we want to know how, as well as to catch the burglar."

"How are the signals given?" I asked.

"Well, when the day's business is over, for instance, Schloss would swing the heavy safe doors together and over them place the doors of a wooden cabinet. That signals an alarm to us here. We answer it and if the proper signal is returned, all right. After that no one can tamper with the safe later in the night without sounding an alarm that would bring a quick investigation."

"But suppose that it became necessary to open the safe before the next morning. Might not some trusted employee return to the office, open it, give the proper signals and loot the safe?"

"No indeed," he answered confidently. "The very moment anyone touches the cabinet, the alarm is sounded. Even if the proper code signal is returned, it is not sufficient. A couple of our trusted men from the central office hustle around there anyhow and they don't leave until they are satisfied that everything is right. We have the authorized signatures on hand of those who are supposed to open the safe and a duplicate of one of them must be given or there is an arrest."

McLear considered for a moment.

"For instance, Schloss, like all the rest, was assigned a box in which was deposited a sealed envelope containing a key to the office and his own signature, in this case, since he alone knew the combination. Now, when an alarm is sounded, as it was last night, and the key removed to gain entrance to the office, a record is made and the key has to be sealed up again by Schloss. A report is also submitted showing when the signals are received and anything else that is worth recording. Last night our men found nothing wrong, apparently. But this morning we learn of the robbery."

"The point is, then," ruminated Kennedy, "what happened in the interval between the ringing of the alarm and the arrival of the special officers? I think I'll drop around and look Schloss' place over," he added quietly, evidently eager to begin at the actual scene of the crime.

On the door of the office to which McLear took us was one of those small blue plates which chance visitors to Maiden Lane must have seen often. To the initiated—be he crook or jeweler—this simple sign means that the merchant is a member of the Jewelers' Security Alliance, enough in itself, it would seem, to make the boldest burglar hesitate. For it is the motto of this organization to "get" the thief at any cost and at any time. Still, it had not deterred the burglar in this instance.

"I know people are going to think it is a fake burglary," exclaimed Schloss, a stout, prosperous-looking gem broker, as we introduced ourselves. "But over two hundred thousands dollars' worth of stones are gone," he half groaned. "Think of it, man," he added, "one of the greatest robberies since the Dead Line was established. And if they can get away with it, why, no one down here is protected any more. Half a billion dollars in jewels in Maiden Lane and John Street are easy prey for the cracksmen!"

Staggering though the loss must have been to him, he had apparently recovered from the first shock of the discovery and had begun the fight to get back what had been lost.

It was, as McLear had intimated, a most amazing burglary, too. The door of Schloss' safe was open when Kennedy and I arrived and found the excited jeweler nervously pacing the office. Surrounding the safe, I noticed a wooden framework constructed in such a way as to be a part of the decorative scheme of the office.

Schloss banged the heavy doors shut.

"There, that's just how it was—shut as tight as a drum. There was absolutely no mark of anyone tampering with the combination lock. And yet the safe was looted!"

"How did you discover it?" asked Craig. "I presume you carry burglary insurance?"

Schloss looked up quickly. "That's what I expected as a first question. No, I carried very little insurance. You see, I thought the safe, one of those new chrome steel affairs, was about impregnable. I never lost a moment's sleep over it; didn't think it possible for anyone to get into it. For, as you see, it is completely wired by the Hale Electric Protection—that wooden framework about it. No one could touch that when it was set without jangling a bell at the central office which would send men scurrying here to protect the place."

"But they must have got past it," suggested Kennedy.

"Yes—they must have. At least this morning I received the regular Hale report. It said that their wires registered last night as though some one was tampering with the safe. But by the time they got around, in less than five minutes, there was no one here, nothing seemed to be disturbed. So they set it down to induction or electrolysis, or something the matter with the wires. I got the report the first thing when I arrived here with my assistant, Muller."

Kennedy was on his knees, going over the safe with a fine brush and some powder, looking now and then through a small magnifying glass.

"Not a finger print," he muttered. "The cracksman must have worn gloves. But how did he get in? There isn't a mark of 'soup' having been used to blow it up, nor of a 'can-opener' to rip it open, if that were possible, nor of an electric or any other kind of drill."

"I've read of those fellows who burn their way in," said Schloss.

"But there is no hole," objected Kennedy, "not a trace of the use of thermit to burn the way in or of the oxyacetylene blowpipe to cut a piece out. Most extraordinary," he murmured.

"You see," shrugged Schloss, "everyone will say it must have been opened by one who knew the combination. But I am the only one. I have never written it down or told anyone, not even Muller. You understand what I am up against?"

"There's the touch system," I suggested. "You

remember, Craig, the old fellow who used to file his finger tips to the quick until they were so sensitive that he could actually feel when he had turned the combination to the right plunger? Might not that explain the lack of finger prints also?" I added eagerly.

"Nothing like that in this case, Walter," objected Craig positively. "This fellow wore gloves, all right. No, this safe has been opened and looted by no ordinarily known method. It's the most amazing case I ever saw in that respect—almost as if we had a cracksman in the fourth dimension to whom the inside of a closed cube is as accessible as is the inside of a plane square to us three dimensional creatures. It is almost incomprehensible."

I fancied I saw Schloss' face brighten as Kennedy took this view. So far, evidently, he had run across only skepticism.

"The stones were unset?" resumed Craig.

"Mostly. Not all."

"You would recognize some of them if you saw them?"

"Yes indeed. Some could be changed only by recutting. Even some of those that were set were of odd cut and size—some from a diamond necklace which belonged to a——"

There was something peculiar in both his tone and manner as he cut short the words.

"To whom?" asked Kennedy casually.

"Oh, once to a well-known woman in society," he said carefully. "It is mine, though, now—at least it was mine. I should prefer to mention no names. I will give a description of the stones."

"Mrs. Lynn Moulton, for instance?" suggested Craig quietly.

Schloss jumped almost as if a burglar alarm had sounded under his very ears. "How did you know? Yes—but it was a secret. I made a large loan on it, and the time has expired."

"Why did she need money so badly?" asked Kennedy.

"How should I know?" demanded Schloss.

Here was a deepening mystery, not to be elucidated by continuing this line of inquiry with Schloss, it seemed.

CHAPTER XVII

THE PASTE REPLICA

CAREFULLY Craig was going over the office. Outside of the safe, there had apparently been nothing of value. The rest of the office was not even wired, and it seemed to have been Schloss' idea that the few thousands of burglary insurance amply protected him against such loss. As for the safe, its own strength and the careful wiring might well have been considered quite sufficient under any hitherto to-be-foreseen circumstances.

A glass door, around the bend of a partition, opened from the hallway into the office and had apparently been designed with the object of making visible the safe so that anyone passing might see whether an intruder was tampering with it.

Kennedy had examined the door, perhaps in the expectation of finding finger prints there, and was passing on to other things, when a change in his position caused his eye to catch a large oval smudge on the glass, which was visible when the light struck it at the right angle. Quickly he dusted it over with the powder, and brought out the detail more clearly. As I examined it, while Craig made preparations to cut out the glass to preserve it, it seemed to contain a number of minute points and several more or less broken parallel lines. The edges gradually trailed off into an indistinct faintness.

172

Business, naturally, was at a standstill, and as we were working near the door, we could see that the news of Schloss' strange robbery had leaked out and was spreading rapidly. Scores of acquaintances in the trade stopped at the door to inquire about the rumor.

To each, it seemed that Morris Muller, the working jeweler employed by Schloss, repeated the same story.

"Oh," he said, "it is a big loss—yes—but big as it is, it will not break Mr. Schloss. And," he would add with the tradesman's idea of humor, "I guess he has enough to play a game of poker—eh?"

"Poker?" asked Kennedy smiling. "Is he much of a player?"

"Yes. Nearly every night with his friends he plays."

Kennedy made a mental note of it. Evidently Schloss trusted Muller implicitly. He seemed like a partner, rather than an employee, even though he had not been entrusted with the secret combination.

Outside, we ran into city detective Lieutenant Winters, the officer who was stationed at the Maiden Lane post, guarding that famous section of the Dead Line established by the immortal Byrnes at Fulton Street, below which no crook was supposed to dare even to be seen. Winters had been detailed on the case.

"You have seen the safe in there?" asked Kennedy, as he was leaving to carry on his investigation elsewhere.

Winters seemed to be quite as skeptical as Schloss had intimated the public would be. "Yes," he replied, "there's been an epidemic of robbery with the

dull times—people who want to collect their burglary insurance, I guess."

"But," objected Kennedy, "Schloss carried so
little."

"Well, there was the Hale Protection. How
about that?"

Craig looked up quickly, unruffled by the patroniz-
ing air of the professional toward the amateur detective.

"What is your theory?" he asked. "Do you
think he robbed himself?"

Winters shrugged his shoulders. "I've been interested in Schloss for some time," he said enigmat-
ically. "He has had some pretty swell customers.
I'll keep you wised up, if anything happens," he
added in a burst of graciousness, walking off.

On the way to the subway, we paused again to see
McLear.

"Well," he asked, "what do you think of it,
now?"

"All most extraordinary," ruminated Craig.
"And the queerest feature of all is that the chief
loss consists of a diamond necklace that belonged
once to Mrs. Antoinette Moulton."

"Mrs. Lynn Moulton?" repeated McLear.

"The same," assured Kennedy.

McLear appeared somewhat puzzled. "Her husband is one of our old subscribers," he pursued.
"He is a lawyer on Wall Street and quite a gem
collector. Last night his safe was tampered with,
but this morning he reports no loss. Not half an
hour ago he had us on the wire congratulating us
on scaring off the burglars, if there had been any."

"What is your opinion," I asked. "Is there a
gang operating?"

"My belief is," he answered, reminiscently of his days on the detective force, "that none of the loot will be recovered until they start to 'fence' it. That would be my lay—to look for the fence. Why, think of all the big robberies that have been pulled off lately. Remember," he went on, "the spoils of a burglary consist generally of precious stones. They are not currency. They must be turned into currency—or what's the use of robbery?

"But merely to offer them for sale at an ordinary jeweler's would be suspicious. Even pawnbrokers are on the watch. You see what I am driving at? I think there is a man or a group of men whose business it is to pay cash for stolen property and who have ways of returning gems into the regular trade channels. In all these robberies we get a glimpse of as dark and mysterious a criminal as has ever been recorded. He may be—anybody. About his legitimacy, I believe, no question has ever been raised. And, I tell you, his arrest is going to create a greater sensation than even the remarkable series of robberies that he has planned or made possible. The question is, to my mind, who is this fence?"

McLear's telephone rang and he handed the instrument to Craig.

"Yes, this is Professor Kennedy," answered Craig. "Oh, too bad you've had to try all over to get me. I've been going from one place to another gathering clues and have made good progress, considering I've hardly started. Why—what's the matter? Really?"

An interval followed, during which McLear left to answer a personal call on another wire.

As Kennedy hung up the receiver, his face wore a peculiar look. "It was Mrs. Moulton," he blurted

out. "She thinks that her husband has found out
that the necklace is paste."

"How?" I asked.

"The paste replica is gone from her wall safe in
the Deluxe."

I turned, startled at the information. Even Kennedy himself was perplexed at the sudden succession
of events. I had nothing to say.

Evidently, however, his rule was when in doubt
play a trump, for, twenty minutes later found us in
the office of Lynn Moulton, the famous corporation
lawyer, in Wall Street.

Moulton was a handsome man of past fifty with
a youthful face against his iron gray hair and mustache, well dressed, genial, a man who seemed keenly
in love with the good things of life.

"It is rumored," began Kennedy, "that an attempt was made on your safe here at the office last
night."

"Yes," he admitted, taking off his glasses and
polishing them carefully. "I suppose there is no
need of concealment, especially as I hear that a
somewhat similar attempt was made on the safe of
my friend Herman Schloss in Maiden Lane."

"You lost nothing?"

Moulton put his glasses on and looked Kennedy
in the face frankly.

"Nothing, fortunately," he said, then went on
slowly. "You see, in my later years, I have been
something of a collector of precious stones myself.
I don't wear them, but I have always taken the
keenest pleasure in owning them and when I was
married it gave me a great deal more pleasure to
have them set in rings, pendants, tiaras, necklaces,
and other forms for my wife."

He had risen, with the air of a busy man who had given the subject all the consideration he could afford and whose work proceeded almost by schedule. "This morning I found my safe tampered with, but, as I said, fortunately something must have scared off the burglars."

He bowed us out politely. What was the explanation, I wondered. It seemed, on the face of things, that Antoinette Moulton feared her husband. Did he know something else already, and did she know he knew? To all appearances he took it very calmly, if he did know. Perhaps that was what she feared, his very calmness.

"I must see Mrs. Moulton again," remarked Kennedy, as we left.

The Moultons lived, we found, in one of the largest suites of a new apartment hotel, the Deluxe, and in spite of the fact that our arrival had been announced some minutes before we saw Mrs. Moulton, it was evident that she had been crying hysterically over the loss of the paste jewels and what it implied.

"I missed it this morning, after my return from seeing you," she replied in answer to Craig's inquiry, then added, wide-eyed with alarm, "What shall I do? He must have opened the wall safe and found the replica. I don't dare ask him point-blank."

"Are you sure he did it?" asked Kennedy, more, I felt, for its moral effect on her than through any doubt in his own mind.

"Not sure. But then the wall safe shows no marks, and the replica is gone."

"Might I see your jewel case?" he asked.

"Surely. I'll get it. The wall safe is in Lynn's

room. I shall probably have to fuss a long time with the combination."

In fact she could not have been very familiar with it for it took several minutes before she returned. Meanwhile, Kennedy, who had been drumming absently on the arms of his chair, suddenly rose and walked quietly over to a scrap basket that stood beside an escritoire. It had evidently just been emptied, for the rooms must have been cleaned several hours before. He bent down over it and picked up two scraps of paper adhering to the wicker work. The rest had evidently been thrown away.

I bent over to read them. One was:

—rest Nettie—
—dying to see—

The other read:

—cherche to-d
—love and ma
—rman.

What did it mean? Hastily, I could fill in "Dearest Nettie," and "I am dying to see you." Kennedy added, "The Recherche to-day," that being the name of a new apartment uptown, as well as "love and many kisses." But "—rman"—what did that mean? Could it be Herman—Herman Schloss?

She was returning and we resumed our seats quickly.

Kennedy took the jewel case from her and examined it carefully. There was not a mark on it.

"Mrs. Moulton," he said slowly, rising and handing it back to her, "have you told me all?"

"Why—yes," she answered.

Kennedy shook his head gravely.

"I'm afraid not. You must tell me everything."

"No—no," she cried vehemently, "there is nothing more."

We left and outside the Deluxe he paused, looked about, caught sight of a taxicab and hailed it.

"Where?" asked the driver.

"Across the street," he said, " and wait. Put the window in back of you down so I can talk. I'll tell you where to go presently. Now, Walter, sit back as far as you can. This may seem like an underhand thing to do, but we've got to get what that woman won't tell us or give up the case."

Perhaps half an hour we waited, still puzzling over the scraps of paper. Suddenly I felt a nudge from Kennedy. Antoinette Moulton was standing in the doorway across the street. Evidently she preferred not to ride in her own car, for a moment later she entered a taxicab.

"Follow that black cab," said Kennedy to our driver.

Sure enough, it stopped in front of the Recherche Apartments and Mrs. Moulton stepped out and almost ran in.

We waited a moment, then Kennedy followed. The elevator that had taken her up had just returned to the ground floor.

"The same floor again," remarked Kennedy, jauntily stepping in and nodding familiarly to the elevator boy.

Then he paused suddenly, looked at his watch, fixed his gaze thoughtfully on me an instant, and exclaimed. "By George—no. I can't go up yet.

I clean forgot that engagement at the hotel. One moment, son. Let us out. We'll be back again."

Considerably mystified, I followed him to the sidewalk.

"You're entitled to an explanation," he laughed catching my bewildered look as he opened the cab door. "I didn't want to go up now while she is there, but I wanted to get on good terms with that boy. We'll wait until she comes down, then go up."

"Where?" I asked.

"That's what I am going through all this elaborate preparation to find out. I have no more idea than you have."

It could not have been more than twenty minutes later when Mrs. Moulton emerged rather hurriedly, and drove away.

While we had been waiting I had observed a man on the other side of the street who seemed unduly interested in the Recherche, too, for he had walked up and down the block no less than six times. Kennedy saw him, and as he made no effort to follow Mrs M.oulton, Kennedy did not do so either. In fact a little quick glance which she had given at our cab had raised a fear that she might have discovered that she was being followed.

Kennedy and I paid off our cabman and sauntered into the Recherche in the most debonair manner we could assume.

"Now, son, we'll go up," he said to the boy who, remembering us, and now not at all clear in his mind that he might not have seen us before that, whisked us to the tenth floor.

"Let me see," said Kennedy, "it's number one hundred and—er——"

"Three," prompted the boy.

He pressed the buzzer and a neatly dressed colored maid responded.

"I had an appointment here with Mrs. Moulton this morning," remarked Kennedy.

"She has just gone," replied the maid, off her guard.

"And was to meet Mr. Schloss here in half an hour," he added quickly.

It was the maid's turn to look surprised.

"I didn't think he was to be here," she said. "He's had some——"

"Trouble at the office," supplied Kennedy. "That's what it was about. Perhaps he hasn't been able to get away yet. But I had the appointment. Ah, I see a telephone in the hall. May I?"

He had stepped politely in, and by dint of cleverly keeping his finger on the hook in the half light, he carried on a one-sided conversation with himself long enough to get a good chance to look about.

There was an air of quiet and refinement about the apartment in the Recherche. It was darkened to give the little glowing electric bulbs in their silken shades a full chance to simulate night. The deep velvety carpets were noiseless to the foot, and the draperies, the pictures, the bronzes, all bespoke taste.

But the chief objects of interest to Craig were the little square green baize-covered tables on one of which lay neatly stacked a pile of gilt-edged cards and a mahogany box full of ivory chips of red, white and blue.

It was none of the old-time gambling places, like Danfield's, with its steel door which Craig had once cut through with an oxyacetylene blowpipe in order to rescue a young spendthrift from himself.

Kennedy seemed perfectly well satisfied merely with a cursory view of the place, as he hung up the receiver and thanked the maid politely for allowing him to use it.

"This is up-to-date gambling in cleaned-up New York," he remarked as we waited for the elevator to return for us. "And the worst of it all is that it gets the women as well as the men. Once they are caught in the net, they are the most powerful lure to men that the gamblers have yet devised."

We rode down in silence, and as we went down the steps to the street, I noticed the man whom we had seen watching the place, lurking down at the lower corner. Kennedy quickened his pace and came up behind him.

"Why, Winters!" exclaimed Craig. "You here?"

"I might say the same to you," grinned the detective not displeased evidently that our trail had crossed his. "I suppose you are looking for Schloss, too. He's up in the Recherche a great deal, playing poker. I understand he owns an interest in the game up there."

Kennedy nodded, but said nothing.

"I just saw one of the cappers for the place go out before you went in."

"Capper?" repeated Kennedy surprised. "Antoinette Moulton a steerer for a gambling joint? What can a rich society woman have to do with a place like that or a man like Schloss?"

Winters smiled sardonically. "Society ladies today often get into scrapes of which their husbands know nothing," he remarked. "You didn't know before that Antoinette Moulton, like many of her

friends in the smart set, was a gambler—and loser
—did you?"

Craig shook his head. He had more of human
than scientific interest in a case of a woman of her
caliber gone wrong.

"But you must have read of the famous Moulton
diamonds?"

"Yes," said Craig, blankly, as if it were all news
to him.

"Schloss has them—or at least had them. The
jewels she wore at the opera this winter were paste,
I understand."

"Does Moulton play?" he asked.

"I think so—but not here, naturally. In a way,
I suppose, it is his fault. They all do it. The
example of one drives on another."

Instantly there flashed over my mind a host of
possibilities. Perhaps, after all, Winters had been
right. Schloss had taken this way to make sure of
the jewels so that she could not redeem them. Suddenly another explanation crowded that out. Had
Mrs. Moulton robbed the safe herself, or hired
some one else to do it for her, and had that person
gone back on her?

Then a horrid possibility occurred to me. Whatever Antoinette Moulton may have been and done,
some one must have her in his power. What a
situation for the woman! My sympathy went out
to her in her supreme struggle. Even if it had been
a real robbery, Schloss might easily recover from it.
But for her every event spelled ruin and seemed
only to be bringing that ruin closer.

We left Winters, still watching on the trail of
Schloss, and went on uptown to the laboratory.

CHAPTER XVIII

THE BURGLAR'S MICROPHONE

THAT night I was sitting, brooding over the case, while Craig was studying a photograph which he made of the smudge on the glass door down at Schloss'. He paused in his scrutiny of the print to answer the telephone.

"Something has happened to Schloss," he exclaimed seizing his hat and coat. "Winters has been watching him. He didn't go to the Recherche. Winters wants me to meet him at a place several blocks below it. Come on. He wouldn't say over the wire what it was. Hurry."

We met Winters in less than ten minutes at the address he had given, a bachelor apartment in the neighborhood of the Recherche.

"Schloss kept rooms here," explained Winters, hurrying us quickly upstairs. "I wanted you to see before anyone else."

As we entered the large and luxuriously furnished living room of the jeweler's suite, a gruesome sight greeted us.

There lay Schloss on the floor, face down, in a horribly contorted position. In one hand, clenched under him partly, the torn sleeve of a woman's dress was grasped convulsively. The room bore unmistakable traces of a violent struggle, but except for the hideous object on the floor was vacant.

Kennedy bent down over him. Schloss was dead.

In a corner, by the door, stood a pile of grips, stacked up, packed, and undisturbed.

Winters who had been studying the room while we got our bearings picked up a queer-looking revolver from the floor. As he held it up I could see that along the top of the barrel was a long cylinder with a ratchet or catch at the butt end. He turned it over and over carefully.

"By George," he muttered, "it has been fired off."

Kennedy glanced more minutely at the body. There was not a mark on it. I stared about vacantly at the place where Winters had picked the thing up.

"Look," I cried, my eye catching a little hole in the baseboard of the woodwork near it.

"It must have fallen and exploded on the floor," remarked Kennedy. "Let me see it, Winters."

Craig held it at arm's length and pulled the catch. Instead of an explosion, there came a cone of light from the top of the gun. As Kennedy moved it over the wall, I saw in the center of the circle of light a dark spot.

"A new invention," Craig explained. "All you need to do is to move it so that little dark spot falls directly on an object. Pull the trigger—the bullet strikes the dark spot. Even a nervous and unskilled marksman becomes a good shot in the dark. He can even shoot from behind the protection of something—and hit accurately."

It was too much for me. I could only stand and watch Kennedy as he deftly bent over Schloss again and placed a piece of chemically prepared paper flat on the forehead of the dead man.

13

When he withdrew it, I could see that it bore marks of the lines on his head. Without a word, Kennedy drew from his pocket a print of the photograph of the smudge on Schloss' door.

"It is possible," he said, half to himself, "to identify a person by means of the arrangement of the sweat glands or pores. Poroscopy, Dr. Edmond Locard, director of the Police Laboratory at Lyons, calls it. The shape, arrangement, number per square centimeter, all vary in different individuals. Besides, here we have added the lines of the forehead."

He was studying the two impressions intensely. When he looked up from his examination, his face wore a peculiar expression.

"This is not the head which was placed so close to the glass of the door of Schloss' office, peering through, on the night of the robbery, in order to see before picking the lock whether the office was empty and everything ready for the hasty attack on the safe."

"That disposes of my theory that Schloss robbed himself," remarked Winters reluctantly. "But the struggle here, the sleeve of the dress, the pistol— could he have been shot?"

"No, I think not," considered Kennedy. "It looks to me more like a case of apoplexy."

"What shall we do?" asked Winters. "Far from clearing anything up, this complicates it."

"Where's Muller?" asked Kennedy. "Does he know? Perhaps he can shed some light on it."

The clang of an ambulance bell outside told that the aid summoned by Winters had arrived.

We left the body in charge of the surgeon and

of a policeman who arrived about the same time, and followed Winters.

Muller lived in a cheap boarding house in a shabbily respectable street downtown, and without announcing ourselves we climbed the stairs to his room. He looked up surprised but not disconcerted as we entered.

"What's the matter?" he asked.

"Muller," shot out Winters, "we have just found Mr. Schloss dead!"

"D-dead!" he stammered.

The man seemed speechless with horror.

"Yes, and with his grips packed as if to run away."

Muller looked dazedly from one of us to the other, but shut up like a clam.

"I think you had better come along with us as a material witness," burst out Winters roughly.

Kennedy said nothing, leaving that sort of third degree work to the detective. But he was not idle, as Winters tried to extract more than the monosyllables, "I don't know," in answer to every inquiry of Muller about his employer's life and business.

A low exclamation from Craig attracted my attention from Winters. In a corner he had discovered a small box and had opened it. Inside was a dry battery and a most peculiar instrument, something like a little flat telephone transmitter yet attached by wires to earpieces that fitted over the head after the manner of those of a wireless detector.

"What's this?" asked Kennedy, dangling it before Muller.

He looked at it phlegmatically. "A deaf instrument I have been working on," replied the jeweler. "My hearing is getting poor."

Kennedy looked hastily from the instrument to the man.

"I think I'll take it along with us," he said quietly.

Winters, true to his instincts, had been searching Muller in the meantime. Besides the various assortment that a man carries in his pockets usually, including pens, pencils, notebooks, a watch, a handkerchief, a bunch of keys, one of which was large enough to open a castle, there was a bunch of blank and unissued pawntickets bearing the name, "Stein's One Per Cent. a Month Loans," and an address on the Bowery.

Was Muller the "fence" we were seeking, or only a tool for the "fence" higher up? Who was this Stein?

What it all meant I could only guess. It was a far cry from the wealth of Diamond Lane to a dingy Bowery pawnshop, even though pawnbroking at one per cent. a month—and more, on the side—pays. I knew, too, that diamonds are hoarded on the East Side as nowhere else in the world, outside of India. It was no uncommon thing, I had heard, for a pawnbroker whose shop seemed dirty and greasy to the casual visitor to have stored away in his vault gems running into the hundreds of thousands of dollars.

"Mrs. Moulton must know of this," remarked Kennedy. "Winters, you and Jameson bring Muller along. I am going up to the Deluxe."

I must say that I was surprised at finding Mrs. Moulton there. Outside the suite Winters and I waited with the unresisting Muller, while Kennedy entered. But through the door which he left ajar I could hear what passed.

"Mrs. Moulton," he began, "something terrible has happened——"

He broke off, and I gathered that her pale face and agitated manner told him that she knew already.

"Where is Mr. Moulton?" he went on, changing his question.

"Mr. Moulton is at his office," she answered tremulously. "He telephoned while I was out that he had to work to-night. Oh, Mr. Kennedy—he knows—he knows. I know it. He has avoided me ever since I missed the replica from——"

"Sh!" cautioned Craig. He had risen and gone to the door.

"Winters," he whispered, "I want you to go down to Lynn Moulton's office. Meanwhile Jameson can take care of Muller. I am going over to that place of Stein's presently. Bring Moulton up there. You will wait here, Walter, for the present," he nodded.

He returned to the room where I could hear her crying softly.

"Now, Mrs. Moulton," he said gently, "I'm afraid I must trouble you to go with me. I am going over to a pawnbroker's on the Bowery."

"The Bowery?" she repeated, with a genuinely surprised shudder. "Oh, no, Mr. Kennedy. Don't ask me to go anywhere to-night. I am—I am in no condition to go anywhere—to do anything—I——"

"But you must," said Kennedy in a low voice.

"I can't. Oh—have mercy on me. I am terribly upset. You——"

"It is your duty to go, Mrs. Moulton," he repeated.

"I don't understand," she murmured. "A pawnbroker's?"

"Come," urged Kennedy, not harshly but firmly, then, as she held back, added, playing a trump card, "We must work quickly. In his hands we found the fragments of a torn dress. When the police——"

She uttered a shriek. A glance had told her, if she had deceived herself before, that Kennedy knew her secret.

Antoinette Moulton was standing before him, talking rapidly.

"Some one has told Lynn. I know it. There is nothing now that I can conceal. If you had come half an hour later you would not have found me. He had written to Mr. Schloss, threatening him that if he did not leave the country he would shoot him at sight. Mr. Schloss showed me the letter.

"It had come to this. I must either elope with Schloss, or lose his aid. The thought of either was unendurable. I hated him—yet was dependent on him.

"To-night I met him, in his empty apartment, alone. I knew that he had what was left of his money with him, that everything was packed up. I went prepared. I would not elope. My plan was no less than to make him pay the balance on the necklace that he had lost—or to murder him.

"I carried a new pistol in my muff, one which Lynn had just bought. I don't know how I did it. I was desperate.

"He told me he loved me, that Lynn did not, never had—that Lynn had married me only to show off his wealth and diamonds, to give him a social position—that I was merely a—a piece of property —a dummy.

"He tried to kiss me. It was revolting. I struggled away from him.

"And in the struggle, the revolver fell from my muff and exploded on the floor.

"At once he was aflame with suspicion.

" 'So—it's murder you want!' he shouted. 'Well, murder it shall be!'

"I saw death in his eye as he seized my arm. I was defenseless now. The old passion came over him. Before he killed—he—would have his way with me.

"I screamed. With a wild effort I twisted away from him.

"He raised his hand to strike me, I saw his eyes, glassy. Then he sank back—fell to the floor—dead of apoplexy—dead of his furious emotions.

"I fled.

"And now you have found me."

She had turned, hastily, to leave the room. Kennedy blocked the door.

"Mrs. Moulton," he said firmly, "listen to me. What was the first question you asked me? 'Can I trust you?' And I told you you could. This is no time for—for suicide." He shot the word out bluntly. "All may not be lost. I have sent for your husband. Muller is outside."

"Muller?" she cried. "He made the replica."

"Very well. I am going to clear this thing up. Come. You *must.*"

It was all confused to me, the dash in a car to the little pawnbroker's on the first floor of a five-story tenement, the quick entry into the place by one of Muller's keys.

Over the safe in back was a framework like that which had covered Schloss' safe. Kennedy tore it away, regardless of the alarm which it must have sounded. In a moment he was down before it on his knees.

"This is how Schloss' safe was opened so quickly," he muttered, working feverishly. "Here is some of their own medicine."

He had placed the peculiar telephone-like transmitter close to the combination lock and was turning the combination rapidly.

Suddenly he rose, gave the bolts a twist, and the ponderous doors swung open.

"What is it?" I asked eagerly.

"A burglar's microphone," he answered, hastily looking over the contents of the safe. "The microphone is now used by burglars for picking combination locks. When you turn the lock, a slight sound is made when the proper number comes opposite the working point. It can be heard sometimes by a sensitive ear, although it is imperceptible to most persons. But by using a microphone it is an easy matter to hear the sounds which allow of opening the lock."

He had taken a yellow chamois bag out of the safe and opened it.

Inside sparkled the famous Moulton diamonds. He held them up—in all their wicked brilliancy. No one spoke.

Then he took another yellow bag, more dirty and worn than the first. As he opened it, Mrs. Moulton could restrain herself no longer.

"The replica!" she cried. "The replica!"

Without a word, Craig handed the real necklace to her. Then he slipped the paste jewels into the newer of the bags and restored both it and the empty one to their places, banged shut the door of the safe, and replaced the wooden screen.

"Quick!" he said to her, "you have still a minute to get away. Hurry—anywhere—away—only away!"

The look of gratitude that came over her face, as she understood the full meaning of it was such as I had never seen before.

"Quick!" he repeated.

It was too late.

"For God's sake, Kennedy," shouted a voice at the street door, "what are you doing here?"

It was McLear himself. He had come with the Hale patrol, on his mettle now to take care of the epidemic of robberies.

Before Craig could reply a cab drew up with a rush at the curb and two men, half fighting, half cursing, catapulted themselves into the shop.

They were Winters and Moulton.

Without a word, taking advantage of the first shock of surprise, Kennedy had clapped a piece of chemical paper on the foreheads of Mrs. Moulton, then of Moulton, and on Muller's. Oblivious to the rest of us, he studied the impressions in the full light of the counter.

Moulton was facing his wife with a scornful curl of the lip.

"I've been told of the paste replica—and I wrote Schloss that I'd shoot him down like the dog he is, you—you traitress," he hissed.

She drew herself up scornfully.

"And I have been told why you married me—to show off your wicked jewels and help you in your——"

"You lie!" he cried fiercely. "Muller—some one

—open this safe—whoever it is. If what I have been told is true, there is in it one new bag containing the necklace. It was stolen from Schloss to whom you sold *my* jewels. The other old bag, stolen from me, contains the paste replica you had made to deceive me."

It was all so confused that I do not know how it happened. I think it was Muller who opened the safe.

"There is the new yellow bag," cried Moulton, "from Schloss' own safe. Open it."

McLear had taken it. He did so. There sparkled not the real gems, but the replica.

"The devil!" Moulton exclaimed, breaking from Winters and seizing the old bag.

He tore it open and—it was empty.

"One moment," interrupted Kennedy, looking up quietly from the counter. "Seal that safe again, McLear. In it are the Schloss jewels and the products of half a dozen other robberies which the dupe Muller—or Stein, as you please—pulled off, some as a blind to conceal the real criminal. You may have shown him how to leave no finger prints, but you yourself have left what is just as good—your own forehead print. McLear—you were right. There's your criminal—Lynn Moulton, professional fence, the brains of the thing."

CHAPTER XIX

THE GERM LETTER

Lynn Moulton made no fight and Kennedy did not pursue the case, for, with the rescue of Antoinette Moulton, his interest ceased.

Blackmail takes various forms, and the Moulton affair was only one phase of it. It was not long before we had to meet a much stranger attempt.

"Read the letter, Professor Kennedy. Then I will tell you the sequel."

Mrs. Hunter Blake lay back in the cushions of her invalid chair in the sun parlor of the great Blake mansion on Riverside Drive, facing the Hudson with its continuous reel of maritime life framed against the green-hilled background of the Jersey shore.

Her nurse, Miss Dora Sears, gently smoothed out the pillows and adjusted them so that the invalid could more easily watch us. Mrs. Blake, wealthy, known as a philanthropist, was not an old woman, but had been for years a great sufferer from rheumatism.

I watched Miss Sears eagerly. Full-bosomed, fine of face and figure, she was something more than a nurse; she was a companion. She had bright, sparkling black eyes and an expression about her well-cut mouth which made one want to laugh with her. It seemed to say that the world was a huge joke and she invited you to enjoy the joke with her.

Kennedy took the letter which Miss Sears proffered him, and as he did so I could not help noticing her full, plump forearm on which gleamed a handsome plain gold bracelet. He spread the letter out on a dainty wicker table in such a way that we both could see it.

We had been summoned over the telephone to the Blake mansion by Reginald Blake, Mrs. Blake's eldest son. Reginald had been very reticent over the reason, but had seemed very anxious and insistent that Kennedy should come immediately.

Craig read quickly and I followed him, fascinated by the letter from its very opening paragraph.

"Dear Madam," it began. "Having received my diploma as doctor of medicine and bacteriology at Heidelberg in 1909, I came to the United States to study a most serious disease which is prevalent in several of the western mountain states."

So far, I reflected, it looked like an ordinary appeal for aid. The next words, however, were queer: "I have four hundred persons of wealth on my list. Your name was——"

Kennedy turned the page. On the next leaf of the letter sheet was pasted a strip of gelatine. The first page had adhered slightly to the gelatine.

"Chosen by fate," went on the sentence ominously.

"By opening this letter," I read, "you have liberated millions of the virulent bacteria of this disease. Without a doubt you are infected by this time, for no human body is impervious to them, and up to the present only one in one hundred has fully recovered after going through all its stages."

I gasped. The gelatine had evidently been arranged so that when the two sheets were pulled apart, the germs would be thrown into the air about the person opening the letter. It was a very ingenious device.

The letter continued, "I am happy to say, however, that I have a prophylactic which will destroy any number of these germs if used up to the ninth day. It is necessary only that you should place five thousand dollars in an envelope and leave it for me to be called for at the desk of the Prince Henry Hotel. When the messenger delivers the money to me, the prophylactic will be sent immediately.

"First of all, take a match and burn this letter to avoid spreading the disease. Then change your clothes and burn the old ones. Enclosed you will find in a germ-proof envelope an exact copy of this letter. The room should then be thoroughly fumigated. Do not come into close contact with anyone near and dear to you until you have used the prophylactic. Tell no one. In case you do, the prophylactic will not be sent under any circumstances. Very truly yours,   DR. HANS HOPF."

"Blackmail!" exclaimed Kennedy, looking intently again at the gelatine on the second page, as I involuntarily backed away and held my breath.

"Yes, I know," responded Mrs. Blake anxiously, "but is it true?"

There could be no doubt from the tone of her voice that she more than half believed that it was true.

"I cannot say—yet," replied Craig, still cautiously scanning the apparently innocent piece of gelatine on the original letter which Mrs. Blake had not destroyed. "I shall have to keep it and examine it."

On the gelatine I could see a dark mass which evidently was supposed to contain the germs.

"I opened the letter here in this room," she went on. "At first I thought nothing of it. But this morning, when Buster, my prize Pekinese, who had been with me, sitting on my lap at the time and closer to the letter even than I was, when Buster was taken suddenly ill, I—well, I began to worry."

She finished with a little nervous laugh, as people will to hide their real feelings.

"I should like to see the dog," remarked Kennedy simply.

"Miss Sears," asked her mistress, "will you get Buster, please?"

The nurse left the room. No longer was there the laughing look on her face. This was serious business.

A few minutes later she reappeared, carrying gingerly a small dog basket. Mrs. Blake lifted the lid. Inside was a beautiful little "Peke," and it was easy to see that Buster was indeed ill.

"Who is your doctor?" asked Craig, considering.

"Dr. Rae Wilson, a very well-known woman physician."

Kennedy nodded recognition of the name. "What does she say?" he asked, observing the dog narrowly.

"We haven't told anyone, outside, of it yet," replied Mrs. Blake. "In fact until Buster fell sick, I thought it was a hoax."

"You haven't told anyone?"

"Only Reginald and my daughter Betty. Betty is frantic—not with fear for herself, but with fear for me. No one can reassure her. In fact it was as much for her sake as anyone's that I sent for you. Reginald has tried to trace the thing down himself, but has not succeeded."

She paused. The door opened and Reginald Blake entered. He was a young fellow, self confident and no doubt very efficient at the new dances, though scarcely fitted to rub elbows with a cold world which, outside of his own immediate circle, knew not the name of Blake. He stood for a moment regarding us through the smoke of his cigarette.

"Tell me just what you have done," asked Kennedy of him as his mother introduced him, although he had done the talking for her over the telephone.

"Done?" he drawled. "Why, as soon as mother told me of the letter, I left an envelope up at the Prince Henry, as it directed."

"With the money?" put in Craig quickly.

"Oh, no—just as a decoy."

"Yes. What happened?"

"Well, I waited around a long time. It was far along in the day when a woman appeared at the desk. I had instructed the clerk to be on the watch for anyone who asked for mail addressed to a Dr. Hopf. The clerk slammed the register. That was the signal. I moved up closer."

"What did she look like?" asked Kennedy keenly.

"I couldn't see her face. But she was beautifully dressed, with a long light flowing linen duster, a veil that hid her features and on her hands and arms a long pair of motoring doeskin gloves. By George, she was a winner—in general looks, though. Well, something about the clerk, I suppose, must have aroused her suspicions. For, a moment later, she was gone in the crowd. Evidently she had thought of the danger and had picked out a time when the lobby would be full and everybody busy. But she did not leave by the front entrance through which she entered. I concluded that she must have left by one of the side street carriage doors."

"And she got away?"

"Yes. I found that she asked one of the boys at the door to crank up a car standing at the curb. She slid into the seat, and was off in a minute."

Kennedy said nothing. But I knew that he was making a mighty effort to restrain comment on the bungling amateur detective work of the son of our client.

Reginald saw the look on his face. "Still," he hastened, "I got the number of the car. It was 200859 New York."

"You have looked it up?" queried Kennedy quickly.

"I didn't need to do it. A few minutes later Dr. Rae Wilson herself came out—storming like mad. Her car had been stolen at the very door of the hotel by this woman with the innocent aid of the hotel employees."

Kennedy was evidently keenly interested. The mention of the stolen car had apparently at once suggested an idea to him.

"Mrs. Blake," he said, as he rose to go, "I shall take this letter with me. Will you see that Buster is sent up to my laboratory immediately?"

She nodded. It was evident that Buster was a great pet with her and that it was with difficulty she kept from smoothing his silky coat.

"You—you won't hurt Buster?" she pleaded.

"No. Trust me. More than that, if there is any possible way of untangling this mystery, I shall do it."

Mrs. Blake looked rather than spoke her thanks. As we went downstairs, accompanied by Miss Sears, we could see in the music room a very interesting couple, chatting earnestly over the piano.

Betty Blake, a slip of a girl in her first season, was dividing her attention between her visitor and the door by which we were passing.

She rose as she heard us, leaving the young man standing alone at the piano. He was of an age perhaps a year or two older than Reginald Blake. It was evident that, whatever Miss Betty might think, he had eyes for no one else but the pretty débutante. He even seemed to be regarding Kennedy sullenly, as if he were a possible rival.

"You—you don't think it is serious?" whispered Betty in an undertone, scarcely waiting to be introduced. She had evidently known of our visit, but had been unable to get away to be present upstairs.

"Really, Miss Blake," reassured Kennedy, "I can't say. All I can do is to repeat what I have already said to your mother. Keep up a good heart and trust me to work it out."

"Thank you," she murmured, and then, impulsively extending her small hand to Craig, she added, "Mr. Kennedy, if there is anything I can do to help you, I beg that you will call on me."

"I shall not forget," he answered, relinquishing the hand reluctantly. Then, as she thanked him, and turned again to her guest, he added in a low tone to me, "A remarkable girl, Walter, a girl that can be depended on."

We followed Miss Sears down the hall.

"Who was that young man in the music room?" asked Kennedy, when we were out of earshot.

14

"Duncan Baldwin," she answered. "A friend and bosom companion of Reginald."

"He seems to think more of Betty than of her brother," Craig remarked dryly.

Miss Sears smiled. "Sometimes, we think they are secretly engaged," she returned. We had almost reached the door. "By the way," she asked anxiously, "do you think there are any precautions that I should take for Mrs. Blake—and the rest?"

"Hardly," answered Kennedy, after a moment's consideration, "as long as you have taken none in particular already. Still, I suppose it will do no harm to be as antiseptic as possible."

"I shall try," she promised, her face showing that she considered the affair now in a much more serious light than she had before our visit.

"And keep me informed of anything that turns up," added Kennedy handing her a card with the telephone number of the laboratory.

As we left the Blake mansion, Kennedy remarked, "We must trace that car somehow—at least we must get someone working on that."

Half an hour later we were in a towering office building on Liberty Street, the home of various kinds of insurance. Kennedy stopped before a door which bore the name, "Douglas Garwood: Insurance Adjuster."

Briefly, Craig told the story of the stolen car, omitting the account of the dastardly method taken to blackmail Mrs. Blake. As he proceeded a light seemed to break on the face of Garwood, a heavy-set man, whose very gaze was inquisitorial.

"Yes, the theft has been reported to us already by Dr. Wilson herself," he interrupted. "The car was insured in a company I represent."

"I had hoped so," remarked Kennedy. "Do you know the woman?" he added, watching the insurance adjuster who had been listening intently as he told about the fair motor car thief.

"Know her?" repeated Garwood emphatically. "Why, man, we have been so close to that woman that I feel almost intimate with her. The descriptions are those of a lady, well-dressed, and with a voice and manner that would carry her through any of the fashionable hotels, perhaps into society itself."

"One of a gang of blackmailers, then," I hazarded.

Garwood shrugged his shoulders. "Perhaps," he acquiesced. "It is automobile thieving that interests me, though. "Why, he went on, rising excitedly, "the gangs of these thieves are getting away with half a million dollars' worth of high-priced cars every year. The police seem to be powerless to stop it. We appeal to them, but with no result. So, now we have taken things into our own hands."

"What are you doing in this case?" asked Kennedy.

"What the insurance companies have to do to recover stolen automobiles," Garwood replied. "For, with all deference to your friend, Deputy O'Connor, it is the insurance companies rather than the police who get stolen cars back."

He had pulled out a postal card from a pigeon hole in his desk, selecting it from several apparently similar. We read:

$250.00 REWARD

We will pay $100.00 for car, $150.00 additional for information which will convict the thief. When

last seen, driven by a woman, name not known, who
is described as dark-haired, well-dressed, slight, apparently thirty years old. The car is a Dixon, 1912,
seven-passenger, touring, No. 193,222, license No.
200,859, New York; dark red body, mohair top,
brass lamps, has no wind shield; rear axle brake
band clevice has extra nut on turnbuckle not painted.
Car last seen near Prince Henry Hotel, New York
City, Friday, the 10th.

Communicate by telegraph or telephone, after
notifying nearest police department, with Douglas
Garwood, New York City.

"The secret of it is," explained Garwood, as we
finished reading, "that there are innumerable people
who keep their eyes open and like to earn money
easily. Thus we have several hundreds of amateur
and enthusiastic detectives watching all over the city
and country for any car that looks suspicious."

Kennedy thanked him for his courtesy, and we
rose to go. "I shall be glad to keep you informed
of anything that turns up," he promised.

CHAPTER XX

In the laboratory, Kennedy quietly set to work. He began by tearing from the germ letter the piece of gelatine and first examining it with a pocket lens. Then, with a sterile platinum wire, he picked out several minute sections of the black spot on the gelatine and placed them in agar, blood serum, and other media on which they would be likely to grow.

"I shall have to wait until to-morrow to examine them properly," he remarked. "There are colonies of something there, all right, but I must have them more fully developed."

A hurried telephone call late in the day from Miss Sears told us that Mrs. Blake herself had begun to complain, and that Dr. Wilson had been summoned but had been unable to give an opinion on the nature of the malady.

Kennedy quickly decided on making a visit to the doctor, who lived not far downtown from the laboratory.

Dr. Rae Wilson proved to be a nervous little woman, inclined, I felt, to be dictatorial. I thought that secretly she felt a little piqued at our having been taken into the Blakes' confidence before herself, and Kennedy made every effort to smooth that aspect over tactfully.

"Have you any idea what it can be?" he asked finally.

She shook her head noncommitally. "I have taken blood smears," she answered, "but so far haven't been able to discover anything. I shall have to have her under observation for a day or two before I can answer that. Still, as Mrs. Blake is so ill, I have ordered another trained nurse to relieve Miss Sears of the added work, a very efficient nurse, a Miss Rogers."

Kennedy had risen to go. "You have had no word about your car?" he asked casually.

"None yet. I'm not worrying. It was insured."

"Who is this arch criminal, Dr. Hopf?" I mused as we retraced our steps to the laboratory. "Is Mrs. Blake stricken now by the same trouble that seems to have affected Buster?"

"Only my examination will show," he said. "I shall let nothing interfere with that now. It must be the starting point for any work that I may do in the case."

We arrived at Kennedy's workshop of scientific crime and he immediately plunged into work. Looking up he caught sight of me standing helplessly idle.

"Walter," he remarked thoughtfully adjusting a microscope, "suppose you run down and see Garwood. Perhaps he has something to report. And, by the way, while you are out, make inquiries about the Blakes, young Baldwin, Miss Sears and this Dr. Wilson. I have heard of her before, at least by name. Perhaps you may find something interesting."

Glad to have a chance to seem to be doing something whether it amounted to anything or not, I

dropped in to see Garwood.   So far he had nothing
to report except the usual number of false alarms.
From his office I went up to the *Star* where fortunately I found one of the reporters who wrote
society notes.

The Blakes, I found, as we already knew, to be
well known and moving in the highest social circles.
As far as known they had no particular enemies,
other than those common to all people of great
wealth.   Dr. Wilson had a large practice, built up
in recent years, and was one of the best known
society physicians for women.   Miss Sears was unknown, as far as I could determine.   As for Duncan
Baldwin, I found that he had become acquainted
with Reginald Blake in college, that he came of no
particular family and seemed to have no great
means, although he was very popular in the best
circles.   In fact he had had, thanks to his friend, a
rather meteoric rise in society, though it was reported that he was somewhat involved in debt as a
result.

I returned to the laboratory to find that Craig
had taken out of a cabinet a peculiar looking arrangement.   It consisted of thirty-two tubes, each
about sixteen inches long, with S-turns, like a minute
radiator.   It was altogether not over a cubic foot
in size, and enclosed in a glass cylinder.   There were
in it, perhaps, fifty feet of tubes, a perfectly-closed
tubular system which I noticed Kennedy was keeping absolutely sterile in a germicidal solution of
some kind.

Inside the tubes and surrounding them was a
saline solution which was kept at a uniform temperature by a special heating apparatus.

Kennedy had placed the apparatus on the laboratory table and then gently took the little dog from his basket and laid him beside it. A few minutes later the poor little suffering Buster was mercifully under the influence of an anesthetic.

Quickly Craig worked. First he attached the end of one of the tubes by means of a little cannula to the carotid artery of the dog. Then the other was attached to the jugular vein.

As he released the clamp which held the artery, the little dog's feverishly beating heart spurted the arterial blood from the carotid into the tubes holding the normal salt solution and that pressure, in turn, pumped the salt solution which filled the tubes into the jugular vein, thus replacing the arterial blood that had poured into the tubes from the other end and maintaining the normal hydrostatic conditions in the body circulation. The dog was being kept alive, although perhaps a third of his blood was out of his body.

"You see," he said at length, after we had watched the process a few minutes, "what I have here is in reality an artificial kidney. It is a system that has been devised by several doctors at Johns Hopkins.

"If there is any toxin in the blood of this dog, the kidneys are naturally endeavoring to eliminate it. Perhaps it is being eliminated too slowly. In that case this arrangement which I have here will aid them. We call it vividiffusion and it depends for its action on the physical principle of osmosis, the passage of substances of a certain kind through a porous membrane, such as these tubes of celloidin.

"Thus any substance, any poison that is dialyzable is diffused into the surrounding salt solution and the blood is passed back into the body, with no air in it, no infection, and without alteration. Clotting is prevented by the injection of a harmless substance derived from leeches, known as hirudin. I prevent the loss of anything in the blood which I want retained by placing in the salt solution around the tubes an amount of that substance equal to that held in solution by the blood. Of course that does not apply to the colloidal substances in the blood which would not pass by osmosis under any circumstances. But by such adjustments I can remove and study any desired substance in the blood, provided it is capable of diffusion. In fact this little apparatus has been found in practice to compare favorably with the kidneys themselves in removing even a lethal dose of poison."

I watched in amazement. He was actually cleaning the blood of the dog and putting it back again, purified, into the little body. Far from being cruel, as perhaps it might seem, it was in reality probably the only method by which the animal could be saved, and at the same time it was giving us a clue as to some elusive, subtle substance used in the case.

"Indeed," Kennedy went on reflectively, "this process can be kept up for several hours without injury to the dog, though I do not think that will be necessary to relieve the unwonted strain that has been put upon his natural organs. Finally, at the close of the operation, serious loss of blood is overcome by driving back the greater part of it into his body, closing up the artery and vein, and taking good care of the animal so that he will make a quick recovery."

For a long time I watched the fascinating process of seeing the life blood coursing through the porous tubes in the salt solution, while Kennedy gave his undivided attention to the success of the delicate experiment. It was late when I left him, still at work over Buster, and went up to our apartment to turn in, convinced that nothing more would happen that night.

The next morning, with characteristic energy, Craig was at work early, examining the cultures he had made from the black spots on the gelatine.

By the look of perplexity on his face, I knew that he had discovered something that instead of clearing the mystery up, further deepened it.

"What do you find?" I asked anxiously.

"Walter," he exclaimed, laying aside the last of the slides which he had been staining and looking at intently through the microscope, "that stuff on the gelatine is entirely harmless. There was nothing in it except common mold."

For the moment I did not comprehend. "Mold?" I repeated.

"Yes," he replied, "just common, ordinary mold such as grows on the top of a jar of fruit or preserves when it is exposed to the air."

I stifled an exclamation of incredulity. It seemed impossible that the deadly germ note should be harmless, in view of the events that had followed its receipt.

Just then the laboratory door was flung open and Reginald Blake, pale and excited, entered. He had every mark of having been up all night.

"What's the matter?" asked Craig.

"It's about my mother," he blurted out. "She seems to be getting worse all the time. Miss Sears is alarmed, and Betty is almost ill herself with worry. Dr. Wilson doesn't seem to know what it is that affects her, and neither does the new nurse. Can you *do* something?"

There was a tone of appeal in his voice that was not like the self-sufficient Reginald of the day before.

"Does there seem to be any immediate danger?" asked Kennedy.

"Perhaps not—I can't say," he urged. "But she is gradually getting worse instead of better."

Kennedy thought a moment. "Has anything else happened?" he asked slowly.

"N-no. That's enough, isn't it?"

"Indeed it is," replied Craig, trying to be reassuring. Then, recollecting Betty, he added, "Reginald, go back and tell your sister for me that she must positively make the greatest effort of her life to control herself. Tell her that her mother needs her—needs her well and brave. I shall be up at the house immediately. Do the best you can. I depend on you."

Kennedy's words seemed to have a bracing effect on Reginald and a few moments later he left, much calmer.

"I hope I have given him something to do which will keep him from mussing things up again," remarked Kennedy, mindful of Reginald's former excursion into detective work.

Meanwhile Craig plunged furiously into his study of the substances he had isolated from the saline solution in which he had "washed" the blood of the little Pekinese.

"There's no use doing anything in the dark," he explained. "Until we know what it is we are fighting we can't very well fight."

For the moment I was overwhelmed by the impending tragedy that seemed to be hanging over

Mrs. Blake. The more I thought of it, the more inexplicable became the discovery of the mold.

"That is all very well about the mold on the gelatine strip in the letter," I insisted at length. "But, Craig, there must be something wrong somewhere. Mere molds could not have made Buster so ill, and now the infection, or whatever it is, has spread to Mrs. Blake herself. What have you found out by studying Buster?"

He looked up from his close scrutiny of the material in one of the test tubes which contained something he had recovered from the saline solution of the diffusion apparatus.

I could read on his face that whatever it was, it was serious. "What is it?" I repeated almost breathlessly.

"I suppose I might coin a word to describe it," he answered slowly, measuring his phrases. "Perhaps it might be called hyper-amino-acidemia."

I puckered my eyes at the mouth-filling term Kennedy smiled. "It would mean," he explained, "a great quantity of the amino-acids, non-coagulable, nitrogenous compounds in the blood. You know the indols, the phenols, and the amins are produced both by putrefactive bacteria and by the process of metabolism, the burning up of the tissues in the process of utilizing the energy that means life. But under normal circumstances, the amins are not present in the blood in any such quantities as I have discovered by this new method of diffusion."

He paused a moment, as if in deference to my inability to follow him on such an abstruse topic, then resumed, "As far as I am able to determine, this poison or toxin is an amin similar to that secreted by certain cephalopods found in the borhood of Naples. It is an aromatic amin. Smell it."

I bent over and inhaled the peculiar odor.

"Those creatures," he continued, "catch their prey by this highly active poison secreted by the so-called salivary glands. Even a little bit will kill a crab easily."

I was following him now with intense interest, thinking of the astuteness of a mind capable of thinking of such a poison.

"Indeed, it is surprising," he resumed thoughtfully, "how many an innocent substance can be changed by bacteria into a virulent poison. In fact our poisons and our drugs are in many instances the close relations of harmless compounds that represent the intermediate steps in the daily process of metabolism."

"Then," I put in, "the toxin was produced by germs, after all?"

"I did not say that," he corrected. "It might have been. But I find no germs in the blood of Buster. Nor did Dr. Wilson find any in the blood smears which she took from Mrs. Blake."

He seemed to have thrown the whole thing back again into the limbo of the unexplainable, and I felt nonplussed.

"The writer of that letter," he went on, waving the piece of sterile platinum wire with which he had been transferring drops of liquid in his search for germs, "was a much more skillful bacteriologist than I thought, evidently. No, the trouble does not seem to be from germs breathed in, or from germs at all—it is from some kind of germ-free toxin that has been injected or otherwise introduced."

Vaguely now I began to appreciate the terrible significance of what he had discovered.

"But the letter?" I persisted mechanically.

"The writer of that was quite as shrewd a psychologist as bacteriologist," pursued Craig impressively. "He calculated the moral effect of the letter, then of Buster's illness, and finally of reaching Mrs. Blake herself."

"You think Dr. Rae Wilson knows nothing of it yet?" I queried.

Kennedy appeared to consider his answer carefully. Then he said slowly: "Almost any doctor with a microscope and the faintest trace of a scientific education could recognize disease germs either naturally or feloniously implanted. But when it comes to the detection of concentrated, filtered, germ-free toxins, almost any scientist might be baffled. Walter," he concluded, "this is not mere blackmail, although perhaps the visit of that woman to the Prince Henry—a desperate thing in itself, although she did get away by her quick thinking—perhaps that shows that these people are ready to stop at nothing. No, it goes deeper than blackmail."

I stood aghast at the discovery of this new method of scientific murder. The astute criminal, whoever he might be, had planned to leave not even the slender clue that might be afforded by disease germs. He was operating, not with disease itself, but with something showing the ultimate effects, perhaps, of disease with none of the preliminary symptoms, baffling even to the best of physicians.

I scarcely knew what to say. Before I realized it, however, Craig was at last ready for the promised visit to Mrs. Blake. We went together, carrying Buster, in his basket, not recovered, to be sure, but a very different little animal from the dying creature that had been sent to us at the laboratory.

CHAPTER XXI

THE POISON BRACELET

WE reached the Blake mansion and were promptly admitted. Miss Betty, bearing up bravely under Reginald's reassurances, greeted us before we were fairly inside the door, though she and her brother were not able to conceal the fact that their mother was no better. Miss Sears was out, for an airing, and the new nurse, Miss Rogers, was in charge of the patient.

"How do you feel, this morning?" inquired Kennedy as we entered the sun-parlor, where Mrs. Blake had first received us.

A single glance was enough to satisfy me of the seriousness of her condition. She seemed to be in almost a stupor from which she roused herself only with difficulty. It was as if some overpowering toxin were gradually undermining her already weakened constitution.

She nodded recognition, but nothing further.

Kennedy had set the dog basket down near her wheel-chair and she caught sight of it.

"Buster?" she murmured, raising her eyes. "Is —he—all right?"

For answer, Craig simply raised the lid of the basket. Buster already seemed to have recognized the voice of his mistress, and, with an almost human instinct, to realize that though he himself was still weak and ill, she needed encouragement.

As Mrs. Blake stretched out her slender hand, drawn with pain, to his silky head, he gave a little yelp of delight and his little red tongue eagerly caressed her hand.

It was as though the two understood each other. Although Mrs. Blake, as yet, had no more idea what had happened to her pet, she seemed to feel by some subtle means of thought transference that the intelligent little animal was conveying to her a message of hope. The caress, the sharp, joyous yelp, and the happy wagging of the bushy tail seemed to brighten her up, at least for the moment, almost as if she had received a new impetus.

"Buster!" she exclaimed, overjoyed to get her pet back again in so much improved condition.

"I wouldn't exert myself too much, Mrs. Blake," cautioned Kennedy.

"Were—were there any germs in the letter?" she asked, as Reginald and Betty stood on the other side of the chair, much encouraged, apparently, at this show of throwing off the lethargy that had seized her.

"Yes, but about as harmless as those would be on a piece of cheese," Kennedy hastened.

"But I—I feel so weak, so played out—and my head——"

Her voice trailed off, a too evident reminder that her improvement had been only momentary and prompted by the excitement of our arrival.

Betty bent down solicitously and made her more comfortable as only one woman can make another. Kennedy, meanwhile. had been talking to Miss

15

Rogers, and I could see that he was secretly taking her measure.

"Has Dr. Wilson been here this morning?" I heard him ask.

"Not yet," she replied. "But we expect her soon."

"Professor Kennedy?" announced a servant.

"Yes?" answered Craig.

"There is someone on the telephone who wants to speak to you. He said he had called the laboratory first and that they told him to call you here."

Kennedy hurried after the servant, while Betty and Reginald joined me, waiting, for we seemed to feel that something was about to happen.

"One of the unofficial detectives has unearthed a clue," he whispered to me a few moments later when he returned. "It was Garwood." Then to the others he added, "A car, repainted, and with the number changed, but otherwise answering the description of Dr. Wilson's has been traced to the West Side. It is somewhere in the neighborhood of a saloon and garage where drivers of taxicabs hang out. Reginald, I wish you would come along with us."

To Betty's unspoken question Craig hastened to add, "I don't think there is any immediate danger. If there is any change—let me know. I shall call up soon. And meanwhile," he lowered his voice to impress the instruction on her, "don't leave your mother for a moment—not for a moment," he emphasized.

Reginald was ready and together we three set off to meet Garwood at a subway station near the point where the car had been reported. We had scarcely closed the front door, when we ran into Duncan

Baldwin, coming down the street, evidently bent on inquiring how Mrs. Blake and Betty were.

"Much better," reassured Kennedy. "Come on, Baldwin. We can't have too many on whom we can rely on an expedition like this."

"Like what?" he asked, evidently not comprehending.

"There's a clue, they think, to that car of Dr. Wilson's," hastily explained Reginald, linking his arm into that of his friend and falling in behind us, as Craig hurried ahead.

It did not take long to reach the subway, and as we waited for the train, Craig remarked: "This is a pretty good example of how the automobile is becoming one of the most dangerous of criminal weapons. All one has to do nowadays, apparently, after committing a crime, is to jump into a waiting car and breeze away, safe."

We met Garwood and under his guidance picked our way westward from the better known streets in the heart of the city, to a section that was anything but prepossessing.

The place which Garwood sought was a typical Raines Law hotel on a corner, with a saloon on the first floor, and apparently the requisite number of rooms above to give it a legal license.

We had separated a little so that we would not attract undue attention. Kennedy and I entered the swinging doors boldly, while the others continued across to the other corner to wait with Garwood and take in the situation. It was a strange expedition and Reginald was fidgeting while Duncan seemed nervous.

Among the group of chauffeurs lounging at the bar and in the back room anyone who had ever had any dealings with the gangs of New York might have recognized the faces of men whose pictures were in the rogues' gallery and who were members of those various aristocratic organizations of the underworld.

Kennedy glanced about at the motley crowd. "This is a place where you need only to be introduced properly," he whispered to me, "to have any kind of crime committed for you."

As we stood there, observing, without appearing to do so, through an open window on the side street I could tell from the sounds that there was a garage in the rear of the hotel.

We were startled to hear a sudden uproar from the street.

Garwood, impatient at our delay, had walked down past the garage to reconnoiter. A car was being backed out hurriedly, and as it turned and swung around the corner, his trained eye had recognized it.

Instantly he had reasoned that it was an attempt to make a getaway, and had raised an alarm.

Those nearest the door piled out, keen for any excitement. We, too, dashed out on the street. There we saw passing an automobile, swaying and lurching at the terrific speed with which its driver, urged it up the avenue. As he flashed by he looked like an Italian to me, perhaps a gunman.

Garwood had impressed a passing trolley car into service and was pursuing the automobile in it, as it swayed on its tracks as crazily as the motor did on the roadway, running with all the power the motorman could apply.

A mounted policeman galloped past us, blazing away at the tires. The avenue was stirred, as seldom even in its strenuous life, with reports of shots, honking of horns, the clang of trolley bells and the shouts of men.

The pursuers were losing when there came a rattle and roar from the rear wheels which told that the tires were punctured and the heavy car was riding on its rims. A huge brewery wagon crossing a side street paused to see the fun, effectually blocking the road.

The car jolted to a stop. The chauffeur leaped out and a moment later dived down into a cellar. In that congested district, pursuit was useless.

"Only an accomplice," commented Kennedy. "Perhaps we can get him some other way if we can catch the man—or woman—higher up."

Down the street now we could see Garwood surrounded by a curious crowd but in possession of the car. I looked about for Duncan and Reginald. They had apparently been swallowed up in the crowds of idlers which seemed to be pouring out of nowhere, collecting to gape at the excitement, after the manner of a New York crowd.

As I ran my eye over them, I caught sight of Reginald near the corner where we had left him in an incipient fight with someone who had a fancied grievance. A moment later we had rescued him.

"Where's Duncan?" he panted. "Did anything happen to him? Garwood told us to stay here—but we got separated."

Policemen had appeared on the heels of the crowd and now, except for a knot following Garwood, things seemed to be calming down.

The excitement over, and the people thinning out, Kennedy still could not find any trace of Duncan. Finally he glanced in again through the swinging doors. There was Duncan, evidently quite upset by what had occurred, fortifying himself at the bar.

Suddenly from above came a heavy thud, as if someone had fallen on the floor above us, followed by a suppressed shuffling of feet and a cry of help.

Kennedy sprang toward a side door which led out into the hall to the hotel room above. It was locked. Before any of the others he ran out on the street and into the hall that way, taking the stairs two at a time, past a little cubby-hole of an "office" and down the upper hall to a door from which came the cry.

It was a peculiar room into which we burst, half bedroom, half workshop, or rather laboratory, for on a deal table by a window stood a rack of test-tubes, several beakers, and other paraphernalia.

A chambermaid was shrieking over a woman who was lying lethargic on the floor.

I looked more closely.

It was Dora Sears.

For the moment I could not imagine what had happened. Had the events of the past few days worked on her mind and driven her into temporary insanity? Or had the blackmailing gang of automobile thieves, failing in extorting money by their original plan, seized her?

Kennedy bent over and tried to lift her up. As he did so, the gold bracelet, unclasped, clattered to the floor.

He picked it up and for a moment looked at it. It was hollow, but in that part of it where it unclasped could be seen a minute hypodermic needle and traces of a liquid.

"A poison bracelet," he muttered to himself, "one in which enough of a virulent poison could be hidden so that in an emergency death could cheat the law."

"But this Dr. Hopf," exclaimed Reginald, who stood behind us looking from the insensible girl to the bracelet and slowly comprehending what it all meant, "she alone knows where and who he is!"

We looked at Kennedy. What was to be done? Was the criminal higher up to escape because one of his tools had been cornered and had taken the easiest way to get out?

Kennedy had taken down the receiver of the wall telephone in the room. A moment later he was calling insistently for his laboratory. One of the students in another part of the building answered. Quickly he described the apparatus for vividiffusion and how to handle it without rupturing any of the delicate tubes."

"The large one," he ordered, "with one hundred and ninety-two tubes. And hurry."

Before the student appeared, came an ambulance which some one in the excitement had summoned. Kennedy quickly commandeered both the young doctor and what surgical material he had with him.

Briefly he explained what he proposed to do and before the student arrived with the apparatus, they had placed the nurse in such a position that they were ready for the operation.

The next room which was unoccupied had been thrown open to us and there I waited with Reginald and Duncan, endeavoring to explain to them the mysteries of the new process of washing the blood.

The minutes lengthened into hours, as the blood of the poisoned girl coursed through its artificial channel, literally being washed of the toxin from the poisoned bracelet.

Would it succeed? It had saved the life of

Buster. But would it bring back the unfortunate before us, long enough even for her to yield her secret and enable us to catch the real criminal. What if she died?

As Kennedy worked, the young men with me became more and more fascinated, watching him. The vividiffusion apparatus was now in full operation.

In the intervals when he left the apparatus in charge of the young ambulance surgeon Kennedy was looking over the room. In a trunk which was open he found several bundles of papers. As he ran his eye over them quickly, he selected some and stuffed them into his pocket, then went back to watch the working of the apparatus.

Reginald, who had been growing more and more nervous, at last asked if he might call up Betty to find out how his mother was.

. He came back from the telephone, his face wrinkled.

"Poor mother," he remarked anxiously, "do you think she will pull through, Professor? Betty says that Dr. Wilson has given her no idea yet about the nature of the trouble."

Kennedy thought a moment. "Of course," he said, "your mother has had no such relative amount of the poison as Buster has had. I think that undoubtedly she will recover by purely natural means. I hope so. But if not, here is the apparatus," and he patted the vividiffusion tubes in their glass case, "that will save her, too."

As well as I could I explained to Reginald the nature of the toxin that Kennedy had discovered. Duncan listened, putting in a question now and then. But it was evident that his thoughts were on something else, and now and then Reginald, breaking into his old humor, rallied him about thinking of Betty.

A low exclamation from both Kennedy and the surgeon attracted us.

Dora Sears had moved.

The operation of the apparatus was stopped, the artery and vein had been joined up, and she was slowly coming out from under the effects of the anesthetic.

As we gathered about her, at a little distance, we heard her cry in her delirium, "I—I would have— done—anything—for him."

We strained our ears. Was she talking of the blackmailer, Dr. Hopf?

"Who?" asked Craig, bending over close to her ear.

"I—I would—have done anything," she repeated as if someone had contradicted her. She went on, dreamily, ramblingly, "He—is—is—my brother. I——"

She stopped through weakness.

"Where is Dr. Hopf?" asked Kennedy, trying to recall her fleeting attention.

"Dr. Hopf? Dr. Hopf?" she repeated, then smiling to herself as people will when they are leaving the borderline of anesthesia, she repeated the name, "Hopf?"

"Yes," persisted Kennedy.

"There is no Dr. Hopf," she added. "Tell me— did—did they——"

"No Dr. Hopf?" Kennedy insisted.

She had lapsed again into half insensibility.

He rose and faced us, speaking rapidly.

"New York seems to have a mysterious and uncanny attraction for odds and ends of humanity, among them the great army of adventuresses. In

fact there often seems to be something decidedly
adventurous about the nursing profession. This is
a girl of unusual education in medicine. Evidently
she has traveled—her letters show it. Many of
them show that she has been in Italy. Perhaps it
was there that she heard of the drug that has been
used in this case. It was she who injected the germ-
free toxin, first into the dog, then into Mrs. Blake,
she who wrote the blackmail letter which was to
have explained the death."

He paused. Evidently she had heard dimly, was
straining every effort to hear. In her effort she
caught sight of our faces.

Suddenly, as if she had seen an apparition, she
raised herself with almost superhuman strength.

"Duncan!" she cried. "Duncan! Why—didn't
you—get away—while there was time—after you
warned me?"

Kennedy had wheeled about and was facing us.
He was holding in his hand some of the letters he
had taken from the trunk. Among others was a
folded piece of parchment that looked like a diploma. He unfolded it and we bent over to read.

It was a diploma from the Central Western College of Nursing. As I read the name written in, it
was with a shock. It was not Dora Sears, but Dora
Baldwin.

"A very clever plot," he ground out, taking a
step nearer us. "With the aid of your sister and a
disreputable gang of chauffeurs you planned to
hasten the death of Mrs. Blake, to hasten the in-
heritance of the Blake fortune by your future wife.
I think your creditors will have less chance of collecting now than ever, Duncan Baldwin."

CHAPTER XXII

THE DEVIL WORSHIPERS

TRAGIC though the end of the young nurse, Dora Baldwin, had been, the scheme of her brother, in which she had become fatally involved, was by no means as diabolical as that in the case that confronted us a short time after that.

I recall this case particularly not only because it was so weird but also because of the unique manner in which it began.

"I am damned—Professor Kennedy—damned!"

The words rang out as the cry of a lost soul. A terrible look of inexpressible anguish and fear was written on the face of Craig's visitor, as she uttered them and sank back, trembling, in the easy chair, mentally and physically convulsed.

As nearly as I had been able to follow, Mrs. Veda Blair's story had dealt mostly with a Professor and Madame Rapport and something she called the "Red Lodge" of the "Temple of the Occult."

She was not exactly a young woman, although she was a very attractive one. She was of an age that is, perhaps, even more interesting than youth.

Veda Blair, I knew, had been, before her recent marriage to Seward Blair, a Treacy, of an old, though somewhat unfortunate, family. Both the Blairs and the Treacys had been intimate and old Seward Blair, when he died about a year before, had left his fortune to his son on the condition that he marry Veda Treacy.

"Sometimes," faltered Mrs. Blair, "it is as though I had two souls. One of them is dispossessed of its body and the use of its organs and is frantic at the sight of the other that has crept in."

She ended her rambling story, sobbing the terrible words, "Oh—I have committed the unpardonable sin—I am anathema—I am damned—damned!"

She said nothing of what terrible thing she had done and Kennedy, for the present, did not try to lead the conversation. But of all the stories that I have heard poured forth in the confessional of the detective's office, hers, I think, was the wildest.

Was she insane? At least I felt that she was sincere. Still, I wondered what sort of hallucination Craig had to deal with, as Veda Blair repeated the incoherent tale of her spiritual vagaries.

Almost, I had begun to fancy that this was a case for a doctor, not for a detective, when suddenly she asked a most peculiar question.

"Can people affect you for good or evil, merely by thinking about you?" she queried. Then a shudder passed over her. "They may be thinking about me now!" she murmured in terror.

Her fear was so real and her physical distress so evident that Kennedy, who had been listening silently for the most part, rose and hastened to reassure her.

"Not unless you make your own fears affect yourself and so play into their hands," he said earnestly.

Veda looked at him a moment, then shook her head mournfully. "I have seen Dr. Vaughn," she said slowly.

Dr. Gilbert Vaughn, I recollected, was a well-known alienist in the city.

"He tried to tell me the same thing," she resumed doubtfully. "But—oh—I know what I know! I have felt the death thought—and he knows it!"

"What do you mean?" inquired Kennedy, leaning forward keenly.

"The death thought," she repeated, "a malicious psychic attack. Some one is driving me to death by it. I thought I could fight it off. I went away to escape it. Now I have come back—and I have not escaped. There is always that disturbing influence —always—directed against me. I know it will— kill me!"

I listened, startled. The death thought! What did it mean? What terrible power was it? Was it hypnotism? What was this fearsome, cruel belief, this modern witchcraft that could unnerve a rich and educated woman? Surely, after all, I felt that this was not a case for a doctor alone; it called for a detective.

"You see," she went on, heroically trying to control herself, "I have always been interested in the mysterious, the strange, the occult. In fact my father and my husband's father met through their common interest. So, you see, I come naturally by it.

"Not long ago I heard of Professor and Madame Rapport and their new Temple of the Occult. I went to it, and later Seward became interested, too. We have been taken into a sort of inner circle," she continued fearfully, as though there were some evil power in the very words themselves, "the Red Lodge."

"You have told Dr. Vaughn?" shot out Ken-

nedy suddenly, his eyes fixed on her face to see what
it would betray.

Veda leaned forward, as if to tell a secret, then
whispered in a low voice, "He knows. Like us—
he—he is a—Devil Worshiper!"

"What?" exclaimed Kennedy in wide-eyed astonishment.

"A Devil Worshiper," she repeated. "You
haven't heard of the Red Lodge?"

Kennedy nodded negatively. "Could you get us
—initiated?" he hazarded.

"P-perhaps," she hesitated, in a half-frightened
tone. "I—I'll try to get you in to-night."

She had risen, half dazed, as if her own temerity
overwhelmed her.

"You—poor girl," blurted out Kennedy, his sym-
pathies getting the upper hand for the moment as
he took the hand she extended mutely. "Trust me.
I will do all in my power, all in the power of modern
science to help you fight off this—influence."

There must have been something magnetic, hypnotic in his eye.

"I will stop here for you," she murmured, as she
almost fled from the room.

Personally, I cannot say that I liked the idea of
spying. It is not usually clean and wholesome. But
I realized that occasionally it was necessary.

"We are in for it now," remarked Kennedy half
humorously, half seriously, "to see the Devil in the
twentieth century."

"And I," I added, "I am, I suppose, to be the reporter to Satan."

We said nothing more about it, but I thought
much about it, and the more I thought, the more
incomprehensible the thing seemed. I had heard

of Devil Worship, but had always associated it with far-off Indian and other heathen lands—in fact never among Caucasians in modern times, except possibly in Paris. Was there such a cult here in my own city? I felt skeptical.

That night, however, promptly at the appointed time, a cab called for us, and in it was Veda Blair, nervous but determined.

"Seward has gone ahead," she explained. "I told him that a friend had introduced you, that you had studied the occult abroad. I trust you to carry it out."

Kennedy reassured her.

The curtains were drawn and we could see nothing outside, though we must have been driven several miles, far out into the suburbs.

At last the cab stopped. As we left it we could see nothing of the building, for the cab had entered a closed courtyard.

"Who enters the Red Lodge?" challenged a sepulchral voice at the porte-cochère. "Give the password!"

"The Serpent's Tooth," Veda answered.

"Who are these?" asked the voice.

"Neophytes," she replied, and a whispered parley followed.

"Then enter!" announced the voice at length.

It was a large room into which we were first ushered, to be inducted into the rites of Satan.

There seemed to be both men and women, perhaps half a dozen votaries. Seward Blair was already present. As I met him, I did not like the look in his eye; it was too stary. Dr. Vaughn was there, too, talking in a low tone to Madame Rapport. He shot a quick look at us. His were not eyes but gimlets that tried to bore into your very soul. Chatting with Seward Blair was a Mrs. Langhorne, a very beautiful woman. To-night she seemed to be unnaturally excited.

All seemed to be on most intimate terms, and, as we waited a few minutes, I could not help recalling a sentence from Huysmans: "The worship of the Devil is no more insane than the worship of God. The worshipers of Satan are mystics—mystics of an unclean sort, it is true, but mystics none the less."

I did not agree with it, and did not repeat it, of course, but a moment later I overheard Dr. Vaughn saying to Kennedy: "Hoffman brought the Devil into modern life. Poe forgoes the aid of demons and works patiently and precisely by the scientific method. But the result is the same."

"Yes," agreed Kennedy for the sake of appearances, "in a sense, I suppose, we are all devil worshipers in modern society—always have been. It is fear that rules and we fear the bad—not the good."

As we waited, I felt, more and more, the sense of the mysterious, the secret, the unknown which have always exercised a powerful attraction on the human mind. Even the aeroplane and the submarine, the X-ray and wireless have not banished the occult.

In it, I felt, there was fascination for the frivolous and deep appeal to the intellectual and spiritual. The Temple of the Occult had evidently been designed to appeal to both types. I wondered how, like Lucifer, it had fallen. The prime requisite, I could guess already, however, was—money. Was it in its worship of the root of all evil that it had fallen?

We passed soon into another room, hung entirely in red, with weird, cabalistic signs all about, on the walls. It was uncanny, creepy.

A huge reproduction in plaster of one of the most sardonic of Notre Dame's gargoyles seemed to preside over everything—a terrible figure in such an atmosphere.

As we entered, we were struck by the blinding glare of the light, in contrast with the darkened room in which we had passed our brief novitiate, if it might be called such.

Suddenly the lights were extinguished.

The great gargoyle shone with an infernal light of its own!

"Phosphorescent paint," whispered Kennedy to me.

Still, it did not detract from the weird effect to know what caused it.

There was a startling noise in the general hush.

"Sata!" cried one of the devotees.

A door opened and there appeared the veritable priest of the Devil—pale of face, nose sharp, mouth bitter, eyes glassy.

"That is Rapport," Vaughn whispered to me.

The worshipers crowded forward.

Without a word, he raised his long, lean forefinger and began to single them out impressively. As he did so, each spoke, as if imploring aid.

He came to Mrs. Langhorne.

"I have tried the charm," she cried earnestly, "and the one whom I love still hates me, while the one I hate loves me!"

"Concentrate!" replied the priest, "concentrate! Think always 'I love him. He must love me. I want him to love me. I love him. He must love
16

me.' Over and over again you must think it. Then
the other side, 'I hate him. He must leave me. I
want him to leave me. I hate him—hate him.' "

Around the circle he went.

At last his lean finger was outstretched at Veda.
It seemed as if some imp of the perverse were compelling her unwilling tongue to unlock its secrets.

"Sometimes," she cried in a low, tremulous voice,
"something seems to seize me, as if by the hand
and urge me onward. I canot flee from it."

"Defend yourself!" answered the priest subtly.
"When you know that some one is trying to kill you
mentally, defend yourself! Work against it by
every means in your power. Discourage! Intimi-
date! Destroy!"

I marveled at these cryptic utterances. They
shadowed a modern Black Art, of which I had had
no conception—a recrudescence in other language of
the age-old dualism of good and evil. It was a sort
of mental malpractice.

"Over and over again," he went on speaking to
her, "the same thought is to be repeated against an
enemy. 'You know you are going to die! You
know you are going to die!' Do it an hour, two
hours, at a time. Others can help you, all thinking
in unison the same thought."

What was this, I asked myself breathlessly—a
new transcendental toxicology?

Slowly, a strange mephitic vapor seemed to ex-
hale into the room—or was it my heightened imagination?

CHAPTER XXIII

THE PSYCHIC CURSE

THERE came a sudden noise—nameless—striking terror, low, rattling. I stood rooted to the spot. What was it that held me? Was it an atavistic joy in the horrible or was it merely a blasphemous curiosity?

I scarcely dared to look.

At last I raised my eyes. There was a live snake, upraised, his fangs striking out viciously—a rattler!

I would have drawn back and fled, but Craig caught my arm.

"Caged," he whispered monosyllabically.

I shuddered. This, at least, was no drawing-room diablerie.

"It is Ophis," intoned Rapport, "the Serpent—the one active form in Nature that cannot be ungraceful!"

The appearance of the basilisk seemed to heighten the tension.

At last it broke loose and then followed the most terrible blasphemies. The disciples, now all frenzied, surrounded closer the priest, the gargoyle and the serpent.

They worshiped with howls and obscenities. Mad laughter mingled with pale fear and wild scorn in turns were written on the hectic faces about me.

They had risen—it became a dance, a reel.

The votaries seemed to spin about on their axes, as it were, uttering a low, moaning chant as they whirled. It was a mania, the spirit of demonism. Something unseen seemed to urge them on.

Disgusted and stifled at the surcharged atmosphere, I would have tried to leave, but I seemed frozen to the spot. I could think of nothing except Poe's Masque of the Red Death.

Above all the rest whirled Seward Blair himself. The laugh of the fiend, for the moment, was in his mouth. An instant he stood—the oracle of the Demon—devil-possessed. Around whirled the frantic devotees, howling.

Shrilly he cried, "The Devil is in me!"

Forward staggered the devil dancer—tall, haggard, with deep sunken eyes and matted hair, face now smeared with dirt and blood-red with the reflection of the strange, unearthly phosphorescence.

He reeled slowly through the crowd, crooning a quatrain, in a low, monotonous voice, his eyelids drooping and his head forward on his breast:

> If the Red Slayer think he slays,
>   Or the slain think he is slain,
> They know not well the subtle ways
>   I keep and pass and turn again!

Entranced the whirling crowd paused and watched. One of their number had received the "power."

He was swaying slowly to and fro.

"Look!" whispered Kennedy.

His fingers twitched, his head wagged uncannily. Perspiration seemed to ooze from every pore. His breast heaved.

He gave a sudden yell—ear-piercing. Then followed a screech of hellish laughter.

The dance had ended, the dancers spellbound at the sight.

He was whirling slowly, eyes protruding now, mouth foaming, chest rising and falling like a bellows, muscles quivering.

Cries, vows, imprecations, prayers, all blended in an infernal hubbub.

With a burst of ghastly, guttural laughter, he shrieked, "I *am* the Devil!"

His arms waved—cutting, sawing, hacking the air.

The votaries, trembling, scarcely moved, breathed, as he danced.

Suddenly he gave a great leap into the air—then fell, motionless. They crowded around him. The fiendish look was gone—the demoniac laughter stilled.

It was over.

The tension of the orgy had been too much for us. We parted, with scarcely a word, and yet I could feel that among the rest there was a sort of unholy companionship.

Silently, Kennedy and I drove away in the darkened cab, this time with Seward and Veda Blair and Mrs. Langhorne.

For several minutes not a word was said. I was, however, much occupied in watching the two women. It was not because of anything they said or did. That was not necessary. But I felt that there was a feud, something that set them against each other.

"How would Rapport use the death thought, I wonder?" asked Craig speculatively, breaking the silence.

Blair answered quickly. "Suppose some one tried to break away, to renounce the Lodge, expose its secrets. They would treat him so as to make him harmless—perhaps insane, confused, afraid to talk, paralyzed, or even to commit suicide or be killed in an accident. They would put the death thought on him!"

Even in the prosaic jolting of the cab, away from the terrible mysteries of the Red Lodge, one could feel the spell.

The cab stopped. Seward was on his feet in a moment and handing Mrs. Langhorne out at her home. For a moment they paused on the steps for an exchange of words.

In that moment I caught flitting over the face of Veda a look of hatred, more intense, more real, more awful than any that had been induced under the mysteries of the rites at the Lodge.

It was gone in an instant, and as Seward rejoined us I felt that, with Mrs. Langhorne gone, there was less restraint. I wondered whether it was she who had inspired the fear in Veda.

Although it was more comfortable, the rest of our journey was made in silence and the Blairs dropped us at our apartment with many expressions of cordiality as we left them to proceed to their own.

"Of one thing I'm sure," I remarked, entering the room where only a few short hours before Mrs. Blair had related her strange tale. "Whatever the cause of it, the devil dancers don't sham."

Kennedy did not reply. He was apparently wrapped up in the consideration of the remarkable events of the evening.

As for myself, it was a state of affairs which, the

day before, I should have pronounced utterly beyond the wildest bounds of the imagination of the
most colorful writer. Yet here it was; I had seen it.

I glanced up to find Kennedy standing by the
light examining something he had apparently picked
up at the Red Lodge. I bent over to look at it,
too. It was a little glass tube.

"An ampoule, I believe the technical name of such
a container is," he remarked, holding it closer to the
light.

In it were the remains of a dried yellow substance, broken up minutely, resembling crystals.

"Who dropped it?" I asked.

"Vaughn, I think," he replied. "At least, I saw
him near Blair, stooping over him, at the end, and
I imagine this is what I saw gleaming for an instant
in the light."

Kennedy said nothing more, and for my part I
was thoroughly at sea and could make nothing out
of it all.

"What object can such a man as Dr. Vaughn possibly have in frequenting such a place?" I asked at
length, adding, "And there's that Mrs. Langhorne
—she was interesting, too."

Kennedy made no direct reply. "I shall have
them shadowed to-morrow," he said briefly, "while
I am at work in the laboratory over this ampoule."

As usual, also, Craig had begun on his scientific
studies long before I was able to shake myself loose
from the nightmares that haunted me after our
weird experience of the evening.

He had already given the order to an agency for
the shadowing, and his next move was to start me
out, also, looking into the history of those concerned in the case. As far as I was able to deter-

mine, Dr. Vaughn had an excellent reputation, and I could find no reason whatever for his connection with anything of the nature of the Red Lodge. The Rapports seemed to be nearly unknown in New York, although it was reported that they had come from Paris lately. Mrs. Langhorne was a divorcée from one of the western states, but little was known about her, except that she always seemed to be well supplied with money. It seemed to be well known in the circle in which Seward Blair moved that he was friendly with her, and I had about reached the conclusion that she was unscrupulously making use of his friendship, perhaps was not above such a thing as blackmail.

Thus the day passed, and we heard no word from Veda Blair, although that was explained by the shadows, whose trails crossed in a most unexpected manner. Their reports showed that there was a meeting at the Red Lodge during the late afternoon, at which all had been present except Dr. Vaughn. We learned also from them the exact location of the Lodge, in an old house just across the line in Westchester.

It was evidently a long and troublesome analysis that Craig was engaged in at the laboratory, for it was some hours after dinner that night when he came into the apartment, and even then he said nothing, but buried himself in some of the technical works with which his library was stocked. He said little, but I gathered that he was in great doubt about something, perhaps, as much as anything, about how to proceed with so peculiar a case.

It was growing late, and Kennedy was still steeped in his books, when the door of the apartment, which we happened to have left unlocked, was suddenly thrown open and Seward Blair burst in on us, wildly excited.

"Veda is gone!" he cried, before either of us could ask him what was the matter.

"Gone?" repeated Kennedy. "How—where?"

"I don't know," Blair blurted out breathlessly. "We had been out together this afternoon, and I returned with her. Then I went out to the club after dinner for a while, and when I got back I missed her—not quarter of an hour ago. I burst into her room—and there I found this note. Read it. I don't know what to do. No one seems to know what has become of her. I've called up all over and then thought perhaps you might help me, might know some friend of hers that I don't know, with whom she might have gone out."

Blair was plainly eager for us to help him. Kennedy took the paper from him. On it, in a trembling hand, were scrawled some words, evidently addressed to Blair himself:

"You would forgive me and pity me if you knew what I have been through.

"When I refused to yield my will to the will of the Lodge I suppose I aroused the enmity of the Lodge.

"To-night as I lay in bed, alone, I felt that my hour had come, that mental forces that were almost irresistible were being directed against me.

"I realized that I must fight not only for my sanity but for my life.

"For hours I have fought that fight.

"But during those hours, some one, I won't say who, seemed to have developed such psychic faculties of penetration that they were able to make their bodies pass through the walls of my room.

"At last I am conquered. I pray that you———"

The writing broke off abruptly, as if she had left it in wild flight.

"What does that mean?" asked Kennedy, "the 'will of the Lodge'?"

Blair looked at us keenly. I fancied that there was even something accusatory in the look. "Perhaps it was some mental reservation on her part," he suggested. "You do not know yourself of any reason why she should fear anything, do you?" he asked pointedly.

Kennedy did not betray even by the motion of an eyelash that we knew more than we should ostensibly.

There was a tap at the door. I sprang to open it, thinking perhaps, after all, it was Veda herself.

Instead, a man, a stranger, stood there.

"Is this Professor Kennedy?" he asked, touching his hat.

Craig nodded.

"I am from the psychopathic ward of the City Hospital—an orderly, sir," the man introduced.

"Yes," encouraged Craig, "what can I do for you?"

"A Mrs. Blair has just been brought in, sir, and we can't find her husband. She's calling for you now."

Kennedy stared from the orderly to Seward Blair, startled, speechless.

"What has happened?" asked Blair anxiously. "I am Mr. Blair."

The orderly shook his head. He had delivered his message. That was all he knew.

"What do you suppose it is?" I asked, as we sped

across town in a taxicab. "Is it the curse that she dreaded?"

Kennedy said nothing and Blair appeared to hear nothing. His face was drawn in tense lines.

The psychopathic ward is at once one of the most interesting and one of the most depressing departments of a large city hospital, harboring, as it does, all from the more or less harmless insane to violent alcoholics and wrecked drug fiends.

Mrs. Blair, we learned, had been found hatless, without money, dazed, having fallen, after an apparently aimless wandering in the streets.

For the moment she lay exhausted on the white bed of the ward, eyes glazed, pupils contracted, pulse now quick, now almost evanescent, face drawn, breathing difficult, moaning now and then in physical and mental agony.

Until she spoke it was impossible to tell what had happened, but the ambulance surgeon had found a little red mark on her white forearm and had pointed it out, evidently with the idea that she was suffering from a drug.

At the mere sight of the mark, Blair stared as though hypnotized. Leaning over to Kennedy, so that the others could not hear, he whispered, "It is the mark of the serpent!"

Our arrival had been announced to the hospital physician, who entered and stood for a moment looking at the patient.

"I think it is a drug—a poison," he said meditatively.

"You haven't found out yet what is is, then?" asked Craig.

The physician shook his head doubtfully. "Whatever it is," he said slowly, "it is closely allied to the

cyanide groups in its rapacious activity. I haven't
the slightest idea of its true nature, but it seems to
have a powerful affinity for important nerve centers
of respiration and muscular coördination, as well as
for disorganizing the blood. I should say that it
produces death by respiratory paralysis and convulsions. To my mind it is an exact, though perhaps
less active, counterpart of hydrocyanic acid."

Kennedy had been listening intently at the start,
but before the physician had finished he had bent
over and made a ligature quickly with his handkerchief.

Then he dispatched a messenger with a note.
Next he cut about the minute wound on her arm
until the blood flowed, cupping it to increase the
flow. Now and then he had them administer a little
stimulant.

He had worked rapidly, while Blair watched him
with a sort of fascination.

"Get Dr. Vaughn," ordered Craig, as soon as he
had a breathing spell after his quick work, adding,
"and Professor and Madame Rapport. Walter, attend to that, will you? I think you will find an officer outside. You'll have to compel them to come,
if they won't come otherwise," he added, giving the
address of the Lodge, as we had found it.

Blair shot a quick look at him, as though Craig in
his knowledge were uncanny. Apparently, the address had been a secret which he thought we did
not know.

I managed to find an officer and dispatch him for
the Rapports. A hospital orderly, I thought, would
serve to get Dr. Vaughn.

CHAPTER XXIV

THE SERPENT'S TOOTH

I HAD scarcely returned to the ward when, suddenly, an unnatural strength seemed to be infused into Veda.

She had risen in bed.

"It shall not catch me!" she cried in a new paroxysm of nameless terror. "No—no—it is pursuing me. I am never out of its grasp. I have been thought six feet underground—I know it. There it is again—still driving me—still driving me!

"Will it never stop? Will no one stop it? Save me! It—is the death thought!"

She had risen convulsively and had drawn back in abject, cowering terror. What was it she saw? Evidently it was very real and very awful. It pursued her relentlessly.

As she lay there, rolling her eyes about, she caught sight of us and recognized us for the first time, although she had been calling for us.

"They had the thought on you, too, Professor Kennedy," she almost screamed. "Hour after hour, Rapport and the rest repeated over and over again, 'Why does not some one kill him? Why does he not die?' They knew you—even when I brought you to the Red Lodge. They thought you were a spy."

I turned to Kennedy. He had advanced and was

leaning over to catch every word. Blair was standing behind me and she had not seen her husband
yet. A quick glance showed me that he was trembling from head to foot like a leaf, as though he,
too, were pursued by the nameless terror.

"What did they do?" Kennedy asked in a low
tone.

Fearfully, gripping the bars of the iron bed, as
though they were some tangible support for her
mind, she answered: "They would get together.
'Now, all of you,' they said, 'unite yourselves in
thought against our enemy, against Kennedy, that
he must leave off persecuting us. He is ripe for
destruction!'"

Kennedy glanced sidewise at me, with a significant look.

"God grant," she implored, "that none haunt me
for what I have done in my ignorance!"

Just then the door opened and my messenger entered, accompanied by Dr. Vaughn.

I had turned to catch the expression on Blair's
face just in time. It was a look of abject appeal.

Before Dr. Vaughn could ask a question, or fairly
take in the situation, Kennedy had faced him.

"What was the purpose of all that elaborate
mummery out at the Red Lodge?" asked Kennedy
pointblank.

I think I looked at Craig in no less amazement
than Vaughn. In spite of the dramatic scenes
through which we had passed, the spell of the occult had not fallen on him for an instant.

"Mummery?" repeated Dr. Vaughn, bending his
penetrating eyes on Kennedy, as if he would force
him to betray himself first.

"Yes," reiterated Craig. "You know as well as

I do that it has been said that it is a well-established
fact that the world wants to be deceived and is willing to pay for the privilege."

Dr. Vaughn still gazed from one to the other of
us defiantly.

"You know what I mean," persisted Kennedy,
"the mumbo-jumbo—just as the Haitian obi man
sticks pins in a doll or melts a wax figure of his
enemy. That is supposed to be an outward sign.
But back of this terrible power that people believe
moves in darkness and mystery is something tangible—something real."

Dr. Vaughn looked up sharply at him, I think
mistaking Kennedy's meaning. If he did, all doubt
that Kennedy attributed anything to the supernatural
was removed as he went on: "At first I had no explanation of the curious events I have just witnessed,
and the more I thought about them, the more obscure did they seem.

"I have tried to reason the thing out," he continued thoughtfully. "Did auto-suggestion, self-
hypnotism explain what I have seen? Has Veda
Blair been driven almost to death by her own fears
only?"

No one interrupted and he answered his own
question. "Somehow the idea that it was purely
fear that had driven her on did not satisfy me. As
I said, I wanted something more tangible. I could
not help thinking that it was not merely subjective.
There was something objective, some force at work,
something more than psychic in the result achieved
by this criminal mental marauder, whoever it is."

I was following Kennedy's reasoning now closely.
As he proceeded, the point that he was making
seemed more clear to me.

Persons of a certain type of mind could be really mentally unbalanced by such methods which we had heard outlined, where the mere fact of another trying to exert power over them became known to them.   They would, as a matter of fact, unbalance themselves, thinking about and fighting off imaginary terrors.

Such people, I could readily see, might be quickly controlled, and in the wake of such control would follow stifled love, wrecked homes, ruined fortunes, suicide and even death.

Dr. Vaughn leaned forward critically.   "What did you conclude, then, was the explanation of what you saw last night?" he asked sharply.

Kennedy met his question squarely, without flinching.   "It looks to me," he replied quietly, "like a sort of hystero-epilepsy.   It is well known, I believe, to demonologists—those who have studied this sort of thing.   They have recognized the contortions, the screams, the wild, blasphemous talk, the cataleptic rigidity.   They are epileptiform."

Vaughn said nothing, but continued to weigh Kennedy as if in a balance.   I, who knew him, knew that it would take a greater than Vaughn to find him wanting, once Kennedy chose to speak.   As for Vaughn, was he trying to hide behind some technicality in medical ethics?

"Dr. Vaughn," continued Craig, as if goading him to the point of breaking down his calm silence, "you are specialist enough to know these things as well, better than I do.   You must know that epilepsy is one of the most peculiar diseases.

"The victim may be in good physical condition, apparently.   In fact, some hardly know that they have it.   But it is something more than merely the fits. Always there is something wrong mentally. It is not the motor disturbance so much as the disturbance of consciousness."

Kennedy was talking slowly, deliberately, so that none could drop a link in the reasoning.

"Perhaps one in ten epileptics has insane periods, more or less," he went on, "and there is no more dangerous form of insanity. Self-consciousness is lost, and in this state of automatism the worst of crimes have been committed without the subsequent knowledge of the patient. In that state they are no more responsible than are the actors in one's dreams."

The hospital physician entered, accompanied by Craig's messenger, breathless. Craig almost seized the package from his hands and broke the seal.

"Ah—this is what I wanted," he exclaimed, with an air of relief, forgetting for the time the exposition of the case that he was engaged in. "Here I have some anti-crotalus venine, of Drs. Flexner and Noguchi. Fortunately, in the city it is within easy reach."

Quickly, with the aid of the physician he injected it into Veda's arm.

"Of all substances in nature," he remarked, still at work over the unfortunate woman, "none is so little known as the venom of serpents."

It was a startling idea which the sentence had raised in my mind. All at once I recalled the first remark of Seward Blair, in which he had repeated the password that had admitted us into the Red Lodge—"the Serpent's Tooth." Could it have been that she had really been bitten at some of the orgies by the serpent which they worshiped hideously hissing in its cage? I was sure that, at least until they

17

were compelled, none would say anything about it. Was that the interpretation of the almost hynotized look on Blair's face?

"We know next to nothing of the composition of the protein bodies in the venoms which have such terrific, quick physiological effects," Kennedy was saying. "They have been studied, it is true, but we cannot really say that they are understood—or even that there are any adequate tests by which they can be recognized. The fact is, that snake venoms are about the safest of poisons for the criminal."

Kennedy had scarcely propounded this startling idea when a car was heard outside. The Rapports had arrived, with the officer I had sent after them, protesting and threatening.

They quieted down a bit as they entered, and after a quick glance around saw who was present.

Professor Rapport gave one glance at the victim lying exhausted on the bed, then drew back, melodramatically, and cried, "The Serpent—the mark of the serpent!"

For a moment Kennedy gazed full in the eyes of them all.

"*Was* it a snake bite?" he asked slowly, then, turning to Mrs. Blair, after a quick glance, he went on rapidly, "The first thing to ascertain is whether the mark consists of two isolated punctures, from the poison-conducting teeth or fangs of the snake, which are constructed like a hypodermic needle."

The hospital physician had bent over her at the words, and before Kennedy could go on interrupted: "This was not a snake bite; it was more likely from an all-glass hypodermic syringe with a platinum-iridium needle."

Professor Rapport, priest of the Devil, advanced

a step menacingly toward Kennedy. "Remember,"
he said in a low, angry tone, "remember—you are
pledged to keep the secrets of the Red Lodge!"

Craig brushed aside the sophistry with a sentence.
"I do not recognize any secrets that I have to keep
about the meeting this afternon to which you summoned the Blairs and Mrs. Langhorne, according
to reports from the shadows I had placed on Mrs.
Langhorne and Dr. Vaughn."

If there is such a thing as the evil eye, Rapport's
must have been a pair of them, as he realized that
Kennedy had resorted to the simple devices of shadowing the devotees.

A cry, almost a shriek, startled us. Kennedy's
encounter with Rapport had had an effect which
none of us had considered. The step or two in ad-
vance which the prophet had taken had brought him
into the line of vision of the still half-stupefied Veda
lying back of Kennedy on the hospital cot.

The mere sight of him, the sound of his voice and
the mention of the Red Lodge had been sufficient
to penetrate that stupor. She was sitting bolt up-
right, a ghastly, trembling specter. Slowly a smile
seemed to creep over the cruel face of the mystic.
Was it not a recognition of his hypnotic power?

Kennedy turned and laid a gentle hand on the
quaking convulsed figure of the woman. One could
feel the electric tension in the air, the battle of two
powers for good or evil. Which would win—the
old fascination of the occult or the new power of
science?

It was a dramatic moment. Yet not so dramatic
as the outcome. To my surprise, neither won.

Suddenly she caught sight of her husband. Her

face changed. All the prehistoric jealousy of which woman is capable seemed to blaze forth.

"I will defend myself!" she cried. "I will fight back! She shall not win—she shall not have you— no—she shall not—never!"

I recalled the strained feeling between the two women that I had noticed in the cab. Was it Mrs. Langhorne who had been the disturbing influence, whose power she feared, over herself and over her husband?

Rapport had fallen back a step, but not from the mind of Kennedy.

"Here," challenged Craig, facing the group and drawing from his pocket the glass ampoule, "I picked this up at the Red Lodge last night."

He held it out in his hand before the Rapports so that they could not help but see it. Were they merely good actors? They betrayed nothing, at least by face or action.

"It is crotalin," he announced, "the venom of the rattlesnake—crotalus horridus. It has been noticed that persons suffering from certain diseases of which epilepsy is one, after having been bitten by a rattle-snake, if they recover from the snake bite, are cured of the disease."

Kennedy was forging straight ahead now in his exposure. "Crotalin," he continued, "is one of the new drugs used in the treatment of epilepsy. But it is a powerful two-edged instrument. Some one who knew the drug, who perhaps had used it, has tried an artificial bite of a rattler on Veda Blair, not for epilepsy, but for another, diabolical purpose, think-ing to cover up the crime, either as the result of the so-called death thought of the Lodge or as the bite of the real rattler at the Lodge."

Kennedy had at last got under Dr. Vaughn's guard. All his reticence was gone.

"I joined the cult," he confessed. "I did it in order to observe and treat one of my patients for epilepsy. I justified myself. I said, 'I will be the exposer, not the accomplice, of this modern Satanism.' I joined it and——"

"There is no use trying to shield anyone, Vaughn," rapped out Kennedy, scarcely taking time to listen. "An epileptic of the most dangerous criminal type has arranged this whole elaborate setting as a plot to get rid of the wife who brought him his fortune and now stands in the way of his unholy love of Mrs. Langhorne. He used you to get the poison with which you treated him. He used the Rapports with money to play on her mysticism by their so-called death thought, while he watched his opportunity to inject the fatal crotalin."

Craig faced the criminal, whose eyes now showed more plainly than words his deranged mental condition, and in a low tone added, "The Devil *is* in you, Seward Blair!"

CHAPTER XXV

THE "HAPPY DUST"

VEDA BLAIR'S rescue from the strange use that was made of the venom came at a time when the city was aroused as it never had been before over the nation-wide agitation against drugs.

Already, it will be recalled, Kennedy and I had had some recent experience with dope fiends of various kinds, but this case I set down because it drew us more intimately into the crusade.

"I've called on you, Professor Kennedy, to see if I can't interest you in the campaign I am planning against drugs."

Mrs. Claydon Sutphen, social leader and suffragist, had scarcely more than introduced herself when she launched earnestly into the reason for her visit to us.

"You don't realize it, perhaps," she continued rapidly, "but very often a little silver bottle of tablets is as much a necessary to some women of the smart set as cosmetics."

"I've heard of such cases," nodded Craig encouragingly.

"Well, you see I became interested in the subject," she added, "when I saw some of my own friends going down. That's how I came to plan the campaign in the first place."

She paused, evidently nervous. "I've been threat-

254

ened, too," she went on, "but I'm not going to give up the fight. People think that drugs are a curse only to the underworld, but they have no idea what inroads the habit has made in the upper world, too. Oh, it is awful!" she exclaimed.

Suddenly, she leaned over and whispered, "Why, there's my own sister, Mrs. Garrett. She began taking drugs after an operation, and now they have a terrible hold on her. I needn't try to conceal anything. It's all been published in the papers—everybody knows it. Think of it—divorced, disgraced, all through these cursed drugs! Dr. Coleman, our family physician, has done everything known to break up the habit, but he hasn't succeeded."

Dr. Coleman, I knew, was a famous society physician. If he had failed, I wondered why she thought a detective might succeed. But it was evidently another purpose she had in mind in introducing the subject.

"So you can understand what it all means to me, personally," she resumed, with a sigh. "I've studied the thing—I've been forced to study it. Why, now the exploiters are even making drug fiends of mere—children!"

Mrs. Sutphen spread out a crumpled sheet of note paper before us on which was written something in a trembling scrawl. "For instance, here's a letter I received only yesterday."

Kennedy glanced over it carefully. It was signed "A Friend," and read:

"I have heard of your drug war in the newspapers and wish to help you, only I don't dare to do so openly. But I can assure you that if you will investigate what I am about to tell you, you will soon be on the trail of those higher up in this terrible drug business. There is a little center of the traffic on West 66th Street, just off Broadway. I cannot tell you more, but if you can investigate it, you will be doing more good than you can possibly realize now. There is one girl there, whom they call 'Snowbird.' If you could only get hold of her quietly and place her in a sanitarium you might save her yet."

Craig was more than ordinarily interested. "And the children—what did you mean by that?"

"Why, it's literally true," asserted Mrs. Sutphen in a horrified tone. "Some of the victims are actually school children. Up there in 66th Street we have found a man named Armstrong, who seems to be very friendly with this young girl whom they call 'Snowbird.' Her real name, by the way, is Sawtelle, I believe. She can't be over eighteen, a mere child, yet she's a slave to the stuff."

"Oh, then you have actually already acted on the hint in the letter?" asked Craig.

"Yes," she replied, "I've had one of the agents of our Anti-Drug Society, a social worker, investigating the neighborhood."

Kennedy nodded for her to go on.

"I've even investigated myself a little, and now I want to employ some one to break the thing up. My husband had heard of you and so here I am. Can you help me?"

There was a note of appeal in her voice that was irresistible to a man who had the heart of Kennedy.

"Tell me just what you have discovered so far," he asked simply.

"Well," she replied slowly, "after my agent verified the contents of the letter, I watched until I saw this girl—she's a mere child, as I said—going to a cabaret in the neighborhood. What struck me was that I saw her go in looking like a wreck and come out a beautiful creature, with bright eyes, flushed cheeks, almost youthful again. A most remarkable girl she is, too," mused Mrs. Sutphen, "who always wears a white gown, white hat, white shoes and white stockings. It must be a mania with her."

Mrs. Sutphen seemed to have exhausted her small store of information, and as she rose to go Kennedy rose also. "I shall be glad to look into the case, Mrs. Sutphen," he promised. "I'm sure there is something that can be done—there must be."

"Thank you, ever so much," she murmured, as she paused at the door, something still on her mind. "And perhaps, too," she added, "you may run across my sister, Mrs. Garrett."

"Indeed," he assured her, "if there is anything I can possibly do that will assist you personally, I shall be only too happy to do it."

"Thank you again, ever so much," she repeated with just a little choke in her voice.

For several moments Kennedy sat contemplating the anonymous letter which she had left with him, studying both its contents and the handwriting.

"We must go over the ground up there again," he remarked finally. "Perhaps we can do better than Mrs. Sutphen and her drug investigator have done."

Half an hour later we had arrived and were sauntering along the street in question, walking slowly up and down in the now fast-gathering dusk. It was a typical cheap apartment block of variegated character, with people sitting idly on the narrow front steps and children spilling out into the roadway in imminent danger of their young lives from every passing automobile.

On the crowded sidewalk a creation in white hurried past us. One glance at the tense face in the flickering arc light was enough for Kennedy. He pulled my arm and we turned and followed at a safe distance.

She looked like a girl who could not have been more than eighteen, if she was as old as that. She was pretty, too, but already her face was beginning to look old and worn from the use of drugs. It was unmistakable.

In spite of the fact that she was hurrying, it was not difficult to follow her in the crowd, as she picked her way in and out, and finally turned into Broadway where the white lights were welcoming the night.

Under the glare of a huge electric sign she stopped a moment, then entered one of the most notorious of the cabarets.

We entered also at a discreet distance and sat down at a table.

"Don't look around, Walter," whispered Craig, as the waiter took our order, "but to your right is Mrs. Sutphen."

If he had mentioned any other name in the world, I could not have been more surprised. I waited impatiently until I could pick her out from the corner of my eye. Sure enough, it was Mrs. Sutphen and another woman. What they were doing there I could not imagine, for neither had the look of habitués of such a place.

I followed Kennedy's eye and found that he was gazing furtively at a flashily dressed young man who was sitting alone at the far end in a sort of booth upholstered in leather.

The girl in white, whom I was now sure was Miss

Sawtelle, went over and greeted him.   It was too
far to see just what happened, but the young woman
after sitting down rose and left almost immediately.
As nearly as I could make out, she had got something from him which she had dropped into her
handbag and was now hugging the handbag close to
herself almost as if it were gold.

We sat for a few minutes debating just what to
do, when Mrs. Sutphen and her friend rose.   As
she passed out, a quick, covert glance told us to follow.   We did so and the two turned into Broadway.

"Let me present you to Miss McCann," introduced Mrs. Sutphen as we caught up with them.
"Miss McCann is a social worker and trained investigator whom I'm employing."

We bowed, but before we could ask a question,
Mrs. Sutphen cried excitedly: "I think I have a clue,
anyway.   We've traced the source of the drugs at
least as far as that young fellow, 'Whitecap,' whom
you saw in there."

I had not recognized his face, although I had
undoubtedly seen pictures of him before.   But no
sooner had I heard the name than I recognized it as
that of one of the most notorious gang leaders on
the West Side.

Not only that, but Whitecap's gang played an important part in local politics.   There was scarcely
a form of crime or vice to which Whitecap and his
followers could not turn a skilled hand, whether it
was swinging an election, running a gambling club,
or dispensing "dope."

"You see," she explained, "even before I saw you,
my suspicions were aroused and I determined to obtain some of the stuff they are using up here, if possible.   I realized it would be useless for me to try to

get it myself, so I got Miss McCann from the Neighborhood House to try it. She got it and has turned the bottle over to me."

"May I see it?" asked Craig eagerly.

Mrs. Sutphen reached hastily into her handbag, drew forth a small brown glass bottle and handed it to him. Craig retreated into one of the less dark side streets. There he pulled out the paraffinned cork from the bottle, picked out a piece of cotton stuffed in the neck of the bottle and poured out some flat tablets that showed a glistening white in the palm of his hand. For an instant he regarded them.

"I may keep these?" he asked.

"Certainly," replied Mrs. Sutphen. "That's what I had Miss McCann get them for."

Kennedy dropped the bottle into his pocket.

"So that was the gang leader, 'Whitecap,'" he remarked as we turned again to Broadway.

"Yes," replied Mrs. Sutphen. "At certain hours, I believe he can be found at that cabaret selling this stuff, whatever it is, to anyone who comes properly introduced. The thing seems to be so open and notorious that it amounts to a scandal."

We parted a moment later, Mrs. Sutphen and Miss McCann to go to the settlement house, Craig and I to continue our investigations.

"First of all, Walter," he said as we swung aboard an uptown car, "I want to stop at the laboratory."

In his den, which had been the scene of so many triumphs, Kennedy began a hasty examination of the tablets, powdering one and testing it with one chemical after another.

"What are they?" I asked at length when he

seemed to have found the right reaction which gave him the clue.

"Happy dust," he answered briefly.

"Happy dust?" I repeated, looking at him a moment in doubt as to whether he was joking or serious. "What is that?"

"The Tenderloin name for heroin—a comparatively new derivative of morphine. It is really morphine treated with acetic acid which renders it more powerful than morphine alone."

"How do they take them? What's the effect?" I asked.

"The person who uses heroin usually powders the tablets and snuffs the powder up the nose," he answered. "In a short time, perhaps only two or three weeks, one can become a confirmed victim of 'happy dust.' And while one is under its influence he is morally, physically and mentally irresponsible."

Kennedy was putting away the paraphernalia he had used, meanwhile talking about the drug. "One of the worst aspects of it, too," he continued, "is the desire of the user to share his experience with some one else. This passing on of the habit, which seems to be one of the strongest desires of the drug fiend, makes him even more dangerous to society than he would otherwise be. It makes it harder for anyone once addicted to a drug to shake it off, for his friends will give him no chance. The only thing to do is to get the victim out of his environment and into an entirely new scene."

The laboratory table cleared again, Kennedy had dropped into a deep study.

"Now, why was Mrs. Sutphen there?" he asked aloud. "I can't think it was solely through her interest for that girl they call Snowbird. She was interested in her, but she made no attempt to interfere or to follow her. No, there must have been another reason."

"You don't think she's a dope fiend herself, do you?" I asked hurriedly.

Kennedy smiled. "Hardly, Walter. If she has any obsession on the subject, it is more likely to lead her to actual fanaticism against all stimulants and narcotics and everything connected with them. No, you might possibly persuade me that two and two equal five—but not seventeen. It's not very late. I think we might make another visit to that cabaret and see whether the same thing is going on yet."

CHAPTER XXVI

THE BINET TEST

WE rode downtown again and again sauntered in, this time with the theater crowd. Our first visit had been so quiet and unostentatious that the second attracted no attention or comment from the waiters, or anyone else.

As we sat down we glanced over, and there in his corner still was Whitecap. Apparently his supply of the dope was inexhaustible, for he was still dispensing it. As we watched the tenderloin habitués come and go, I came soon to recognize the signs by the mere look on the face—the pasty skin, the vacant eye, the nervous quiver of the muscles as though every organ and every nerve were crying out for more of the favorite nepenthe. Time and again I noticed the victims as they sat at the tables, growing more and more haggard and worn, until they could stand it no longer. Then they would retire, sometimes after a visit across the floor to Whitecap, more often directly, for they had stocked themselves up with the drug evidently after the first visit to him. But always they would come back, changed in appearance, with what seemed to be a new lease of life, but nevertheless still as recognizable as drug victims.

It was not long, as we waited, before another woman, older than Miss Sawtelle, but dressed in an extreme fashion, hurried into the cabaret and with scarcely a look to right or left went directly to Whitecap's corner. I noticed that she, too, had the look.

There was a surreptitious passing of a bottle in exchange for a treasury note, and she dropped into the seat beside him.

Before he could interfere, she had opened the bottle, crushed a tablet or two in a napkin, and was holding it to her face as though breathing the most exquisite perfume. With one quick inspiration of her breath after another, she was snuffing the powder up her nose.

Whitecap with an angry gesture pulled the napkin from her face, and one could fancy his snarl under his breath, "Say—do you want to get me in wrong here?"

But it was too late. Some at least of the happy dust had taken effect, at least enough to relieve the terrible pangs she must have been suffering.

As she rose and retired, with a hasty apology to Whitecap for her indiscretion, Kennedy turned to me and exclaimed, "Think of it. The deadliest of all habits is the simplest. No hypodermic; no pipe; no paraphernalia of any kind. It's terrible."

She returned to sit down and enjoy herself, careful not to obtrude herself on Whitecap lest he might become angry at the mere sight of her and treasure his anger up against the next time when she would need the drug.

Already there was the most marvelous change in her. She seemed captivated by the music, the dancing, the life which a few moments before she had totally disregarded.

She was seated alone, not far from us, and as

she glanced about Kennedy caught her eye. She allowed her gaze to rest on us for a moment, the signal for a mild flirtation which ended in our exchange of tables and we found ourselves opposite the drug fiend, who was following up the taking of the dope by a thin-stemmed glass of a liqueur.

I do not recall the conversation, but it was one of those inconsequential talks that Bohemians consider so brilliant and everybody else so vapid. As we skimmed from one subject to another, treating the big facts of life as if they were mere incidents and the little as if they overshadowed all else, I could see that Craig, who had a faculty of probing into the very soul of anyone, when he chose, was gradually leading around to a subject which I knew he wanted, above all others, to discuss.

It was not long before, as the most natural remark in the world following something he had made her say, just as a clever prestidigitator forces a card, he asked, "What was it I saw you snuffing over in the booth—happy dust?"

She did not even take the trouble to deny it, but nodded a brazen "Yes."

"How did you come to use it first?" he asked, careful not to give offense in either tone or manner.

"The usual way, I suppose," she replied with a laugh that sounded harsh and grating. "I was ill and I found out what it was the doctor was giving me."

"And then?"

"Oh, I thought I would use it only as long as it served my purpose and, when that was over, give it up."

"But——?" prompted Craig hypnotically.

"Instead, I was soon using six, eight, ten tablets

18

of heroin a day. I found that I needed that amount in order to live. Then it went up by leaps to twenty, thirty, forty."

"Suppose you couldn't get it, what then?"

"Couldn't get it?" she repeated with an unspeakable horror. "Once I thought I'd try to stop. But my heart skipped beats; then it seemed to pound away, as if trying to break through my ribs. I don't think heroin is like other drugs. When one has her 'coke'—that's cocaine—taken away, she feels like a rag. Fill her up and she can do anything again. But, heroin—I think one might murder to get it!"

The expression on the woman's face was almost tragic. I verily believe that she meant it.

"Why," she cried, "if anyone had told me a year ago that the time would ever come when I would value some tiny white tablets above anything else in the world, yes, and even above my immortal soul, I would have thought him a lunatic."

It was getting late, and as the woman showed no disposition to leave, Kennedy and I excused ourselves.

Outside Craig looked at me keenly. "Can you guess who that was?"

"Although she didn't tell us her name," I replied, "I am morally certain that it was Mrs. Garrett."

"Precisely," he answered, "and what a shame, too, for she must evidently once have been a woman of great education and refinement."

He shook his head sadly. "Walter, there isn't likely to be anything that we can do for some hours now. I have a little experiment I'd like to make. Suppose you publish for me a story in the *Star* about the campaign against drugs. Tell about what we have seen to-night, mention the cabaret by indirection and Whitecap directly. Then we can sit back and see what happens. We've got to throw a scare into them somehow, if we are going to smoke out anyone higher up than Whitecap. But you'll have to be careful, for if they suspect us our usefulness in the case will be over."

Together, Kennedy and I worked over our story far into the night down at the *Star* office, and the following day waited to see whether anything came of it.

It was with a great deal of interest tempered by fear that we dropped into the cabaret the following evening. Fortunately no one suspected us. In fact, having been there the night before, we had established ourselves, as it were, and were welcomed as old patrons and good spenders.

I noticed, however, that Whitecap was not there. The story had been read by such of the dope fiends as had not fallen too far to keep abreast of the times and these and the waiters were busy quietly warning off a line of haggard-eyed, disappointed patrons who came around, as usual.

Some of them were so obviously dependent on Whitecap that I almost regretted having written the story, for they must have been suffering the tortures of the damned.

It was in the midst of a reverie of this sort that a low exclamation from Kennedy recalled my attention. There was Snowbird with a man considerably older than herself. They had just come in and were looking about frantically for Whitecap. But Whitecap had been too frightened by the story in the *Star* to sell any more of the magic happy dust openly in the cabaret, at least.

The pair, nerve-racked and exhausted, sat down

mournfully in a seat near us, and as they talked earnestly in low tones we had an excellent opportunity for studying Armstrong for the first time.

He was not a bad-looking man, or even a weak one. In back of the dissipation of the drugs one fancied he could read the story of a brilliant life wrecked. But there was little left to admire or respect. As the couple talked earnestly, the one so old, the other so young in vice, I had to keep a tight rein on myself to prevent my sympathy for the wretched girl getting the better of common sense and kicking the older man out of doors.

Finally Armstrong rose to go, with a final imploring glance from the girl. Obviously she had persuaded him to forage about to secure the heroin, by hook or crook, now that the accustomed source of supply was cut off so suddenly.

It was also really our first chance to study the girl carefully under the light, for her entrance and exit the night before had been so hurried that we had seen comparatively little of her. Craig was watching her narrowly. Not only were the effects of the drug plainly evident on her face, but it was apparent that the snuffing the powdered tablets was destroying the bones in her nose, through shrinkage of the blood vessels, as well as undermining the nervous system and causing the brain to totter.

I was wondering whether Armstrong knew of any depot for the secret distribution of the drug. I could not believe that Whitecap was either the chief distributer or the financial head of the illegal traffic. I wondered who indeed was the man higher up. Was he an importer of the drug, or was he the representative of some chemical company not averse to making an illegal dollar now and then by dragging down his fellow man?

Kennedy and I were trying to act as if we were enjoying the cabaret show and not too much interested in the little drama that was being acted before us. I think little Miss Sawtelle noticed, however, that we were looking often her way. I was amazed, too, on studying her more closely to find that there was something indefinably queer about her, aside from the marked effect of the drugs she had been taking. What it was I was at a loss to determine, but I felt sure from the expression on Kennedy's face that he had noticed it also.

I was on the point of asking him if he, too, observed anything queer in the girl, when Armstrong hurried in and handed her a small package, then almost without a word stalked out again, evidently as much to Snowbird's surprise as to our own.

She had literally seized the package, as though she were drowning and grasping at a life buoy. Even the surprise at his hasty departure could not prevent her, however, from literally tearing the wrapper off, and in the sheltering shadow of the table cloth pouring forth the little white pellets in her lap, counting them as a miser counts his gold.

"The old thief!" she exclaimed aloud. "He's held out twenty-five!"

I don't know which it was that amazed me most, the almost childish petulance and ungovernable temper of the girl which made her cry out in spite of her surroundings and the circumstances, or the petty rapacity of the man who could stoop to such a low level as to rob her in this seeming underhand manner.

There was no time for useless repining now. The

call of outraged nature for its daily and hourly
quota of poison was too imperative. She dumped
the pellets back into the bottle hastily, and disappeared.

When she came back, it was with that expression
I had come to know so well. At least for a few
hours there was a respite for her from the terrific
pangs she had been suffering. She was almost happy,
smiling. Even that false happiness, I felt, was su-
perior to Armstrong's moral sense blunted by drugs.
I had begun to realize how lying, stealing, crimes of
all sorts might be laid at the door of this great evil.

In her haste to get where she could snuff the
heroin she had forgotten a light wrap lying on her
chair. As she returned for it, it fell to the floor.
Instantly Kennedy was on his feet, bending over to
pick it up.

She thanked him, and the smile lingered a moment on her face. It was enough. It gave Kennedy the chance to pursue a conversation, and in the
free and easy atmosphere of the cabaret to invite
her to sit over at our table.

At least all her nervousness was gone and she
chatted vivaciously. Kennedy said little. He was
too busy watching her. It was quite the opposite
of the case of Mrs. Garrett. Yet I was at a loss to
define what it was that I sensed.

Still the minutes sped past and we seemed to be
getting on famously. Unlike his action in the case
of the older woman where he had been sounding the
depths of her heart and mind, in this case his idea
seemed to be to allow the childish prattle to come
out and perhaps explain itself.

However, at the end of half an hour when we
seemed to be getting no further along, Kennedy did

not protest at her desire to leave us, "to keep a date," as she expressed it.

"Waiter, the check, please," ordered Kennedy leisurely.

When he received it, he seemed to be in no great hurry to pay it, but went over one item after another, then added up the footing again.

"Strange how some of these waiters grow rich?" Craig remarked finally with a gay smile.

The idea of waiters and money quickly brought some petty reminiscences to her mind. While she was still talking, Craig casually pulled a pencil out of his pocket and scribbled some figures on the back of the waiter's check.

From where I was sitting beside him, I could see that he had written some figures similar to the following:

5183
47395
654726
2964375
47293815
924738651
2146073859

"Here's a stunt," he remarked, breaking into the conversation at a convenient point. "Can you repeat these numbers after me?"

Without waiting for her to make excuse, he said quickly "5183." "5183," she repeated mechanically.

"47395," came in rapid succession, to which she replied, perhaps a little slower than before, "47395."

"Now, 654726," he said.

"654726," she repeated, I thought with some hesitation.

"Again, 2964375," he shot out.

"269," she hesitated, "73——" she stopped.

It was evident that she had reached the limit.

Kennedy smiled, paid the check and we parted at the door.

"What was all that rigmarole?" I inquired as the white figure disappeared down the street.

"Part of the Binet test, seeing how many digits one can remember. An adult ought to remember from eight to ten, in any order. But she has the mentality of a child. That is the queer thing about her. Chronologically she may be eighteen years or so old. Mentally she is scarcely more than eight. Mrs. Sutphen was right. They have made a fiend out of a mere child—a defective who never had a chance against them."

CHAPTER XXVII

THE LIE DETECTOR

As the horror of it all dawned on me, I hated Armstrong worse than ever, hated Whitecap, hated the man higher up, whoever he might be, who was enriching himself out of the defective, as well as the weakling, and the vicious—all three typified by Snowbird, Armstrong and Whitecap.

Having no other place to go, pending further developments of the publicity we had given the drug war in the *Star,* Kennedy and I decided on a walk home in the bracing night air.

We had scarcely entered the apartment when the hall boy called to us frantically: "Some one's been trying to get you all over town, Professor Kennedy. Here's the message. I wrote it down. An attempt has been made to poison Mrs. Sutphen. They said at the other end of the line that you'd know."

We faced each other aghast.

"My God!" exclaimed Kennedy. "Has that been the effect of our story, Walter? Instead of smoking out anyone—we've almost killed some one."

As fast as a cab could whisk us around to Mrs. Sutphen's we hurried.

"I warned her that if she mixed up in any such fight as this she might expect almost anything," remarked Mr. Sutphen nervously, as he met us in the reception room. "She's all right, now, I guess, but if it hadn't been for the prompt work of the ambulance surgeon I sent for, Dr. Coleman says she would have died in fifteen minutes."

"How did it happen?" asked Craig.

"Why, she usually drinks a glass of vichy and milk before retiring," replied Mr. Sutphen. "We don't know yet whether it was the vichy or the milk that was poisoned, but Dr. Coleman thinks it was chloral in one or the other, and so did the ambulance surgeon. I tell you I was scared. I tried to get Coleman, but he was out on a case, and I happened to think of the hospitals as probably the quickest. Dr. Coleman came in just as the young surgeon was bringing her around. He—oh, here he is now."

The famous doctor was just coming downstairs. He saw us, but, I suppose, inasmuch as we did not belong to the Sutphen and Coleman set, ignored us.

"Mrs. Sutphen will be all right now," he said reassuringly as he drew on his gloves. "The nurse has arrived, and I have given her instructions what to do. And, by the way, my dear Sutphen, I should advise you to deal firmly with her in that matter about which her name is appearing in the papers. Women nowadays don't seem to realize the dangers they run in mixing in in all these reforms. I have ordered an analysis of both the milk and vichy, but that will do little good unless we can find out who poisoned it. And there are so many chances for things like that, life is so complex nowadays——"

He passed out with scarcely a nod at us. Kennedy did not attempt to question him. He was thinking rapidly.

"Walter, we have no time to lose," he exclaimed, seizing a telephone that stood on a stand near by.

"This is the time for action. Hello—Police Head-quarters, First Deputy O'Connor, please."

As Kennedy waited I tried to figure out how it could have happened. I wondered whether it might not have been Mrs. Garrett. Would she stop at anything if she feared the loss of her favorite drug? But then there were so many others and so many ways of "getting" anybody who interfered with the drug traffic that it seemed impossible to figure it out by pure deduction.

"Hello, O'Connor," I heard Kennedy say; "you read that story in the *Star* this morning about the drug fiends at that Broadway cabaret? Yes? Well, Jameson and I wrote it. It's part of the drug war that Mrs. Sutphen has been waging. O'Connor, she's been poisoned—oh, no—she's all right now. But I want you to send out and arrest Whitecap and that fellow Armstrong immediately. I'm going to put them through a scientific third degree up in the laboratory to-night. Thank you. No—no matter how late it is, bring them up."

Dr. Coleman had gone long since, Mr. Sutphen had absolutely no interest further than the recovery of Mrs. Sutphen just now, and Mrs. Sutphen was resting quietly and could not be seen. Accordingly Kennedy and I hastened up to the laboratory to wait until O'Connor could "deliver the goods."

It was not long before one of O'Connor's men came in with Whitecap.

"While we're waiting," said Craig, "I wish you would just try this little cut-out puzzle."

I don't know what Whitecap thought, but I know I looked at Craig's invitation to "play blocks" as a joke scarcely higher in order than the number repe-tition of Snowbird. Whitecap did it, however, sullenly, and under compulsion, in, I should say about two minutes.

"I have Armstrong here myself," called out the voice of our old friend O'Connor, as he burst into the room.

"Good!" exclaimed Kennedy. "I shall be ready for him in just a second. Have Whitecap held here in the anteroom while you bring Armstrong into the laboratory. By the way, Walter, that was another of the Binet tests, putting a man at solving puzzles. It involves reflective judgment, one of the factors in executive ability. If Whitecap had been defective, it would have taken him five minutes to do that puzzle, if at all. So you see he is not in the class with Miss Sawtelle. The test shows him to be shrewd. He doesn't even touch his own dope. Now for Armstrong."

I knew enough of the underworld to set Whitecap down, however, as a "lobbygow"—an agent for some one higher up, recruiting both the gangs and the ranks of street women.

Before us, as O'Connor led in Armstrong, was a little machine with a big black cylinder. By means of wires and electrodes Kennedy attached it to Armstrong's chest.

"Now, Armstrong," he began in an even tone, "I want you to tell the truth—the whole truth. You have been getting heroin tablets from Whitecap."

"Yes, sir," replied the dope fiend defiantly.

"To-day you had to get them elsewhere."

No answer.

"Never mind," persisted Kennedy, still calm, "I know. Why, Armstrong, you even robbed that girl of twenty-five tablets."

"I did not," shot out the answer.

"There were twenty-five short," accused Kennedy.

The two faced each other. Craig repeated his remark.

"Yes," replied Armstrong, "I held out the tablets, but it was not for myself. I can get all I want. I did it because I didn't want her to get above seventy-five a day. I have tried every way to break her of the habit that has got me—and failed. But seventy-five—is the limit!"

"A pretty story!" exclaimed O'Connor.

Craig laid his hand on his arm to check him, as he examined a record registered on the cylinder of the machine.

"By the way, Armstrong, I want you to write me out a note that I can use to get a hundred heroin tablets. You can write it all but the name of the place where I can get them."

Armstrong was on the point of demurring, but the last sentence reassured him. He would reveal nothing by it—yet.

Still the man was trembling like a leaf. He wrote:

"Give Whitecap one hundred shocks—A Victim."

For a moment Kennedy studied the note carefully. "Oh—er—I forgot, Armstrong, but a few days ago an anonymous letter was sent to Mrs. Sutphen, signed 'A Friend.' Do you know anything about it?"

"A note?" the man repeated. "Mrs. Sutphen? I don't know anything about any note, or Mrs. Sutphen either."

Kennedy was still studying his record. "This," he remarked slowly, "is what I call my psychophysical test for falsehood. Lying, when it is practiced by an expert, is not easily detected by the most care‹ ful scrutiny of the liar's appearance and manner.

"However, successful means have been developed for the detection of falsehood by the study of experimental psychology. Walter, I think you will recall the test I used once, the psychophysical factor of the character and rapidity of the mental process known as the association of ideas?"

I nodded acquiescence.

"Well," he resumed, "in criminal jurisprudence, I find an even more simple and more subjective test which has been recently devised. Professor Stoerring of Bonn has found out that feelings of pleasure and pain produce well-defined changes in respiration. Similar effects are produced by lying, according to the famous Professor Benussi of Graz.

"These effects are unerring, unequivocal. The utterance of a false statement increases respiration; of a true statement decreases. The importance and scope of these discoveries are obvious."

Craig was figuring rapidly on a piece of paper. "This is a certain and objective criterion," he continued as he figured, "between truth and falsehood. Even when a clever liar endeavors to escape detection by breathing irregularly, it is likely to fail, for Benussi has investigated and found that voluntary changes in respiration don't alter the result. You see, the quotient obtained by dividing the time of inspiration by the time of expiration gives me the result."

He looked up suddenly. "Armstrong, you are telling the truth about some things—downright lies about others. You are a drug fiend—but I will be lenient with you, for one reason. Contrary to everything that I would have expected, you are really trying to save that poor half-witted girl whom you love from the terrible habit that has gripped you. That is why you held out the quarter of the one hundred tablets. That is why you wrote the note to Mrs. Sutphen, hoping that she might be treated in some institution."

Kennedy paused as a look of incredulity passed over Armstrong's face.

"Another thing you said was true," added Kennedy. "You can get all the heroin you want. Armstrong, you will put the address of that place on the outside of the note, or both you and Whitecap go to jail. Snowbird will be left to her own devices—she can get all the 'snow,' as some of you fiends call it, that she wants from those who might exploit her."

"Please, Mr. Kennedy," pleaded Armstrong.

"No," interrupted Craig, before the drug fiend could finish. "That is final. I must have the name of that place."

In a shaky hand Armstrong wrote again. Hastily Craig stuffed the note into his pocket, and ten minutes later we were mounting the steps of a big brownstone house on a fashionable side street just around the corner from Fifth Avenue.

As the door was opened by an obsequious colored servant, Craig handed him the scrap of paper signed by the password, "A Victim."

Imitating the cough of a confirmed dope user, Craig was led into a large waiting room.

"You're in pretty bad shape, sah," commented the servant.

Kennedy nudged me and, taking the cue, I coughed myself red in the face.

"Yes," he said. "Hurry—please."

The servant knocked at a door, and as it was

opened we caught a glimpse of Mrs. Garrett in negligee.

"What is it, Sam?" she asked.

"Two gentlemen for some heroin tablets, ma'am."

"Tell them to go to the chemical works—not to my office, Sam," growled a man's voice inside.

With a quick motion, Kennedy had Mrs. Garrett by the wrist.

"I knew it," he ground out. "It was all a fake about how you got the habit. You wanted to get it, so you could get and hold him. And neither one of you would stop at anything, not even the murder of your sister, to prevent the ruin of the devilish business you have built up in manufacturing and marketing the stuff."

He pulled the note from the hand of the surprised negro. "I had the right address, the place where you sell hundreds of ounces of the stuff a week—but I preferred to come to the doctor's office where I could find you both."

Kennedy had firmly twisted her wrist until, with a little scream of pain, she let go the door handle. Then he gently pushed her aside, and the next instant Craig had his hand inside the collar of Dr. Coleman, society physician, proprietor of the Coleman Chemical Works downtown, the real leader of the drug gang that was debauching whole sections of the metropolis.

CHAPTER XXVIII

THE FAMILY SKELETON

SURPRISED though we were at the unmasking of Dr. Coleman, there was nothing to do but to follow the thing out. In such cases we usually ran into the greatest difficulty—organized vice. This was no exception.

Even when cases involved only a clever individual or a prominent family, it was the same. I recall, for example, the case of a well-known family in a New York suburb, which was particularly difficult. It began in a rather unusual manner, too.

"Mr. Kennedy—I am ruined—ruined."

It was early one morning that the telephone rang and I answered it. A very excited German, breathless and incoherent, was evidently at the other end of the wire.

I handed the receiver to Craig and picked up the morning paper lying on the table.

"Minturn—dead?" I heard Craig exclaim. "In the paper this morning? I'll be down to see you directly."

Kennedy almost tore the paper from me. In the next to the end column where late news usually is dropped was a brief account of the sudden death of Owen Minturn, one of the foremost criminal lawyers of the city, in Josephson's Baths downtown.

It ended: "It is believed by the coroner that Mr.

Minturn was shocked to death and evidence is being sought to show that two hundred and forty volts
of electricity had been thrown into the attorney's
body while he was in the electric bath. Joseph Josephson, the proprietor of the bath, who operated
the switchboard, is being held, pending the completion of the inquiry."

As Kennedy hastily ran his eye over the paragraphs, he became more and more excited himself.

"Walter," he cried, as he finished, "I don't believe that that was an accident at all."

"Why?" I asked.

He already had his hat on, and I knew he was
going to Josephson's breakfastless. I followed reluctantly.

"Because," he answered, as we hustled along in
the early morning crowd, "it was only yesterday
afternoon that I saw Minturn at his office and he
made an appointment with me for this very morning. He was a very secretive man, but he did tell
me this much, that he feared his life was in danger
and that it was in some way connected with that
Pearcy case up in Stratfield, Connecticut, where he
has an estate. You have read of the case?"

Indeed I had. It had seemed to me to be a particularly inexplicable affair. Apparently a whole
family had been poisoned and a few days before old
Mr. Randall Pearcy, a retired manufacturer, had
died after a brief but mysterious illness.

Pearcy had been married a year or so ago to Annette Oakleigh, a Broadway comic opera singer, who
was his second wife. By his first marriage he had
had two children, a son, Warner, and a daughter,
Isabel.

Warner Pearcy, I had heard, had blazed a ver-

milion trail along the Great White Way, but his
sister was of the opposite temperament, interested
in social work, and had attracted much attention by
organizing a settlement in the slums of Stratfield
for the uplift of the workers in the Pearcy and other
mills.

Broadway, as well as Stratfield, had already
woven a fantastic background, for the mystery and
hints had been broadly made that Annette Oakleigh
had been indiscreetly intimate with a young physician in the town, a Dr. Gunther, a friend, by the
way, of Minturn.

"There has been no trial yet," went on Kennedy,
"but Minturn seems to have appeared before the
coroner's jury at Stratfield and to have asserted the
innocence of Mrs. Pearcy and that of Dr. Gunther so
well that, although the jury brought in a verdict of
murder by poison by some one unknown, there has
been no mention of the name of anyone else. The
coroner simply adjourned the inquest so that a more
careful analysis might be made of the vital organs.
And now comes this second tragedy in New York."

"What was the poison?" I asked. "Have they
found out yet?"

"They are pretty sure, so Minturn told me, that
it was lead poisoning. The fact not generally known
is," he added in a lower tone, "that the cases were
not confined to the Pearcy house. They had even
extended to Minturn's too, although about that he
said little yesterday. The estates up there adjoin,
you know."

Owen Minturn, I recalled, had gained a formida-
ble reputation by his successful handling of cases
from the lowest strata of society to the highest.
Indeed it was a byword that his appearance in court

indicated two things—the guilt of the accused and a verdict of acquittal.

"Of course," Craig pursued as we were jolted from station to station downtown, "you know they say that Minturn never kept a record of a case. But written records were as nothing compared to what that man must have carried only in his head."

It was a common saying that, if Minturn should tell all he knew, he might hang half a dozen prominent men in society. That was not strictly true, perhaps, but it was certain that a revelation of the things confided to him by clients which were never put down on paper would have caused a series of explosions that would have wrecked at least some portions of the social and financial world. He had heard much and told little, for he had been a sort of "father confessor."

Had Minturn, I wondered, known the name of the real criminal?

Josephson's was a popular bath on Forty-second Street, where many of the "sun-dodgers" were accustomed to recuperate during the day from their arduous pursuit of pleasure at night and prepare for the resumption of their toil during the coming night. It was more than that, however, for it had a reputation for being conducted really on a high plane.

We met Josephson downstairs. He had been released under bail, though the place was temporarily closed and watched over by the agents of the coroner and the police. Josephson appeared to be a man of some education and quite different from what I had imagined from hearing him over the telephone.

"Oh, Mr. Kennedy," he exclaimed, "who now will

come to my baths?   Last night they were crowded, but to-day——."

He ended with an expressive gesture of his hands.

"One customer I have surely lost, young Mr. Pearcy," he went on.

"Warner Pearcy?" asked Craig.   "Was he here last night?"

"Nearly every night," replied Josephson, now glib enough as his first excitement subsided and his command of English returned.   "He was a neighbor of Mr. Minturn's, I hear.   Oh, what luck!" growled Josephson as the name recalled him to his present troubles.

"Well," remarked Kennedy with an attempt at reassurance as if to gain the masseur's confidence, "I know as well as you that it is often amazing what a tremendous shock a man may receive and yet not be killed, and no less amazing how small a shock may kill.   It all depends on circumstances."

Josephson shot a covert look at Kennedy.   "Yes," he reiterated, "but I cannot see how it *could* be. If the lights had become short-circuited with the bath, that might have thrown a current into the bath.   But they were not.   I know it."

"Still," pursued Kennedy, watching him keenly, "it is not all a question of current.   To kill, the shock must pass through a vital organ—the brain, the heart, the upper spinal cord.   So, a small shock may kill and a large one may not.   If it passes in one foot and out by the other, the current isn't likely to be as dangerous as if it passes in by a hand or foot and then out by a foot or hand.   In one case it passes through no vital organ; in the other it is very likely to do so.   You see, the current can flow through the body only when it has a place of entrance and a place of exit. In all cases of accident from electric light wires, the victim is touching some conductor—damp earth, salty earth, water, something that gives the current an outlet and——"

"But even if the lights had been short-circuited," interrupted Josephson, "Mr. Minturn would have escaped injury unless he had touched the taps of the bath. Oh, no, sir, accidents in the medical use of electricity are rare. They don't happen here in my establishment," he maintained stoutly. "The trouble was that the coroner, without any knowledge of the physiological effects of electricity on the body, simply jumped at once to the conclusion that it was the electric bath that did it."

"Then it was for medical treatment that Mr. Minturn was taking the bath?" asked Kennedy, quickly taking up the point.

"Yes, of course," answered the masseur, eager to explain. "You are acquainted with the latest treatment for lead poisoning by means of the electric bath?"

Kennedy nodded. "I know that Sir Thomas Oliver, the English authority who has written much on dangerous trades, has tried it with marked success."

"Well, sir, that was why Mr. Minturn was here. He came here introduced by a Dr. Gunther of Stratfield."

"Indeed?" remarked Kennedy colorlessly, though I could see that it interested him, for evidently Minturn had said nothing of being himself a sufferer from the poison. "May I see the bath?"

"Surely," said Josephson, leading the way upstairs.

It was an oaken tub with metal rods on the two

long sides, from which depended prismatic carbon rods. Kennedy examined it closely.

"This is what we call a hydro-electric bath," Josephson explained. "Those rods on the sides are the electrodes. You see there are no metal parts in the tub itself. The rods are attached by wiring to a wall switch out here."

He pointed to the next room. Kennedy examined the switch with care.

"From it," went on Josephson, "wires lead to an accumulator battery of perhaps thirty volts. It uses very little current. Dr. Gunther tested it and found it all right."

Craig leaned over the bath, and from the carbon electrodes scraped off a white powder in minute crystals.

"Ordinarily," Josephson pursued, "lead is eliminated by the skin and kidneys. But now, as you know, it is being helped along by electrolysis. I talked to Dr. Gunther about it. It is his opinion that it is probably eliminated as a chloride from the tissues of the body to the electrodes in the bath in which the patient is wholly or partly immersed. On the positive electrodes we get the peroxide. On the negative there is a spongy metallic form of lead. But it is only a small amount."

"The body has been removed?" asked Craig.

"Not yet," the masseur replied. "The coroner has ordered it kept here under guard until he makes up his mind what disposition to have made of it."

We were next ushered into a little room on the same floor, at the door of which was posted an official from the coroner.

"First of all," remarked Craig, as he drew back the sheet and began a minute examination of the earthly remains of the great lawyer, "there are to be considered the safeguards of the human body against the passage through it of a fatal electric current—the high electric resistance of the body itself. It is particularly high when the current must pass through joints such as wrists, knees, elbows, and quite high when the bones of the head are concerned. Still, there might have been an incautious application of the current to the head, especially when the subject is a person of advanced age or latent cerebral disease, though I don't know that that fits Mr. Minturn. That's strange," he muttered, looking up, puzzled. "I can find no mark of a burn on the body—absolutely no mark of anything."

"That's what I say," put in Josephson, much pleased by what Kennedy said, for he had been waiting anxiously to see what Craig discovered on his own examination. "It's impossible."

"It's all the more remarkable," went on Craig, half to himself and ignoring Josephson, "because burns due to electric currents are totally unlike those produced in other ways. They occur at the point of contact, usually about the arms and hands, or the head. Electricity is much to be feared when it involves the cranial cavity."

He completed his examination of the head which once had carried secrets which themselves must have been incandescent.

"Then, too, such burns are most often something more than superficial, for considerable heat is developed which leads to massive destruction and carbonization of the tissues to a considerable depth. I have seen actual losses of substance—a lump of killed flesh surrounded by healthy tissues. Besides, such burns show an unexpected indolence when compared to the violent pains of ordinary burns. Perhaps that is due to the destruction of the nerve endings. How did Minturn die? Was he alone? Was he dead when he was discovered?"

"He was alone," replied Josephson, slowly endeavoring to tell it exactly as he had seen it, "but that's the strange part of it. He seemed to be suffering from a convulsion. I think he complained at first of a feeling of tightness of his throat and a twitching of the muscles of his hands and feet. Anyhow, he called for help. I was up here and we rushed in. Dr. Gunther had just brought him and then had gone away, after introducing him, and showing him the bath."

Josephson proceeded slowly, evidently having been warned that anything he said might be used against him. "We carried him, when he was this way, into this very room. But it was only for a short time. Then came a violent convulsion. It seemed to extend rapidly all over his body. His legs were rigid, his feet bent, his head back. Why, he was resting only on his heels and the back of his head. You see, Mr. Kennedy, that simply could not be the electric shock."

"Hardly," commented Kennedy, looking again at the body. "It looks more like a tetanus convulsion. Yet there does not seem to be any trace of a recent wound that might have caused lockjaw. How did he look?"

"Oh, his face finally became livid," replied Josephson. "He had a ghastly, grinning expression, his eyes were wide, there was foam on his mouth, and his breathing was difficult."

"Not like tetanus, either," revised Craig. "There

the convulsion usually begins with the face and progresses to the other muscles. Here it seems to have gone the other way."

"That lasted a minute or so," resumed the masseur. "Then he sank back—perfectly limp. I thought he was dead. But he was not. A cold sweat broke out all over him and he was as if in a deep sleep."

"What did you do?" prompted Kennedy.

"I didn't know what to do. I called an ambulance. But the moment the door opened, his body seemed to stiffen again. He had one other convulsion—and when he grew limp he was dead."

CHAPTER XXIX

THE LEAD POISONER

IT was a gruesome recital and I was glad to leave the baths finally with Kennedy. Josephson was quite evidently relieved at the attitude Craig had taken toward the coroner's conclusion that Minturn had been shocked to death. As far as I could see, however, it added to rather than cleared up the mystery.

Craig went directly uptown to his laboratory, in contrast with our journey down, in abstracted silence, which was his manner when he was trying to reason out some particularly knotty problem.

As Kennedy placed the white crystals which he had scraped off the electrodes of the tub on a piece of dark paper in the laboratory, he wet the tip of his finger and touched just the minutest grain to his tongue.

The look on his face told me that something unexpected had happened. He held a similar minute speck of the powder out to me.

It was an intensely bitter taste and very persistent, for even after we had rinsed out our mouths it seemed to remain, clinging persistently to the tongue.

He placed some of the grains in some pure water. They dissolved only slightly, if at all. But in

a tube in which he mixed a little ether and chloro-
form they dissolved fairly readily.

Next, without a word, he poured just a drop of
strong sulphuric acid on the crystals. There was not
a change in them.

Quickly he reached up into the rack and took
down a bottle labeled "Potassium Bichromate."

"Let us see what an oxidizing agent will do," he
remarked.

As he gently added the bichromate, there came a
most marvelous, kaleidoscopic change. From being
almost colorless, the crystals turned instantly to a
deep blue, then rapidly to purple, lilac, red, and then
the red slowly faded away and they became colorless again.

"What is it?" I asked, fascinated. "Lead?"

"N-no," he replied, the lines of his forehead deepening. "No. This is sulphate of strychnine."

"Sulphate of strychnine?" I repeated in astonishment.

"Yes," he reiterated slowly. "I might have suspected that from the convulsions, particularly when
Josephson said that the noise and excitement of the
arrival of the ambulance brought on the fatal
paroxysm. That is symptomatic. But I didn't fully
realize it until I got up here and tasted the stuff.
Then I suspected, for that taste is characteristic.
Even one part diluted seventy thousand times gives
that decided bitter taste."

"That's all very well," I remarked, recalling the
intense bitterness yet on my tongue. "But how do
you suppose it was possible for anyone to administer it? It seems to me that he would have said something, if he had swallowed even the minutest part
of it. He must have known it. Yet apparently

he didn't.   At least he said nothing about it—or else Josephson is concealing something."

"Did he swallow it—necessarily?" queried Kennedy, in a tone calculated to show me that the chemical world, at least, was full of a number of things, and there was much to learn.

"Well, I suppose if it had been given hypodermically, it would have a more violent effect," I persisted, trying to figure out a way that the poison might have been given.

"Even more unlikely," objected Craig, with a delight at discovering a new mystery that to me seemed almost fiendish.   "No, he would certainly have felt a needle, have cried out and said something about it, if anyone had tried that.   This poisoned needle business isn't as easy as some people seem to think nowadays."

"Then he might have absorbed it from the water," I insisted, recalling a recent case of Kennedy's and adding, "by osmosis."

"You saw how difficult it was to dissolve in water," Craig rejected quietly.

"Well, then," I concluded in desperation.   "How could it have been introduced?"

"I have a theory," was all he would say, reaching for the railway guide, "but it will take me up to Stratfield to prove it."

His plan gave us a little respite and we paused long enough to lunch, for which breathing space I was duly thankful.   The forenoon saw us on the train, Kennedy carrying a large and cumbersome package which he brought down with him from the laboratory and which we took turns in carrying, though he gave no hint of its contents.

We arrived in Stratfield, a very pretty little mill

town, in the middle of the afternoon, and with very
little trouble were directed to the Pearcy house, after
Kennedy had checked the parcel with the station
agent.

Mrs. Pearcy, to whom we introduced ourselves
as reporters of the *Star,* was a tall blonde.   I could
not help thinking that she made a particularly dash-
ing widow.   With her at the time was Isabel Pearcy,
a slender girl whose sensitive lips and large, earnest
eyes indicated a fine, high-strung nature.

Even before we had introduced ourselves, I could
not help thinking that there was a sort of hostility
between the women.   Certainly it was evident that
there was as much difference in temperament as between the butterfly and the bee.

"No," replied the elder woman quickly to a re-
quest from Kennedy for an interview, "there is nothing that I care to say to the newspapers.   They have
said too much already about this—unfortunate affair."

Whether it was imagination or not, I fancied that
there was an air of reserve about both women.   It
struck me as a most peculiar household.   What was
it?   Was each suspicious of the other?   Was each
concealing something?

I managed to steal a glance at Kennedy's face
to see whether there was anything to confirm my
own impression.   He was watching Mrs. Pearcy
closely as she spoke.   In fact his next few questions, inconsequential as they were, seemed addressed to her solely for the purpose of getting her
to speak.

I followed his eyes and found that he was watching her mouth, in reality.   As she answered I noted
her beautiful white teeth.   Kennedy himself had

trained me to notice small things, and at the time, though I thought it was trivial, I recall noticing on her gums, where they joined the teeth, a peculiar bluish-black line.

Kennedy had been careful to address only Mrs. Pearcy at first, and as he continued questioning her, she seemed to realize that he was trying to lead her along.

"I must positively refuse to talk any more," she repeated finally, rising. "I am not to be tricked into saying anything."

She had left the room, evidently expecting that Isabel would follow. She did not. In fact I felt that Miss Pearcy was visibly relieved by the departure of her stepmother. She seemed anxious to ask us something and now took the first opportunity.

"Tell me," she said eagerly, "how did Mr. Minturn die? What do they really think of it in New York?"

"They think it is poisoning," replied Craig, noting the look on her face.

She betrayed nothing, as far as I could see, except a natural neighborly interest. "Poisoning?" she repeated. "By what?"

"Lead poisoning," he replied evasively.

She said nothing. It was evident that, slip of a girl though she was, she was quite the match of anyone who attempted leading questions. Kennedy changed his method.

"You will pardon me," he said apologetically, "for recalling what must be distressing. But we newspapermen often have to do things and ask questions that are distasteful. I believe it is rumored that your father suffered from lead poisoning?"

"Oh, I don't know what it was—none of us do,"

she cried, almost pathetically. "I had been living at the settlement until lately. When father grew worse, I came home. He had such strange visions —hallucinations, I suppose you would call them. In the daytime he would be so very morose and melancholy. Then, too, there were terrible pains in his stomach, and his eyesight began to fail. Yes, I believe that Dr. Gunther did say it was lead poisoning. But—they have said so many things—so many things," she repeated, plainly distressed at the subject of her recent bereavement.

"Your brother is not at home?" asked Kennedy, quickly changing the subject.

"No," she answered, then with a flash as though lifting the veil of a confidence, added: "You know, neither Warner nor I have lived here much this year. He has been in New York most of the time and I have been at the settlement, as I already told you."

She hesitated, as if wondering whether she should say more, then added quickly: "It has been repeated often enough; there is no reason why I shouldn't say it to you. Neither of us exactly approved of father's marriage."

She checked herself and glanced about, somewhat with the air of one who has suddenly considered the possibility of being overheard.

"May I have a glass of water?" asked Kennedy suddenly.

"Why, certainly," she answered, going to the door, apparently eager for an excuse to find out whether there was some one on the other side of it.

There was not, nor any indication that there had been.

"Evidently she does not have any suspicions of

that," remarked Kennedy in an undertone, half to himself.

I had no chance to question him, for she returned almost immediately. Instead of drinking the water, however, he held it carefully up to the light. It was slightly turbid.

"You drink the water from the tap?" he asked, as he poured some of it into a sterilized vial which he drew quickly from his vest pocket.

"Certainly," she replied, for the moment non-plussed at his strange actions. "Everybody drinks the town water in Stratfield."

A few more questions, none of which were of importance, and Kennedy and I excused ourselves.

At the gate, instead of turning toward the town, however, Kennedy went on and entered the grounds of the Minturn house next door. The lawyer, I had understood, was a widower and, though he lived in Stratfield only part of the time, still maintained his house there.

We rang the bell and a middle-aged housekeeper answered.

"I am from the water company," he began politely. "We are testing the water, perhaps will supply consumers with filters. Can you let me have a sample?"

She did not demur, but invited us in. As she drew the water, Craig watched her hands closely. She seemed to have difficulty in holding the glass, and as she handed it to him, I noticed a peculiar hanging down of the wrist. Kennedy poured the sample into a second vial, and I noticed that it was turbid, too. With no mention of the tragedy to her employer, he excused himself, and we walked slowly back to the road.

20

Between the two houses Kennedy paused, and for several moments appeared to be studying them.

We walked slowly back along the road to the town. As we passed the local drug store, Kennedy turned and sauntered in.

He found it easy enough to get into conversation with the druggist, after making a small purchase, and in the course of a few minutes we found ourselves gossiping behind the partition that shut off the arcana of the prescription counter from the rest of the store.

Gradually Kennedy led the conversation around to the point which he wanted, and asked, "I wish you'd let me fix up a little sulphureted hydrogen."

"Go ahead," granted the druggist good-naturedly. "I guess you can do it. You know as much about drugs as I do. I can stand the smell, if you can."

Kennedy smiled and set to work.

Slowly he passed the gas through the samples of water he had taken from the two houses. As he did so the gas, bubbling through, made a blackish precipitate.

"What is it?" asked the druggist curiously.

"Lead sulphide," replied Kennedy, stroking his chin. "This is an extremely delicate test. Why, one can get a distinct brownish tinge if lead is present in even incredibly minute quantities."

He continued to work over the vials ranged on the table before him.

"The water contains, I should say, from ten to fifteen hundredths of a grain of lead to the gallon," he remarked finally.

"Where did it come from?" asked the druggist, unable longer to restrain his curiosity.

"I got it up at Pearcy's," Kennedy replied frankly,

turning to observe whether the druggist might betray any knowledge of it.

"That's strange," he replied in genuine surprise. "Our water in Stratfield is supplied by a company to a large area, and it has always seemed to me to be of great organic purity."

"But the pipes are of lead, are they not?" asked Kennedy.

"Y-yes," answered the druggist, "I think in most places the service pipes are of lead. But," he added earnestly as he saw the implication of his admission, "water has never to my knowledge been found to attack the pipes so as to affect its quality injuriously."

He turned his own faucet and drew a glassful. "It is normally quite clear," he added, holding the glass up.

It was in fact perfectly clear, and when he passed some of the gas through it nothing happened at all.

Just then a man lounged into the store.

"Hello, Doctor," greeted the druggist. "Here are a couple of fellows that have been investigating the water up at Pearcy's. They've found lead in it. That ought to interest you. This is Dr. Gunther," he introduced, turning to us.

It was an unexpected encounter, one I imagine that Kennedy might have preferred to take place under other circumstances. But he was equal to the occasion.

"We've been sent up here to look into the case for the New York *Star*," Kennedy said quickly. "I intended to come around to see you, but you have saved me the trouble."

Dr. Gunther looked from one of us to the other. "Seems to me the New York papers ought to have

enough to do without sending men all over the country making news," he grunted.

"Well," drawled Kennedy quietly, "there seems
to be a most remarkable situation up there at
Pearcy's and Minturn's, too. As nearly as I can
make out several people there are suffering from unmistakable signs of lead poisoning. There are the
pains in the stomach, the colic, and then on the gums
is that characteristic line of plumbic sulphide, the
distinctive mark produced by lead. There is the
wrist-drop, the eyesight affected, the partial paralysis, the hallucinations and a condition in old Pearcy's
case almost bordering on insanity—to enumerate the
symptoms that seem to be present in varying degrees
in various persons in the two houses."

Gunther looked at Kennedy, as if in doubt just
how to take him.

"That's what the coroner says, too—lead poisoning," put in the druggist, himself as keen as anyone
else for a piece of local news, and evidently not
averse to stimulating talk from Dr. Gunther, who
had been Pearcy's physician.

"That all seems to be true enough," replied Gunther at length guardedly. "I recognized that some
time ago."

"Why do you think it affects each so differently?"
asked the druggist.

Dr. Gunther settled himselr easily back in a chair
to speak as one having authority. "Well," he began
slowly, "Miss Pearcy, of course, hasn't been living
there much until lately. As for the others, perhaps
this gentleman here from the *Star* knows that lead,
once absorbed, may remain latent in the system and
then make itself felt. It is like arsenic, an accumula-
tive poison, slowly collecting in the body until the

limit is reached, or until the body, becoming weakened from some other cause, gives way to it."

He shifted his position slowly, and went on, as if defending the course of action he had taken in the case.

"Then, too, you know, there is an individual as well as family and sex susceptibility to lead. Women are especially liable to lead poisoning, but then perhaps in this case Mrs. Pearcy comes of a family that is very resistant. There are many factors. Personally, I don't think Pearcy himself was resistant. Perhaps Minturn was not, either. At any rate, after Pearcy's death, it was I who advised Minturn to take the electrolysis cure in New York. I took him down there," added Gunther. "Confound it, I wish I had stayed with him. But I always found Josephson perfectly reliable in hydrotherapy with other patients I sent to him, and I understood that he had been very successful with cases sent to him by many physicians in the city."

He paused and I waited anxiously to see whether Kennedy would make some reference to the discovery of the strychnine salts.

"Have you any idea how the lead poisoning could have been caused?" asked Kennedy instead.

Dr. Gunther shook his head. "It is a puzzle to me," he answered. "I am sure of only one thing. It could not be from working in lead, for it is needless to say that none of them worked."

"Food?" Craig suggested.

The doctor considered. "I had thought of that. I know that many cases of lead poisoning have been traced to the presence of the stuff in ordinary foods, drugs and drinks. I have examined the foods, especially the bread. They don't use canned goods.

I even went so far as to examine the kitchen ware to see if there could be anything wrong with the glazing. They don't drink wines and beers, into which now and then the stuff seems to get."

"You seem to have a good grasp of the subject," flattered Kennedy, as we rose to go. "I can hardly blame you for neglecting the water, since everyone here seems to be so sure of the purity of the supply."

Gunther said nothing. I was not surprised, for, at the very least, no one likes to have an outsider come in and put his finger directly on the raw spot. What more there might be to it, I could only conjecture.

We left the druggist's and Kennedy, glancing at his watch, remarked: "If you will go down to the station, Walter, and get that package we left there, I shall be much obliged to you. I want to make just one more stop, at the office of the water company, and I think I shall just about have time for it. There's a pretty good restaurant across the street. Meet me there, and by that time I shall know whether to carry out a little plan I have outlined or not."

CHAPTER XXX

THE ELECTROLYTIC MURDER

WE dined leisurely, which seemed strange to me, for it was not Kennedy's custom to let moments fly uselessly when he was on a case. However, I soon found out why it was. He was waiting for darkness.

As soon as the lights began to glow in the little stores on the main street, we sallied forth, taking the direction of the Pearcy and Minturn houses.

On the way he dropped into the hardware store and purchased a light spade and one of the small pocket electric flashlights, about which he wrapped a piece of cardboard in such a way as to make a most effective dark lantern.

We trudged along in silence, occasionally changing from carrying the heavy package to the light spade.

Both the Pearcy and Minturn houses were in nearly total darkness when we arrived. They set well back from the road and were plentifully shielded by shrubbery. Then, too, at night it was not a much frequented neighborhood. We could easily hear the footsteps of anyone approaching on the walk, and an occasional automobile gliding past did not worry us in the least.

"I have calculated carefully from an examination of the water company's map," said Craig, "just

303

where the water pipe of the two houses branches off
from the main in the road."

After a measurement or two from some land-
mark, we set to work a few feet inside, under cover
of the bushes and the shadows, like two grave dig-
gers.

Kennedy had been wielding the spade vigorously
for a few minutes when it touched something metallic. There, just beneath the frost line, we came upon
the service pipe.

He widened the hole, and carefully scraped off
the damp earth that adhered to the pipe. Next he
found a valve where he shut off the water and cut
out a small piece of the pipe.

"I hope they don't suspect anything like this in
the houses with their water cut off," he remarked as
he carefully split the piece open lengthwise and examined it under the light.

On the interior of the pipe could be seen patchy
lumps of white which projected about an eighth of
an inch above the internal surface. As the pipe
dried in the warm night air, they could easily be
brushed off as a white powder.

"What is it—strychnine?" I asked.

"No," he replied, regarding it thoughtfully with
some satisfaction. "That is lead carbonate. There
can be no doubt that the turbidity of the water was
due to this powder in suspension. A little dissolves
in the water, while the scales and incrustations in
fine particles are carried along in the current. As a
matter of fact the amount necessary to make the water poisonous need not be large."

He applied a little instrument to the cut ends of
the pipe. As I bent over, I could see the needle on
its dial deflected just a bit.

"My voltmeter," he said, reading it, "shows that there is a current of about 1.8 volts passing through this pipe all the time."

"Electrolysis of water pipes!" I exclaimed, thinking of statements I had heard by engineers. "That's what they mean by stray or vagabond currents, isn't it?"

He had seized the lantern and was eagerly following up and down the line of the water pipe. At last he stopped, with a low exclamation, at a point where an electric light wire supplying the Minturn cottage crossed overhead. Fastened inconspicuously to the trunk of a tree which served as a support for the wire was another wire which led down from it and was buried in the ground.

Craig turned up the soft earth as fast as he could, until he reached the pipe at this point. There was the buried wire wound several times around it.

As quickly and as neatly as he could he inserted a connection between the severed ends of the pipe to restore the flow of water to the houses, turned on the water and covered up the holes he had dug. Then he unwrapped the package which we had tugged about all day, and in a narrow path between the bushes which led to the point where the wire had tapped the electric light feed he placed in a shallow hole in the ground a peculiar apparatus.

As nearly as I could make it out, it consisted of two flat platforms between which, covered over and projected, was a slip of paper which moved forward, actuated by clockwork, and pressed on by a sort of stylus. Then he covered it over lightly with dirt so that, unless anyone had been looking for it, it would never be noticed.

It was late when we reached the city again, but

Kennedy had one more piece of work and that de-
volved on me. All the way down on the train he
had been writing and rewriting something.

"Walter," he said, as the train pulled into the station, "I want that published in to-morrow's papers."

I looked over what he had written. It was one
of the most sensational stories I have ever fathered,
beginning, "Latest of the victims of the unknown
poisoner of whole families in Stratfield, Connecticut,
is Miss Isabel Pearcy, whose father, Randall Pearcy,
died last week."

I knew that it was a "plant" of some kind, for
so far he had discovered no evidence that Miss
Pearcy had been affected. What his purpose was, I
could not guess, but I got the story printed.

The next morning early Kennedy was quietly at
work in the laboratory.

"What is this treatment of lead poisoning by
electrolysis?" I asked, now that there had come a
lull when I might get an intelligible answer. "How
does it work?"

"Brand new, Walter," replied Kennedy. "It has
been discovered that ions will flow directly through
the membranes."

"Ions?" I repeated. "What are ions?"

"Travelers," he answered, smiling, "so named by
Faraday from the Greek verb, *io,* to go. They are
little positive and negative charges of electricity of
which molecules are composed. You know some believe now that matter is really composed of electrical
energy. I think I can explain it best by a simile I use
with my classes. It is as though you had a ballroom
in which the dancers in couples represent the neutral
molecules. There are a certain number of isolated
ladies and gentlemen—dissociated ions——"

"Who don't know these new dances?" I interrupted.

"They all know this dance," he laughed. "But, to be serious in the simile, suppose at one end of the room there is a large mirror and at the other a buffet with cigars and champagne. What happens to the dissociated ions?"

"Well, I suppose you want me to say that the ladies gather about the mirror and the men about the buffet."

"Exactly. And some of the dancing partners separate and follow the crowd. Well, that room presents a picture of what happens in an electrolytic solution at the moment when the electric current is passing through it."

"Thanks," I laughed. "That was quite adequate to my immature understanding."

Kennedy continued at work, checking up and arranging his data until the middle of the afternoon, when he went up to Stratfield.

Having nothing better to do, I wandered out about town in the hope of running across some one with whom to while away the hours until Kennedy returned. I found out that, since yesterday, Broadway had woven an entirely new background for the mystery. Now it was rumored that the lawyer Minturn himself had been on very intimate terms with Mrs. Pearcy. I did not pay much attention to the rumor, for I knew that Broadway is constitutionally unable to believe that anybody is straight.

Kennedy had commissioned me to keep in touch with Josephson and I finally managed to get around to the Baths, to find them still closed.

As I was talking with him, a very muddy and

dusty car pulled up at the door and a young man whose face was marred by the red congested blood vessels that are in some a mark of dissipation burst in on us.

"What — closed up yet — Joe?" he asked. "Haven't they taken Minturn's body away?"

"Yes, it was sent up to Stratfield to-day," replied the masseur, "but the coroner seems to want to worry me all he can."

"Too bad. I was up almost all last night, and to-day I have been out in my car—tired to death. Thought I might get some rest here. Where are you sending the boys—to the Longacre?"

"Yes. They'll take good care of you till I open up again. Hope to see you back again, then, Mr. Pearcy," he added, as the young man turned and hurried out to his car again. "That was that young Pearcy, you know. Nice boy—but living the life too fast. What's Kennedy doing—anything?"

I did not like the jaunty bravado of the masseur which now seemed to be returning, since nothing definite had taken shape. I determined that he should not pump me, as he evidently was trying to do. I had at least fulfilled Kennedy's commission and felt that the sooner I left Josephson the better for both of us.

I was surprised at dinner to receive a wire from Craig saying that he was bringing down Dr. Gunther, Mrs. Pearcy and Isabel to New York and asking me to have Warner Pearcy and Josephson at the laboratory at nine o'clock.

By strategy I managed to persuade Pearcy to come, and as for Josephson, he could not very well escape, though I saw that as long as nothing more had happened, he was more interested in "fixing" the police so that he could resume business than anything else.

As we entered the laboratory that night, Kennedy, who had left his party at a downtown hotel to freshen up, met us each at the door. Instead of conducting us in front of his laboratory table, which was the natural way, he led us singly around through the narrow space back of it.

I recall that as I followed him, I half imagined that the floor gave way just a bit, and there flashed over me, by a queer association of ideas, the recollection of having visited an amusement park not long before where merely stepping on an innocent-looking section of the flooring had resulted in a tremendous knocking and banging beneath, much to the delight of the lovers of slap-stick humor. This was serious business, however, and I quickly banished the frivolous thought from my mind.

"The discovery of poison, and its identification," began Craig at last when we had all arrived and were seated about him, "often involves not only the use of chemistry but also a knowledge of the chemical effect of the poison on the body, and the gross as well as microscopic changes which it produces in various tissues and organs—changes, some due to mere contact, others to the actual chemico-physiological reaction between the poison and the body."

His hand was resting on the poles of a large battery, as he proceeded: "Every day the medical detective plays a more and more important part in the detection of crime, and I might say that, except in the case of crime complicated by a lunacy plea, his work has earned the respect of the courts and of detectives, while in the case of insanity the discredit

is the fault rather of the law itself. The ways in
which the doctor can be of use in untangling the
facts in many forms of crime have become so nu-
merous that the profession of medical detective may
almost be called a specialty."

Kennedy repeated what he had already told me
about electrolysis, then placed between the poles of
the battery a large piece of raw beef.

He covered the negative electrode with blotting
paper and soaked it in a beaker near at hand.

"This solution," he explained, "is composed of
potassium iodide. In this other beaker I have a
mixture of ordinary starch."

He soaked the positive electrode in the starch and
then jammed the two against the soft red meat.
Then he applied the current.

A few moments later he withdrew the positive
electrode. Both it and the meat under it were blue!

"What has happened?" he asked. "The iodine
ions have actually passed through the beef to the
positive pole and the paper on the electrode. Here
we have starch iodide."

It was a startling idea, this of the introduction of
a substance by electrolysis.

"I may say," he resumed, "that the medical view
of electricity is changing, due in large measure to
the genius of the Frenchman, Dr. Leduc. The body,
we know, is composed largely of water, with salts
of soda and potash. It is an excellent electrolyte.
Yet most doctors regard the introduction of substances by the electric current as insignificant or non-
existent. But on the contrary the introduction of
drugs by electrolysis is regular and far from being
insignificant may very easily bring about death.

"That action," he went on, looking from one of

us to another, "may be therapeutic, as in the cure for lead poisoning by removing the lead, or it may be toxic—as in the case of actually introducing such a poison as strychnine into the body by the same forces that will remove the lead."

He paused a moment, to enforce the point which had already been suggested. I glanced about hastily. If anyone in his little audience was guilty, no one betrayed it, for all were following him, fascinated. Yet in the wildly throbbing brain of some one of them the guilty knowledge must be seared indelibly. Would the mere accusation be enough to dissociate the truth from that brain or would Kennedy have to resort to other means?

"Some one," he went on, in a low, tense voice, leaning forward, "some one who knew this effect placed strychnine salts on one of the electrodes of the bath which Owen Minturn was to use."

He did not pause. Evidently he was planning to let the force of his exposure be cumulative, until from its sheer momentum it carried everything before it.

"Walter," he ordered quickly. "Lend me a hand."

Together we moved the laboratory table as he directed.

There, in the floor, concealed by the shadow, he had placed the same apparatus which I had seen him bury in the path between the Pearcy and Minturn estates at Stratfield.

We scarcely breathed.

"This," he explained rapidly, "is what is known as a kinograph—the invention of Professor Hele-Shaw of London. It enables me to identify a person by his or her walk. Each of you as you entered this room has passed over this apparatus and has left a different mark on the paper which registers."

For a moment he stopped, as if gathering strength for the final assault.

"Until late this afternoon I had this kinograph secreted at a certain place in Stratfield. Some one had tampered with the leaden water pipes and the electric light cable. Fearful that the lead poisoning brought on by electrolysis might not produce its result in the intended victim, that person took advantage of the new discoveries in electrolysis to complete that work by introducing the deadly strychnine during the very process of cure of the lead poisoning."

He slapped down a copy of a newspaper. "In the news this morning I told just enough of what I had discovered and colored it in such a way that I was sure I would arouse apprehension. I did it because I wanted to make the criminal revisit the real scene of the crime. There was a double motive now—to remove the evidence and to check the spread of the poisoning."

He reached over, tore off the paper with a quick, decisive motion, and laid it beside another strip, a little discolored by moisture, as though the damp earth had touched it.

"That person, alarmed lest something in the cleverly laid plot, might be discovered, went to a certain spot to remove the traces of the diabolical work which were hidden there. My kinograph shows the footsteps, shows as plainly as if I had been present, the exact person who tried to obliterate the evidence."

An ashen pallor seemed to spread over the face of Miss Pearcy, as Kennedy shot out the words.

"That person," he emphasized, "had planned to

put out of the way one who had brought disgrace on the Pearcy family. It was an act of private justice."

Mrs. Pearcy could stand the strain no longer. She had broken down and was weeping incoherently. I strained my ears to catch what she was murmuring. It was Minturn's name, not Gunther's, that was on her lips.

"But," cried Kennedy, raising an accusatory finger from the kinograph tracing and pointing it like the finger of Fate itself, "but the self-appointed avenger forgot that the leaden water pipe was common to the two houses. Old Mr. Pearcy, the wronged, died first. Isabel has guessed the family skeleton—has tried hard to shield you, but, Warner Pearcy, you are the murderer!"

21

CHAPTER XXXI

THE EUGENIC BRIDE

SCANDAL, such as that which Kennedy unearthed in this Pearcy case, was never much to his liking, yet he seemed destined, about this period of his career, to have a good deal of it.

We had scarcely finished with the indictment that followed the arrest of young Pearcy, when we were confronted by a situation which was as unique as it was intensely modern.

"There's absolutely no insanity in Eugenia's family," I heard a young man remark to Kennedy, as my key turned in the lock of the laboratory door.

For a moment I hesitated about breaking in on a confidential conference, then reflected that, as they had probably already heard me at the lock, I had better go in and excuse myself.

As I swung the door open, I saw a young man pacing up and down the laboratory nervously, too preoccupied even to notice the slight noise I had made.

He paused in his nervous walk and faced Kennedy, his back to me.

"Kennedy," he said huskily, "I wouldn't care if there was insanity in her family—for, my God!—the tragedy of it all now—I love her!"

He turned, following Kennedy's eyes in my direction, and I saw on his face the most haggard, haunt-

314

ing look of anxiety that I had ever seen on a young person.

Instantly I recognized from the pictures I had seen in the newspapers young Quincy Atherton, the last of this famous line of the family, who had attracted a great deal of attention several months previously by what the newspapers had called his search through society for a "eugenics bride," to infuse new blood into the Atherton stock.

"You need have no fear that Mr. Jameson will be like the other newspaper men," reassured Craig, as he introduced us, mindful of the prejudice which the unpleasant notoriety of Atherton's marriage had already engendered in his mind.

I recalled that when I had first heard of Atherton's "eugenic marriage," I had instinctively felt a prejudice against the very idea of such cold, calculating, materialistic, scientific mating, as if one of the last fixed points were disappearing in the chaos of the social and sex upheaval.

Now, I saw that one great fact of life must always remain. We might ride in hydroaeroplanes, delve into the very soul by psychanalysis, perhaps even run our machines by the internal forces of radium—even marry according to Galton or Mendel. But there would always be love, deep passionate love of the man for the woman, love which all the discoveries of science might perhaps direct a little less blindly, but the consuming flame of which not all the coldness of science could ever quench. No tampering with the roots of human nature could ever change the roots.

I must say that I rather liked young Atherton. He had a frank, open face, the most prominent feature of which was his somewhat aristocratic nose.

Otherwise he impressed one as being the victim of heredity in faults, if at all serious, against which he was struggling heroically.

It was a most pathetic story which he told, a story of how his family had degenerated from the strong stock of his ancestors until he was the last of the line. He told of his education, how he had fallen, a rather wild youth bent in the footsteps of his father who had been a notoriously good clubfellow, under the influence of a college professor, Dr. Crafts, a classmate of his father's, of how the professor had carefully and persistently fostered in him an idea that had completely changed him.

"Crafts always said it was a case of eugenics against euthenics," remarked Atherton, "of birth against environment. He would tell me over and over that birth gave me the clay, and it wasn't such bad clay after all, but that environment would shape the vessel."

Then Atherton launched into a description of how he had striven to find a girl who had the strong qualities his family germ plasm seemed to have lost, mainly, I gathered, resistance to a taint much like manic depressive insanity. And as he talked, it was borne in on me that, after all, contrary to my first prejudice, there was nothing very romantic indeed about disregarding the plain teachings of science on the subject of marriage and one's children.

In his search for a bride, Dr. Crafts, who had founded a sort of Eugenics Bureau, had come to advise him. Others may have looked up their brides in Bradstreet's, or at least the Social Register. Atherton had gone higher, had been overjoyed to find that a girl he had met in the West, Eugenia Gilman, measured up to what his friend told him were the latest teachings of science. He had been overjoyed because, long before Crafts had told him, he had found out that he loved her deeply.

"And now," he went on, half choking with emotion, "she is apparently suffering from just the same sort of depression as I myself might suffer from if the recessive trait became active."

"What do you mean, for instance?" asked Craig.

"Well, for one thing, she has the delusion that my relatives are persecuting her."

"Persecuting her?" repeated Craig, stifling the remark that that was not in itself a new thing in this or any other family. "How?"

"Oh, making her feel that, after all, it is Atherton family rather than Gilman health that counts— little remarks that when our baby is born, they hope it will resemble Quincy rather than Eugenia, and all that sort of thing, only worse and more cutting, until the thing has begun to prey on her mind."

"I see," remarked Kennedy thoughtfully. "But don't you think this is a case for a—a doctor, rather than a detective?"

Atherton glanced up quickly. "Kennedy," he answered slowly, "where millions of dollars are involved, no one can guess to what lengths the human mind will go—no one, except you."

"Then you have suspicions of something worse?"

"Y-yes—but nothing definite. Now, take this case. If I should die childless, after my wife, the Atherton estate would descend to my nearest relative, Burroughs Atherton, a cousin."

"Unless you willed it to——"

"I have already drawn a will," he interrupted, "and in case I survive Eugenia and die childless, the money goes to the founding of a larger Eugenics

Bureau, to prevent in the future, as much as possible, tragedies such as this of which I find myself a part. If the case is reversed, Eugenia will get her third and the remainder will go to the Bureau or the Foundation, as I call the new venture. But," and here young Atherton leaned forward and fixed his large eyes keenly on us, "Burroughs might break the will. He might show that I was of unsound mind, or that Eugenia was, too."

"Are there no other relatives?"

"Burroughs is the nearest," he replied, then added frankly, "I have a second cousin, a young lady named Edith Atherton, with whom both Burroughs and I used to be very friendly."

It was evident from the way he spoke that he had thought a great deal about Edith Atherton, and still thought well of her.

"Your wife thinks it is Burroughs who is persecuting her?" asked Kennedy.

Atherton shrugged his shoulders.

"Does she get along badly with Edith? She knows her I presume?"

"Of course. The fact is that since the death of her mother, Edith has been living with us. She is a splendid girl, and all alone in the world now, and I had hopes that in New York she might meet some one and marry well."

Kennedy was looking squarely at Atherton, wondering whether he might ask a question without seeming impertinent. Atherton caught the look, read it, and answered quite frankly, "To tell the truth, I suppose I might have married Edith, before I met Eugenia, if Professor Crafts had not dissuaded me. But it wouldn't have been real love—nor wise. You know," he went on more frankly, now that the first hesitation was over and he realized that if he were to gain anything at all by Kennedy's services, there must be the utmost candor between them, "you know cousins may marry if the stocks are known to be strong. But if there is a defect, it is almost sure to be intensified. And so I—I gave up the idea—never had it, in fact, so strongly as to propose to her. And when I met Eugenia all the Athertons on the family tree couldn't have bucked up against the combination."

He was deadly in earnest as he arose from the chair into which he had dropped after I came in.

"Oh, it's terrible--this haunting fear, this obsession that I have had, that, in spite of all I have tried to do, some one, somehow, will defeat me. Then comes the situation, just at a time when Eugenia and I feel that we have won against Fate, and she in particular needs all the consideration and care in the world—and—and I am defeated."

Atherton was again pacing the laboratory.

"I have my car waiting outside," he pleaded. "I wish you would go with me to see Eugenia—now."

It was impossible to resist him. Kennedy rose and I followed, not without a trace of misgiving.

The Atherton mansion was one of the old houses of the city, a somber stone dwelling with a garden about it on a downtown square, on which business was already encroaching. We were admitted by a servant who seemed to walk over the polished floors with stealthy step as if there was something sacred about even the Atherton silence. As we waited in a high-ceilinged drawing-room with exquisite old tapestries on the walls, I could not help feeling myself the influence of wealth and birth that seemed to cry out from every object of art in the house.

On the longer wall of the room, I saw a group of paintings. One, I noted especially, must have been Atherton's ancestor, the founder of the line. There was the same nose in Atherton, for instance, a striking instance of heredity. I studied the face carefully. There was every element of strength in it, and I thought instinctively that, whatever might have been the effects of in-breeding and bad alliances, there must still be some of that strength left in the present descendant of the house of Atherton. The more I thought about the house, the portrait, the whole case, the more unable was I to get out of my head a feeling that though I had not been in such a position before, I had at least read or heard something of which it vaguely reminded me.

Eugenia Atherton was reclining listlessly in her room in a deep leather easy chair, when Atherton took us up at last. She did not rise to greet us, but I noted that she was attired in what Kennedy once called, as we strolled up the Avenue, "the expensive sloppiness of the present styles." In her case the looseness with which her clothes hung was exaggerated by the lack of energy with which she wore them.

She had been a beautiful girl, I knew. In fact, one could see that she must have been. Now, however, she showed marks of change. Her eyes were large, and protruding, not with the fire of passion which is often associated with large eyes, but dully, set in a puffy face, a trifle florid. Her hands seemed, when she moved them, to shake with an involuntary tremor, and in spite of the fact that one almost could feel that her heart and lungs were speeding with energy, she had lost weight and no longer had the full, rounded figure of health. Her manner showed severe mental disturbance, indifference, depression, a distressing deterioration. All her attractive Western breeziness was gone. One felt the tragedy of it only too keenly.

"I have asked Professor Kennedy, a specialist, to call, my dear," said Atherton gently, without mentioning what the specialty was.

"Another one?" she queried languorously.

There was a colorless indifference in the tone which was almost tragic. She said the words slowly and deliberately, as though even her mind worked that way.

From the first, I saw that Kennedy had been observing Eugenia Atherton keenly. And in the rôle of specialist in nervous diseases he was enabled to do what otherwise would have been difficult to accomplish.

Gradually, from observing her mental condition of indifference which made conversation extremely difficult as well as profitless, he began to consider her physical condition. I knew him well enough to gather from his manner alone as he went on that what had seemed at the start to be merely a curious case, because it concerned the Athertons, was looming up in his mind as unusual in itself, and was interesting him because it baffled him.

Craig had just discovered that her pulse was abnormally high, and that consequently she had a high temperature, and was sweating profusely.

"Would you mind turning your head, Mrs. Atherton?" he asked.

She turned slowly, half way, her eyes fixed vacantly on the floor until we could see the once striking profile.

"No, all the way around, if you please," added Kennedy.

She offered no objection, not the slightest resistance. As she turned her head as far as she could, Kennedy quickly placed his forefinger and thumb gently on her throat, the once beautiful throat, now with skin harsh and rough. Softly he moved his fingers just a fraction of an inch over the so-called "Adam's apple" and around it for a little distance.

"Thank you," he said. "Now around to the other side."

He made no other remark as he repeated the process, but I fancied I could tell that he had had an instant suspicion of something the moment he touched her throat.

He rose abstractedly, bowed, and we started to leave the room, uncertain whether she knew or cared. Quincy had fixed his eyes silently on Craig, as if imploring him to speak, but I knew how unlikely that was until he had confirmed his suspicion to the last slightest detail.

We were passing through a dressing room in the suite when we met a tall young woman, whose face I instantly recognized, not because I had ever seen it before, but because she had the Atherton nose so prominently developed.

"My cousin, Edith," introduced Quincy.

We bowed and stood for a moment chatting. There seemed to be no reason why we should leave the suite, since Mrs. Atherton paid so little attention to us even when we had been in the same room. Yet a slight movement in her room told me that in spite of her lethargy she seemed to know that we were there and to recognize who had joined us.

Edith Atherton was a noticeable woman, a woman

of temperament, not beautiful exactly, but with a stateliness about her, an aloofness. The more I studied her face, with its thin sensitive lips and commanding, almost imperious eyes, the more there seemed to be something peculiar about her. She was dressed very simply in black, but it was the simplicity that costs. One thing was quite evident— her pride in the family of Atherton.

And as we talked, it seemed to be that she, much more than Eugenia in her former blooming health, was a part of the somber house. There came over me again the impression I had received before that I had read or heard something like this case before.

She did not linger long, but continued her stately way into the room where Eugenia sat. And at once it flashed over me what my impression, indefinable, half formed, was. I could not help thinking, as I saw her pass, of the lady Madeline in "The Fall of the House of Usher."

CHAPTER XXXII

THE GERM PLASM

I REGARDED her with utter astonishment and yet found it impossible to account for such a feeling. I looked at Atherton, but on his face I could see nothing but a sort of questioning fear that only increased my illusion, as if he, too, had only a vague, haunting premonition of something terrible impending. Almost I began to wonder whether the Atherton house might not crumble under the fierceness of a sudden whirlwind, while the two women in this case, one representing the wasted past, the other the blasted future, dragged Atherton down, as the whole scene dissolved into some ghostly tarn. It was only for a moment, and then I saw that the more practical Kennedy had been examining some bottles on the lady's dresser before which we had paused.

One was a plain bottle of pellets which might have been some homeopathic remedy.

"Whatever it is that is the matter with Eugenia," remarked Atherton, "it seems to have baffled the doctors so far."

Kennedy said nothing, but I saw that he had clumsily overturned the bottle and absently set it up again, as though his thoughts were far away. Yet with a cleverness that would have done credit to a professor of legerdemain he had managed to extract two or three of the pellets.

"Yes," he said, as he moved slowly toward the staircase in the wide hall, "most baffling."

Atherton was plainly disappointed. Evidently he had expected Kennedy to arrive at the truth and set matters right by some sudden piece of wizardry, and it was with difficulty that he refrained from saying so.

"I should like to meet Burroughs Atherton," he remarked as we stood in the wide hall on the first floor of the big house. "Is he a frequent visitor?"

"Not frequent," hastened Quincy Atherton, in a tone that showed some satisfaction in saying it. "However, by a lucky chance he has promised to call to-night—a mere courtesy, I believe, to Edith, since she has come to town on a visit."

"Good!" exclaimed Kennedy. "Now, I leave it to you, Atherton, to make some plausible excuse for our meeting Burroughs here."

"I can do that easily."

"I shall be here early," pursued Kennedy as we left.

Back again in the laboratory to which Atherton insisted on accompanying us in his car, Kennedy busied himself for a few minutes, crushing up one of the tablets and trying one or two reactions with some of the powder dissolved, while I looked on curiously.

"Craig," I remarked contemplatively, after a while, "how about Atherton himself? Is he really free from the—er—stigmata, I suppose you call them, of insanity?"

"You mean, may the whole trouble lie with him?" he asked, not looking up from his work.

"Yes—and the effect on her be a sort of reflex, say, perhaps the effect of having sold herself for

money and position.   In other words, does she, did
she, ever love him?   We don't know that.   Might
it not prey on her mind, until with the kind help of
his precious relatives even Nature herself could not
stand the strain—especially in the delicate condition
in which she now finds herself?"

I must admit that I felt the utmost sympathy for
the poor girl whom we had just seen such a pitiable
wreck.

Kennedy closed his eyes tightly until they wrinkled
at the corners.

"I think I have found out the immediate cause of
her trouble," he said simply, ignoring my suggestion.

"What is it?" I asked eagerly.

"I can't imagine how they could have failed to
guess it, except that they never would have suspected to look for anything resembling exophthalmic goiter in a person of her stamina," he answered,
pronouncing the word slowly.   "You have heard of
the thyroid gland in the neck?"

"Yes?" I queried, for it was a mere name to me.

"It is a vascular organ lying under the chin with
a sort of little isthmus joining the two parts on
either side of the windpipe," he explained.   "Well,
when there is any deterioration of those glands
through any cause, all sorts of complications may
arise.   The thyroid is one of the so-called ductless
glands, like the adrenals above the kidneys, the
pineal gland and the pituitary body.   In normal activity they discharge into the blood substances which
are carried to other organs and are now known to
be absolutely essential.

"The substances which they secrete are called
'hormones'—those chemical messengers, as it were,

by which many of the processes of the body are regulated. In fact, no field of experimental physiology is richer in interest than this. It seems that few ordinary drugs approach in their effects on metabolism the hormones of the thyroid. In excess they produce such diseases as exophthalmic goiter, and goiter is concerned with the enlargement of the glands and surrounding tissues beyond anything like natural size. Then, too, a defect in the glands causes the disease known as myxedema in adults and cretinism in children. Most of all, the gland seems to tell on the germ plasm of the body, especially in women."

I listened in amazement, hardly knowing what to think. Did his discovery portend something diabolical, or was it purely a defect in nature which Dr. Crafts of the Eugenics Bureau had overlooked?

"One thing at a time, Walter," cautioned Kennedy, when I put the question to him, scarcely expecting an answer yet.

That night in the old Atherton mansion, while we waited for Borroughs to arrive, Kennedy, whose fertile mind had contrived to kill at least two birds with one stone, busied himself by cutting in on the regular telephone line and placing an extension of his own in a closet in the library. To it he attached an ordinary telephone receiver fastened to an arrangement which was strange to me. As nearly as I can describe it, between the diaphragm of the regular receiver and a brownish cylinder, like that of a phonograph, and with a needle attached, was fitted an air chamber of small size, open to the outer air by a small hole to prevent compression.

The work was completed expeditiously, but we had plenty of time to wait, for Borroughs Atherton evidently did not consider that an evening had fairly begun until nine o'clock.

He arrived at last, however, rather tall, slight of figure, narrow-shouldered, designed for the latest models of imported fabrics. It was evident merely by shaking hands with Burroughs that he thought both the Athertons and the Burroughses just the right combination. He was one of those few men against whom I conceive an instinctive prejudice, and in this case I felt positive that, whatever faults the Atherton germ plasm might contain, he had combined others from the determiners of that of the other ancestors he boasted. I could not help feeling that Eugenia Atherton was in about as unpleasant an atmosphere of social miasma as could be imagined.

Burroughs asked politely after Eugenia, but it was evident that the real deference was paid to Edith Atherton and that they got along very well together. Burroughs excused himself early, and we followed soon after.

"I think I shall go around to this Eugenics Bureau of Dr. Crafts," remarked Kennedy the next day, after a night's consideration of the case.

The Bureau occupied a floor in a dwelling house uptown which had been remodeled into an office building. Huge cabinets were stacked up against the walls, and in them several women were engaged in filing blanks and card records. Another part of the office consisted of an extensive library on eugenic subjects.

Dr. Crafts, in charge of the work, whom we found in a little office in front partitioned off by ground glass, was an old man with an alert, vigorous mind on whom the effects of plain living and high thinking showed plainly. He was looking over some new blanks with a young woman who seemed to be working with him, directing the force of clerks as well as the "field workers," who were gathering the vast mass of information which was being studied. As we introduced ourselves, he introduced Dr. Maude Schofield.

"I have heard of your eugenic marriage contests," began Kennedy, "more especially of what you have done for Mr. Quincy Atherton."

"Well—not exactly a contest in that case, at least," corrected Dr. Crafts with an indulgent smile for a layman.

"No," put in Dr. Schofield, "the Eugenics Bureau isn't a human stock farm."

"I see," commented Kennedy, who had no such idea, anyhow. He was always lenient with anyone who had what he often referred to as the "illusion of grandeur."

"We advise people sometimes regarding the desirability or the undesirability of marriage," mollified Dr. Crafts. "This is a sort of clearing house for scientific race investigation and improvement."

"At any rate," persisted Kennedy, "after investigation, I understand, you advised in favor of his marriage with Miss Gilman."

"Yes, Eugenia Gilman seemed to measure well up to the requirements in such a match. Her branch of the Gilmans has always been of the vigorous, pioneering type, as well as intellectual. Her father was one of the foremost thinkers in the West; in fact had long held ideas on the betterment of the race. You see that in the choice of a name for his daughter—Eugenia."

"Then there were no recessive traits in her fam-
22

ily," asked Kennedy quickly, "of the same sort that you find in the Athertons?"

"None that we could discover," answered Dr. Crafts positively.

"No epilepsy, no insanity of any form?"

"No. Of course, you understand that almost no one is what might be called eugenically perfect. Strictly speaking, perhaps not over two or three per cent. of the population even approximates that standard. But it seemed to me that in everything essential in this case, weakness latent in Atherton was mating strength in Eugenia and the same way on her part for an entirely different set of traits."

"Still," considered Kennedy, "there might have been something latent in her family germ plasm back of the time through which you could trace it?"

Dr. Crafts shrugged his shoulders. "There often is, I must admit, something we can't discover because it lies too far back in the past."

"And likely to crop out after skipping generations," put in Maude Schofield.

She evidently did not take the same liberal view in the practical application of the matter expressed by her chief. I set it down to the ardor of youth in a new cause, which often becomes the saner conservatism of maturity.

"Of course, you found it much easier than usual to get at the true family history of the Athertons," pursued Kennedy. "It is an old family and has been prominent for generations."

"Naturally," assented Dr. Crafts.

"You know Burroughs Atherton on both lines of descent?" asked Kennedy, changing the subject abruptly.

"Yes, fairly well," answered Crafts.

"Now, for example," went on Craig, "how would you advise him to marry?"

I saw at once that he was taking this subterfuge as a way of securing information which might otherwise have been withheld if asked for directly. Maude Schofield also saw it, I fancied, but this time said nothing.

"They had a grandfather who was a manic depressive on the Atherton side," said Crafts slowly. "Now, no attempt has ever been made to breed that defect out of the family. In the case of Burroughs, it is perhaps a little worse, for the other side of his ancestry is not free from the taint of alcoholism."

"And Edith Atherton?"

"The same way. They both carry it. I won't go into the Mendelian law on the subject. We are clearing up much that is obscure. But as to Burroughs, he should marry, if at all, some one without that particular taint. I believe that in a few generations by proper mating most taints might be bred out of families."

Maude Schofield evidently did not agree with Dr. Crafts on some point, and, noticing it, he seemed to be in the position both of explaining his contention to us and of defending it before his fair assistant.

"It is my opinion, as far as I have gone with the data," he added, "that there is hope for many of those whose family history shows certain nervous taints. A sweeping prohibition of such marriages would be futile, perhaps injurious. It is necessary that the mating be carefully made, however, to prevent intensifying the taint. You see, though I am a eugenist I am not an extremist."

He paused, then resumed argumentatively:

"Then there are other questions, too, like that of genius with its close relation to manic depressive insanity. Also, there is decrease enough in the birth rate, without adding an excuse for it. No, that a young man like Atherton should take the subject seriously, instead of spending his time in wild dissipation, like his father, is certainly creditable, argues in itself that there still must exist some strength in his stock.

"And, of course," he continued warmly, "when I say that weakness in a trait—not in all traits, by any means—should marry strength and that strength may marry weakness, I don't mean that all matches should be like that. If we are too strict we may prohibit practically all marriages. In Atherton's case, as in many another, I felt that I should interpret the rule as sanely as possible."

"Strength should marry strength, and weakness should never marry," persisted Maude Schofield. "Nothing short of that will satisfy the true eugenist."

"Theoretically," objected Crafts. "But Atherton was going to marry, anyhow. The only thing for me to do was to lay down a rule which he might follow safely. Besides, any other rule meant sure disaster."

"It was the only rule with half a chance of being followed and at any rate," drawled Kennedy, as the eugenists wrangled, "what difference does it make in this case? As nearly as I can make out it is Mrs. Atherton herself, not Atherton, who is ill."

Maude Schofield had risen to return to supervising a clerk who needed help. She left us, still unconvinced.

"That is a very clever girl," remarked Kennedy as

she shut the door and he scanned Dr. Crafts' face closely.

"Very," assented the Doctor.

"The Schofields come of good stock?" hazarded Kennedy.

"Very," assented Dr. Crafts again.

Evidently he did not care to talk about individual cases, and I felt that the rule was a safe one, to prevent Eugenics from becoming Gossip. Kennedy thanked him for his courtesy, and we left apparently on the best of terms both with Crafts and his assistant.

CHAPTER XXXIII

THE SEX CONTROL

I DID not see Kennedy again that day until late in the afternoon, when he came into the laboratory carrying a small package.

"Theory is one thing, practice is another," he remarked, as he threw his hat and coat into a chair.

"Which means—in this case?" I prompted.

"Why, I have just seen Atherton. Of course I didn't repeat our conversation of this morning, and I'm glad I didn't. He almost makes me think you are right, Walter. He's obsessed by the fear of Burroughs. Why, he even told me that Burroughs had gone so far as to take a leaf out of his book, so to speak, get in touch with the Eugenics Bureau as if to follow his footsteps, but really to pump them about Atherton himself. Atherton says it's all Burroughs' plan to break his will and that the fellow has even gone so far as to cultivate the acquaintance of Maude Schofield, knowing that he will get no sympathy from Crafts."

"First it was Edith Atherton, now it is Maude Schofield that he hitches up with Burroughs," I commented. "Seems to me that I have heard that one of the first signs of insanity is belief that everyone about the victim is conspiring against him. I haven't any love for any of them—but I must be fair."

"Well," said Kennedy, unwrapping the package,

334

"there *is* this much to it. Atherton says Burroughs and Maude Schofield have been seen together more than once—and not at intellectual gatherings either. Burroughs is a fascinating fellow to a woman, if he wants to be, and the Schofields are at least the social equals of the Burroughs. Besides," he added, "in spite of eugenics, feminism, and all the rest—sex, like murder, will out. There's no use having any false ideas about *that*. Atherton may see red—but, then, he was quite excited."

"Over what?" I asked, perplexed more than ever at the turn of events.

"He called me up in the first place. 'Can't you do something?' he implored. 'Eugenia is getting worse all the time.' She is, too. I saw her for a moment, and she was even more vacant than yesterday."

The thought of the poor girl in the big house somehow brought over me again my first impression of Poe's story.

Kennedy had unwrapped the package which proved to be the instrument he had left in the closet at Atherton's. It was, as I had observed, like an ordinary wax cylinder phonograph record.

"You see," explained Kennedy, "it is nothing more than a successful application at last of, say, one of those phonographs you have seen in offices for taking dictation, placed so that the feebler vibrations of the telephone affect it. Let us see what we have here."

He had attached the cylinder to an ordinary phonograph, and after a number of routine calls had been run off, he came to this, in voices which we could only guess at but not recognize, for no names were used.

"How is she to-day?"

"Not much changed—perhaps not so well."

"It's all right, though.   That is natural.   It is working well.   I think you might increase the dose, one tablet."

"You're sure it is all right?" (with anxiety).

"Oh, positively—it has been done in Europe."

"I hope so.   It must be a boy—and an *Atherton*."

"Never fear."

That was all.   Who was it?   The voices were unfamiliar to me, especially when repeated mechanically.   Besides they may have been disguised.   At any rate we had learned something.   Some one was trying to control the sex of the expected Atherton heir.   But that was about all.   Who it was, we knew no better, apparently, than before.

Kennedy did not seem to care much, however. Quickly he got Quincy Atherton on the wire and arranged for Atherton to have Dr. Crafts meet us at the house at eight o'clock that night, with Maude Schofield.   Then he asked that Burroughs Atherton be there, and of course, Edith and Eugenia.

We arrived almost as the clock was striking, Kennedy carrying the phonograph record and another blank record, and a boy tugging along the machine itself.   Dr. Crafts was the next to appear, expressing surprise at meeting us, and I thought a bit annoyed, for he mentioned that it had been with reluctance that he had had to give up some work he had planned for the evening.   Maude Schofield, who came with him, looked bored.   Knowing that she disapproved of the match with Eugenia, I was not surprised.   Burroughs arrived, not as late as I had expected, but almost insultingly supercilious at finding so many strangers at what Atherton had told

him was to be a family conference, in order to get
him to come.   Last of all Edith Atherton descended
the staircase, the personification of dignity, bowing
to each with a studied graciousness, as if distributing
largess, but greeting Burroughs with an air that
plainly showed how much thicker was blood than water.   Eugenia remained upstairs, lethargic, almost
cataleptic, as Atherton told us when we arrived.

"I trust you are not going to keep us long,
Quincy," yawned Burroughs, looking ostentatiously
at his watch.

"Only long enough for Professor Kennedy to say
a few words about Eugenia," replied Atherton nervously, bowing to Kennedy.

Kennedy cleared his throat slowly.

"I don't know that I have much to say," began
Kennedy, still seated.   "I suppose Mr. Atherton has
told you I have been much interested in the peculiar
state of health of Mrs. Atherton?"

No one spoke, and he went on easily: "There is
something I might say, however, about the—er—
what I call the chemistry of insanity.   Among the
present wonders of science, as you doubtless know,
none stirs the imagination so powerfully as the doc-
trine that at least some forms of insanity are the result of chemical changes in the blood.   For instance,
ill temper, intoxication, many things are due to
chemical changes in the blood acting on the brain.

"Go further back.   Take typhoid fever with its
delirium, influenza with its suicide mania.   All due
to toxins—poisons.   Chemistry—chemistry—all of
them chemistry."

Craig had begun carefully so as to win their attention.   He had it as he went on: "Do we not
brew within ourselves poisons which enter the cir-

culation and pervade the system? A sudden emotion
upsets the chemistry of the body. Or poisonous
food. Or a drug. It affects many things. But we
could never have had this chemical theory unless we
had had physiological chemistry—and some carry it
so far as to say that the brain secretes thought, just
as the liver secretes bile, that thoughts are the results of molecular changes."

"You are, then, a materialist of the most pronounced type," asserted Dr. Crafts.

Kennedy had been reaching over to a table, toying with the phonograph. As Crafts spoke he
moved a key, and I suspected that it was in order
to catch the words.

"Not entirely," he said. "No more than some
eugenists."

"In our field," put in Maude Schofield, "I might
express the thought this way—the sociologist has
had his day; now it is the biologist, the eugenist."

"That expresses it," commented Kennedy, still
tinkering with the record. "Yet it does not mean
that because we have new ideas, they abolish the
old. Often they only explain, amplify, supplement.
For instance," he said, looking up at Edith Atherton, "take heredity. Our knowledge seems new, but
is it? Marriages have always been dictated by a
sort of eugenics. Society is founded on that."

"Precisely," she answered. "The best families
have always married into the best families. These
modern notions simply recognize what the best people have always thought—except that it seems to
me," she added with a sarcastic flourish, "people of
no ancestry are trying to force themselves in among
their betters."

"Very true, Edith," drawled Burroughs, "but we

did not have to be brought here by Quincy to learn that."

Quincy Atherton had risen during the discussion and had approached Kennedy. Craig continued to finger the phonograph abstractedly, as he looked up.

"About this—this insanity theory," he whispered eagerly. "You think that the suspicions I had have been justified?"

I had been watching Kennedy's hand. As soon as Atherton had started to speak, I saw that Craig, as before, had moved the key, evidently registering what he said, as he had in the case of the others during the discussion.

"One moment, Atherton," he whispered in reply, "I'm coming to that. Now," he resumed aloud, "there is a disease, or a number of diseases, to which my remarks about insanity a while ago might apply very well. They have been known for some time to arise from various affections of the thyroid glands in the neck. These glands, strange to say, if acted on in certain ways can cause degenerations of mind and body, which are well known, but in spite of much study are still very little understood. For example, there is a definite interrelation between them and sex—especially in woman."

Rapidly he sketched what he had already told me of the thyroid and the hormones. "These hormones," added Kennedy, "are closely related to many reactions in the body, such as even the mother's secretion of milk at the proper time and then only. That and many other functions are due to the presence and character of these chemical secretions from the thyroid and other ductless glands. It is a fascinating study. For we know that anything that will upset—reduce or increase—the hormones is a matter intimately concerned with health. Such changes," he said earnestly, leaning forward, "might be aimed directly at the very heart of what otherwise would be a true eugenic marriage. It is even possible that loss of sex itself might be made to follow deep changes of the thyroid."

He stopped a moment. Even if he had accomplished nothing else he had struck a note which had caused the Athertons to forget their former superciliousness.

"If there is an oversupply of thyroid hormones," continued Craig, "that excess will produce many changes, for instance a condition very much like exophthalmic goiter. And," he said, straightening up, "I find that Eugenia Atherton has within her blood an undue proportion of these thyroid hormones. Now, is it overfunction of the glands, hypersecretion—or is it something else?"

No one moved as Kennedy skillfully led his disclosure along step by step.

"That question," he began again slowly, shifting his position in the chair, "raises in my mind, at least, a question which has often occurred to me before. Is it possible for a person, taking advantage of the scientific knowledge we have gained, to devise and successfully execute a murder without fear of discovery? In other words, can a person be removed with that technical nicety of detail which will leave no clue and will be set down as something entirely natural, though unfortunate?"

It was a terrible idea he was framing, and he dwelt on it so that we might accept it at its full value. "As one doctor has said," he added, "although toxicologists and chemists have not always possessed infallible tests for practical use, it is at present a pretty certain observation that every poison leaves its mark. But then on the other hand, students of criminology have said that a skilled physician or surgeon is about the only person now capable of carrying out a really scientific murder.

"Which is true? It seems to me, at least in the latter case, that the very nicety of the handiwork must often serve as a clue in itself. The trained hand leaves the peculiar mark characteristic of its training. No matter how shrewdly the deed is planned, the execution of it is daily becoming a more and more difficult feat, thanks to our increasing knowledge of microbiology and pathology."

He had risen, as he finished the sentence, every eye fixed on him, as if he had been a master hypnotist.

"Perhaps," he said, taking off the cylinder from the phonograph and placing on one which I knew was that which had lain in the library closet over night, "perhaps some of the things I have said will explain or be explained by the record on this cylinder."

He had started the machine. So magical was the effect on the little audience that I am tempted to repeat what I had already heard, but had not myself yet been able to explain:

"How is she to-day?"
"Not much changed—perhaps not so well."
"It's all right, though. That is natural. It is working well. I think you might increase the dose one tablet."
"You're sure it is all right?"
"Oh, positively—it has been done in Europe."
"I hope so. It must be a boy—and an *Atherton*."
"Never fear."

No one moved a muscle. If there was anyone in the room guilty of playing on the feelings and the health of an unfortunate woman, that person must have had superb control of his own feelings.

"As you know," resumed Kennedy thoughtfully, "there are and have been many theories of sex control. One of the latest, but by no means the only one, is that it can be done by use of the extracts of various glands administered to the mother. I do not know with what scientific authority it was stated, but I do know that some one has recently said that adrenalin, derived from the suprarenal glands, induces boys to develop—cholin, from the bile of the liver, girls. It makes no difference—in this case. There may have been a show of science. But it was to cover up a crime. Some one has been administering to Eugenia Atherton tablets of thyroid extract—ostensibly to aid her in fulfilling the dearest ambition of her soul—to become the mother of a new line of Athertons which might bear the same relation to the future of the country as the great family of the Edwards mothered by Elizabeth Tuttle."

He was bending over the two phonograph cylinders now, rapidly comparing the new one which he had made and that which he had just allowed to reel off its astounding revelation.

"When a voice speaks into a phonograph," he said, half to himself, "its modulations received on the diaphragm are written by a needle point upon the surface of a cylinder or disk in a series of fine waving or zigzag lines of infinitely varying depth or breadth. Dr. Marage and others have been able to distinguish vocal sounds by the naked eye on phonograph records. Mr. Edison has studied them with the microscope in his world-wide search for the perfect voice.

"In fact, now it is possible to identify voices by the records they make, to get at the precise meaning of each slightest variation of the lines with mathematical accuracy. They can no more be falsified than handwriting can be forged so that modern science cannot detect it or than typewriting can be concealed and attributed to another machine. The voice is like a finger print, a portrait parlé—unescapable."

He glanced up, then back again. "This microscope shows me," he said, "that the voices on that cylinder you heard are identical with two on this record which I have just made in this room."

"Walter," he said, motioning to me, "look."

I glanced into the eyepiece and saw a series of lines and curves, peculiar waves lapping together and making an appearance in some spots almost like tooth marks. Although I did not understand the details of the thing, I could readily see that by study one might learn as much about it as about loops, whorls, and arches on finger tips.

"The upper and lower lines," he explained, "with long regular waves, on that highly magnified section of the record, are formed by the voice with no overtones. The three lines in the middle, with rhythmic ripples, show the overtones."

He paused a moment and faced us. "Many a person," he resumed, "is a biotype in whom a full complement of what are called inhibitions never develops. That is part of your eugenics. Throughout life, and in spite of the best of training, that person reacts now and then to a certain stimulus directly. A man stands high; once a year he falls with a lethal quantity of alcohol. A woman, brilliant, accomplished, slips away and spends a day with a lover as unlike herself as can be imagined.

"The voice that interests me most on these records," he went on, emphasizing the words with one of the cylinders which he still held, "is that of a person who has been working on the family pride of another. That person has persuaded the other to administer to Eugenia an extract because 'it must be a boy and an Atherton.' That person is a high-class defective, born with a criminal instinct, reacting to it in an artful way. Thank God, the love of a man whom theoretical eugenics condemned, roused us in——"

A cry at the door brought us all to our feet, with hearts thumping as if they were bursting.

It was Eugenia Atherton, wild-eyed, erect, staring.

I stood aghast at the vision. Was she really to be the Lady Madeline in this fall of the House of Atherton?

"Edith—I—I missed you. I heard voices. Is—is it true—what this man—says? Is my—my baby——"

Quincy Atherton leaped forward and caught her as she reeled. Quickly Craig threw open a window for air, and as he did so leaned far out and blew shrilly on a police whistle.

The young man looked up from Eugenia, over whom he was bending, scarcely heeding what else went on about him. Still, there was no trace of anger on his face, in spite of the great wrong that had been done him. There was room for only one great emotion—only anxiety for the poor girl who had suffered so cruelly merely for taking his name.

Kennedy saw the unspoken question in his eyes.

"Eugenia is a pure normal, as Dr. Crafts told you," he said gently. "A few weeks, perhaps only days, of treatment—the thyroid will revert · to its normal state—and Eugenia Gilman will be the mother of a new house of Atherton which may eclipse even the proud record of the founder of the old."

"Who blew the whistle?" demanded a gruff voice at the door, as a tall bluecoat puffed past the scandalized butler.

"Arrest that woman," pointed Kennedy. "She is the poisoner. Either as wife of Burroughs, whom she fascinates and controls as she does Edith, she planned to break the will of Quincy or, in the other event, to administer the fortune as head of the Eugenics Foundation after the death of Dr. Crafts, who would have followed Eugenia and Quincy Atherton."

I followed the direction of Kennedy's accusing finger. Maude Schofield's face betrayed more than even her tongue could have confessed.

CHAPTER XXXIV

THE BILLIONAIRE BABY

COMING to us directly as a result of the talk that the Atherton case provoked was another that involved the happiness of a wealthy family to a no less degree.

"I suppose you have heard of the 'billionaire baby,' Morton Hazleton III?" asked Kennedy of me one afternoon shortly afterward.

The mere mention of the name conjured up in my mind a picture of the lusty two-year-old heir of two fortunes, as the feature articles in the *Star* had described that little scion of wealth—his luxurious nursery, his magnificent toys, his own motor car, a trained nurse and a detective on guard every hour of the day and night, every possible precaution for his health and safety.

"Gad, what a lucky kid!" I exclaimed involuntarily.

"Oh, I don't know about that," put in Kennedy. "The fortune may be exaggerated. His happiness is, I'm sure."

He had pulled from his pocketbook a card and handed it to me. It read: "Gilbert Butler, American representative, Lloyd's."

"Lloyd's?" I queried. "What has Lloyd's to do with the billion-dollar baby?"

"Very much. The child has been insured with

them for some fabulous sum against accident, including kidnaping."

"Yes?" I prompted, "sensing" a story.

"Well, there seem to have been threats of some kind, I understand. Mr. Butler has called on me once already to-day to retain my services and is going to—ah—there he is again now."

Kennedy had answered the door buzzer himself, and Mr. Butler, a tall, sloping-shouldered Englishman, entered.

"Has anything new developed?" asked Kennedy, introducing me.

"I can't say," replied Butler dubiously. "I rather think we have found something that may have a bearing on the case. You know Miss Haversham, Veronica Haversham?"

"The actress and professional beauty? Yes—at least I have seen her. Why?"

"We hear that Morton Hazleton knows her, anyhow," remarked Butler dryly.

"Well?"

"Then you don't know the gossip?" he cut in. "She is said to be in a sanitarium near the city. I'll have to find that out for you. It's a fast set she has been traveling with lately, including not only Hazleton, but Dr. Maudsley, the Hazleton physician, and one or two others, who if they were poorer might be called desperate characters."

"Does Mrs. Hazleton know of—of his reputed intimacy?"

"I can't say that, either. I presume that she is no fool."

Morton Hazleton, Jr., I knew, belonged to a rather smart group of young men. He had been mentioned in several near-scandals, but as far as

I knew there had been nothing quite as public and definite as this one.

"Wouldn't that account for her fears?" I asked.

"Hardly," replied Butler, shaking his head. "You see, Mrs. Hazleton is a nervous wreck, but it's about the baby, and caused, she says, by her fears for its safety. It came to us only in a roundabout way, through a servant in the house who keeps us in touch. The curious feature is that we can seem to get nothing definite from her about her fears. They may be groundless."

Butler shrugged his shoulders and proceeded, "And they may be well-founded. But we prefer to run no chances in a case of this kind. The child, you know, is guarded in the house. In his perambulator he is doubly guarded, and when he goes out for his airing in the automobile, two men, the chauffeur and a detective, are always there, besides his nurse, and often his mother or grandmother. Even in the nursery suite they have iron shutters which can be pulled down and padlocked at night and are constructed so as to give plenty of fresh air even to a scientific baby. Master Hazleton was the best sort of risk, we thought. But now—we don't know."

"You can protect yourselves, though," suggested Kennedy.

"Yes, we have, under the policy, the right to take certain measures to protect ourselves in addition to the precautions taken by the Hazletons. We have added our own detective to those already on duty. But we—we don't know what to guard against," he concluded, perplexed. "We'd like to know—that's all. It's too big a risk."

"I may see Mrs. Hazleton?" mused Kennedy.

"Yes. Under the circumstances she can scarcely

refuse to see anyone we send.   I've arranged already
for you to meet her within an hour.   Is that all
right?"

"Certainly."

The Hazleton home in winter in the city was
uptown, facing the river.   The large grounds adjoining made the Hazletons quite independent of the
daily infant parade which one sees along Riverside
Drive.

As we entered the grounds we could almost feel
the very atmosphere on guard.   We did not see the
little subject of so much concern, but I remembered
his much heralded advent, when his grandparents
had settled a cold million on him, just as a reward
for coming into the world.   Evidently, Morton, Sr.,
had hoped that Morton, Jr., would calm down, now
that there was a third generation to consider.   It
seemed that he had not.   I wondered if that had
really been the occasion of the threats or whatever
it was that had caused Mrs. Hazleton's fears, and
whether Veronica Haversham or any of the fast set
around her had had anything to do with it.

Millicent Hazleton was a very pretty little
woman, in whom one saw instinctively the artistic
temperament.   She had been an actress, too, when
young Morton Hazleton married her, and at first,
at least, they had seemed very devoted to each other.

We were admitted to see her in her own library,
a tastefully furnished room on the second floor of
the house, facing a garden at the side.

"Mrs. Hazleton," began Butler, smoothing the
way for us, "of course you realize that we are working in your interests.   Professor Kennedy, therefore,
in a sense, represents both of us."

"I am quite sure I shall be delighted to help

you," she said with an absent expression, though not ungraciously.

Butler, having introduced us, courteously withdrew. "I leave this entirely in your hands," he said, as he excused himself. "If you want me to do anything more, call on me."

I must say that I was much surprised at the way she had received us. Was there in it, I wondered, an element of fear lest if she refused to talk suspicion might grow even greater? One could see anxiety plainly enough on her face, as she waited for Kennedy to begin.

A few moments of general conversation then followed.

"Just what is it you fear?" he asked, after having gradually led around to the subject. "Have there been any threatening letters?"

"N-no," she hesitated, "at least nothing—definite."

"Gossip?" he hinted.

"No." She said it so positively that I fancied it might be taken for a plain "Yes."

"Then what is it?" he asked, very deferentially, but firmly.

She had been looking out at the garden. "You couldn't understand," she remarked. "No detective——" she stopped.

"You may be sure, Mrs. Hazleton, that I have not come here unnecessarily to intrude," he reassured her. "It is exactly as Mr. Butler put it. We —want to help you."

I fancied there seemed to be something compelling about his manner. It was at once sympathetic and persuasive. Quite evidently he was taking pains to break down the prejudice in her mind which she had already shown toward the ordinary detective.

"You would think me crazy," she remarked slowly. "But it is just a—a dream—just dreams."

I don't think she had intended to say anything, for she stopped short and looked at him quickly as if to make sure whether he could understand. As for myself, I must say I felt a little skeptical. To my surprise, Kennedy seemed to take the statement at its face value.

"Ah," he remarked, "an anxiety dream? You will pardon me, Mrs. Hazleton, but before we go further let me tell you frankly that I am much more than an ordinary detective. If you will permit me, I should rather have you think of me as a psychologist, a specialist, one who has come to set your mind at rest rather than to worm things from you by devious methods against which you have to be on guard. It is just for such an unusual case as yours that Mr. Butler has called me in. By the way, as our interview may last a few minutes, would you mind sitting down? I think you'll find it easier to talk if you can get your mind perfectly at rest, and for the moment trust to the nurse and the detectives who are guarding the garden, I am sure, perfectly."

She had been standing by the window during the interview and was quite evidently growing more and more nervous. With a bow Kennedy placed her at her ease on a chaise lounge.

"Now," he continued, standing near her, but out of sight, "you must try to remain free from all external influences and impressions. Don't move. Avoid every use of a muscle. Don't let anything distract you. Just concentrate your attention on your psychic activities. Don't suppress one idea as unimportan., irrelevant, or nonsensical. Simply tell me what occurs to you in connection with the dreams —everything," emphasized Craig.

I could not help feeling surprised to find that she accepted Kennedy's deferential commands, for after all that was what they amounted to. Almost I felt that she was turning to him for help, that he had broken down some barrier to her confidence. He seemed to exert a sort of hypnotic influence over her.

"I have had cases before which involved dreams," he was saying quietly and reassuringly. "Believe me, I do not share the world's opinion that dreams are nothing. Nor yet do I believe in them superstitiously. I can readily understand how a dream can play a mighty part in shaping the feelings of a high-tensioned woman. Might I ask exactly what it is you fear in your dreams?"

She sank her head back in the cushions, and for a moment closed her eyes, half in weariness, half in tacit obedience to him.

"Oh, I have such horrible dreams," she said at length, "full of anxiety and fear for Morton and little Morton. I can't explain it. But they are so horrible."

Kennedy said nothing. She was talking freely at last.

"Only last night," she went on, "I dreamt that Morton was dead. I could see the funeral, all the preparations, and the procession. It seemed that in the crowd there was a woman. I could not see her face, but she had fallen down and the crowd was around her. Then Dr. Maudsley appeared. Then all of a sudden the dream changed. I thought I was on the sand, at the seashore, or perhaps a lake. I was with Junior and it seemed as if he were wading in the water, his head bobbing up and down in the waves. It was like a desert, too—the sand. I turned, and there was a lion behind me. I did not seem to be afraid of him, although I was so close that I could almost feel his shaggy mane. Yet I feared that he might bite Junior. The next I knew I was running with the child in my arms. I escaped —and—oh, the relief!"

She sank back, half exhausted, half terrified still by the recollection.

"In your dream when Dr. Maudsley appeared," asked Kennedy, evidently interested in filling in the gap, "what did he do?"

"Do?" she repeated. "In the dream? Nothing."

"Are you sure?" he asked, shooting a quick glance at her.

"Yes. That part of the dream became indistinct. I'm sure he did nothing, except shoulder through the crowd. I think he had just entered. Then that part of the dream seemed to end and the second part began."

Piece by piece Kennedy went over it, putting it together as if it were a mosaic.

"Now, the woman. You say her face was hidden?"

She hesitated. "N-no. I saw it. But it was no one I knew."

Kennedy did not dwell on the contradiction, but added, "And the crowd?"

"Strangers, too."

"Dr. Maudsley is your family physician?" he questioned.

"Yes."

"Did he call—er—yesterday?"

"He calls every day to supervise the nurse who has Junior in charge."

"Could one always be true to oneself in the face of any temptation?" he asked suddenly.

It was a bold question. Yet such had been the gradual manner of his leading up to it that, before she knew it, she had answered quite frankly, "Yes —if one always thought of home and her child, I cannot see how one could help controlling herself."

She seemed to catch her breath, almost as though the words had escaped her before she knew it.

"Is there anything besides your dream that alarms you," he asked, changing the subject quickly, "any suspicion of—say the servants?"

"No," she said, watching him now. "But some time ago we caught a burglar upstairs here. He managed to escape. That has made me nervous. I didn't think it was possible."

"Anything else?"

"No," she said positively, this time on her guard.

Kennedy saw that she had made up her mind to say no more.

"Mrs. Hazleton," he said, rising. "I can hardly thank you too much for the manner in which you have met my questions. It will make it much easier for me to quiet your fears. And if anything else occurs to you, you may rest assured I shall violate no confidences in your telling me."

I could not help the feeling, however, that there was just a little air of relief on her face as we left.

CHAPTER XXXV

"H-M," mused Kennedy as we walked along after leaving the house. "There were several 'complexes,' as they are called, there—the most interesting and important being the erotic, as usual. Now, take the lion in the dream, with his mane. That, I suspect, was Dr. Maudsley. If you are acquainted with him, you will recall his heavy, almost tawny beard."

Kennedy seemed to be revolving something in his mind and I did not interrupt. I had known him too long to feel that even a dream might not have its value with him. Indeed, several times before he had given me glimpses into the fascinating possibilities of the new psychology.

"In spite of the work of thousands of years, little progress has been made in the scientific understanding of dreams," he remarked a few moments later. "Freud, of Vienna—you recall the name?— has done most, I think in that direction."

I recalled something of the theories of the Freudists, but said nothing.

"It is an unpleasant feature of his philosophy," he went on, "but Freud finds the conclusion irresistible that all humanity underneath the shell is sensuous and sensual in nature. Practically all dreams betray some delight of the senses and sexual dreams are a large proportion. There is, according to the theory, always a wish hidden or expressed in a dream. The dream is one of three things, the open, the disguised or the distorted fulfillment of a wish, sometimes recognized, sometimes repressed.

"Anxiety dreams are among the most interesting and important. Anxiety may originate in psycho-sexual excitement, the repressed libido, as the Freud-ists call it. Neurotic fear has its origin in sexual life and corresponds to a libido which has been turned away from its object and has not succeeded in being applied. All so-called day dreams of women are erotic; of men they are either ambition or love.

"Often dreams, apparently harmless, turn out to be sinister if we take pains to interpret them. All have the mark of the beast. For example, there was that unknown woman who had fallen down and was surrounded by a crowd. If a woman dreams that, it is sexual. It can mean only a fallen woman. That is the symbolism. The crowd always denotes a secret.

"Take also the dream of death. If there is no sorrow felt, then there is another cause for it. But if there is sorrow, then the dreamer really desires death or absence. I expect to have you quarrel with that. But read Freud, and remember that in child-hood death is synonymous with being away. Thus for example, if a girl dreams that her mother is dead, perhaps it means only that she wishes her away so that she can enjoy some pleasure that her strict parent, by her presence, denies.

"Then there was that dream about the baby in the water. That, I think, was a dream of birth. You see, I asked her practically to repeat the dreams because there were several gaps. At such points one usually finds first hesitation, then something that shows one of the main complexes. Perhaps the subject grows angry at the discovery.

"Now, from the tangle of the dream thought, I find that she fears that her husband is too intimate with another woman, and that perhaps unconsciously she has turned to Dr. Maudsley for sympathy. Dr. Maudsley, as I said, is not only bearded, but somewhat of a social lion. He had called on her the day before. Of such stuff are all dream lions when there is no fear. But she shows that she has been guilty of no wrongdoing—she escaped, and felt relieved."

"I'm glad of that," I put in. "I don't like these scandals. On the *Star* when I have to report them, I do it always under protest. I don't know what your psychanalysis is going to show in the end, but I for one have the greatest sympathy for that poor little woman in the big house alone, surrounded by and dependent on servants, while her husband is out collecting scandals."

"Which suggests our next step," he said, turning the subject. "I hope that Butler has found out the retreat of Veronica Haversham."

We discovered Miss Haversham at last at Dr. Klemm's sanitarium, up in the hills of Westchester County, a delightful place with a reputation for its rest cures. Dr. Klemm was an old friend of Kennedy's, having had some connection with the medical school at the University.

She had gone up there rather suddenly, it seemed, to recuperate. At least that was what was given out, though there seemed to be much mystery about her, and she was taking no treatment as far as was known.

"Who is her physician?" asked Kennedy of Dr. Klemm as we sat in his luxurious office.

"A Dr. Maudsley of the city."

Kennedy glanced quickly at me in time to check an exclamation.

"I wonder if I could see her?"

"Why, of course—if she is willing," replied Dr. Klemm.

"I will have to have some excuse," ruminated Kennedy. "Tell her I am a specialist in nervous troubles from the city, have been visiting one of the other patients, anything."

Dr. Klemm pulled down a switch on a large oblong oak box on his desk, asked for Miss Haversham, and waited a moment.

"What is that?" I asked.

"A vocaphone," replied Kennedy. "This sanitarium is quite up to date, Klemm."

The doctor nodded and smiled. "Yes, Kennedy," he replied. "Communicating with every suite of rooms we have the vocaphone. I find it very convenient to have these microphones, as I suppose you would call them, catching your words without talking into them directly as you have to do in the telephone and then at the other end emitting the words without the use of an earpiece, from the box itself, as if from a megaphone horn. Miss Haversham, this is Dr. Klemm. There is a Dr. Kennedy here visiting another patient, a specialist from New York. He'd like very much to see you if you can spare a few minutes."

"Tell him to come up." The voice seemed to come from the vocaphone as though she were in the room with us.

Veronica Haversham was indeed wonderful, one

of the leading figures in the night life of New York, a statuesque brunette of striking beauty, though I had heard of often ungovernable temper. Yet there was something strange about her face here. It seemed perhaps a little yellow, and I am sure that her nose had a peculiar look as if she were suffering from an incipient rhinitis. The pupils of her eyes were as fine as pin heads, her eyebrows were slightly elevated. Indeed, I felt that she had made no mistake in taking a rest if she would preserve the beauty which had made her popularity so meteoric.

"Miss Haversham," began Kennedy, "they tell me that you are suffering from nervousness. Perhaps I can help you. At any rate it will do no harm to try. I know Dr. Maudsley well, and if he doesn't approve—well, you may throw the treatment into the waste basket."

"I'm sure I have no reason to refuse," she said. "What would you suggest?"

"Well, first of all, there is a very simple test I'd like to try. You won't find that it bothers you in the least—and if I can't help you, then no harm is done."

Again I watched Kennedy as he tactfully went through the preparations for another kind of psychanalysis, placing Miss Haversham at her ease on a davenport in such a way that nothing would distract her attention. As she reclined against the leather pillows in the shadow it was not difficult to understand the lure by which she held together the little coterie of her intimates. One beautiful white arm, bare to the elbow, hung carelessly over the edge of the davenport, displaying a plain gold bracelet.

"Now," began Kennedy, on whom I knew the

charms of Miss Haversham produced a negative effect, although one would never have guessed it from his manner, "as I read off from this list of words, I wish that you would repeat the first thing, anything," he emphasized, "that comes into your head, no matter how trivial it may seem. Don't force yourself to think. Let your ideas flow naturally. It depends altogether on your paying attention to the words and answering as quickly as you can—remember, the first word that comes into your mind. It is easy to do. We'll call it a game," he reassured.

Kennedy handed a copy of the list to me to record the answers. There must have been some fifty words, apparently senseless, chosen at random, it seemed. They were:

head	to dance	salt	white	lie
green	sick	new	child	to fear
water	pride	to pray	sad	stork
to sing	ink	money	to marry	false
death	angry	foolish	dear	anxiety
long	needle	despise	to quarrel	to kiss
ship	voyage	finger	old	bride
to pay	to sin	expensive	family	pure
window	bread	to fall	friend	ridicule
cold	rich	unjust	luck	to sleep

"The Jung association word test is part of the Freud psychanalysis, also," he whispered to me. "You remember we tried something based on the same idea once before?"

I nodded. I had heard of the thing in connection with blood-pressure tests, but not this way.

Kennedy called out the first word, "Head," while

in his hand he held a stop watch which registered to one-fifth of a second.

Quickly she replied, "Ache," with an involuntary movement of her hand toward her beautiful forehead.

"Good," exclaimed Kennedy. "You seem to grasp the idea better than most of my patients."

I had recorded the answer, he the time, and we found out, I recall afterward, that the time averaged something like two and two-fifths seconds.

I thought her reply to the second word, "green," was curious. It came quickly, "Envy."

However, I shall not attempt to give all the replies, but merely some of the most significant. There did not seem to be any hesitation about most of the words, but whenever Kennedy tried to question her about a word that seemed to him interesting she made either evasive or hesitating answers, until it became evident that in the back of her head was some idea which she was repressing and concealing from us, something that she set off with a mental "No Thoroughfare."

He had finished going through the list, and Kennedy was now studying over the answers and comparing the time records.

"Now," he said at length, running his eye over the words again, "I want to repeat the performance. Try to remember and duplicate your first replies," he said.

Again we went through what at first had seemed to me to be a solemn farce, but which I began to see was quite important. Sometimes she would repeat the answer exactly as before. At other times a new word would occur to her. Kennedy was keen to note all the differences in the two lists.

One which I recall because the incident made an impression on me had to do with the trio, "Death—life—inevitable."

"Why that?" he asked casually.

"Haven't you ever heard the saying, 'One should let nothing which one can have escape, even if a little wrong is done; no opportunity should be missed; life is so short, death inevitable'?"

There were several others which to Kennedy seemed more important, but long after we had finished I pondered this answer. Was that her philosophy of life? Undoubtedly she would never have remembered the phrase if it had not been so, at least in a measure.

She had begun to show signs of weariness, and Kennedy quickly brought the conversation around to subjects of apparently a general nature, but skillfully contrived so as to lead the way along lines her answers had indicated.

Kennedy had risen to go, still chatting. Almost unintentionally he picked up from a dressing table a bottle of white tablets, without a label, shaking it to emphasize an entirely, and I believe purposely, irrelevant remark.

"By the way," he said, breaking off naturally, "what is that?"

"Only something Dr. Maudsley had prescribed for me," she answered quickly.

As he replaced the bottle and went on with the thread of the conversation, I saw that in shaking the bottle he had abstracted a couple of the tablets before she realized it.

"I can't tell you just what to do without thinking the case over," he concluded, rising to go. "Yours is a peculiar case, Miss Haversham, baffling. I'll have to study it over, perhaps ask Dr. Maudsley if I may see you again.   Meanwhile, I am sure what he is doing is the correct thing."

Inasmuch as she had said nothing about what Dr. Maudsley was doing, I wondered whether there was not just a trace of suspicion in her glance at him from under her long dark lashes.

"I can't see that you have done anything," she remarked pointedly.   "But then doctors are queer—queer."

That parting shot also had in it, for me, something to ponder over.   In fact I began to wonder if she might not be a great deal more clever than even Kennedy gave her credit for being, whether she might not have submitted to his tests for pure love of pulling the wool over his eyes.

Downstairs again, Kennedy paused only long enough to speak a few words with his friend Dr. Klemm.

"I suppose you have no idea what Dr. Maudsley has prescribed for her?" he asked carelessly.

"Nothing, as far as I know, except rest and simple food."

He seemed to hesitate, then he said under his voice, "I suppose you know that she is a regular dope fiend, seasons her cigarettes with opium, and all that."

"I guessed as much," remarked Kennedy, "but how does she get it here?"

"She doesn't."

"I see," remarked Craig, apparently weighing now the man before him.   At length he seemed to decide to risk something.

"Klemm," he said, "I wish you would do something for me.   I see you have the vocaphone here.

Now if—say Hazleton—should call—will you listen in on that vocaphone for me?"

Dr. Klemm looked squarely at him.

"Kennedy," he said, "it's unprofessional, but——"

"So it is to let her be doped up under guise of a
cure."

"What?" he asked, startled. "She's getting the
stuff now?"

"No, I didn't say she was getting opium, or from
anyone here. All the same, if you would just keep
an ear open——"

"It's unprofessional, but—you'd not ask it without a good reason. I'll try."

It was very late when we got back to the city and
we dined at an uptown restaurant which we had almost to ourselves.

Kennedy had placed the little whitish tablets in a
small paper packet for safe keeping. As we waited
for our order he drew one from his pocket, and
after looking at it a moment crushed it to a powder
in the paper.

"What is it?" I asked curiously. "Cocaine?"

"No," he said, shaking his head doubtfully.

He had tried to dissolve a little of the powder in
some water from the glass before him, but it would
not dissolve.

As he continued to look at it his eye fell on the cut-
glass vinegar cruet before us. It was full of the
white vinegar.

"Really acetic acid," he remarked, pouring out a
little.

The white powder dissolved.

For several minutes he continued looking at the
stuff.

"That, I think," he remarked finally, "is heroin."

"More 'happy dust'?" I replied with added interest now, thinking of our previous case. "Is the habit so extensive?"

"Yes," he replied, "the habit is comparatively new, although in Paris, I believe, they call the drug fiends, 'heroinomaniacs.' It is, as I told you before, a derivative of morphine. Its scientific name is diacetyl-morphin. It is New York's newest peril, one of the most dangerous drugs yet. Thousands are slaves to it, although its sale is supposedly restricted. It is rotting the heart out of the Tenderloin. Did you notice Veronica Haversham's yellowish whiteness, her down-drawn mouth, elevated eyebrows, and contracted eyes? She may have taken it up to escape other drugs. Some people have—and have just got a new habit. It can be taken hypodermically, or in a tablet, or by powdering the tablet to a white crystalline powder and snuffing up the nose. That's the way she takes it. It produces rhinitis of the nasal passages, which I see you observed, but did not understand. It has a more profound effect than morphine, and is ten times as powerful as codeine. And one of the worst features is that so many people start with it, thinking it is as harmless as it has been advertised. I wouldn't be surprised if she used from seventy-five to a hundred one-twelfth grain tablets a day. Some of them do, you know."

"And Dr. Maudsley," I asked quickly, "do you think it is through him or in spite of him?"

"That's what I'd like to know. About those words," he continued, "what did you make of the list and the answers?"

I had made nothing and said so, rather quickly.

"Those," he explained, "were words selected and arranged to strike almost all the common complexes

in analyzing and diagnosing. You'd think any intelligent person could give a fluent answer to them,
perhaps a misleading answer. But try it yourself,
Walter. You'll find you can't. You may start all
right, but not all the words will be reacted to in the
same time or with the same smoothness and ease.
Yet, like the expressions of a dream, they often
seem senseless. But they have a meaning as soon
as they are 'psychanalyzed.' All the mistakes in answering the second time, for example, have a reason, if we can only get at it. They are not arbi-
trary answers, but betray the inmost subconscious
thoughts, those things marked, split off from consciousness and repressed into the unconscious. As-
sociations, like dreams, never lie. You may try to
conceal the emotions and unconscious actions, but
you can't."

I listened, fascinated by Kennedy's explanation.

"Anyone can see that that woman has something
on her mind besides the heroin habit. It may be
that she is trying to shake the habit off in order to
do it; it may be that she seeks relief from her
thoughts by refuge in the habit; and it may be that
some one has purposely caused her to contract this
new habit in the guise of throwing off an old. The
only way by which to find out is to study the
case."

He paused. He had me keenly on edge, but I
knew that he was not yet in a position to answer his
queries positively.

"Now I found," he went on, "that the religious
complexes were extremely few; as I expected the
erotic were many. If you will look over the three
lists you will find something queer about every such
word as, 'child,' 'to marry,' 'bride,' 'to lie,' 'stork,'

and so on. We're on the right track. That woman does know something about that child."

"My eye catches the words 'to sin,' 'to fall,' 'pure,' and others," I remarked, glancing over the list.

"Yes, there's something there, too. I got the hint for the drug from her hesitation over 'needle' and 'white.' But the main complex has to do with words relating to that child and to love. In short, I think we are going to find it to be the reverse of the rule of the French, that it will be a case of 'cherchez l'homme.'"

Early the next day Kennedy, after a night of studying over the case, journeyed up to the sanitarium again. We found Dr. Klemm eager to meet us.

"What is it?" asked Kennedy, equally eager.

"I overheard some surprising things over the vocaphone," he hastened. "Hazleton called. Why, there must have been some wild orgies in that precious set of theirs, and, would you believe it, many of them seem to have been at what Dr. Maudsley calls his 'stable studio,' a den he has fixed up artistically over his garage on a side street."

"Indeed?"

"I couldn't get it all, but I did hear her repeating over and over to Hazleton, 'Aren't you all mine? Aren't you all mine?' There must be some vague jealousy lurking in the heart of that ardent woman. I can't figure it out."

"I'd like to see her again," remarked Kennedy. "Will you ask her if I may?"

CHAPTER XXXVI

THE ENDS OF JUSTICE

'A FEW minutes later we were in the sitting room of her suite. She received us rather ungraciously, I thought.

"Do you feel any better?" asked Kennedy.

"No," she replied curtly. "Excuse me for a moment. I wish to see that maid of mine. Clarisse!"

She had hardly left the room when Kennedy was on his feet. The bottle of white tablets, nearly empty, was still on the table. I saw him take some very fine white powder and dust it quickly over the bottle. It seemed to adhere, and from his pocket he quickly drew a piece of what seemed to be specially prepared paper, laid it over the bottle where the powder adhered, fitting it over the curves. He withdrew it quickly, for outside we heard her light step, returning. I am sure she either saw or suspected that Kennedy had been touching the bottle of tablets, for there was a look of startled fear on her face.

"Then you do not feel like continuing the tests we abandoned last night?" asked Kennedy, apparently not noticing her look.

"No, I do not," she almost snapped. "You— you are detectives. Mrs. Hazleton has sent you."

"Indeed, Mrs. Hazleton has not sent us," in-

368

sisted Kennedy, never for an instant showing his surprise at her mention of the name.

"You are. You can tell her, you can tell everybody. I'll tell—I'll tell myself. I won't wait. That child is mine—mine—not hers. Now—go!"

Veronica Haversham on the stage never towered in a fit of passion as she did now in real life, as her ungovernable feelings broke forth tempestuously on us.

I was astounded, bewildered at the revelation, the possibilities in those simple words, "The child is mine." For a moment I was stunned. Then as the full meaning dawned on me I wondered in a flood of consciousness whether it was true. Was it the product of her drug-disordered brain? Had her desperate love for Hazleton produced a hallucination?

Kennedy, silent, saw that the case demanded quick action. I shall never forget the breathless ride down from the sanitarium to the Hazleton house on Riverside Drive.

"Mrs. Hazleton," he cried, as we hurried in, "you will pardon me for this unceremonious intrusion, but it is most important. May I trouble you to place your fingers on this paper—so?"

He held out to her a piece of the prepared paper. She looked at him once, then saw from his face that he was not to be questioned. Almost tremulously she did as he said, saying not a word. I wondered whether she knew the story of Veronica, or whether so far only hints of it had been brought to her.

"Thank you," he said quickly. "Now, if I may see Morton?"

It was the first time we had seen the baby about whom the rapidly thickening events were crowding.

He was a perfect specimen of well-cared-for, scientific infant.

Kennedy took the little chubby fingers playfully in his own. He seemed at once to win the child's confidence, though he may have violated scientific rules. One by one he pressed the little fingers on the paper, until little Morton crowed with delight as one little piggy after another "went to market." He had deserted thousands of dollars' worth of toys just to play with the simple piece of paper Kennedy had brought with him. As I looked at him, I thought of what Kennedy had said at the start. Perhaps this innocent child was not to be envied after all. I could hardly restrain my excitement over the astounding situation which had suddenly developed.

"That will do," announced Kennedy finally, carelessly folding up the paper and slipping it into his pocket. "You must excuse me now."

"You see," he explained on the way to the laboratory, "that powder adheres to fresh finger prints, taking all the gradations. Then the paper with its paraffine and glycerine coating takes off the powder."

In the laboratory he buried himself in work, with microscope compasses, calipers, while I fumed impotently at the window.

"Walter," he called suddenly, "get Dr. Maudsley on the telephone. Tell him to come immediately to the laboratory."

Meanwhile Kennedy was busy arranging what he had discovered in logical order and putting on it the finishing touches.

As Dr. Maudsley entered Kennedy greeted him and began by plunging directly into the case in answer to his rather discourteous inquiry as to why he had been so hastily summoned.

"Dr. Maudsley," said Craig, "I have asked you to call alone because, while I am on the verge of discovering the truth in an important case affecting Morton Hazleton and his wife, I am frankly perplexed as to how to go ahead."

The doctor seemed to shake with excitement as Kennedy proceeded.

"Dr. Maudsley," Craig added, dropping his voice, "is Morton III the son of Millicent Hazleton or not? You were the physician in attendance on her at the birth. Is he?"

Maudsley had been watching Kennedy furtively at first, but as he rapped out the words I thought the doctor's eyes would pop out of his head. Perspiration in great beads collected on his face.

"P-professor K-Kennedy," he muttered, frantically rubbing his face and lower jaw as if to compose the agitation he could so ill conceal, "let me explain."

"Yes, yes—go on," urged Kennedy.

"Mrs. Hazleton's baby was born—dead. I knew how much she and the rest of the family had longed for an heir, how much it meant. And I—substituted for the dead child a newborn baby from the maternity hospital. It—it belonged to Veronica Haversham—then a poor chorus girl. I did not intend that she should ever know it. I intended that she should think her baby was dead. But in some way she found out. Since then she has become a famous beauty, has numbered among her friends even Hazleton himself. For nearly two years I have tried to keep her from divulging the secret. From time to time hints of it have leaked out. I knew that if Hazleton with his infatuation of her were to learn——"

"And Mrs. Hazleton, has she been told?" interrupted Kennedy.

"I have been trying to keep it from her as long as I can, but it has been difficult to keep Veronica from telling it. Hazleton himself was so wild over her. And she wanted her son as she——"

"Maudsley," snapped out Kennedy, slapping down on the table the mass of prints and charts which he had hurriedly collected and was studying, "you lie! Morton is Millicent Hazleton's son. The whole story is blackmail. I knew it when she told me of her dreams and I suspected first some such devilish scheme as yours. Now I know it scientifically."

He turned over the prints.

"I suppose that study of these prints, Maudsley, will convey nothing to you. I know that it is usually stated that there are no two sets of finger prints in the world that are identical or that can be confused. Still, there are certain similarities of finger prints and other characteristics, and these similarities have recently been exhaustively studied by Bertillon, who has found that there are clear relationships sometimes between mother and child in these respects. If Solomon were alive, doctor, he would not now have to resort to the expedient to which he did when the two women disputed over the right to the living child. Modern science is now deciding by exact laboratory methods the same problem as he solved by his unique knowledge of feminine psychology.

"I saw how this case was tending. Not a moment too soon, I said to myself, 'The hand of the child will tell.' By the very variations in unlike things, such as finger and palm prints, as tabulated and arranged by Bertillon after study in thousands of cases, by the very loops, whorls, arches and composites, I have proved my case.

"The dominancy, not the identity, of heredity through the infinite varieties of finger markings is sometimes very striking. Unique patterns in a parent have been repeated with marvelous accuracy in the child. I knew that negative results might prove nothing in regard to parentage, a caution which it is important to observe. But I was prepared to meet even that.

"I would have gone on into other studies, such as Tammasia's, of heredity in the veining of the back of the hands; I would have measured the hands, compared the relative proportion of the parts; I would have studied them under the X-ray as they are being studied to-day; I would have tried the Reichert blood crystal test which is being perfected now so that it will tell heredity itself. There is no scientific stone I would have left unturned until I had delved at the truth of this riddle. Fortunately it was not necessary. Simple finger prints have told me enough. And best of all, it has been in time to frustrate that devilish scheme you and Veronica Haversham have been slowly unfolding."

Maudsley crumpled up, as it were, at Kennedy's denunciation. He seemed to shrink toward the door.

"Yes," cried Kennedy, with extended forefinger, "you may go—for the present. Don't try to run away. You're watched from this moment on."

Maudsley had retreated precipitately.

I looked at Kennedy inquiringly. What to do? It was indeed a delicate situation, requiring the utmost care to handle. If the story had been told to Hazleton, what might he not have already done? He must be found first of all if we were to meet the conspiracy of these two.

Kennedy reached quickly for the telephone. "There is one stream of scandal that can be dammed at its source," he remarked, calling a number. "Hello. Klemm's Sanitarium? I'd like to speak with Miss Haversham. What—gone? Disappeared? Escaped?"

He hung up the receiver and looked at me blankly. I was speechless.

A thousand ideas flew through our minds at once. Had she perceived the import of our last visit and was she now on her way to complete her plotted slander of Millicent Hazleton, though it pulled down on herself in the end the whole structure?

Hastily Kennedy called Hazleton's home, Butler, and one after another of Hazleton's favorite clubs. It was not until noon that Butler himself found him and came with him, under protest, to the laboratory.

"What is it—what have you found?" cried Butler, his lean form a-quiver with suppressed excitement.

Briefly, one fact after another, sparing Hazleton nothing, Kennedy poured forth the story, how by hint and innuendo Maudsley had been working on Millicent, undermining her, little knowing that he had attacked in her a very tower of strength, how Veronica, infatuated by him, had infatuated him, had led him on step by step.

Pale and agitated, with nerves unstrung by the life he had been leading, Hazleton listened. And as Kennedy hammered one fact after another home, he

clenched his fists until the nails dug into his very
palms.

"The scoundrels," he ground out, as Kennedy finished by painting the picture of the brave little
broken-hearted woman fighting off she knew not
what, and the golden-haired, innocent baby stretching out his arms in glee at the very chance to prove
that he was what he was. "The scoundrels—take
me to Maudsley now. I must see Maudsley.
Quick!"

As we pulled up before the door of the recon-
structed stable-studio, Kennedy jumped out. The
door was unlocked. Up the broad flight of stairs,
Hazleton went two at a time. We followed him
closely.

Lying on the divan in the room that had been the
scene of so many orgies, locked in each other's arms,
were two figures—Veronica Haversham and Dr.
Maudsley.

She must have gone there directly after our visit
to Dr. Klemm's, must have been waiting for him
when he returned with his story of the exposure to
answer her fears of us as Mrs. Hazleton's detectives. In a frenzy of intoxication she must have
flung her arms blindly about him in a last wild em-
brace.

Hazleton looked, aghast.

He leaned over and took her arm. Before he
could frame the name, "Veronica!" he had recoiled.

The two were cold and rigid.

"An overdose of heroin this time," muttered Kennedy.

My head was in a whirl.

Hazleton stared blankly at the two figures ab-
jectly lying before him, as the truth burned itself

indelibly into his soul. He covered his face with his hands. And still he saw it all.

Craig said nothing. He was content to let what he had shown work in the man's mind.

"For the sake of—that baby—would she—would she forgive?" asked Hazleton, turning desperately toward Kennedy.

Deliberately Kennedy faced him, not as scientist and millionaire, but as man and man.

"From my psychanalysis," he said slowly, "I should say that it *is* within your power, in time, to change those dreams."

Hazleton grasped Kennedy's hand before he knew it.

"Kennedy—home—quick. This is the first manful impulse I have had for two years. And, Jameson—you'll tone down that part of it in the newspapers that Junior—might read—when he grows up?"

THE END